A CONNECTICUT GUMSHOE

IN

the Cavern of the Weird Sisters

BY

RANDY MCCHARLES

A CONNECTICUT GUMSHOE

IN

the Cavern of the Weird Sisters

BY

RANDY MCCHARLES

TYCHE BOOKS LTD.

A Connecticut Gumshoe in the Cavern of the Weird Sisters

Copyright © 2022 Randy McCharles

Published by Tyche Books Ltd.
Calgary, Alberta, Canada
www.TycheBooks.com

Cover Design by Indigo Chick Designs
Interior Layout by M.L.D. Curelas
Editorial by M.L.D. Curelas

First Tyche Books Ltd Edition 2022
Print ISBN: 978-1-989407-46-2
Ebook ISBN: 978-1-989407-49-3

Author photograph: Leonard Halmrast

This book was funded in part by a grant from the Alberta Media Fund.

This book is dedicated to the great playwright William Shakespeare for envisioning his strong repertoire of timeless plays that have enthralled audiences for generations. While The Scottish Play is a tragedy, as is the Bogart film *Casablanca*, at least for Rick, I have always tried to seek out the positive. I also relish when villains receive their comeuppance.

1

A THUNDERING CONFUSION

A thundering confusion of snow and ice pounded against the Volvo's windshield faster than the wipers could clear it. Not that there was much to see beyond the weather-splattered safety glass; the afternoon sky was as dark as night, and a slushy mess of heavy snow shrouded the highway like a dirty blanket. Though Sam knew the effort was futile, he hunched over the steering wheel and fiddled with the rotating wiper switch in search of a faster setting.

"Do you want me to drive?" Sam's business partner, Nora, spoke in a manner that was calm, considerate, and wholly inappropriate given the circumstances.

Abandoning the wiper switch, he gripped the steering wheel with both hands. "I've got this."

Though inwardly he had doubts.

Truth was, Sam had never driven in weather this bad. He couldn't even see where the shoulder ended and the verge began. On the car radio, the talking head on WTIC—1080 on your dial— had called it the worst winter storm in a hundred years. Easy enough to say when you're safe and snug inside a radio station. Why did Connecticut have to have such wonky weather?

1

Sweltering hot in the summer. And in the winter, cold enough to freeze fire.

"That's weird," Nora said, interrupting Sam's private pity party.

"What's weird?" Preoccupied with the maelstrom outside the window, he wasn't sure what his partner was referring to.

"On the radio." Nora reached forward and increased the volume. "Zack Hutchinson just cackled."

"Zack Hutchinson?"

"The news anchor. He cackled. In the middle of his weather report."

Sam had only been half-listening to the radio. The announcer was still talking weather. Something about things warming up on the weekend. No apology for laughing when people's lives were at risk, especially those driving on Route 5 toward New Year's Eve dinner with a business partner's family.

But something was off. Sam worked his jaw, trying to clear his ears. The radio sounded muffled. And he was certain the wind he heard came from the car speakers and not the storm outside. "What is that? Static?"

As though answering his question, the blustery wind shaped itself into whispers: *"Bubble, bubble, toil and trouble."*

"Like no static I've ever heard," Nora said.

The radio continued. *"Fire burn and caldron bubble."*

Sam felt a ringing in his ears, and his eyes began to blur. "Maybe you should drive. If I can get us onto the shoulder." He nudged the car toward where he hoped the verge was, then felt himself falling sideways. Instead of lodging against the inside of the door, however, he kept falling, falling, falling until the side of his face hit something hard. And cold.

The sense of movement was gone. Had he stopped the car? He remembered taking his foot off the gas as he steered off the highway onto the snow-covered shoulder, but then what? Why was he lying on his side? And where was the storm?

Sam listened, hearing wind, but the gusts echoed as though he were in a tunnel. The static was still there, louder and clearer, no longer muffled. *"Eye of newt and toe of frog. Wool of bat and tongue of dog."*

It wasn't static, but a rasping voice. No. More than one voice.

Two, three voices, grating and scratching like someone trying to cut through a sheet of tin with a metal file. *"Adder's fork and blind-worm's sting. Lizard's leg and howlet's wing."*

And there were smells. Was someone cooking? Whatever soup was being made, Sam would take a pass. A hard pass. Howlet's wing? What was that anyway? Owl? And who would make soup in the middle of the worst storm of the century?

Sam pressed his hand against the cold ground, expecting snow, but found only hard, dry stone. The air was also chill, but not as chill as it had been when he and Nora had bundled themselves into his Volvo S60 and rubbed their hands together while the in-car heater gathered steam. The wind howled in the distance, but the air around him was as still as in a morgue.

"Cool it with a baboon's blood," the rasping chorus continued. *"Then the charm is firm and good."*

The three voices cackled. Then a single, droning hiss cried out: "Sam Spade! Arise!"

Sam Spade? Well, that explained a lot.

It was only then that Sam realized his eyes were closed. The fluttering of his lids seemed more an obedience to the sibilant command than a response to his will. Not that opening his eyes made much difference. Wherever he was, the lights were out. Though, after a moment, he began to make out rough shapes.

Uneven walls rose up around him, possibly ending at a high ceiling. At this point, it wouldn't surprise him if this particular abyss had no ceiling. Perhaps thirty feet away stood the source of the poor lighting. A campfire. Of sorts. The fire would have been brighter, except someone had set a giant pot directly on top of it— the source of the awful soup smells.

As his eyes adjusted to the low light, Sam made out three figures standing around the pot. They were either very tall, very skinny, or both. Throw in the giant pot, and everything seemed out of proportion. The scene was something one might see in a funhouse mirror at a carnival, or in a rundown gallery that featured bad surrealist art.

He figured the three personages for elderly women, elderly because of the shrill rasp of their chanting, and women because the voice that had hissed out his unfortunate alias sounded familiar.

"Do not lie there like a lump," the familiar voice grated. "We have work to do."

It couldn't be. But it was. Morgan Le Fay.

Setting aside the horrible woman's impossible height, Le Fay was barely recognizable as the petite beauty he had first encountered in Camelot. Or the more weathered version who had advised the Sheriff of Nottingham twelve years later. Add six more years, and any beauty Morgan Le Fay once possessed was gone. Instead, her face was a mass of heavy wrinkles, with hollow cheeks and a pointed chin. The woman's hair, once a lustrous crown of raven black, reflected dull grey in the weak firelight. Only Le Fay's eyes, deep blue with a hint of violet, remained undiminished.

Had it only been six years since their last encounter?

Three weeks earlier, Sam had sat at his desk in his office, waiting. His previous three journeys to the past had occurred, almost to the day, at six-month intervals. Six months in Hartford, but with six years passing in jolly old England. But when hour after hour then day after day went by with no unlikely client darkening his doorway, Pendragon coin in hand and a desperate case in the past only Sam Spade could solve, he'd figured that was it. Sam Spade was out of business. Long live Sam Sparrow.

Apparently, he'd been wrong. Not that that was unusual. Sam Sparrow was often wrong. He freely admitted it. Such was the lot of a private investigator—following red herrings and dead ends until only the one true path remained. You were only right after being repeatedly wrong. But finding himself here, wherever here was, now, whenever now was, was the mother of all wrongs.

If time still passed at the same rate, it should be six years plus a few months since he left Sherwood Forest. That would land him in the fall sometime. Where though, he had no idea.

"Mr. Spade," Le Fay growled. "Need I cast another spell?"

Probably not a good idea. "Gimme me a sec," Sam said. "It's been a long trip, and I need to work out some kinks."

All three women cackled. Like old crones. Did they think they were witches or something? Well, they did look like witches. And they were casting spells. Only, back in Nottingham, Le Fay had denied being a witch. She'd even taken offence at the word. She had called herself a sorceress. Of course, a lot could happen in six, seven years. Or longer, if the woman's rough appearance was any indication.

Sam climbed to his feet and searched for his fedora, then remembered it was still in his office. He hadn't been out beating Hartford's mean streets when Le Fay had dragged him back into the past. He'd been driving—"Nora!"

"Who?" one of the other witch-women standing near the big pot shrilled. This one was similar to Le Fay in appearance, only her skin was rough like broken clay and held a reddish-brown hue.

"My business partner," Sam said. "I was driving when—"

Le Fay cut him off. "That is no concern of ours. We have a task for you."

Sam clenched his fingers into fists. "Whatever game you got goin', I ain't interested. You left Nora in a moving vehicle in the middle of a snow storm with no driver."

Le Fay frowned, adding years to her already ancient face. "I fail to see a problem. The carriage shall slow of its own accord. Or, if the horse is well trained, it shall keep on to its destination without a driver."

"The horse," Sam growled, "has no training whatsoever." There was no time for this. "Send me back. Maybe I can stop the car safely."

"Of course, we shall send you back," Le Fay purred. That is, if hyenas could purr. "After you complete our task."

Sam reached into the pocket of the fleece-lined Burberry trench coat he wore over his dress clothes, and casually slid his hand through the tear he had made through the lining. Not finding his Smith and Wesson M&P semi-automatic strapped to his belt, he belatedly remembered that, like his fedora, he'd left the weapon in his office.

It was New Year's Eve and Nora, aware that he had no plans, had invited him to dinner with her family. Showing up locked and loaded might have made the wrong impression with Nora's parents and kid sister, so here he was without his hat and bean-shooter.

With his semi-automatic, Sam might have been able to threaten Le Fay into returning him to Hartford. But the only weapons he could muster were the cell phone in his shirt pocket and maybe a pinch of lint. Not even MacGyver could work a decent bluff from that. "A task, huh?" Sam rubbed his ear. "And you'll send me back afterward?"

The three witches nodded.

"Back to where and when you took me from?"

A wide grin split Le Fay's hideous face, revealing uneven rows of broken and rotting teeth. "Nothing could be simpler."

Sam had been in this situation before. He knew it didn't matter how much time went by on one of these jaunts into the past. He could get sent back to the moment he left. Or even before he left, as had happened on his second trip. The question was: could he trust Le Fay to send him back at all?

He felt his cheek twitch, an involuntary stress response reminiscent of the real Sam Spade. As a teenager, Sam had done everything he could to walk and talk like his hero, Humphrey Bogart. He'd even smoked two packs a day and acquired a taste for whiskey. He'd gone so far as to practice in a mirror Bogart's signature facial twitch, the result of nerve damage caused by beatings his father, Belmont Bogart, had given him as a child. At first Sam could perform the twitch on command. Later it had become second nature, and Sam found he couldn't get rid of it.

The twitch came in handy now, a less than subtle reminder that Le Fay couldn't be trusted. But what choice did he have? He was, literally, at the evil woman's mercy. Though it was the last thing on Earth he wanted right now, once again, Sam Spade had a job to do.

2
A NEW AND NOVEL IDEA

Sam stepped closer to the giant, foul-smelling pot, and immediately noted he hadn't been wrong. Morgan Le Fay and her two pals stood eight feet tall if they stood an inch, and were rail thin, something the long black robes they wore couldn't hide. Maybe it was the result of a steady diet of owl feather and lizard leg soup. "A job, huh? Well, you'd better give me the bad news."

Instead of speaking, Le Fay reached out one hand and uncurled a fistful of long emaciated fingers. There, on a shrivelled palm, sat a dull, silver ring.

Sam glanced up toward the impossibly tall woman's deep blue eyes, and noticed a raw line crossing through the wrinkles of her left cheek. A scar. A mark he himself had left when he'd tried to shoot the sorceress in the Sheriff of Nottingham's keep. Le Fay had used magic to divert the bullet, but it had still managed to graze her. Just when he thought things couldn't get worse. Le Fay was the type of woman to not just hold a grudge, but to coddle it like a lover while waiting for an opportune moment to dish out a disproportionate amount of revenge.

"A ring?" Sam said, hoping to distract his nemesis from whatever vengeful thoughts she was brewing. "What am I supposed to do with that?"

Le Fay snorted. "What one is wont to do with a ring. Wear it."

Against his better judgement, Sam slowly reached forward to pluck the ring from its shrivelled resting place. The dull metal felt like a lump of ice, numbing his hand, but he held on rather than drop it. Before he could pull back, however, the woman's long fingers wrapped themselves around his wrist.

Le Fay leaned down and hissed into his face. "Could I have summoned another, I would have. You are not to my liking, Sam Spade."

Resisting the urge to scream, Sam grunted through clenched teeth, "I could recommend someone."

Le Fay let go of his wrist and straightened. "I have cast the bones. You are the one."

Sam pulled back his hand, the ring clutched like an oddly shaped stone against his palm. "You sure? I know a guy who knows a guy."

"Get on with it," growled the third witch, who up till now had remained silent. Though as tall as the others, she looked even more skeletal, with parchment-thin skin the colour of chalk, and hair matted like dead seaweed. Her eyes were so dark they seemed like holes punched through leather.

"Very well, sister." Le Fay waved a bony wrist at Sam. "Place yon ring upon your finger."

Sam wasn't one for jewellery and had never worn rings. Besides, who knew what the customs were in this time and place. "Which finger?"

Le Fay's voice rose with annoyance. "It matters not. The magic works all the same."

"Oh ho! A magic ring, is it?" Sam turned away from the witch's stony gaze and examined the object his nemesis had given him. Having been nestled in his fist, it had lost its chill and now looked ordinary in the glow of the fire. Just a thin band of steel or iron or whatever plain grey rings were made of. He squinted as he peered inside the band.

"What are you looking for?" Le Fay demanded.

"Writing," Sam answered. "*One Ring to rule them all*, or some such. You did say this was a magic ring."

"There is no writing. Simply wear it on whichever finger it fits."

Sam obliged, twisting the ring onto the middle finger of his left hand. The fit was tight, but at least he knew it wouldn't slip off. Holding out his hand, he appraised the look. It didn't make much of a fashion statement. And whatever magic it was supposed to hold didn't make him feel any different. "Now what?"

"Now," Le Fay said, "you are invisible to any mortal man or woman who should gaze upon you."

"Invisible," Sam echoed. "You sure there's no writing on this ring? I mean, the Land of Mordor had a ring with exactly the same magic."

"I have never heard of this Mordor," Le Fay growled.

"It's a nice place," Sam lied. "You'd fit right in."

"Sister!" the chalk-white witch hissed.

Le Fay raised a bony finger and pointed at Sam before waving her arm to one side. "That way leads to the cavern entrance. On your way outside you shall pass a man sitting at a table writing a letter. He is a mighty general who is destined to rule over all of Scotland. Your task is to help him achieve his destiny."

Out of all that, the word Sam caught was *Scotland*. "Is that where we are? Scotland? I thought England was your patch."

Le Fay sniffed. "I am not the same woman I was years ago."

"I can see that," Sam said, then wished he hadn't. "So how am I supposed to help this general of yours? I'm no soldier."

"Macbeth shall need allies to support his rebellion. And money with which to pay them. You shall assist with both by operating a nightclub in his castle at Inverness."

Sam was so busy trying to swallow the name Macbeth that he almost missed the word *nightclub*.

"Nightclub? They have those here?"

Le Fay exhaled a heavy sigh. "Of course not. It shall be a new and novel idea that shall attract thanes and generals like flies to a dung heap. They shall herald Macbeth as a genius and rush to support his cause."

Macbeth.

Like all his classmates in high school, Sam had been required to read Shakespeare. Or at least try. He'd fallen asleep whenever he opened a book. In theory, the plays were written in English. His brain, however, wouldn't buy it. All the *prate*s and *ronyon*s and *alarum*s said otherwise. He'd made good use of CliffsNotes before exams, which actually were written in English, and managed to pass his courses. Barely.

Most of Shakespeare had gone in one ear and out the other, but he did recall Macbeth as the villain in one of the plays. Whoever was supposed to be the good guy occupied an empty void in Sam's mind. Maybe it was an exotic foreigner named Sam Spade, recorded by Shakespeare under an assumed name to protect the innocent and all that.

It irked Sam that Le Fay had dragged him into the past, leaving Nora in danger, only to charge him with helping the bad guy. What was she thinking? He floundered for a moment trying to recall more of Macbeth's story, but drew a blank. He was certain more would come to him as Shakespeare's play played out. Right now, he had bigger concerns. If he waffled much longer, Le Fay would start dwelling on those vengeful thoughts of hers.

"So," Sam said. "A nightclub. How did you come up with that chestnut?"

A smile crossed Le Fay's non-existent lips. "While searching for you I saw much of your land, Connecticut. I was unsure how, precisely, you would help our general, until I saw how your countrymen could not resist your nightclubs, especially the ones called casinos."

Sam rubbed his ear. "I can see you've put a lot of thought into this, but your plan does have one flaw."

"And that is?"

"I have no idea how to run a nightclub. I do, however, know someone who knows someone—"

"It shall be you," Le Fay said. "What you accomplished in Camelot and Nottingham . . . it must be you. If you wish to return to your Connecticut and rescue this Nora person, you shall raise a nightclub and aid Macbeth in becoming king."

3
YOU MUST BE TRIPLETS

Raise a nightclub? Le Fay had no idea what she was asking, and looked in no mood to discuss it.

"Where do you suggest I start?" Sam asked. He had no plan yet for getting back to his own time and place, but he'd figure something out. Arguing with the sorceress-turned-witch wasn't going to do it. He'd have to play her game until he found someone or something that could send him home.

"Once you leave this cavern," Le Fay instructed, "follow the road north past General Macbeth's soldiers. You shall soon meet up with three helpers who shall assist you with your nightclub."

"Helpers? That's more like it. What do they know about nightclubs?"

"Not one whit," Le Fay said. "After leaving Macbeth's soldiers and before you come upon your helpers, remove the ring. Frightening off your help shall not benefit you."

Sam nodded. "Right. Hey, wait. You can see me, can't you? I'm wearing the ring." He held up his middle finger in a way that would get him in trouble in his own time.

"Such magic will not work on me," Le Fay spat. "I am no fool."

Sam figured she had better be a fool. If he couldn't find an alternate solution, he'd have to trick her somehow into sending him back home. He nodded again to disguise his thoughts.

11

"Anyone else I should be concerned about seeing me when they shouldn't?"

"No." Le Fay gestured again in the direction of the cavern entrance.

Sam could take a hint. "Fine. I'll just go set up a nightclub then, shall I?"

All three witches raised an arm and pointed.

"Okay, okay. I'm going."

As Sam left the influence of the campfire, the poor light in the cavern dimmed further. He held out his hands so he wouldn't walk into a wall and stepped carefully along the uneven floor. Soon however, his vision improved. Ahead, he could see where the ceiling lowered and the cavern walls turned. The howling of wind that had echoed around the witches' chamber grew louder, and as he rounded a corner, cold air cut across his face and sent a shiver down his spine. The source of the wind, an opening no larger than a tractor tire, looked out into a leaden sky.

But what caught Sam's attention was a rickety table set just inside the opening. Or rather, the man who sat at the table. Sam figured Macbeth was roughly his own age and build and looked a little like Ned Stark from *Game of Thrones*—the King of the North. It wasn't just the stony features, shoulder-length hair, and trimmed beard. The Scottish general even wore Stark's fur-embellished black leather cloak. Macbeth seemed intent on his writing, and took no notice as Sam approached then passed by on his way through the opening.

Sam did pause long enough to note Macbeth was scribbling on a piece of quality parchment with a quill pen. A stack of similar paper sat at his elbow, weighted down by a stone. The thin sheets fluttered in the breeze, perhaps masking Sam's footsteps. He watched as Macbeth dipped the quill into a jar of ink, tapped off excess liquid, then scratched the quill tip against the parchment. Sam couldn't help but think that texting was a much-improved form of written communication.

Climbing carefully through the rock-strewn hole, Sam still managed a misstep, causing loose gravel to crunch beneath his Thorogood Oxfords. He held his breath as Macbeth looked up before resuming his love letter, or execution orders, or whatever it was the Scottish villain felt compelled to write in a cave in the middle of nowhere.

Once free of the cavern, he discovered the mountain he thought he'd been inside was little more than a pile of boulders. The land about him was hilly—with forests to the south and east, and grassy meadows running north and west—but not what he would call mountainous. Though the sky was a mass of thick, mostly grey clouds, he could see enough of a hazy glow to mark the sun and get his bearings. He didn't know much about Scotland, but knew the place was north of England, so the sun should be to the south.

It had been cold inside the cavern, but the wind and threatening rain made the great outdoors that much worse. Pulling up the collar of his fleece-lined trench coat, Sam mentally kicked himself for stuffing his winter gloves in the door panel of his car instead of his coat pocket.

None of the two dozen men crowded close together a short distance from the jumble of boulders seemed to notice the weather. Dressed in patterned kilts that left their legs bare from the knees on down, they looked much like the Scottish redshank mercenaries Sam had encountered in England during his last visit to the past. Their only acknowledgment of the cold were the heavy cloaks they wore across their shoulders.

Busying themselves with their horses and saddlebags, most of the men wore their hair long, sported thick beards, and had cold, watchful eyes that took in everything around them. Everything except Sam. Le Fay's ring appeared to be doing its job. How that would help him set up a nightclub, he had no idea. He was sure, however, that he'd find a good use for it. If he could get the ring back to Hartford, he'd really be cooking with gas. What an advantage it would give him in his PI business.

But first he had to find a way home. Until then, he'd have to pretend to do what Morgan Le Fay wanted. For now, that was finding this road that led to the helpers she'd promised. Problem was, Sam couldn't see any roads.

As he worked his way out from among the boulders, he noticed the cave behind him was little more than a hole in the ground. He shook his head. How about that? The witches' cavern was bigger on the inside than it was on the outside.

There was no evidence of a path leading away from the

boulders, but as he walked closer to Macbeth's soldiers, he saw that not all of them wore kilts. Several wore long, pale-yellow shirts beneath their cloaks that partly obscured the fact they wore tight pants or stockings. Each soldier also wore a blood-red cloth tied around their right bicep, as if they were participating in a game of capture the flag.

After circling the gathered men and horses, Sam still hadn't found anything he would call a road. He rubbed his ear while watching a V formation of birds fly overhead. There was no snow on the ground. Leaves were still on the trees. But the place felt like winter. Maybe Scotland was like that. How far north was it? On par with Alaska maybe?

Le Fay had said to take the road north, so he walked to a point he guessed was due north of the entrance to the witches' cavern. After tightening his collar again, he studied the ground but saw little more than scrub grass and wild moss. The foliage was flattened in places, and could have been an animal track that ran north and a little to the east. He glanced back at the men and horses, figuring if that's what passed for traffic in these parts, he very well could be looking at a road.

While committing the jumble of boulders to memory in case he had to find his way back, Sam again wondered how he'd get home to Hartford. He couldn't trust Le Fay, but at the moment was out of options. For now, he'd have to stay on the evil woman's good side. That meant going north.

Sam had no idea how verbose Macbeth was in regard to letter writing, but figured he probably didn't have much time. Le Fay hadn't mentioned it, but once he was done, the Scottish villain and his soldiers would no doubt come riding along the same trail. Sam wanted to find his promised help before Macbeth and his soldiers found him.

He set a quick pace and soon found himself breathing hard and sweating inside his clothes. He loosened the collar he had tightened a few minutes earlier, then undid all the buttons along the front of his trench coat.

Underneath, Sam wore an Italian tuxedo, the brand of which he couldn't pronounce. He'd bought the two-button, double-breasted ensemble at JT Ghamo expressly for New Year's Eve dinner with Nora's family, after she'd warned him that her parents took dinner parties seriously. It didn't take a genius to guess they had more money than Nora had led him to believe. The fact they lived on a South Windsor acreage five miles northeast of Hartford was all anyone had to say.

He still wondered about the invitation.

In the days leading up to their unexpected visit to Sherwood Forest, Nora had been increasingly friendly, possibly to the point of flirtatious. Their relationship had always been strictly business, but had recently evolved into an occasional touch as well as comments here and there that had nothing to do with whatever case they were on. Sam figured she had merely grown comfortable around him, but there could be more to it.

Sherwood Forest had changed all that. While stuck in the past, Nora had suffered a concussion, lost her memory, then slowly gained it back through Sam's gentle reminders of who she had been. By the time they returned to Hartford, Nora seemed to have recovered. Certainly, her detective skills hadn't suffered. But her behaviour . . . ?

Nora went back to all business. No more touches or comments. She'd buried herself in the work, and looked at him differently. Before Sherwood, she'd seen enough inexplicable evidence to believe his wild tales of visiting Camelot. But traveling to the past herself, and what had happened to her there, may have been a step too far. After their return, she had put distance between them. He'd even worried she blamed him for what had happened, even though all of it had been out of his control.

Then Christmas approached, and Nora began behaving like her old self again. A smile or remark here. A touch there. Maybe she had finally put behind her what had happened, or had found it within herself to forgive him.

Regardless, he'd begun to feel they were on track again. He even thought there could be a possibility for a budding romance. Nora's invitation to family dinner sure seemed to point in that direction.

Then along came Morgan Le Fay, throwing a wrench in the works. Some days Sam just never caught a break.

The grassy trail continued northward. After a while, Sam could see up ahead where meadow ended and trees began. A flutter of colour just inside the forest edge got him hoping he'd found his helpers. Since good first impressions went a long way, he slowed his pace so he wouldn't be breathing hard when he met up with them. Then he almost bungled it by forgetting to remove Le Fay's magic ring. Slipping the metal band off his finger, he reached inside his two layers of coat and slipped it into his shirt pocket next to his cell phone.

As he drew closer to the treeline, Sam made out three people dressed in unabashedly bright clothing, which seemed disjointed given Macbeth's men all wore black or dark brown. It dawned on him that his helpers weren't men at all, but women. The first wore a blue ankle-length overcoat and had long raven hair that fell almost to her waist. Beside her stood a redhead with short hair, dark eyes, and a dark red coat. The third had mid-length chestnut hair and a coat of bright green that matched her eyes. All three looked to be in their early to mid-twenties. Sam rubbed his ear. What kind of nightclub had Le Fay visited on her tour of Connecticut?

As the three young women watched Sam approach, their expressions remained flat except for their eyes, which seemed to be taking his measure just as he'd taken theirs. When he was close enough, the dark-eyed redhead spoke. "You must be Sam Spade. My name is Ruby." She indicated her two companions. "These are my sisters, Emerald and Sapphire."

"You must be kidding," Sam said.

"Kidding?" This from the green-eyed beauty, Emerald.

"Where do I begin?" Sam asked. "Your unlikely names? Your mismatched genetics? Or the fact you must be triplets because you're all about the same age?"

Emerald's jaw fell open. Then Sapphire stepped forward. "We are not true sisters. And these are our stage names. We are performers."

"Performers," Sam echoed. "What is it you do, exactly?"

"We dance," Ruby blurted out, drawing wide-eyed looks from her two so-called sisters. "Or . . . we shall learn to dance once we find a position."

"I sing," Emerald volunteered. "Sometimes. Though not very well."

"Right," Sam said. "What do you all know about nightclubs?"

Sapphire leaned forward. "What is that? Some kind of weapon?"

Sam knew then he had his work cut out for him. He rubbed his face, then forced a smile. "Ladies, I think this is the beginning of a beautiful friendship."

4
A MISTAKE ON THE BATTLEFIELD

Whatever else Sam's three precious gems had to tell him would have to wait. A thunder of hoofbeats made him turn around, and the four of them stood watching as the Scottish cavalry approached, then slowed to a stop.

The man who had been writing in the cave—Macbeth—leaned forward in his saddle, his expression a severe scowl framed by his neatly trimmed beard. "Are you the Sam Spade who was foretold by the weird sisters?"

Sam looked up at the small man riding a big horse. "The one and only."

"And these are your assistants?" The general waved a hand at Sam's precious gems, then did a double take. "Your oddly dressed assistants?"

"They're performers," Sam explained.

Macbeth relaxed in his saddle, apparently accustomed to oddly dressed performers. "And you," he said, pointing at Sam's trench coat. "Are you also a performer?"

"No," Sam admitted. "I'm merely oddly dressed."

"I see." Macbeth rubbed his bearded chin before turning to the rider next to him. "Banquo, find our friends some mounts. I will not have them slow our progress."

"Yes, General."

Within moments, four of Macbeth's party dismounted. Eagerly, it seemed, they helped Sam's precious gems up into the vacated saddles. Sam was also helped, though with noticeably less enthusiasm. Then Macbeth's cavalry was off, trotting into the thin forest at a pace that left Sam bouncing in his saddle.

There wasn't room among the trees to ride more than two abreast, but after a few minutes, the man Macbeth had called Banquo dropped back beside Sam. Though well into his forties or fifties, if the grey in his beard was any indication, the man carried himself with a boyish cheerfulness. "You are not accustomed to the saddle, are you?"

"Truth be told," Sam said, "I prefer to walk."

Banquo smiled. "As do I. Unfortunately, today we have not the luxury. You will be happier, however, if you move with the saddle rather than fight against it."

Sam had a vague recollection of receiving similar advice when he was in Sherwood Forest. It took a few tries, but soon he was able to move with the motion of the horse rather than be jostled by it.

"That is better," Banquo said, still smiling. "Your backside will thank you when we arrive at our destination."

"And where is that?" Sam asked.

"Forres," Banquo said. "We ride to meet the king."

Sam almost asked, "Which king?" but instead managed to dredge up a name from high school English class: Duncan. Didn't Macbeth murder him? Or was it Macbeth's wife who killed the king? It seemed to Sam that a lot of people had died in that particular play. And that there weren't a lot of laughs.

After an hour or so of riding, the trees parted and they entered a wide field where more of Macbeth's men waited. Le Fay had called Macbeth a general. Sam assumed this was Macbeth's army. Hundreds if not thousands of men and horses lined the field. And beyond them, a mansion of some sort built from dirty white stone sat among a setting of groomed trees and bushes. The central tower rose five stories, with halls that looked to have only two floors running to either side. Appended to the rightmost hall, a three-storey extension ran back further than Sam could see.

"This is Forres?" he asked Banquo.

Macbeth's friend laughed. "Heavens no. This is Cawdor

Castle. The army before us has recently come from battle, where General Macbeth and I routed the invading King of Norway and chased Cawdor's rebellious thane back to his hovel. The traitor cowers within."

"I suppose congratulations are in order," Sam said. "And we're here because . . . ?"

Banquo grinned. "General Macbeth wishes to bestow a present upon our fellow thane. Come, you must see."

Sam kneed his horse so it would follow Banquo's as they rode through the crowd of soldiers up to the castle's main gate. Macbeth and several of his warriors had arrived before them and were dismounting outside an arched gateway behind which sat a small garden and the castle's main doors. The garden stood empty and the doors stood closed. The layout reminded Sam of the Sheriff's Keep in Nottingham, except the lower wall made a poor defence, and the only battlements he could see were at the top of the central tower. Those, too, had been abandoned.

"Not much of a welcome," Sam whispered to Banquo.

"Alas," Banquo whispered back, "the thane's warriors have abandoned his cause."

Sam watched as Macbeth stood facing the gateway, his hands on his hips. The general then signalled one of his men, who brought him a weighted sack. Macbeth reached inside. When he withdrew his hands, his fingers gripped a bodiless head by its hair.

"Uhm," Sam said.

Banquo leaned toward him. "'Tis MacDonwald, Thane Cawdor's general. MacDonwald made a mistake on the battlefield."

"A mistake?" Sam asked, despite his mouth having gone dry.

"MacDonwald allowed General Macbeth to slice him open from loin to throat. Good Macbeth thought it honourable to return Cawdor's general to his master."

"But it's just his head," Sam muttered.

"Did I not say? After exposing MacDonwald's bowels, Macbeth beheaded him. The act turned the tide of battle, which otherwise may not have been won. General Macbeth is a mighty hero."

Sam watched on in horror as the mighty hero impaled his

enemy's head on one of the spikes that jutted from the castle gate. The gathered army responded with an exuberant cheer which nearly caused Sam to jump out of his Thorogood Oxford shoes.

Taking a steadying breath, he muttered to himself, "Here's looking at you, kid."

5
THE PRINCE OF CUMBERLAND

Sam hardly knew what was happening as Banquo led his horse away from the grisly scene. Then once again they were riding through the countryside.

As he regained his bearings, he saw they were on some kind of trail, an actual dirt path wide enough for wagons. There were riders up ahead and more behind, many more than had ridden from the witches' cavern, but not enough to account for the sizable army outside Cawdor Castle. A glance over his shoulder revealed the helpers the witches had provided, his three precious gems, riding side by side.

Eventually, the trees parted and the trail cut through fields, some cultivated, most just wild grass. He couldn't tell what the crops had been, as the harvest seemed to have ended. But in some fields, workmen were bent to the task of planting winter grains.

They rode for what felt like hours, the countryside growing wilder as the trail cut through stands of trees and across the shallows of streambeds. The sun drifted toward the horizon behind them and to the south, and the sky grew darker. Sam figured they were riding east and a bit to the north. Without the cover of trees, a cold wind whipped his face and chilled his fingers that clutched his horse's reins.

"Is it always this cold?" Sam asked Banquo.

His escort let out a heavy breath. "No. The weather has been unnaturally bad since . . ." Whatever provocation Macbeth's friend had been about to mention remained a secret behind pinched lips.

"Then maybe you could tell me what month it is?" Sam suggested.

Banquo turned his head and raised one brow. "You do not know the month?"

Sam felt his cheek twitch. "When I woke up this morning, it was December."

"You are dressed for winter," Banquo admitted, his eyes taking in Sam's fleece-lined trench coat. He paused for a moment, then lowered his voice to a whisper. "What have you to do with the weird sisters?"

That was a good guess, as well as a good question. Sam figured honesty was the best policy. "I'm their captive."

Banquo's eyes remained on Sam's. "And the ladies?"

Sam knew the man meant his precious gems. "I have no idea."

Macbeth's friend let out another heavy breath. "It is September. Haefest monath. Harvest month."

They rode after that in silence.

As the sun began to set, Sam adjusted his Rolex, moving the hour hand from twelve to eight. He wasn't exactly sure when the sun went down in Scotland in September, but was reasonably confident that 8 p.m. was closer than midnight. It had been a long day so far, and there appeared to be hours yet to go.

The sky was storm-cloud purple, at the trailing edge of twilight, when the trail took them through a patch of forest that parted to reveal a castle somewhat larger than the one where Macbeth had left his *present*. The last light of day illuminated yellow-white stone walls and slate-grey roof tiles. Most of the building complex stood four storeys tall, and only the leftmost tower seemed to include battlements. Unlike Cawdor Castle, there was no front courtyard, just a tall, though plain, main doorway. Apparently, Scotland had never heard of moats.

As Sam watched, the main gate opened and a half-dozen warriors stepped outside. Like Macbeth's soldiers, these wore kilts or yellow shirts with strips of red cloth tied around their upper arms. That, and the grins on the men's faces, suggested a battle probably wasn't in the offing.

The warriors parted as a taller man dressed in leather armour stepped outside and approached Macbeth, who remained seated on his horse at the fore of his war band. The new arrival's hair was thick and dark, as was his beard. His sonorous voice was deep and carried well. "Hail Macbeth, defeater of the King of Norway and rebellious Scottish thanes. I, Thane Macduff of Fife, welcome you to Forres, the seat of the King of Scotland." The man dropped all formality as he added, "The other generals and I arrived before midday. Did you encounter trouble on the road?"

"No trouble," Macbeth answered, "merely an errand. My path took me to Cawdor where I imparted a small gift."

Macduff let out a hearty laugh that was instantly taken up by the soldiers behind him.

Macbeth grinned, then shouted over the cheerful voices. "I also left the bulk of my army on Thane Cawdor's doorstep should the traitor think to depart for Norway or England."

The laughter doubled before abating to allow Macduff to resume speaking. "Our good king has plans for the rebellious thane. 'Twould be a shame should Cawdor miss out. But you and your men have fought and ridden hard. Leave your horses for the grooms, and bid your men relax in the courtyard. You and your captains are invited to sup with the king. There is much to celebrate."

Sam didn't know if he was considered a captain or not, but he and his three precious gems climbed off their horses and followed Banquo in through the castle's impressive main gate.

The ceiling inside the main hall was tall with high windows, but since outdoor light was in short supply, ornate lamps set on wooden stands had been lit. Along the walls, smaller oil lamps set in metal sconces also burned. Most everything was made with pinkish-white stone blocks—walls, floor, ceiling, and a set of wide steps leading up to a higher level—but there were also façades of dark wood, thick tapestries, busts of important personages, and giant pots overflowing with shrubs and small trees. The place was homey, and made up for the absence of an exterior garden.

Banquo and the others led the way down a wide corridor, past another set of stairs, around a corner, and into a spacious banquet hall lined with several rows of long tables. Most of the seats were occupied, though a table near the head of the hall stood empty. All conversation stopped as Macbeth and his captains, along with Sam and his precious gems, trooped toward the vacant table. When they arrived, the captains stood by the waiting chairs rather than sit. Sam barely caught himself and remained standing as well.

Movement caught his eye, and he watched as an elderly man with long white hair and a gaunt expression rose from a seat positioned at the centre of the head table. The table itself sat on a raised platform, while the chair the white-haired man occupied was ornate to the point of gaudiness compared to others in the room. Two giant hounds lay beneath the table at the old man's feet. This could only be King Duncan.

"General Macbeth!" the old man grunted. "Well met, if not tardy. We have, I am afraid, begun our celebrations without you."

"My apologies for the delay," Macbeth answered, his tone friendly. "There was the small matter of securing Thane Cawdor. Your rebellious clansman awaits your pleasure at his domicile."

A frown crossed the old man's face. "I trusted Cawdor as a son. His land and title were gifts from my own hand. And he repays me with treason!"

Macbeth smiled and waved his hand. "Norway and Cawdor both have learned a hard lesson. Scotland shall not be undone."

A chorus of voices rose throughout the banquet hall. "Scotland shall not be undone!"

Duncan's frown reversed into a smile. "With generals such as Macbeth leading our armies, Scotland shall never be undone."

Everyone in the room jumped to their feet, shouting, "All hail Macbeth!"

The old man waved a hand and everyone sat, including Macbeth and Banquo. Sam scrambled into the nearest available chair which happened to be next to Banquo and opposite his precious gems. No one took off their riding cloaks, not that there was anywhere to put them.

Quiet descended, and the old king continued speaking. "Let us not forget that General Macbeth is also a thane, the Thane of Glamis. And from this day forward, as reward for his prowess in battle, Thane of Cawdor as well. Cawdor's current occupant shall be executed, his title and associated lands given to our good general."

The room cheered, but not as brightly as the expression on Macbeth's face. Banquo nudged Sam and whispered into his ear, "It is as the weird sisters promised. Macbeth has been named Thane of Cawdor."

Duncan again waved his hand. "But there is more." Macbeth leaned forward, reminding Sam of an overeager dog. "Thane Macbeth is not the only one to prove himself in battle. Malcolm, my eldest, also proved himself this day."

The room responded with scattered applause, then more when the old man's face darkened.

"Malcolm?" Banquo whispered. "The spineless feartie-cat spent the battle cowering in a tent."

Duncan waved for attention, then gestured for a scrawny young man seated at his table to rise. Red-haired and red-faced, the thin twenty-something stood slowly and with trembling hands. "True, Malcolm is young, yet this day's battle has reminded me that the shadow of my own years grows long. It is past time I made formal announcement of my heir. It is with much gladness of heart that I name Malcolm the Prince of Cumberland."

Silence filled the hall. Then one captain rose to his feet and clapped his hands. Several more followed and soon the entire room was standing. Shouts joined the handclaps, the entire cacophony ringing in Sam's ears.

Old King Duncan regarded the room, then nodded and sat.

The noise quieted as the banquet guests returned to their seats. Banquo tugged Sam's arm and they both sat. "Macbeth shall not be happy," Banquo whispered. "The weird sisters told us he would be king after Duncan. This Cumberland declaration must be undone."

6
DYNASTIES ARE MORE EASILY LOST THAN WON

Servants filed into the banquet hall, placing long platters of steaming food onto each of the tables. Dressed like refugees from Medieval Times in Lyndhurst, with bleached white tunics and dark stockings, they paused to give Sam's trench coat a sideways look. His precious gems, with their colourful cloaks, received similar askance glances. "We're from out of town," Sam murmured.

The maze of drafty corridors inside Forres Castle weren't much warmer than the unseasonably cool countryside, but the sheer number of warm bodies in the banquet hall succeeded in heating the crowded room to that of a drafty sauna. Sam's helpers unbuttoned their colourful cloaks, revealing matching blouses underneath. He didn't think it was the colours that drew looks from other table guests, who were all male and acted as one might expect males to act in the presence of a trio of beautiful young women. Had he not known who had sent them, Sam might have felt tempted to cast a few interested looks of his own.

But no. There was something off about the three young women the witches had waiting for him at the edge of the forest. Something more than merely looking like they had walked off the cover of a fashion magazine. Their lips were full, their skin perfect. Even after riding for hours, not a hair on their heads was out of place. Their features looked airbrushed. Put them in a paper box with a plastic window, they could be Barbie dolls.

"Is there something amiss?" Sapphire asked, her violet eyes twinkling.

Sam realized he must have been staring while making his assessment of the young women.

Before he could answer, Banquo spoke up. It was possible the noble Scotsman had been staring as well. "Your clothes. I have never seen such vibrant colours. And the cloth . . ."

Smile lines formed to either side of Sapphire's perfectly symmetrical mouth. "Parisienne. The fashion is all the rage in Paris right now."

"Paris," Banquo said. "France?"

"Bien sûr. Parlez-vous Français?"

Banquo simply stared at her.

"My friends could be from France," Sam suggested, hoping to break the awkwardness. "I'm just not sure which year."

The Scotsman nodded, then ducked his head and busied himself with his plate.

Sam did the same, but quickly realized he was feeling a bit overheated himself. Unbuttoning his trench coat didn't seem to do the trick, so he undid the two buttons on his dinner jacket as well as loosen his bow tie in hopes of coaxing some cool air underneath. When he noticed everyone watching him, he said, "A man can't make himself too comfortable."

Despite the occasion being a celebratory banquet and the table belonging to Scotland's king, Sam found his meal tasteless. Some kind of wild meat, probably sheep or goat, fish with bones in it, and oddly-shaped vegetables that were green, yet bland. The only thing to recommend the meal was the beer, which was heavy and flavourful, probably meant to prevent people from complaining about the food.

"'Tis made from malted barley," Banquo explained. "And herbs known only to the alewife who brewed this particular batch. The king, of course, has Scotland's best alewives at his disposal."

"Cheers," Sam murmured. He couldn't help thinking that,

instead of a crowded banquet hall in medieval Scotland, he should be on an acreage outside Hartford sitting at a table with Nora, her younger sibling, and her parents. But he would be. Of course, he would. Just as soon as he figured out how to get back. Even if that meant completing the ill-defined job Le Fay had given him. He'd get sent back to the exact moment he had left, and safely steer his car back onto the highway.

The hall around him was loud with laughter and boisterous talk. Sam found it odd that none of the men seated near him spoke with his precious gems, who stood out like three roses in a bed of thorns. He'd been curious as to what medieval Scotsmen might use as pickup lines, but the young women collected looks and nothing more. Perhaps the locals were tongue-tied. Or maybe, like him, they felt there was something off about supermodels sharing their table. His witch-supplied helpers didn't seem to mind the looks and otherwise lack of attention. They kept to themselves and their dinner.

The banqueters also all but ignored Sam, so maybe it was foreignness they found off-putting. As that thought crossed his mind, the man at his opposite elbow from Banquo spoke to him. "You and your . . . friends. Foreign?"

Sam barely resisted bursting into laughter. "The short answer? Yes."

The man rubbed his bearded chin, taking his own time to consider things. "And the long answer would be?"

"Confusing," Sam said.

That was the extent of the conversation.

A little after that, Banquo indicated it was time to leave. As Sam rose from his seat he fell toward the table, barely catching himself before making a scene. Apparently, he'd had too much. Drink, not food. Whiskey was Sam's poison of choice, and he knew to the ounce how much he could get away with. He couldn't say the same about Scottish beer, especially not malt beer made with unspecified herbs.

With Banquo holding up one arm and a stranger supporting the other, Sam felt himself being escorted from the banquet hall. The next thing he knew he was waking up in a building that looked and smelled like a barn. What had awoken him was a chorus of snoring men. Normally that wouldn't be so bad, but

Sam also sported a roaring headache.

Taking care not to step on anyone, he maneuvered among dozens of sprawling men wrapped in blankets, and escaped the barn into a large courtyard that lined the entire backside of the castle. Seeing no one about, he reached into his shirt pocket and retrieved the ring Le Fay had given him. If he was going to wander around a strange castle in the middle of the night, he'd do it without the risk of being caught.

Fortunate for him, most of the day's clouds had been replaced by a gibbous moon surrounded by a blanket of unfamiliar stars. This let him see his way along the courtyard and past stalls of horses and a few small gatherings of men, not all of whom were asleep. As a test, he approached several men dressed in clothes that looked to have seen better days, and stood listening to their conversation. None of them noticed him, and he soon discerned they were workmen. Sam could only make out half of their heavily accented discussion, which seemed to revolve around the unseasonable weather and the additional work Duncan's guests had burdened them with.

Sam continued on his way until he reached a narrow door that led inside the castle. No one was around, so he tried the latch, which moved. He waited a moment before unlatching the door from its frame and inching it open. If anyone noticed, they would blame the icy wind that breezed through the courtyard.

Once the gap was wide enough, Sam slipped through and found himself in a vacant hallway. No statues or indoor plants here. Just dreary walls of bare stone. No lighting either, except for a single oil lamp toward the end of the hallway. Sam felt his way along one wall as he moved deeper into the castle.

He had no idea why he had left his straw bed in the courtyard. He only knew he wouldn't get back to sleep, not with a cacophony of snoring bedfellows. It also seemed prudent to verify if Le Fay's ring still worked. Reconnoitring Duncan's castle would be the ideal test.

Or less than ideal. After wandering the length and breadth of the gloomy castle and encountering no one, he eventually found himself back in the banquet hall where a lone candle sat on the head table, providing light. The remains of the food had been cleared and probably fed to the pigs. There were still a few pitchers of beer, however, that weren't quite empty. Sam helped himself. Hair of the dog.

Feeling slightly better, he worked his way back down the hallway until he came to a narrow staircase that led up to the next floor. Of course, he had to go up for a look. Maybe he'd find someplace quiet where he could sleep.

Skipping the middle floors, he climbed the stairs to the top level, figuring it would be reserved for access to the battlements and for hiding away disliked relatives and unwelcome guests. Though the wall hangings were no less magnificent than those on the main level, the corridors seemed narrower and the oil lamps along the walls set further apart. The burning oil gave off a slight, fishy smell, and hardly any light, and cast eerie shadows across the tapestries. Behind the various closed doors, Sam could hear the cadence of fitful snoring or sometimes more interesting noises. A glance at the luminous dial of his Rolex told him the hour was roughly 3 a.m. Hot time in the castle tonight.

Which door, he wondered, on the various levels, belonged to Scotland's king? And where would Macbeth be staying?

He almost passed the alcove without realizing it, except for a voice that spoke out in a whisper. "Whit was that?"

Sam froze, then turned his head. What he had thought was a dark wall hanging was really a sheer curtain. No, not even a curtain, just a wall of knotted threads that extended from ceiling to floor. The whisper had come from behind it.

"Ye'r hearin' things," came an answering whisper. "Ain't no one aboot at this hour."

Sam peered through the spaces between the threads and saw the outline of two soldiers sitting on a bench. They were dressed in leather and held swords across their laps. He figured the king's chamber must be nearby. Penthouse apartment. Who knew?

"Time ye go on patrol, anyway," the first whisperer said.

"Nay, it be yer turn."

"Ye want me to be holdin' yer hand?" the other retorted.

"Sit yerself." One of the soldier outlines stood and adjusted his grip on the pommel of his sword. "Should I die this night, it be on yer head."

"Dinnae be so dramatic," the other answered.

Before Sam had company in the narrow corridor, he backed

away toward the end of the hallway and raced around a corner. He'd only travelled a few feet before the passage ended at a single closed door. Cold air seeped in along the doorframe, and the latch rattled from gusting wind on the other side.

As he paused, listening for pursuit, Sam realized the two guards and the workmen outside had spoken with heavy Scots accents, while everyone else spoke clear English. Well, maybe with a sometimes-odd vocabulary, but English he could understand.

When in Nottingham, he'd hardly understood what the Sheriff's Scots mercenaries—the redshanks—were saying. Now he was in Scotland, everyone spoke as though they'd been born and raised in Hartford. Le Fay's magic that had brought him here must be helping him communicate with those she intended him to communicate with. The nobility. And his three helpers. For everyone else, he was on his own.

Where had his precious gems gotten to, anyway? Were their voices some of the laughter he'd heard near Duncan's rooms? Not that it mattered. Sam wanted nothing to do with them. Le Fay had told him to run a nightclub, then saddled him with a trio of cocktail waitresses. All to help Macbeth? The man was a cold-blooded murderer. Or would be, in the near future.

No. Before that happened, Sam would find someone who could send him back to Hartford. Merlin. The Lady of the Lake, brought back from the dead. The Loch Ness Monster. He didn't care. Anyone with the power to do it, would do. Surely Scotland had its magicians just like England. Morgan Le Fay didn't hold a monopoly. Banquo would probably help him. The fellow had seemed friendly enough, and he must have connections if he was Macbeth's close companion.

With still no sign of the guard making his rounds, Sam slipped the latch on the door blocking his path and stepped out onto the moonlit castle battlements. The space between the parapet wall and the castle proper was wider than he had imagined. Of course, they'd need room for soldiers to move, replenish their arrows, prepare cauldrons of boiling pitch, etc., but Sam figured King Duncan could have held his banquet here with room to spare.

Icy wind blasted Sam's face as he strode toward the crenels. He tried to make out the surrounding countryside, but saw only blackness. In the distance, thunder rumbled. He wasn't sure what he had expected. Camelot Castle had been surrounded by a sprawling city. Nottingham Castle had its own fortified town. The King of Scotland had a castle in the middle of nowhere. Literally nowhere.

Working his way along the parapet, Sam came around to the backside of the castle. He looked down into the yard where the horses were kept and where he had woken up. To either side, the wings of the castle extended quite a distance, and he had to believe that hundreds of souls dwelt within. Maybe the castle was the town.

Whispered voices carried on the breeze caught Sam's attention. He peered again into the yard below, but then the wind shifted and he realized the sounds came from behind him. Turning, he spotted the shape of two figures standing against the castle wall, their shapes illuminated by the moon and stars, but mostly by a narrow wedge of light that escaped from a nearby doorway. Sam crept closer across the battlements until he could discern Macbeth and the slightly taller Banquo standing close together.

He couldn't quite make out what they were saying, as the wind shifted, throwing several words his way, then flinging the rest away. He sidled closer until he was almost on top of them.

"If somewhat were to happen to Malcolm," Macbeth whispered.

"Somewhat untoward?" Banquo whispered back. "That is unlikely. Duncan coddles the boy like a favourite hound."

"Accidents do happen," Macbeth said.

Banquo hesitated. "Malcolm has a younger brother, Donalbain."

Macbeth snorted. "Donalbain? The boy is an idiot. As a child he was kicked in the head by a pony."

"Idiots have sat on thrones before," Banquo said.

Macbeth fingered his beard with gloved fingers. "You have a stake in this, too."

The taller man chuckled. "Yes, yes. The witches claim my offspring shall sit the throne after you are done with it. My friend, I put less stock in soothsaying than you. The weird sisters speak only words you wish to hear."

"But they have spoken true thus far." Macbeth stood a bit taller. "They predicted I would overcome Norway, even though the Irish and rebel Scots should have turned the battle in their favour. They foretold I would be named Thane of Cawdor as well as Glamis, an act almost unheard of."

"And," Banquo continued, "they said you would sit on the Throne of Scone. The witches did not say when. After Malcolm perhaps. Can you imagine young Malcolm spawning children? The boy is frightened of his own shadow."

Macbeth rubbed his beard. "Perhaps you are right. I am still a young man myself, seven years married—"

"And as yet no children," Banquo interrupted. "Best you father a few heirs yourself before setting your gaze on the throne. Dynasties are more easily lost than won."

"You speak wisdom, my good friend. As always. What would I do without your sage counsel? How fares Fleance? He was— what?—fifteen when last I saw him?"

With the conversation changed from murder to children, Sam backed away before he was discovered. Being invisible didn't make you soundless, or odourless. He'd been sweating most of the day and needed a shower. Maybe if he searched the castle long enough, he'd find the bathhouse.

7
TREASON HAS BUT ONE PENALTY

The sun rose before a bath was found, but Sam did discover a medieval bathroom in his travels, similar though not as ritzy as the Necessarium in Camelot. He made liberal use of the facilities. Shortly after that, servants began roaming the corridors, so he returned to the back courtyard, found a quiet corner, and removed Le Fay's ring.

The morning air was frosty and the sky a gunmetal grey, the moon and stars having made a grudging retreat. The chill seeped into his bones and spoke of high humidity. Sure, it was cold, but it was a damp cold.

With fingers cramped from the chill, Sam rebuttoned his trench coat and pulled the belt tight. He should have worn a scarf. But back when he was driving Nora to her parents, he hadn't planned on being out in the cold for more than a few minutes. Who knew Scotland in September would be scarf weather?

Servants bustled about the courtyard chopping wood, packing saddlebags, and saddling horses. Probably keeping extra busy just to keep warm. Near one wall steamed a large pot of what looked and smelled like porridge.

"There you are."

Sam turned and saw Banquo walking toward him.

"If you haven't eaten your porridge yet, you must make haste.

Thane Macbeth wishes us on our way."

"On our way where?" Sam asked.

Banquo smiled. "Inverness. My good friend claims he has been apart from his lovely wife for far too long."

Good friend. And he'd had such high hopes for Banquo.

Sam helped himself to a bowl of the tasteless gruel and strained to remember more of Shakespeare's play. At the mention of Macbeth's wife, images of a dark-haired beauty with a ghostly pale complexion ran through his mind. Lady Macbeth. He must have seen a film version of the play somewhere, probably in high school. He seemed to recall the woman constantly brooding, and now wondered if it were she, rather than her warrior husband, who murdered Duncan.

Sam's thoughts were interrupted by one of the king's hostlers, sent to assist him in mounting his borrowed pony. Within minutes he was swept up in Macbeth's train of soldiers. Sam's trio of helpers appeared behind him, riding their borrowed mounts like they had been born in the saddle. Banquo was nowhere to be seen. Perhaps the noble Scotsman wasn't returning to Inverness with his *good friend*.

They hadn't travelled far before Sam's hips and back resumed their familiar ache from sitting in a saddle. He reminded himself to move with the horse instead of fighting it, and the ache abated to mere discomfort.

Recognizing a turn in the trail, he realized they were heading back the way they had come from Cawdor Castle. Sure enough, a couple of hours later they approached the now-familiar building and crowd of soldiers Macbeth had left there the previous day.

The horse train came to a stop, and Sam was happy to climb down out of the saddle to stretch his legs. He tried to not look toward the castle gate, but eventually his diligence lapsed. Even from a distance he could make out the head of Cawdor's general decorating its spike.

A few minutes later they were on their way again, only the train was now longer.

Banquo rode up beside him. "It is good that is over."

"What's over?" Sam asked.

"Word has reached the ears of Cawdor that Macbeth has been named thane by the king. The castle no longer resists. Life resumes."

"Is that why we stopped?" Sam asked.

Banquo smiled. "No. Thane Macbeth has no wish to dwell at Cawdor. He paused his journey to name a steward in his place."

"Who did he name?"

Macbeth's good friend waved a hand. "'Tis not important. All have seen what became of MacDonwald. Cawdor shall be true to her new thane."

Sam felt his cheek twitch. Something was missing in Banquo's explanation. "What about the old thane?"

"Treason has but one penalty," Banquo said. "Best not to dwell on it. Now, be of good cheer. Inverness lies ahead. Despite this foul weather, we shall arrive ere nightfall."

"About that." Sam hesitated. "There wouldn't happen to be any magicians at Inverness, would there?"

Banquo pursed his lips. "Magicians? You mean witches?" An uncomfortable look spread from the Scotsman's eyes, across his ruddy cheeks, and ending at his ears. "The dark arts are forbidden . . ."

Sam waved a hand. "No, no, no. I'm talking about good magic. Like the wizard Merlin at Camelot, in England. Or the Lady of the Lake."

A pause. "Good magic? I know not of this wizard or lady. But a word of caution. You best not speak of them. The punishment in Scotland for witchcraft is hanging. Your dress and manner draw enough attention. Should you speak of the dark arts, there are those who would name you for a witch."

Sam let out a deep sigh. Getting home to Hartford would be harder than he'd thought. He lowered his voice. "What about those weird sisters you and Macbeth have been hanging with?"

Banquo grimaced. "Soothsayers. Charlatans. Macbeth finds them amusing. Pay them no mind."

"But—"

Macbeth's good friend interrupted. "It is folly to mention them. I advise against it. Strongly." Then he rode on ahead before Sam could commit further folly.

8

THE WORST WELCOME HOME

The afternoon passed with trees to the south and freshly plowed fields to the north. Sam figured much of what was being planted was winter barley destined for brewing into beer such as King Duncan had served at Forres. The leaves on some of the trees were beginning to yellow in the face of the unseasonable cold. Sam didn't blame them. Despite patches of blue peeking out from among the grey clouds, the air never seemed to grow warmer.

Banquo rode by himself just ahead. Probably focused on the soothsayings of the weird sisters as well as Macbeth's ambitions that had grown from them. Macbeth's good friend had warned Sam that consorting with witches was punishable by hanging, yet that's exactly what he and Macbeth had done. Do as I say, not as I do. Sam had already admitted to being summoned to Scotland by those selfsame witches, and he figured the same had happened with his three helpers. Banquo probably knew he was in a pickle and, just like Sam, had no idea how to get out of it.

As the hours passed, the forest trail widened. There were even ruts in the road that looked to have been made by carts. Traffic started flowing in both directions, with riders or people on foot going past on either side. There were even occasional carts pulled off the road to make way for Macbeth's army. The cart drivers sometimes gave Sam curious looks, but their attention quickly moved on to his precious gems, who stood out among the mounted soldiers like three bright flowers in a field of dry grass.

Cottages began to appear just off the trail. Most were farmers' hovels, but a few looked to be selling goods. Commoners too old or too young to work the fields, wearing patched and mended clothing as well as heavy winter cloaks against the disagreeable weather, sat on stools behind rickety tables laden with what looked like pies, wedges of cheese, dried meats, or pitchers of liquids. Several of the soldiers paused to make purchases.

As they continued west, the road widened further and cottages became more common. Above, the clouds cleared, revealing a sky that looked more purple than blue.

Banquo dropped back beside him. "Moray Firth lies to the north. Inverness is just ahead."

"Excuse my ignorance," Sam said. "But . . ." He waved his arm around. "There seems to be more . . . more everything around here than around the king's castle."

Banquo laughed. "You think like an Englishman. The English herald London as their seat of power. Any who would be king must dwell there. But that is madness. A king should dwell wherever his own power lies—the land of his birth, surrounded by kin and friends. Duncan dwells on his family lands, as well he should."

"What you're saying is that Scotland has no capital city?"

"Capital?" Banquo scratched the side of his head. "Do you refer to Scone? True, Scotland's kings must sit on the throne in Scone Abbey for their coronation, but they need not dwell there."

"And Macbeth was born in Inverness," Sam suggested, "so he lives there?"

Again, Banquo took on an uncomfortable look. "Thane Macbeth is cousin to King Duncan. To maintain peace in the family, the king thought it best to award his cousin the Thanedom of Glamis some distance south of the family seat, rather than keep him close in Forres."

Sam rubbed his ear. "So how does Inverness enter into it?"

Banquo smiled. "Castle Inverness is Lady Macbeth's family home." The taller man laughed. "Thane Macbeth now has three seats he may call home. Glamis. Inverness. And Cawdor. In many ways, he has outdone his cousin the king."

It sounded all too complicated for Sam, but he guessed politics was like that.

As they neared their destination, the countryside continued to become more civilized. Soon they crested a low hill and a city sprawled across the horizon, the first city Sam had seen since arriving in Scotland despite having spent most of the past two days on horseback.

To the north, a wall of muddy blue made it difficult to determine where the sky ended and the inland sea Banquo had called Moray Firth began. Southward, fields stretched on forever, though Sam assumed there would be forests somewhere. In front of him, dirt roads lined with modest dwellings ran in several directions, the first evidence he had seen that Scotland supported a population that could spawn Macbeth's army or the redshank mercenaries he had encountered in England.

The train of horses descended into the city of Inverness, riding past houses and markets where common men, women, and children stopped what they were doing to observe the mounted army. If they'd heard Macbeth had won the war, they were at best indifferent about it. Some few cheered or raise a victory fist, but most bowed their heads and stared at their feet. There was not a banner or a balloon in sight. As a cop, Sam had worked security at numerous parades and other Hartford civic events. This was the worst welcome home he'd ever seen.

Even as Inverness Castle rose up in front of them, the town buildings remained modest and the roads unpaved. Sam knew it was the castle because it stood on a hill like a parliament building, with at least six towers he could see. As they drew nearer, he saw that most of the sprawling building was only two storeys, but the various towers made it look grander. The tallest of the towers was slender and rose six storeys, the battlements at the top probably used as a lookout.

Outside the castle, riders split off for stables that sat to either side of the dirt road. Sam spotted his precious gems and followed them to one of the stables where hostlers helped them dismount, pausing only long enough to gawk at the ladies' and at his own odd attire. Left with no further guidance, Sam did the prudent thing and followed several of the army's captains to the castle's main gate.

Banquo appeared at Sam's elbow. "Thane Macbeth has a private entrance. We shall join him inside."

"Do you live here as well?" Sam asked.

The tall Scotsman had laughed before, but this time it was a deep belly laugh that left him almost falling to the ground. "No. No. No, my friend. Though not as accomplished as Lord Macbeth, I too am a thane. My lands lie south of the Loch."

"The Loch?"

Banquo waved a hand past the castle. "The River Ness flows north to Loch Ness and Loch Lochy. An hour's ride beyond lies the seat of my power. Lochaber. On the morrow I shall return to my family and kin. I have long been away."

This just got better and better. No wizards. And now the only Scotsman Sam was on speaking terms with was leaving.

The inside of the castle sported high ceilings and wide corridors. Macbeth, or possibly Lady Macbeth, was big on armoured statues and mile-wide tapestries depicting bloody battlefields. Fortunately, large windows were also a preference. Light shone in through gaps in curtains that Sam assumed were drawn back on warmer days.

"I am told," Banquo announced, "that Lady Macbeth has cleared space for your . . . *night club*? Sufficient space, I am told, that private rooms shall be apportioned for you and your helpers once you advise on how the main area shall be utilized." Macbeth's good friend then gave Sam an expectant look.

"What?" Sam asked. "Today?"

Banquo frowned. "Is there reason to delay?"

He had a point. It wasn't like Sam had a favourite pub nearby where he could kick up his heels for a while.

A tall, thin man approached. Dressed like a king in flowing robes bedecked with glittering chains, he had long limp hair and a brushlike beard, both streaked with grey. As he joined them, he ducked his head slightly in Banquo's direction. "Thane Banquo. It pleases me that you dispatched Norway without personal incident."

Banquo grinned. "Steward Seyton. Well met. However, I must concede our successes to General Macbeth's stratagems. My companion is Sam Spade. I assume Lady Macbeth mentioned him."

The steward eyed Sam from forehead to knees, taking in his long Burberry trench coat. "Indeed, when Lady Macbeth spoke his name, I figured him for a foreigner. It seems I assumed correctly."

"Don't let my keen fashion sense fool you," Sam said. "I'm actually a fairly simple man."

"Simple." Steward Seyton echoed the word in such a way as to make Sam wonder if it meant something different in medieval Scotland than it did in Hartford.

Before he could explore that possibility, the steward turned and led them into the dark interior of the castle.

9
RICK'S CAFÉ

The space Lady Macbeth had set aside was indeed large. And empty. While the castle hallways had been adorned with art and side tables and benches, what met Sam's gaze was floor to ceiling brick with no windows. A single doorless portal was the only way in or out. He suspected this part of the castle had been used for storage, only ever visited by servants.

As he evaluated the space, Sam reminded himself that he knew nothing about nightclubs. But he had to say something. "We'll need tables. Round ones. And chairs." He turned a questioning look to his precious gems. "Five chairs to a table?"

The three pairs of bright eyes that returned his gaze were equally questioning.

Sam turned back to the steward. "Yup. Five. And more lights." He waved at the few lit candles that sat in metal holders along the walls, just enough to make the place feel like a dungeon. The only feature that gave the room any atmosphere at all were the ceiling supports—three rows of four stone pillars, also plain brick. "We'll need some of those candle holders on these pillars as well."

"Sconces," Seyton said.

"Whatever. And the bar will go there." Sam indicated the short wall to the left of the entryway. Conveniently, it contained a high ledge where the nightclub's inventory of fine wines and quality

47

hooch could be displayed.

The steward appeared confused. "Bar?"

While Sam knew nothing about nightclubs, pubs he was intimate with. He quickly described what he wanted complete with backless bar stools and a large ice bucket.

"You require alcohol?" Seyton asked, clearly agitated. "What quantity?"

Sam indicated the bar area. "Enough to line that wall."

The steward choked. "I was told this endeavour was to raise funds for Thane Macbeth. What you ask will bankrupt the castle."

Sam smiled. "We'll sell the hooch for double what it costs. Basic economics."

"Sell?" The steward appeared scandalized. "This is Inverness Castle, not a marketplace."

"A nightclub is a marketplace," Sam said. "Everything's for sale. How do you expect to raise funds otherwise?" Sam hated to admit it, but he was having fun. "And we'll need playing cards."

"Playing cards?"

And just like that, the fun ended. The only gambling game Sam knew was poker. If his nightclub couldn't have playing cards, what was there? Dice? The pages in King Arthur's court had fleeced the knights by introducing them to a dice game called Stones, but Sam had no idea how that was played. He rubbed his ear. "Is there an Abbot in Inverness?"

"Prior Burnett," Seyton answered.

"I'd like to speak with him."

The steward offered a parting frown and made his escape, likely elated to have been given the opportunity.

Sam watched the condescending butler leave through the large room's doorless portal, then rubbed his ear while trying to figure out what exactly the role of a Scottish steward was.

Servants began arriving with a mishmash of tables, chairs, and benches, and Sam found himself directing traffic, making best guesses where to put them. Other servants began hammering at the walls and pillars, placing the additional sconces Seyton had mentioned. Lastly, carpenters arrived hauling lumber and began building the bar.

During brief moments when he had a break, Sam investigated the three rooms that lined the back wall adjacent to the bar. They were all tiny, windowless, and empty. He claimed the first as his office, the second as his private apartment, and the third as accommodations for his precious gems. The servants gawked at his request for beds and furniture but, without the steward to consult, set out to find what they could.

As the work wound down, Sam stood with his hands on his hips and looked about the place. The stone walls were drab, and the absence of windows frustrating, but all-in-all his medieval nightclub didn't look too bad.

Once the bar was finished, he ran a hand along the surface and cocked an eye at the head carpenter. "Polish?"

"What?"

"We can't have our customers getting splinters. The wood must be polished until it glows."

The man frowned. "I am a carpenter, not a craftsman."

"I don't suppose Inverness Castle has a craftsman?"

The man's frown wagged side to side.

Sam rubbed his ear. "How about servants who polish the woodwork?"

"You must speak with Steward Seyton about that."

Here was his chance to find out Seyton's role. "Steward? Is that like a butler?"

"Steward Seyton is the seneschal."

"Good to know," Sam said, though he had no idea what a seneschal was.

As if conjured by speaking his name, Steward Seyton appeared in the entryway. His long robes swirled about his feet as he approached, and the bling hanging from his neck glittered in the light of the many candles that now adorned the room.

"Prior Burnett shall arrive shortly," Seyton said. Then the tall man stood, looking down his nose at the bar, at the tables and chairs about the room, and the augmented lighting. The additional candles on the walls, along with those hanging on the pillars, provided an atmosphere Sam felt was appropriate for intimate dining. Seyton said nothing, but the look on the steward's face suggested he was impressed.

The head carpenter spoke up. "Your Mr. Spade requests someone to polish the counter."

"Bar," Sam said.

"Of course," Seyton grudgingly agreed as he ran his own hand along the rough wooden surface.

"And we'll need a bartender." Sam leaned toward the carpenter. "*Bar-tender*. Someone to pour drinks. He should also be good with money as he'll have to keep track of and collect the tabs."

The steward let out a heavy sigh. "Of course. Is there anything else?"

"The walls could use some colour. Maybe something like the tapestries in the hallways, only less bloodthirsty."

Air pushed out from between Seyton's lips. "Very well. If there is nothing else . . . ?"

Sam rubbed his ear. "A sign."

Seyton looked at him. "A sign?"

"Hung above the entrance. How is anyone going to know we're here unless we have a sign?"

Sam noticed the thin man's back becoming more rigid. Maybe he was pushing too hard. But his nightclub did need a sign.

"And what, perchance," Seyton asked, "should be written upon this sign?"

Sam envisioned the neon sign from a Bogart film—Rick's Café Américain. Never mind the problem of getting neon to work in medieval Scotland, the sign from the movie would never do. Macbeth's customers might interpret *Café* as advertising a coffee house. No, there was only one thing that would work. He told the steward, then spelled it out for him on a piece of parchment using a quill pen not unlike the one Macbeth had used to write his letter.

A half hour later, Sam stepped out through the nightclub's doorless portal into the castle's broad hallway and turned around.

Neon would have been a help, but paint was all that was available. White letters in broad, cursive strokes sprawled across a wide length of wood that had been wedged between the entryway mantle and the corridor ceiling. The letter 'A' looked a bit odd, like four broken-down lean-tos, but the nightclub's name was legible: CASABLANCA.

10
GOD'S WORK

Casablanca?" Prior Burnett stood in the hallway squinting at the sign. The churchman stood shorter than Sam, with receding dark hair and a thin moustache. If eye glasses had been invented yet, he'd be wearing a pair. "What does the word mean?"

"It's Spanish," Sam said. "It means white house."

The prior continued to squint.

"It's also the name of a city in Morocco."

The prior's myopic gaze drifted toward Sam.

"And possibly the most famous nightclub in the world."

The aging churchman nodded. "I see." Though clearly, he didn't. After a moment he asked, "And what is a *night club*?" Like Banquo before him, Prior Burnett enunciated nightclub as two distinct words.

Sam sighed. "It's nothing unless I get some playing cards."

The prior's dim gaze moved past Sam's shoulder toward the casino entrance. "Playing cards?"

Three hours and two bottles of priory wine later, Sam, Prior Burnett, and a nervous young monk who went by the unlikely name of Alison sat back in their chairs at Casablanca's only occupied table. The monk, who had brought the wine, was Beauly Priory's best manuscript illuminator, spending his days adding coloured illustrations to religious texts. In front of them sat a trio of lit candles and a stack of paper fifty-two sheets deep, each spoiled by a hand-drawn image of a playing card. Spoiled because they had been drawn using a quill pen and a jar of ink, not by the artful monk, but by Sam's unsteady hand.

"You get the idea?" Sam asked.

Alison, who had sat mute and shaking with nerves since he had arrived, nodded.

"You don't look like you get the idea," Sam said.

"The d-d-drawings," the young man stuttered, "will b-be of no d-difficulty. B-b-but . . ."

"But what?" Sam asked.

"B-but why?"

That was a good question. Sam rubbed his ear as he glanced about the empty nightclub. Why any of this? He'd gotten so caught up in the prospect of converting this emptied storeroom into a working nightclub, that he'd forgotten what it was for. To help bloody Macbeth murder a king and take over Scotland.

He felt his cheek twitch. What he needed to do was find a way out of here. Get back to Hartford. He cast a look at the prior, then remembered Banquo's description of witches being burned at the stake. Not the time.

His gaze switched to the nervous monk. This one, once Sam got him alone, would be putty in his hands. Sam could see the illuminator spilling everything he knew without narking to the prior.

"It's what Thane Macbeth wants," Sam said in answer to the monk's question. Until he found a way back home, he needed to play along with Le Fay's plan.

"Manuscript paper won't do," the prior announced, lifting the top parchment sheet and squinting at it. "You say people must shuffle the . . . you call them cards?"

"A deck of cards." Sam searched for words. "A real deck is printed on cardstock and coated with plastic." He moved his hands above the table like he was doing an overhand shuffle.

The prior replaced the parchment sheet and tried to watch Sam's hands. "Paper will not do that. Not even if you soak it in urine and let it dry."

Try as Sam did to get that image out of his head, it wouldn't leave.

The illuminator mumbled something.

"What was that, Brother Alison?" the prior asked.

"B-boiled leather," the nervous young man muttered.

Prior Burnett frowned. "You suggest we make these . . . cards . . . from old armour?"

The young monk shook his head. "You c-cut leather into your c-card shape, only th-thinner than you would for armour. The result will be c-close to what Mr. Spade d-describes."

The prior frowned. "And you know this how?"

The monk ducked his head. "I have a c-cousin in F-F-France. He makes b-book casings from leather. A-And t-t-t-travel bags."

"Book casings?" The prior appeared scandalized, then shook his head. "Foreigners do such odd things." Again, he squinted at the monk. "Know you someone who can boil thin leather?"

Alison nodded his head like it was on a spring.

"Good then." The prior searched for the second wine bottle and poured the remaining contents into his cup. "I was afraid we would need to import this special leather from France."

Though the wine wasn't bad, Sam had hardly touched it. Apart from being busy fighting a quill, the previous night's hangover was still fresh in his mind. There were times he needed a drink. This wasn't one of them. Alison hadn't helped kill the two soldiers either. Despite having brought the wine, Burnett hadn't allowed his monk a single drop.

With both bottles now emptied and his cup drained, Prior Burnett rose unsteadily to his feet and blinked myopically at Sam. "Brother Alison shall manufacture you this deck of cards. Or rather, he shall manufacture it for Thane Macbeth. At Beauly Priory we have God's work to do. I do not see how this so-called night club is God's work."

"You've got that right," Sam said. "I'm only here out of necessity, not because this club will do anyone any good."

Burnett gave Sam a sour look, then Brother Alison scooped up the stack of drawings and helped his prior stagger toward the exit, leaving Sam sitting alone in the empty casino.

11
CLEVERER THAN NORWAY

$am sat alone in the darkened casino. Most of the candles had been doused hours earlier, and Sam's three helpers, having grown bored watching him sketch playing cards, had retired to their newly assigned apartment. With the two churchmen now departed, the castle all around him was quiet. Too quiet. A glance at his Rolex told him it was more or less midnight. The witching hour. Time for a little mischief.

Though alone, Sam didn't want to take any chances. Rising from the table, he wandered into his own newly appointed apartment, only to realize he couldn't see a thing in the dull light that spilled in from the three candles out in the casino.

Sam knew a cot had been set against the far wall and that his trench coat rested across it, having tossed it there himself. The castle wasn't cold enough to wear the fleece-lined coat indoors, but it was cold enough that he'd kept his tailored suit jacket on.

Pulling Le Fay's magic ring from his shirt pocket, he slipped it onto his left middle finger and stepped back out into the casino. For an experiment, he walked past the table that still hosted the trio of candles. Like Chuckles the groundhog predicting an early spring for Hartford, he did not see his shadow. Maybe if he could discover where Le Fay had gotten the ring, he'd find someone who could send him back to Connecticut. Yeah, and maybe he could click his heels together and chant, "There's no place like home."

Stepping out into the castle hallway, he had two objectives in mind. First, to discover the lay of the land. What did the castle near Casablanca look like, and who were its occupants? And second, to find something to eat. A sip of wine was all well and good, but while he'd been directing the arrangement of Casablanca, no one had brought him any dinner. And in Macbeth's hurry to reach Inverness, there had been no lunch on the road. Sam hadn't eaten since the morning's bowl of porridge.

He recalled from when he arrived, that the main body of the castle sat left of the nightclub entrance while parts unknown lay to the right. He turned left, and didn't see anyone until he neared the castle's main gate, where two men lounged against one of the interior walls, bored and apparently on guard duty. It was too bad they weren't playing the Stones game like the guards at Camelot. He could watch without being seen and learn the rules.

Sam shuffled to the side of the main foyer opposite the gate, where a spiral staircase rose up against the back wall. A narrow passage stood to either side of the stairwell. Sam figured them for servant corridors. Perhaps one led to the kitchen.

Unlike the hallway, which was illuminated by oil lamps, the passageway he chose was dark. He felt his way along the rough stones until he came to a narrow corridor with a single wall sconce at either end. Tossing a mental coin, he turned right and surprised himself when he came to a kitchen. He was even more surprised by its occupants. A captivating woman with alabaster skin, long dark hair, and handsome features stood hovering over a man seated at a table, a half-eaten plate of food in front of him. Macbeth.

"You have ambition," the striking woman said. "But not enough ambition. Thane of Cawdor! Cawdor is less than Glamis! And Glamis less than Inverness. You saved your cousin's crown and probably his life, and this is how he rewards you?"

Macbeth shrugged. "Banquo believes it a great honour—"

"Banquo! Lochaber is nothing! A fishing village. Banquo believes watching the sun rise is a great honour."

"Then what do you suggest?" Macbeth demanded. "That I turn down Duncan's gift?"

The beguiling woman caressed Macbeth's cheek, then ran her long, creamy fingers through his hair. "If Duncan refuses to give you the gift you deserve, then you must take it."

Macbeth turned his head up to look at the woman. "My sweet lady wife, taking the crown of Scotland is what Norway attempted, and failed. That failure cost hundreds of lives. What would you have me do?"

"Dearest, I would have you be cleverer than Norway."

"And what if my cleverness is inadequate?"

Lady Macbeth straightened, and Sam figured her for a tall woman, certainly taller than her husband. "Then mine shall have to do."

Sam must have made a noise, or perhaps a sound came from elsewhere in the castle. Macbeth looked up, his dark gaze peering toward and past Sam. The ambitious thane listened for a moment before gazing up at his wife. "We should retire to our rooms. A kitchen is no place for such talk."

Lady Macbeth nodded, and the two of them breezed past Sam and continued down the darkened hallway.

He was tempted to follow the unhappy couple, but being invisible didn't let you walk through walls. Odds were, he'd wind up with an ear to the door of their apartment, unable to make out anything they said. Besides, he was in a kitchen and there was food.

The downside of living in a hundred-room medieval castle was that refrigerators hadn't been invented yet. All those mouths to feed, an enormous kitchen, and no way to keep food fresh. He did come across the next best thing, however—a small closet with a crack in the back wall that probably went all the way outside. Cold air blew in, keeping cool the various shelves of breads, cheeses, and dried meats.

Taking a plate from a cupboard, Sam loaded it up with more than he figured he could handle. Then he sat at the table Macbeth had used and went to work. After washing the meal down with cold water from a bucket, he returned to his Casablanca apartment, removed Le Fay's ring, shed his shoes and dinner jacket, and climbed onto the cot. Huddling beneath a thin wool blanket, he was soon fast asleep.

12

AN ACCOMPLISHED BUSINESSMAN

Sam awoke in the dark with no idea what time it was. A glance at his watch told him nothing; the lumination on the dial of his Rolex needed sunlight to recharge. He reached to the floor where he'd set his phone. Above the time display that said it was around nine o'clock in the morning, was a message stating his battery was at forty-seven percent. Nothing good ever lasts. He powered off the phone to preserve its battery before setting it back on the floor.

Swinging his legs off the cot, Sam blinked his eyes at the dull outline of his door. Someone must have relit the candles in the casino, allowing a modicum of light to seep through the gaps in the wooden frame. Enough light, anyway, to see to smooth his shirt and pants, and shrug into his dinner jacket. He also smoothed back his hair and rubbed the forty-eight-hour shadow on his face. Most of the Scotsmen he'd seen had beards, but not all. There must be a barber in the castle somewhere.

As Sam emerged from his apartment into the casino, he almost didn't see the balding, beardless man sitting at one of Casablanca's tables.

"I'm sorry," Sam said. "We're not open for business yet."

The man, who was probably in his fifties as well as being fifty pounds overweight, didn't move, but gave Sam a penetrating

59

look. At last, he said, "I like what you have done with the place."

Uncertain how to respond, Sam said, "I had help."

The man snorted. "I am called Signor Ferrari."

"Really? And I thought I had a strange name."

"My father," Ferrari said, "is a merchant who journeyed here from Italy, fell in love, and stayed."

"You Italians," Sam said. "Such romantics. Are you a merchant like your father?"

"Hardly. I own an alehouse on Ardconnel Street. The Blue Parrot."

"You'll have to excuse me," Sam said. "I'm a stranger here and don't know where that is."

Ferrari nodded toward the nightclub entrance. "Fifteen minutes' walk from your front door."

"Ah," Sam said. "If you're concerned about competition, you'll have to take that up with Thane and Lady Macbeth. I just work here."

"That can change," Ferrari suggested. "What do you know about running a drinking establishment?"

"Can I be honest with you?" Sam asked.

"Of course."

"I don't know jack."

Ferrari smiled. "As I thought. It would benefit us both were you to sign over your role as manager to me."

Sam felt his cheek twitch. "I can see how that might benefit you. But what's in it for me?"

The smile widened. "You get to keep your life."

"Is that a threat?"

Ferrari rested his elbows on the table and clasped his hands together. "Of course not. But have you considered how Thane Macbeth will respond should his investment in you fail to deliver the expected results? I am told he has a terrible temper, exceeded only by that of his lady wife."

An image of a head hanging on a spike outside a castle gate flashed across Sam's mind. "I hear you. Look, I'd gladly take you up on your offer, but I'm afraid I'm not at liberty. Maybe I could hire you . . ."

"You have money?" Ferrari asked.

"Not as such," Sam admitted. "But I could ask that steward

fella to hire you. He's the guy around here with the purse."

A frown crossed Ferrari's face. "I have already spoken with the seneschal. He believes this adventure a misguided boondoggle, but does as his master asks. That and nothing more. Therefore, you must abdicate your position and force Steward Seyton's hand."

"I see you've got this all figured out," Sam said.

Ferrari nodded. "I am an accomplished businessman."

"I can see that. Look. Let me feel out how that might work, and I'll get back to you."

"You are a fool," Ferrari growled as he rose from his seat. "The longer you delay, the closer the noose tightens around your neck."

"I'm sure you're right," Sam said. "I'd just like to make sure my head won't be adorning the castle gate the moment I step out that door."

The Italian alehouse owner opened his mouth to speak, then collected himself. He smoothed his off-white jacket before turning toward the exit. "I shall call on you again in a day or two. If you still live."

Sam felt his cheek twitch. "I appreciate your confidence."

13

THREE DAYS UNTIL THE GRAND SOIREE

Sam's would-be replacement had no sooner left Casablanca, when the devil they'd been discussing strode in through the entryway. Steward Seyton's robes and bling were the same as the day before, but his limp hair appeared to have been washed, and his brushlike beard tamed.

"You are awake at last," the steward announced. "This is my third visit. I was beginning to think you would sleep the day away."

"Something you should know," Sam said. "Nightclub managers tend to keep late hours and sleep past noon."

"Your night club is not yet open for business," Seyton observed.

"No. But I was up late getting things ready."

"And are they ready?" the steward asked. "Lady Macbeth wishes to send out invitations for the grand opening."

Sam rubbed his ear. "Well. I still need a few things."

"Such as?"

"Playing cards."

"Did Prior Burnett not provide those last evening?"

"He's working on it," Sam said. "And the bar is still dry as a bone."

Seyton harrumphed. "Such a large order takes time. Assorted spirits shall begin arriving later today. And I have hired someone to tend them."

It took a moment for Sam to realize that by "tend them" Seyton meant a bartender. "Fellow named Ferrari?"

"That scoundrel? Don't be absurd. If that is all that remains outstanding, then you shall open your night club in three days hence. I shall inform Thane and Lady Macbeth."

Three days. Sam felt his cheek twitch. "There is one other thing. We'll need a piano. And a piano player."

Seyton frowned. "Piano?"

"You know. Strings in a box. A lot of keys?"

The steward shook his head.

"A musical instrument."

"Ah." The unpleasant man smiled for the first time. "Bagpipes."

"Uhm. No. An instrument that doesn't sound like cats being tortured."

So much for the smile. "Perhaps you prefer the harp?"

Sam rubbed his ear, his mind working through how long it might take the carpenters who put together the bar counter to construct a functional piano. More than a couple of days. Maybe a lot more. "You got a big harp? You know? The kind where the harpist sits on a stool and reaches out with both hands to play the strings?"

Seyton's frown deepened. "I shall find one."

"And a harpist?"

A sneer crossed the steward's face. "You shall not play it yourself?"

"Not if you want any customers."

The tall man turned to go.

"Hey!" Sam said. "Where can I find some breakfast?"

A heavy sigh blew between the steward's lips. "The morning meal is long past. You must needs retire to the kitchen. I can show you—"

"That's okay," Sam said. "I'll find it."

Seyton cocked an eye.

"All these castles are pretty much the same," Sam said, though nothing could be further from the truth.

The steward shook his head and practically sprinted for the exit.

With the pompous butler gone, Sam tapped on the door of the apartment assigned to his helpers. Remembering how small the room was, he wondered how the castle staff had managed to squeeze in three cots.

Emerald opened the door, her long chestnut hair hanging loose and a wide-eyed expression on her face. Her eyes, Sam noticed, were dark green with flecks of brown. If her singing career failed to take off, she would do well as a cosmetics model. Provided medieval Scotland had cosmetics models. Or cosmetics.

"Have you had breakfast yet?" Sam asked. "You and your sisters?" he amended, not wanting the question to sound like an invitation for a date.

"Hours ago," the young woman responded. "We did not know if you wished to be awakened. You did work late."

"That's fine," Sam said. "I was just checking." He turned to leave.

"Wait," Emerald said. "Shall you be opening the nightclub this evening?"

"A real eager beaver, aren't you?" Sam responded.

Emerald frowned. "I am an entertainer, not a woodland creature."

Sam found himself momentarily lost for words. "Bad figure of speech. What I meant was that you seem eager to start work."

"It is why we are here," Emerald said, as though that answered everything.

"Right. Well, not this evening. We've got three days until the grand soiree. Should be big. It sounds like the Macbeths are inviting the entire country."

That put a smile on the young woman's face. "Good. Our venture shall be a huge success." Without another word, the precious gem shut the door to their apartment.

Sam stood for a moment, then scratched the two-days-growth on his chin. He couldn't remember the last time he had seen a lowly employee so excited about the success of a business.

14
WHEN IT INVOLVES ALCOHOL, NO ONE IS BETTER

The kitchen, which had seemed large while cloaked in night's shadows, looked even bigger in the light of day. The curtains on the several windows had been pulled back, letting in sunlight as well as fresh, ice-cold air. Several cats lounged on the floor and cupboards. And a bevy of cooks hustled about preparing the next meal—lunch or dinner, Sam couldn't tell.

After giving Sam the once-over, the cooks opened the cupboard he had discovered the night before and assembled a plate of bread, dried meat, and even dryer cheese. Well, what did he expect? Bacon and eggs? The women stood and watched with wide eyes as he cobbled together a sandwich and took a bite.

After swallowing, he asked, "You don't happen to have a glass of milk you can spare?"

Wordlessly, one of the cooks dipped a ladle into a deep pot and poured an off-white liquid into a cup. Despite a tinge of yellow, it smelled like milk and tasted even better.

"Must have a high fat content," Sam said, toasting his audience. The women looked at each other with slightly scandalized expressions.

"Don't mind me," Sam said. "I'm a foreigner."

After finishing his sandwich and milk, he thanked the cooks and made his way back toward Casablanca thinking he should be there when the first of the beer arrived. And that maybe he should sample the local brew, just to make sure it was suitable for Macbeth's guests. But he also needed to know the status of the playing cards Alison the monk was creating.

At the foyer inside the main gate, he noted the two guards giving him the same odd looks they had given him on his way to the kitchen. The pair ducked their eyes as he turned toward them.

"Hey. You two look like you know up from down. Could you tell me how to get to Beauly Priory?"

The guards looked at each other, then one said, "It could nae be simpler."

The other nodded. "Take the bridge to the west bank o' the River Ness."

"And go north tae Telford Road," the first continued.

"From there," the second said, "head west tae Clachnaharry Road along Beauly Firth."

"Follow Clachnaharry past the village o' Rhindui."

"Tae the village o' Inchmore."

"Then turn onto Kirkhill Road and proceed through the village 'til ye come tae the River Beauly."

"This is the only tricky bit," the second guard said. "You mist follow the bank o' the river north 'til ye come tae the Priory crossing."

The first guard shook his head. "'Tis nae tricky. The crossing is weel marked. Here ye wull find monks waiting on one side or t'other tae ferry ye o'er tae the priory."

"Tricky perhaps," the second guard argued, "for a foreigner unfamiliar wi' priory crossings."

The first guard snorted and wagged a finger at his companion. "Surely foreign lands also hae priories and rivers, and therefore crossings. 'Tis pretentious tae assume all foreigners ur idiots."

The second guard waved a hand at Sam. "If this one's country is the same as ours in such respects, then he wid nae be foreign, wid he? Look how he is dressed? Ah hae ne'er seen a foreigner mair foreign."

The first guard's finger-wagging increased in intensity. "Yet he speaks oor language as though born tae it. Surely, he haes dwelt among us fur some time. Ye cannae simply assume he is ignorant o' oor ways."

"Uhm," Sam said, interrupting. Even if he could remember the directions they had given, he wasn't sure he could follow them. "I don't suppose there is a carriage service?"

The two guards looked at each other again, then broke out laughing.

When he could speak, the first guard said, "Inverness is tae wee a town tae require carriages."

The second suggested. "You ur a guest o' Laird 'n' Lady Macbeth, ur ye nae? His Thaneship may be willing tae lend ye a horse."

"That's okay," Sam said. "I had no idea the priory was so far out of the way."

The two guards shrugged, then watched as he turned back toward the nightclub.

Back to plan A—wait in Casablanca for the arrival of his bar stock.

As it happened, he didn't have long to wait. Sam had just returned and taken a seat at the empty bar, when in waltzed a twenty-something fellow with wavy light-brown hair and a pencil-thin moustache.

The man danced his way behind the bar and leaned across it on his elbows, his lips turned up in a sardonic grin. "You must be Sam Spade."

"And you must be Sacha, the bartender."

The grin faded. "I am indeed a barman, but my name is Donnachac Mhic Dhuinhne."

"Right," Sam said. "In here we'll call you Sacha."

"Sacha." The name rolled off the bartender's tongue. "Sounds foreign, but I like it."

"Are you good at math, Sacha?" Sam asked.

"When it involves alcohol, no one is better."

Sam rested his elbows on the bar as well. "Well Sacha, I think this is the beginning of a beautiful friendship."

The bartender jerked back slightly and an uneasy smile crossed his face. "Yes, we shall get along. But you should know I have a wife."

Sam laughed at the misunderstanding. "Of course, you do.

And I have a lady friend."

He thought of his business partner Nora, and the on-and-off-again flirtation they had shared over the past year. And her welcome, albeit unexpected, invitation to meet her parents on New Year's Eve. There was something going on there. There had to be.

He sobered and rubbed the two-days' growth on his chin. Morgan Le Fay had left Nora speeding down a highway in a driverless car in a blizzard. He had to get back. Back before something tragic happened.

"And everything is well with you and your lady friend?" Sacha asked. In the spirit of true bartending, Sacha was going to be Sam's psychoanalyst as well.

"Maybe," Sam said. "I hope so."

Sam considered the friendliness of his new employee and how it reminded him of Banquo, now gone to his own family in Lochaber. Bartenders were like priests. You could confide in them, get advice, and they'd keep your secrets. He opened his mouth to explain his situation with Le Fay and his need to return to Hartford, when a commotion from the direction of the nightclub entrance drew their attention.

A big man, with bulging biceps and a chest like a mountain, strode toward them and thunked a wooden crate onto the counter. "Mair whaur this cam from," the man grunted. He turned and left.

Sacha rose up on his toes and peered into the crate. "Looks like I have a shelf to stock."

15
THE SLEAGH MAITH

Sam left Sacha to the business of setting up the bar and retired to the room he had designated as his office. It contained a desk, several hardback chairs, and, of course, no window. The only light came from the open doorway connecting the office to the casino. He surveyed his kingdom in silence, all the while wondering if he even needed an office. Then he sat in the lone chair behind the desk, rubbed his forehead, then stood up again and walked back out into the nightclub and through the neighbouring doorway into his private apartment.

The apartment was the same size and shape as the office. But instead of a desk, it contained a cot—a flimsy contraption that was low to the ground with a thin, wool-stuffed mattress set across a slat-lined frame. The pillow was nice, however. Soft and stuffed with feathers.

Though a far cry from his walnut-finish Concorde platform bed in Hartford, the cot was more comfortable than the office chair. Maybe he'd take a nap.

He did manage to fall asleep, but wasn't sure for how long before Sacha rapped on his open door. "We have a man out here with a harp."

Sam sighed, shrugged on his ivory dinner jacket, fastened the buttons, then strolled out into the nightclub.

When Seyton said he'd find a harp and harpist, Sam had expected a sea nymph. Some leggy blonde with hair down to her waist and fingers like the legs of a spider. The man who stood before him could have played defence for the UConn Huskies' football team. He was clean-shaven with short-cropped hair, and stood six foot six if not taller. His height wasn't the only thing that made him unusual for a Scotsman. He was black.

"You Sam Spade?" the man asked in unaccented English. Without waiting for an answer, he grinned and said, "My name is also Sam."

"Sam what?" Sam asked.

"Just Sam."

"Well, Just Sam. I understand you play the harp."

"And sing," Just Sam said, his smile highlighting a mouthful of large, perfect teeth.

"Okay. Why don't you give us a sample?"

Just Sam turned his towering frame toward the far corner of the nightclub, where a monstrosity of a stringed instrument stood almost as tall as the ceiling. Snatching up one of the backless bar stools in one hand like it weighed nothing, he carried it over and plopped it down behind the harp. He then sat on the stool, reached out to either side of the strings, and strummed a few notes.

Music—gentle, resonant, mellow, and melodious—resonated throughout the room.

Sacha stepped up beside Sam. "The fellow isn't half bad."

Sam nodded. "Funny how much more you can say with a few bars of music then a basketful of words."

As though overhearing the conversation, Just Sam began to sing.

"Och ochan a Rìgh, gur tinn an galair an gràdh—"

"Wait, wait," Sam said. "Do you have anything in English?"

The huge man scowled. "English?"

"Never mind. I'll teach you a tune or two later. You're hired. Why don't you leave things where you've set up. That's as good a spot as any. Maybe we can shuffle some of those tables around so you're not so crowded."

Just Sam grinned and went about shifting some of the tables. Then sat back down and resumed strumming the tuneful piece he had started earlier, without the singing.

Sam was no expert, but he had to admit the harpist knew his strings.

Following Sacha back to the bar counter, he sat on a stool and scratched his chin as the bartender danced to the music while plucking small wooden casks, tall clay bottles, and ornate metal jars out of crates and placed them on the high ledge along the wall. A mirror above the ledge would have made it perfect, but Sam knew he was on a budget. And a tight timeline.

"Hey Sacha!" he called. It was now or never.

The bartender looked over his shoulder. "Mr. Spade?"

"Call me Sam."

Sacha glanced at the harpist. "I thought his name was Sam."

"You're right. Call me Mr. Spade."

"Very well. Mr. Spade. What can I do for you?"

Sam knew he'd have to tackle this carefully. "You've probably noticed I'm not from around here."

Sacha nodded. "There are many foreigners in Scotland." He smiled and threw a meaningful look at the harpist.

"Yeah, well," Sam said. "Just Sam's got nothing on me. I'm from further away. And from the future."

The bartender continued to smile. "Anything you say."

"No. I'm serious. A witch stole me from my home and brought me here."

More smiles. "If you say so, but you should know there is no such thing as witches."

Sam's heart fell. "I wish that were true. Have you heard anything, anything at all, of someone in Scotland who may have magic?"

The smile grew uncomfortable. "I am sorry, Mr. Spade. I have no doubt you are right in what you say, but there is no such thing as magic."

Sam had to hand it to him. Sacha knew how to walk around a mine field. He tried another tack. "You haven't heard of anyone named Merlin?"

A shake of the head.

"The Lady of the Lake?"

More shaking.

Sam pursed his lips, and a deep, gut-wrenching hopelessness

encompassed his soul. If tricking Morgan Le Fay into sending him home was his only option, he had his work cut out for him.

"You don't mean," Sacha whispered, "the daoine sìth?"

Sam whispered back, "The who?"

"The sídhe?"

When Sam still had nothing, Sacha said, "The Sleagh Maith. Fairies."

"Ah!" Sam reacted so strongly, Just Sam paused in his strumming.

"Fairies," Sam whispered once the music resumed. "Perfect. Where do I find them?"

Light glittered in Sacha's eyes. "The Sleagh Maith. The Good People. You should know there are two courts: the Seelie, dangerous though often helpful; and the Unseelie, dangerous and never helpful."

Now they were cooking with gas. "This Seelie Court. Where is it?"

"Where is it?" Sacha appeared troubled. "There is no *where*. It is a folk tale."

Sam felt his cheek twitch. "Doesn't the folk tale give them a location?"

"Of course. The realm of faerie."

"Then where is that?"

Sacha shrugged. "Everywhere. And nowhere. It is not here."

The bartender began talking in circles. No matter what Sam asked, the answer was: you can't get there from here. It was obvious Sacha didn't believe any of it, anyway.

Sam gave up. He needed to find someone who did believe in fairies.

16
THERE IS THE MATTER OF CUPS

Having failed at coaxing the name and location of a magic worker out of Sacha, Sam carried his barstool over to Just Sam and his harp, where he spent the next twenty minutes crooning the melody and lyrics of the love theme from *Casablanca*'s "As Time Goes By". It sounded awful in his own ears, and his feelings were vindicated by his three precious gems who emerged from their apartment to listen and giggle.

Just Sam, however, listened patiently, recreating with his standing harp stanza by stanza Herman Hupfeld's classic jazz tune. Once he had the melody, the harpist ran through the song from beginning to end without a sour note or missed lyric.

Sam was tempted to sing along, but figured he'd just throw the harpist off. Besides, he'd endured as much ridicule from his so-called helpers as he could stand.

The fun over, his precious gems returned to their hibernation, and for the next while time did go by. Just Sam continued to practice his repertoire for the grand soiree, occasionally throwing in Casablanca's theme song, a tune which Warner Brothers later also used for their production logo for films and television. Just Sam's harp rendition of the familiar melody was perfect every time.

Once again seated at the bar, Sam watched as Sacha placed a

final jug of beer on the ledge behind the counter, then dance a happy dance reminiscent of Snoopy, Charlie Brown's faithful and fun-loving beagle.

"It is gorgeous, is it not?" the bartender asked with apparent pride.

Sam had to admit there was something majestic about a wall of liquor. "Here's looking at you, kid. Now how about you pour me one of those. Give it a trial run."

Before Sacha could oblige, more footsteps echoed from the nightclub entryway. Sam looked over hoping to see Alison the Illuminator and his deck of leather playing cards, but it was only castle servants bringing Sam and his crew their dinner. Unlike King Duncan, Thane Macbeth had chosen to not invite him to the royal banquet. On the other hand, this was the first meal in Inverness he hadn't missed, so he at least had that.

While they were eating, Steward Seyton arrived and stood looking about the room. The tall man's gaze lingered on Just Sam, who hulked in his seat across from Sam and Sacha at one of Casablanca's tables. "Who is this?"

Sam set down the stick of mystery meat he was chewing. "The harpist you sent me. He's good, by the way."

Seyton frowned, but when he saw the size of the harp occupying the far corner of the room, he sighed. "Not what I expected."

Sam smiled. "I suppose the fates intervened."

"Do not let Prior Burnett hear you speak of fates," the steward warned. "The Church will hang you as a witch."

"Not popular around here?" Sam hedged. "Witches, I mean."

"The scripture is clear," Seyton said. "Witches, wizards, and necromancers shall be put to death."

"What about fairies?" Sam asked.

Confusion twisted the tall man's features. "Fairies are not Human. I mean, they do not exist. Why would scripture forbid that which does not exist?"

"So?" Sam asked. "You're saying witches and wizards do exist? And necromancers?"

"The foulest of the lot," Seyton grumbled. "The dead should be left alone. But this is dangerous talk. We shall speak of it no more."

"Okay," Sam said. "What shall we speak of?"

The steward lifted his chin. "I see liquor aplenty behind your bar. And a source of music. Is all ready for your grand opening tomorrow evening?"

"Tomorrow? You said three days."

The tall man fingered one of the gold chains that hung from his neck. "Lady Macbeth felt that too long a wait. King Duncan and his sons arrive tomorrow. As do many of the thanes. Lady Macbeth and her good husband have decided to welcome them with the grand opening of your night club."

"Well, that's . . . we're not ready. I still need my playing cards."

The steward shook his head and let go of his bling. "If Lord and Lady Macbeth say the night club opens tomorrow, then it opens tomorrow."

Sam could tell the arrogant butler was enjoying this. "Have you heard anything from the priory?"

"Nothing," Seyton said, unable to keep a smile from his face. "But for good or ill our guests arrive tomorrow. Following the evening meal with our lord and lady, they shall be entertained in your night club."

"It won't be much of a soiree without the cards," Sam said.

Still smiling, and with a malicious twinkle in his eye, Seyton said, "Irrelevant."

"Sir?" Sacha, the third party at their table, looked up at the steward. Though they could have crowded in a sixth chair, Sam's precious gems had elected to sit several tables away where they kept their conversation to themselves and picked at their food. "There is the matter of cups."

"Cups?" Seyton seemed confused.

"I cannot pour drinks without something to pour drinks into. We have a handful of tankards here and several drinking bowls, but we require dozens. Many dozens."

The steward sighed. "Cups."

Sam mentally kicked himself for not thinking of that. He quickly searched his mind for anything else he might have missed. "Snacks would be helpful," he suggested. "Something salty. That's a trick pubs use to get customers to drink more."

Both Seyton and Sacha gave him a quizzical look. "It is?" Sacha asked.

"It is where I come from."

"Your countrymen are devious," Seyton suggested, his tone implying he was impressed rather than appalled.

Sam laughed. "You have no idea."

After the steward left, the food eaten, and the plates cleared, a troop of servants entered Casablanca carrying trays of pewter mugs and metal cups. Sacha directed them to set the trays in the space below the back of the counter where he could easily access them.

Then Sam and his bartender sat on a pair of backless stools at the counter where they sipped barley beer and listened as Just Sam entertained them with yet one more rendition of "As Time Goes By".

17
WHAT DO YOU KNOW ABOUT WITCHES?

The evening grew late and castle servants arrived to extinguish the candles. Sacha and Just Sam took that as a cue to leave Casablanca and return to wherever they called home in the town of Inverness. Sam's precious gems also disappeared into their apartment. He still had half a drink left, so he remained at the bar counter nursing it. Without saying a word, the servants left a few candles burning near where he sat.

Sometime later, Sam was slumped over the bar counter, his head resting on his arms, half asleep, when Alison the illuminator entered the nightclub so quietly Sam didn't know he was there until the monk cleared his throat at Sam's shoulder.

"Your p-playing cards, s-sir."

Sam blinked the sleep from his eyes as the priory's best illuminator placed a tall stack of leather coasters in front of him. Then he blinked again. They weren't coasters. They were the playing cards he had sketched the night before, only these were elaborately drawn and in full colour, painted onto hardened leather rectangles. The fifty-two leather plates stood about five times the height of a normal deck. Sam could work with that.

Slowly, he scooped up a double handful of cards and attempted a riffle shuffle. The stiff edges of the leather cards bounced against each other, and several went flying across the counter and onto the floor. Alison bent down to retrieve the fruit of his labours while Sam gathered up the nearer escapees. Looked like the Irish Shuffle would have to do.

Turning the cards face down on the counter, Sam swirled them around, applying pressure to force random cards under other random cards.

"You painted nothing on the back?" Sam asked.

The monk sighed. "The suggestions you made would have t-taken an extra day. You s-said you were in a hurry."

Sam continued smooshing the cards. "That's okay. These will work fine."

With a riffle shuffle, it took only seven passes to randomize a proper deck of poker cards. He had no idea how much smooshing was required. And this deck was anything but proper. After about a minute, he stopped, piled the cards back into a deck, then flipped them over to show Alison they were no longer in sequence. Brightly coloured face cards sat like orphans among the more plentiful, plainer, numbered cards.

"You do not wish them in order?" the monk asked.

"That would defeat the purpose," Sam said. He paused and raised an eyebrow. "Your mother named you Alison?"

"T-t-'tis a good Sc-Scottish name," the monk retorted. "My m-mother's name is Alice. I am her son."

"I'm not judging," Sam said. "Just curious. Thank you for the excellent work. Uh. Where are the other decks?"

Alison's eyes grew wide. "Other decks? I have given you what you requested."

Sam picked up five cards and fanned them out in his hands. "Each deck has fifty-two cards. But that's only good for one game. A nightclub like this needs several games going at once."

As the young man swayed to one side, Sam dropped the cards and reached to catch him before he hit the floor, but the monk recovered himself. Raising one hand to each side of his head, Alison said, "If I w-work all night, I can have you a s-second deck by this time tomorrow."

It was tempting. But Sam could see by the tiredness in the young man's eyes, and hear in the roughness of his voice, that Alice's son had already missed one night's sleep.

"I'll make a deal with you," Sam said. "You go back to the

priory and get a good night's sleep. Once you're well rested, you can work on a second deck and it will be done when it is done. How does that sound?"

The monk narrowed his eyes. "You mentioned a deal. What is in this arrangement for you?"

"How come you're not stuttering?" Sam asked. "You sounded like a broken record last time you were here. Tonight, you've hardly stuttered at all."

Alison ducked his head. "Prior B-Burnett makes me nervous."

Sam chuckled. "I get that. No need to be nervous around me. I'm as gentle as a kitten. But you're right about the deal. I do want something. Where I come from, we have no prohibition against talking about wizards and witches."

The young monk's eyes nearly burst from their sockets. "It is f-f-forbidden."

"I get that," Sam said. "But I'm in kind of a jam. This witch, you see—"

"W-Witch!"

"No need for you to worry," Sam said. "She's a long way from here. Other side of the country. But she put a curse on me." Sam figured that was the easiest way to describe his relationship with Le Fay without making things complicated. "I need to get that curse lifted, so I need to speak with someone who knows something about witches."

The monk simply stared at him.

"Are you that someone?" Sam asked. "What do you know about witches?"

Alison finally worked his jaw loose. "I-I know . . . not to speak of them."

Sam forced a smile to his lips. "You can see how that won't help me. Do you know of anyone who can help?" Sam held his breath.

Alison held his tongue.

It was a race to see who could hold out the longest.

Just as Sam was about to suck in a mouthful of air, the monk murmured, "Prior B-Burnett."

Sam slowly inhaled. "Prior Burnett knows about witches?"

Alison nodded. "He put one to death once."

Sam felt a muscle in his cheek twitch. If Burnett had had an argument with a witch—a real witch—he didn't think the prior would have won. "How about wizards? What do you know about wizards?"

18
FIVE MERKS RICHER THAN FIVE MINUTES AGO

It was a long, restless night. More than once, Sam was tempted to put on Le Fay's magic ring and haunt the castle like a ghost. But what good would it do? Everyone he'd spoken to had been too frightened to talk about, or claimed to have no information on, anyone in Scotland who offered the least shred of magic. Was that why Le Fay had left England? Magic-wise, did she have Scotland all to herself?

As he lay on his cot, Sam wondered how long it would take to walk to England. He could go to Locksley Castle and ask Robin Hood if Merlin was still hanging around Sherwood Forest. Or if the Lady of the Lake had finished coming back from the grave. Walking to England seemed farfetched, but so far it appeared to be his best option. Or maybe he could steal a horse and get there faster.

Well before sun-up, Sam dragged himself out into the casino area of the nightclub only to find his three precious gems huddled together at a table whispering to each other.

Ruby spotted him first. "Did we wake you?"

With only the candles the servants had left the night before, Casablanca was mostly dark. Grim shadows made the young redhead's hair a lurid brown, and her dark eyes a pair of empty pits. Her companions didn't fare much better. Sam assumed he must also look something of a ghoul standing as he did in the gloom.

Idly, he parked himself near a candle and pulled back his coat sleeve. His Rolex suggested it was south of five in the morning. "Why are you all up so early?"

"We were too excited to sleep," Emerald trilled in a voice that was more bird than human. Perhaps the young woman really could sing. "Today is the big day. Grand opening!"

"*Tonight* is the grand opening," Sam corrected. "Not today. We have hours to go yet."

"We are ready now," Sapphire said, the violet in her eyes cutting through the dark shadows. "Casablanca. Casablanca!"

Sam rubbed his ear. "So, you all know how to play poker?"

The three young women exchanged uncertain glances. Then Ruby said, "With the playing cards?"

"Close enough."

After retrieving the monk's deck from the bar counter, Sam sat at their table. The light from the sconces near the bar wasn't going to cut it, so he retrieved one of the lit candles and used it to light several others near the table. Still not the best lighting in the world, but it would have to do.

"Okay. This is how you shuffle between games." Sam spread the cards facedown and smooshed them around. "You'll need to mix them up for a full minute, then stack them like so. Now you're ready to deal. I'm going to teach you a game call Five Card Draw. The rules are pretty simple, but you'll need to be proficient at it and be able to teach the customers how to play."

All three precious gems nodded.

"First, we have the ante. Before the round begins, each player puts a penny in the pot."

"Penny?" Sapphire asked. "Do you not mean a merk?"

"Is that what you call them here?" Sam asked.

Emerald laughed, then quieted when Sapphire gave her a look.

It didn't worry Sam not to be in on the joke. "Merks, then. After shuffling the cards, you deal five to each player, face down." He dealt each of the young women five leather cards off the top of the deck.

"Go ahead and look at your cards."

Ruby began turning hers over.

"No!" Sam reached across the table to stop her. "Watch me."

Sam dealt himself five cards, then picked them up and fanned them out. "Like so. The idea is to not let the other players see your cards."

The ladies all followed his lead. Quick studies.

"Okay. Now. Depending on how good your cards are, you'll either throw another merk in the pot to stay in the game, or you'll fold and lose your ante."

"Which cards are good?" Ruby asked. "The ones with the king and queen painted on them?"

Sam smiled. "It's a bit more complex than that." He quickly ran through the poker ranks from High Card to Royal Flush.

Emerald threw her cards down onto the table. "My hand is worthless."

"Not so hasty." Sam put down his own hand and gathered up Emerald's. "See here? You've got an ace and a king of spades. Ace high isn't bad at this stage. What a player will probably do with this hand is toss anther merk in the pot."

The green-eyed brunette looked uncertain as she took back her cards.

"This is where things get fun," Sam said. "Everyone who hasn't folded gets to trade in some or all of their cards. Emerald, you may want to keep your ace and king and trade in the other three."

"Okay." She threw down three of her cards and Sam dealt her three replacements.

"I shall take two," Ruby said.

Sapphire smiled and wagged her head. "I wish to keep all of my cards."

The other two precious gems gave their sister looks as cold as daggers.

"Are you certain?" Emerald asked.

The raven-haired beauty looked at her two companions, then threw down her hand. "After careful reflection, I shall take five new cards."

Sam felt his cheek twitch as he dealt out five cards. "You'll get the hang of this after a few games. This is now your final hand where the highest rank wins. It's also more interesting because you can bet as many merks as you like. If you feel your hand is a stinker, you can fold. If you feel you might have the best hand, you can play it cool and throw one additional merk into the pot. If you throw in five merks, you may scare off the other players. If everyone else folds, you don't win much."

Ruby stared at her hand. "I don't know what to do."

Sam got up and walked around behind Ruby's chair. Her hand held three nines, a jack, and a two. "That's not a bad hand, especially when everyone is new at the game. You should probably throw one or two merks in the pot, hoping to string along the others and win big. Or you can throw in more and hope everyone else folds, leaving you what's already in the pot. That's called a bluff."

"I shall bet one additional merk," Ruby said.

Sam smiled. "Playing it safe, huh? That's okay."

"I bet two merks," Emerald said, waving her cards like a prize.

Sam walked around behind her chair. The brunette's hand was still only ace high. He wondered if she knew she was bluffing. "Okay, so now to stay in the game Sapphire has to bet at least two merks. Or she can fold."

"I bet two merks," Sapphire said.

Instead of checking Sapphire's cards, Sam looked at Ruby. "That means you need to either fold or throw one more merk into the pot to stay in the game."

Ruby stared at her cards, her lips twisting in indecision. Finally, she said, "I shall stay in the game by betting one additional merk."

"Okay," Sam said. "Since no one raised the bet further, the round is over. None of you folded, so whichever of you has the best hand wins the pot."

All three precious gems laid their cards down in synchronized fashion. The timing couldn't have been more perfect if they had practiced it.

Sam shook his head. He couldn't recall ever meeting a more baffling trio. "Ruby has three of a kind, nine high, which beats Emerald's ace. Sapphire has . . . nothing. You should have folded."

Sapphire merely smiled. "These merks we are betting are a

fabrication, so I risked nothing by continuing in the game."

Sam held back a laugh. "That's true, but your customers will be paying with real merks, so you need to take the game seriously."

"I like this Five Card Draw," Ruby said. "But how does the casino make money?"

"Of course, *you* like the game," Emerald said. "You won. But I too am curious how this benefits Casablanca."

"Good to see your business sense," Sam said. "Ruby won the round, so she wins the pot. After the house takes its cut."

"Cut?" Ruby asked.

Sam waved a hand at the table. "You'll each take a shift as dealer. That's the role I took for this practice game. For your games, you'll have two to four players who will ante up and place bets. The house's cut is ten percent rounded down. That's one merk if the pot is less than twenty merks. Two merks if between twenty and thirty. And so forth. Ruby, you won this round. You put in three merks. The other two players put in three each. So, the house takes one merk and Ruby gets eight, for a profit of five merks."

Ruby's eyes went wide. "I am five merks richer than five minutes ago?"

This time Sam did laugh. "That's why people play. Emerald and Sapphire each lost three merks, but in the next game one of them could be the big winner. The idea is for players to not win or lose too much over time. The house only earns its cut if people stay in the game."

"So," Emerald said, "if someone wins too much, we should make them lose the next few hands."

"And if they lose too much," Ruby said, "we should see to it they win a hand or three."

"Uhm." Sam rubbed his ear. "People are going to play as well or as badly as their nature dictates. There's not much the dealer can do about it. Just be sure you explain the rules well. Hopefully we'll have enough business we can afford to weed out anyone who has difficulty grasping how the game works."

"Of course," Sapphire said. "That makes perfect sense. We should continue to practice now? Correct?"

Sam nodded, then took a candle from one of the sconces and

walked into his makeshift office. Taking a blank sheet of parchment off the desk, he returned to the poker table and began tearing it into small pieces. "You can use these for practice in place of merks."

His precious gems sat staring at him.

"Is something wrong?" Sam asked.

"A waste of good parchment," Ruby said.

Sam paused. "Is it worth more than a merk?"

The three young women shook their heads.

"Then we should be fine with it, financially anyway."

19
I SHALL ENDEAVOUR NOT TO BLEED

By the time castle servants arrived with breakfast, Sam felt his precious gems had Five Card Draw down pat. The young women really were quick studies, even if they did keep suggesting reasons to rig the game. Sam's assurances that there was no need, that the house always wins regardless of what the players do, seemed to fall on deaf ears.

Sacha and Just Sam showed up along with the servants and, after finishing the modest meal, Sam volunteered the two men as poker guinea pigs with the pieces of paper used as money. The bartender was keen on the idea, cracking jokes on how he would use his winnings to buy a stone cottage by the river, while the sombre harpist had some trouble fanning out the cards.

"My fingers are tuned to work the strings," Just Sam complained. "Not fondle these leather drawings."

In the midst of this, Steward Seyton entered the nightclub and observed Sacha dancing in his chair after winning a hand and raking in a small pile of parchment pieces. The stodgy butler shook his head. "This is the game you so desperately needed in order to open your night club? I fail to see the attraction."

"This is just a friendly game," Sam said. "When we open, we'll be playing for money."

"Money," the steward echoed. "How much money?"

"A lot," Sam said. "Which reminds me. This will go a whole lot smoother if we have poker chips."

Seyton frowned.

"Never mind. Our customers will need a lot of merks to play. Maybe Sacha at the bar could exchange merks for larger currencies."

Seyton continued to frown. "Larger currencies?"

"You know," Sam said. "Whatever is worth more than a merk. Silver or gold coins."

"The merk is a silver coin."

Sam flashed a glance at his precious gems, who had implied a merk was a copper penny. Returning his gaze to the irritated butler, he asked, "How much money do you expect your guests to bring with them to Casablanca?"

"Guests are unaccustomed to bringing any money with them. They are accustomed to relying on the generosity of their host."

Sam felt his cheek twitch. "It might have been nice if someone had mentioned that little chestnut before we started this venture."

"Promissory notes," Seyton suggested.

"What?"

The steward let out a heavy sigh. "You shall require your guests to sign promissory notes for anything purchased at the bar—" he turned his gaze toward the poker table "—or spent while gaming."

Sam rubbed his jaw. As a cop he'd seen a lot of people destroy their lives by using credit to support a gambling habit. Or even a drinking habit. "Thane Macbeth is good with this?"

Seyton's forehead tightened. "The political structure of Scotland is built on promises. What Thane Macbeth requires is the support of his peers. If they are indebted to him financially, he shall have that support."

Sam continued to rub his jaw. High stakes gambling on credit. Why not? He'd figured all along that this venture would end in tears. He only hoped those tears weren't his own. "We're going to need a lot of paper."

The steward sneered. "I shall have some official notes drawn up."

Once the contemptuous butler left, Sam rejoined his staff and explained how the casino's guests would pay for things.

Sacha shrugged. "So it is with the peers of the realm. They do not dirty themselves with lesser things such as money. They shall sign away their lands and titles, then feign outrage when a reckoning is due."

"So long as Macbeth is happy, I'm happy," Sam said. "Say, you don't know where a man can get a shave around here?"

The bartender's gaze zeroed in on what was now a thirty-six-hour shadow. "I assumed you were growing out your beard."

"Not by choice."

"Ah." Sacha grinned. "I frequent a barber in the town, but Inverness Castle must have a surgeon. Most castles do."

"A surgeon? I don't need my appendix removed."

Sacha laughed. "Unless you wish to scrape a kitchen knife across your face, you shall visit the surgeon. No one else has the requisite tools and skills."

"Right. Go back to your game and I'll see if I can catch up with Seyton."

The steward's long legs had taken him out of sight, so Sam asked the gate guards for directions. Fortunately, these directions were easier to follow than the way to the priory—just a short distance north along the main hallway.

The castle surgeon, an older man with wild white hair and a bushy moustache reminiscent of Albert Einstein, was busy with a customer. No gallstones or knee replacements. He was trimming a man's beard.

When his turn came up, Sam climbed onto, for lack of a better term, the surgeon's operating stool.

"You are the fellow with the night club," Einstein said.

"What gave me away?"

Einstein gave him an appraising look. "Everything."

"Just a shave, please. I'll leave the trim for another time."

The surgeon stirred the contents of a cup, then slathered foamy soap across Sam's cheeks and chin. "Opening night, I understand."

"Therefore, the shave," Sam said. "It would be a plus if I looked halfway presentable."

Taking a wicked-looking blade in one hand and holding Sam's head steady with the other, Einstein grinned. "I shall endeavour not to bleed you too much."

20
IT IS A CELEBRATION

Sam couldn't remember a time when his face felt so raw. There had been blood. A bit. But that wasn't what bothered him. He was sure he'd paid Einstein for his shave with a pound of flesh. Literally. No wonder so many men in Scotland favoured beards.

On his way back to Casablanca he stopped at a Necessarium he'd discovered earlier in his explorations. After finishing his business, he remained seated on the throne and patted his face with a towel. The bleeding had mostly stopped, but a mirror would have been nice so he could assess the damage.

By force of habit, he searched his pockets for a nicotine patch before remembering he'd declared himself cancer-stick-free back around Halloween. No more patches. It had been a twelve-year struggle to quit his two-pack-a-day habit. The last thing he wanted was to be put down by cancer like his idol Humphrey Bogart, but he sure could use a hit right about now. Maybe one of the containers behind the bar held whiskey.

Sam exchanged the Necessarium throne for a barstool in Casablanca, where he sat rubbing his raw chin.

"Whiskey?" Sacha's forehead wrinkled. "Describe it."

Dropping his hand to the counter, Sam eyed the various containers lined up along the wall behind the bar. "I drink whiskey; I don't make it. I'm pretty sure the good stuff has something to do with malt barley and yeast."

"That sounds like every ale I have ever tasted," Sacha said.

"Well, it's got to age. At least three years."

The bartender's eyes widened. "Three years? The best ales are aged three months."

"Fine. Pour me your oldest ale."

Sacha selected a dusty container from behind the bar, worked off the lid, and poured out a small amount. With his only customer served, the bartender returned to the poker table.

Sam remained sitting on his bar stool and sipped from a wooden cup something undeserving of the name whiskey. It was no Four Roses Single Barrel, but then again, he was no Rick Blaine.

At the poker table, his precious gems and Sacha smooshed illustrator Alison's deck of cards and laughed about their well or poorly played hands. Just Sam had left the game to tune the strings of his harp. Maybe losing imaginary money didn't come as easily to the harpist as it did his other staff members.

Time seemed to drag until, eventually, Sacha returned to the bar to organize things for the opening, and Sam's precious gems retired to their room, hopefully to rest up for the big event.

While nursing the remains of his drink, Sam kept one eye on the nightclub entrance. He expected Macbeth, or at least Lady Macbeth, to drop by and confirm that all was ready for their big soiree, but no dice. He also hoped Banquo would return from his thanedom in the south and poke his head in before the place opened. But nothing. Not even curious castle staff peered in from the hallway. The only person to drop in was a servant delivering Seyton's promised promissory notes. The young man, who was hardly older than a boy, displayed no interest whatsoever in the nightclub.

When less than an hour remained before Casablanca opened for business, Sam couldn't sit any longer. Needing to rid himself of nervous energy, he strode to the nightclub's doorless portal and looked out into the empty corridor. Not a soul. Not a sound. Would anyone even come? No one knew what a casino was. Why would they care? Macbeth would have to order his guests to visit the nightclub.

Hearing voices and then footsteps further down the corridor,

Sam stepped back inside and waited to greet Casablanca's first guests. He was sure his face visibly fell when Seyton stepped in through the doorway followed by a lesser servant of some kind.

"All is in readiness?" the steward asked.

Sam nodded. "Ready or not."

Seyton frowned. "Many of Lord and Lady Macbeth's guests have been arriving throughout the day. I find I am no longer able to keep them amused. That is now your task."

"Fine," Sam said. "Send them in. I'll try out my stand-up comic routine on them."

The frown deepened. "Do not embarrass me in front of Lord and Lady Macbeth or their guests. You may not live to regret it."

"I'm sure I'll have plenty of regrets," Sam said, "but the only person I'll embarrass is myself."

The steward shook his head and stepped back out into the corridor.

Sam turned around and clapped his hands. "All right, boys and girls. I can't keep them out any longer. Be prepared to entertain and extort. Whatever you do, keep an eye on those promissory notes. We mess that up, and our lives won't be worth living."

Sacha laughed from behind the bar and began to whistle. Just Sam strummed his harp with perhaps a bit more feeling. And his precious gems, who had emerged from hiding a while earlier, scurried toward the entryway like excited school girls. If all of Macbeth's guests were of the male persuasion, this evening might just be a success.

Several minutes dragged by, then Seyton appeared leading a string of overdressed, grey-haired, and bearded gentlemen whose lined and drawn faces suggested they had just walked to Inverness from the other end of Scotland. Their expressions brightened when Sam's precious gems rushed up offering to take their cloaks. The guests seemed not to even notice the nightclub manager standing right in front of them.

Sam figured the helpers Le Fay had provided were more qualified at their role than they'd let on. Each of the young ladies quickly made the guests feel welcome, found them a table, gave directions to the bar, and successfully educated them on nightclub etiquette, which the expressions on their faces clearly indicated was a new concept for them.

Virtually all of the guests were indeed men. Sam didn't see Macbeth or Lady Macbeth among them, and figured they would make a grand entrance later. He didn't see Banquo either. Perhaps Macbeth's good friend wouldn't come back from Lochaber.

Ruby took the first turn as dealer at the poker table, with thanes and generals competing to be the first to try their luck. Whether it was the game or the game's dealer that piqued their interest, Sam couldn't decide. Other guests sat at tables, nodding in agreement as Emerald and Sapphire offered to bring them drinks from the bar. The guests happily signed promissory notes without even looking at them. The casino was either going to be a roaring success, or it was going to start a war.

The last tables taken were the ones nearest Just Sam and his sky-scraping harp. The guests at first seemed apprehensive about the towering musical instrument and the giant man who sat behind it, but once Just Sam began playing, they seemed to enjoy the unintelligible, tongue-twisting tunes on offer.

Sam kept station just inside the nightclub entrance, where he greeted new arrivals brought to him by the steward. On one such occasion, the pretentious butler was accompanied by none other than Thane Macbeth and his handsome lady wife. The trio ignored Sam as they entered Casablanca and surveyed the nightclub. Then Seyton loudly cleared his throat.

Just Sam, who must have been watching for this moment, ceased playing in mid-pluck. When the rest of the noise in the room subsided, Macbeth stepped forward and endeavoured to make a speech.

Over the years, Sam had been subjected to his share of political campaign speeches, all unavoidable because he had been assigned by the East Hartford Police Department to provide security. On the obnoxious scale, Macbeth ranked a nine. What prevented him from rating a ten out of ten, was that he kept his remarks short and sat down after only a few minutes.

The wannabe king didn't outright say, "If you help me dethrone my cousin and place the crown on my head, I will ensure your current positions and future advancement," but anyone who was paying attention could have guessed the message.

The result of the speech was to turn the conversations in the room toward Duncan's recent proclamation that his cowardly son be next in line for the throne.

"The people will not stand for it," one octogenarian wheezed to his neighbour.

"We are at war with Norway, the Irish, and the English," said another. "We require a king who inspires the troops."

"Someone like General Macbeth," suggested a third, possibly one of Macbeth's close supporters.

This went on for a while until there was a commotion at the nightclub entrance. Sam had been so preoccupied with eavesdropping that he failed to notice the arrival of King Duncan and his attendants.

Sam was still stationed near the entryway, but hesitated in welcoming Scotland's doomed king. He wasn't sure what to say. Especially after overhearing some of the room's conversations. Fortunately, he was rescued by Lady Macbeth.

"My Lord King!" Macbeth's lady wife had risen from the table she shared with her husband and three of Scotland's prominent thanes. Lifting her voluminous skirts to avoid tripping over them, the Lady of Inverness hurried among the crowded tables before demonstrating a deep curtsy in front of the man she wished her husband to replace.

"Arise, fair lady," Duncan responded, oblivious to the plot against him. "Such obeisance is unnecessary. Are we not family?"

Lady Macbeth straightened. "Even so, you are a visitor in our home and are due the deference owed an honoured guest. We are ever your servants."

"And where is your husband? The new Thane of Cawdor so recently a guest in my own home?"

"Macbeth is near. Here, let me take you to him."

Sam followed the small party to the table furthest from the entrance, one Seyton had commandeered for Macbeth upon his arrival. For the first time, Sam noticed a small platter of what looked like crackers acting as the centrepiece of many of the tables. He assumed they were salty, and that Seyton had listened to him after all.

As they neared the general's table, Sam heard Macbeth

extolling King Duncan's virtues to those gathered near him.

"Our king has been a humble leader," Macbeth commended. "Free of corruption. When he escapes this mortal coil, angels shall play trumpets to extol his virtuous legacy—Ah, Duncan!" The conniving general looked up in surprise. "We were just speaking of you." Macbeth quickly rose from his seat, as did those with him.

"Sit! Sit!" the king responded. "You do me too great an honour." Duncan cast wide one arm, taking in the room. "I have never seen . . . whatever this is. Drink!" He glanced down at the crackers. "Food." Then his gaze took aim at Just Sam, who had resumed playing. "Music. Cousin, you have outdone yourself."

"It is a celebration," Macbeth declared. "In the midst of our dispute with the English, Norway and Ireland sought to take advantage. But under your peerless leadership we have prevailed and are now stronger than ever before."

"You give me too much credit, cousin. I am but an old man. It is you who took the field and turned back our enemies. I declare this night's celebration be in honour of Macbeth, Thane of Glamis and now Cawdor!"

"All hail Macbeth," the men around them shouted.

Sam thought both men were pouring it on a bit thick, but maybe that was normal for political rivals.

He felt an elbow in his side, and turned to find Steward Seyton whispering in his ear. "Why are you not at the door? More guests are arriving."

Sam knew that no explanation would satisfy the steward, so he returned to the entryway and resumed greeting Scotland's curious assortment of movers and shakers.

21
ACT LIKE A MAN

From his station by the entryway, Sam watched as the evening progressed. With the arrival of the king, conversation became more circumspect, drink flowed faster, and voices rose in volume.

Not everyone was in a celebratory mood, however. Two men with watchful eyes and dressed head to toe in leather, sheathed swords at their side, stood near where King Duncan now sat at Macbeth's table. Sam hadn't had a good look at the two soldiers in the alcove outside Duncan's bedroom in Forres Castle, but wondered if these were them. Bodyguards.

When the king decided to try his luck at the poker table, the two guards followed. They looked both professional and capable. Macbeth's murder would not be easy.

Eventually, the number of new arrivals slowed to a trickle and Sam decided he should work the room. He could ask guests if they needed anything, and could see how his precious gems and Sacha were handling the growing pile of promissory notes.

"There was some initial reluctance," Sacha admitted, "with people questioning Inverness hospitality. We told them it was for the war effort, and that seemed to settle things."

"Let me know if anyone gives you trouble," Sam suggested. "We don't have a bouncer, but Just Sam is pretty intimidating. One cool-eyed look from our harpist, and I'm sure folks will sign on the dotted line."

Sacha laughed. "Just Sam is the gentlest of men I have ever encountered. A cool-eyed look may be foreign to him. But fear not, I have been known to comport myself handily at Neffiels and Possing."

Sam had no idea what that meant. Apparently, neither did Le Fay's magic communication spell. Not knowing how to respond, but feeling he should, Sam said, "Never say die. That's my motto."

The evening seemed to be going smoothly, with no call for Neffiels or Possing, until Sam realized Macbeth and his stately wife had left their table. Searching the room with his eyes, he spotted the edge of Lady Macbeth's long skirts sweep out through the nightclub's entryway portal.

He crossed the casino floor at a fast walk and stuck his head out into the corridor. Left toward the main section of the castle, he saw nothing. Looking right toward parts unknown, he spotted the local lord and lady stepping quickly away. They seemed to be arguing.

Sam pulled himself completely into the corridor and, after ensuring that no one was watching, slipped on Le Fay's magic ring. He then followed as softly as he could, down the corridor in hot pursuit.

At the end of a darkened corridor, below what looked like a servant stairway, Macbeth stood speaking with his wife, his voice low yet angry. "We cannot proceed with this plan."

"And pray why not?" Lady Macbeth demanded.

"The king has just honoured me. He declared the celebration in my name, not his. Am I to return his good will with a sword to his belly?"

"An empty honour!" his lady wife growled. "For defeating Norway and saving the king's neck, never mind his crown, he named you a party. A party you arranged. And his coward son who has done nothing—who can do nothing—he has given the kingdom. Are you a man?"

"What kind of question is that?" Macbeth snapped.

"Then act like a man. You know what must be done. Do it. If you will not, I will."

"You?" Macbeth's eyes glowered in the dark. "Women are not meant for such deeds."

"And yet, if you will not be a man, then it falls to me to be one. One way or another, Duncan shall die this night."

Sam had heard enough. Tonight was the night? Le Fay had him under a barrel, forcing him to help Macbeth become king. But she hadn't said anything about helping Macbeth murder the old king. Or . . .

He thought back over his time in the cavern, and what Le Fay had said. His job was to raise capital by managing a nightclub. That was it. She hadn't said anything about murder. Not helping. And not hindering. Didn't that leave him free to do whatever he wanted on his own time? Such as warning the old king? Or sabotaging Macbeth's murder attempt?

As he made his way back along the corridor toward Casablanca, Sam smiled.

22
THE WIND SPEAKS?

Shortly after Sam returned from his hallway eavesdropping, Macbeth and his wife also stepped back inside the nightclub and rejoined the thanes at their table. Sam ignored them and continued his rounds of glad-handing, encouraging Casablanca's guests to enjoy themselves. He avoided the poker table where King Duncan was losing his shirt to several of his peers, and spent an inordinate amount of time in Macbeth's corner of the room, hoping and failing to gain more insight into the plotting couple's plans.

Apart from Sacha's warning that they were running low on beer, there didn't seem to be any emergencies. A second or third poker table would have been useful, but the fact people had to wait their turn to play only seemed to heighten their interest.

Promissory notes were piling up behind the bar counter. Sam figured they were as good as cash, so leaving them out in the open stuck in his craw. He explored his tiny office, and eventually transferred the notices of promised payment to a narrow space between the side of his desk and a wall. Tomorrow, he'd find the head carpenter and have him build either a lock for the office door or a safe for storing valuables.

He resumed his rounds as host until he saw King Duncan, along with the old man's two sons and dutiful guards, heading toward Casablanca's sole exit. Sam had watched for an opportunity to warn the Scottish King of Macbeth's plot, but never found a private moment, what with the crowded room. Maybe this was his chance.

Without attracting attention, he worked his way across the floor toward the nightclub entryway and slipped out into the corridor. Le Fay's ring was on his finger almost before he'd cleared the portal.

Duncan had a good head start, but Sam had an equally good guess which direction he'd gone, and soon caught up. At the castle's main foyer, the king's party was climbing the curving staircase to the higher floor, and stopped only once to check behind them when the heel of Sam's Thorogood Oxford shoe made a scraping sound on the stone steps.

At the top of the stairwell, Sam watched the cluster of men turn off the main corridor into a smaller one that seemed to be its own wing. By the time Sam caught up, Duncan and his sons were safely ensconced behind closed doors, with the two guards standing as rigid as Buckingham Palace Beefeaters to either side of what must be the king's guest room.

Well, Sam had known this wouldn't be easy. Even invisible, there was no way for him to enter Duncan's room without upsetting the guards. That left him no option but to give the guards the warning. That was their job, wasn't it? To protect the king?

Sam reached to slip off the ring, then looked again at the two bodyguards. The men's faces were hard, their eyes alert. Sam figured them for the stab first, ask questions later type. Best to leave the ring where it was.

He took a couple of stealthy steps toward them before speaking in a stage whisper. "Macbeth plans to murder the king."

"What wis that?" the nearer guard whispered.

The other answered, "'Tis the wind."

"The wind speaks?"

"Your muckle ears listen fur whit's nae there."

Sam repeated his whisper. "Macbeth plans to murder the king. Tonight."

"There!" the nearer guard said. "Do ye nae hear it?"

"I hear the wind. Are we nae alone in this hallway? Or dae we share company wi' a ghost?"

"I knew a ghost once," the nearer guard said. "Well, afore she wur a ghost, ah knew her. Efter she died, thare wis no talking tae her."

The further guard chuckled.

"Hey!" Sam growled, raising his voice slightly. "Macbeth plans to murder the king."

Neither guard said anything. Then the further one said, "There is nae such thing as ghosts. Yer deid friend wis just that. Deid."

Sam let out a heavy sigh and turned away. These guys weren't going to respond to anything short of a frontal assault, and he couldn't see himself finding his way back to Nora with a couple of meat cleavers stuck through his belly. Besides, if he was absent from the nightclub for too long, people would notice.

"There you are," Seyton grumbled as Sam re-entered Casablanca. "Where were you?"

"The Necessarium," Sam lied.

"The what?"

"The bathroom."

A frown darkened the steward's face. "The bathhouse is for the sole use of Lord and Lady Macbeth. Who permitted you entrance?"

"Not bathhouse. Bathroom. You know, the water closet."

Seyton continued to frown.

"The place where one relieves oneself?" Sam suggested.

The steward's expression softened. "The garderobe."

"That's where I was. I'm back now."

"Very well." Seyton straightened, his features taking on an official expression. "Our guests are beginning to retire for the night. You must wish them well and bid them return tomorrow for a continuation of this evening's enjoyment."

"Right, sure," Sam said.

"Some few," Seyton added, "who fared well at your gaming table and are unable to return on the morrow, are seeking renumeration."

Sam rubbed his ear. "They're looking for silver?"

"Merks," Seyton said.

Sam continued rubbing his ear. "I'm afraid I'm fresh out of

merks at the moment."

The steward untied a heavy pouch from his waist and placed it in Sam's hands. "I expect a full accounting in the morning of all monies received and disbursed and all promissory notes outstanding, including a list of names with all amounts owed us as well as paid out."

"Uhm," Sam said. "Don't we have an accountant for that?"

"Of course, we do," the steward answered. He smiled, and an evil glint shone in his eyes. "You."

23
YOUR DUTY NOW IS DONE

Given the choice between glad-handing departing guests and doing the books—Sam couldn't do both at once—he picked up the new accumulation of promissory notes from behind the bar and retired to his office.

The windowless room was too dark to get any work done, so he stepped back out into the casino and stole one of the candles from its sconce on the wall. The candle was thick as his fist and twice as tall, and gave off a slight odour of bacon. He could live with that. It was less bright than he would have liked, however, so he set it near the centre of his desk hoping to illuminate a greater workspace.

After closing the office door to shut out the noise and gain a little privacy, he retrieved the promissory notes he'd hidden earlier and set them on top of the rest. The fragile paper mountain looked ready to tumble onto the floor, so he slid his Rolex off his wrist and set it on top as a makeshift paperweight.

When the castle staff first set up the small room to include a stack of blank parchment, a quill pen, and a bottle of ink, Sam had had no idea what he would use them for. The stationery had come in handy for drawing playing cards for Alison the illuminator and for tearing into temporary poker chips, but tonight's business . . . well, he was sure that had been the steward's intended use.

Taking the top promissory note from the stack, he stared at it, the printed letters and numbers barely legible in the bad lighting. Sam had called it correctly. He had no idea what he was doing, and that was the truth of it.

He stared at the note a while longer before setting it down and looking at several additional notes. Each was for a single transaction. A cup of ale, or several cups for a table. The win or loss from a single poker hand. No wonder there were so many receipts. He was going to have to educate his staff in the concept of running a tab.

He began by sorting the notes by customer, which quickly overflowed the desktop into dozens of stacks taking up every inch of the floor. He found himself carrying the candle in one hand while placing notes with the other. It was messy and it was time-consuming, but he eventually worked though the teetering mountain of promissory notes.

Before getting too confident, Sam stepped out into the casino and retrieved another handful from Sacha which he quickly sorted onto the correct piles.

Next, he took each stack and sat at his desk, jotting down numbers and tallying totals, one blank parchment for each customer. It was fortunate he'd had practice with the quill and ink while drawing the playing cards, otherwise his scrawls might not be legible.

Those customers with a balance due, which were not many, he set to one side, then listed their names and amounts on yet another blank parchment. Once done, he tallied that sheet up and took it along with Seyton's bag of coins out to Sacha.

"I understand there may be a few guests looking to collect their poker winnings before they leave."

The bartender nodded. "That mean-looking lot against the far wall. They have been eager to leave, and less than happy when I asked them to wait."

Sam leaned against the bar counter and took a long gander at several leather-clad men who looked military and must be officers of some kind. The Scots didn't seem to have a standard uniform or insignia beyond the blood-red strip of cloth he'd seen the lower ranks wearing. The thanes and senior officers seemed to prefer leather over linen, and no one in Casablanca that evening had bothered with the low-budget armband.

He had planned to ask Sacha to hand out the winnings, but now changed his mind. Sam figured he'd done all the grunt math; he might as well see it through to the end.

The officers watched him approach, their gaze fixed first on his dinner jacket and matching pants, then the clutch of parchments in his hand, and finally the sack of coins he set down on a table. "You are the night club manager," one said, a statement rather than a question.

"Sam Spade, at your service."

The man rubbed his beard. "This *night club*. It is a strange yet amusing thing."

Sam nodded. "That's nightclub. One word. Casablanca is the finest bar and casino in the world. Maybe the only nightclub in the world."

"But why?" another asked.

"Why what?"

"Why did you establish your nightclub here? In Inverness of all places?"

Sam felt his cheek twitch. "I came for the palm trees and tropical breezes."

"But this is the Northern Highlands."

"I was misinformed. Look. I understand each of you did well at the poker table."

The officers brightened visibly at the subtle praise. One of them said, "A most amusing game. Much more interesting than Stones."

"Where can I purchase my own deck of playing cards?" another asked. He was shorter than the others and seemed to have a lazy eye that kept wandering to one side. "My warband leaves Inverness on the morrow."

Another added, "Which is why we cannot wait until tomorrow evening to receive our winnings."

Several of the officers gave Sam a look that suggested a lack of confidence in said winnings being forthcoming, and that there would be repercussions should that be the case.

"I have your money right here," Sam said, giving the bag on the table a friendly pat. "The cards are another story. There's only one deck in existence. The one here in Casablanca. Maybe you'll rotate back in the near future."

The fellow with the lazy eye tried to speak, but Sam interrupted. "If you tell me your names, one at a time, I'll dole out your cash."

That got all the officers shouting their names at him.

"You," Sam said, pointing at the nearest man. "Name?"

"Ingelram," the officer said quickly. "Ingelram Brùn."

Sam leafed through his tallies. "Here you are." He set the tally sheet on the table and counted out coins from the bag. Then he pointed at the next closest fellow.

The final officer waiting for payment was the one with the lazy eye. Gaufrid Mac a' Ghobhainn. That was a tongue teaser. Sam looked at his tally sheet and pursed his lips. "You did quite well."

Mac a' Ghobhainn threw him a Cheshire grin. "I feel this game comes naturally to me."

Sam nodded. "Uh-huh." He counted out the man's coins. "Or maybe you just had a lucky night."

The officer ignored the warning. "About your deck of cards. Perhaps I could purchase yours."

Sam couldn't help but chortle. "Or perhaps you could quit the military and become a full-time gambler."

"That is a profession?" Mac a' Ghobhainn asked.

"Not a long-term one. Anyway, the cards aren't for sale. And don't get any funny ideas. This place isn't mine. It belongs to Thane Macbeth. Mess with it at your own risk."

Without another word, the officer took his winnings and left the casino.

Sam let out a heavy sigh and took his paperwork and Seyton's remaining coins back to his office. He decided to leave the remaining paperwork for morning. There were still a few notes to come in, so why get ahead of himself?

Returning to the bar, Sam sat on a stool at the counter and looked at Sacha. "Is there anything left to drink?"

"Only if you are not picky," the bartender answered.

"Just make sure it's wet. Has Macbeth left yet?"

Sacha nodded toward the poker table where the lord and would-be king sat glowering at his cards.

Sam chortled. "Not much of a poker face."

"Poker face," Sacha echoed, then laughed. "No, he has not. You should see his 'I have a good hand' grin."

"They'll learn," Sam said. "I wasn't great at it either the first time I played."

"It is a strange game," Sacha agreed. "Stones is much simpler." Sam cast his gaze about the room. "I don't see Lady Macbeth."

Sacha topped up Sam's cup. "The bonny lady left some time ago. Shortly after King Duncan."

That wasn't good news. Especially if Macbeth had decided not to be a man. "Do me a favour, will ya? Keep an eye on my office door. Make sure no one goes inside."

"You are leaving again?"

Sam drained his cup and set it on the counter. "For a few minutes."

"You are the boss."

A few minutes was at best optimistic. It took Sam that long just to traverse the castle back to the royal guest room, even with the aid of invisibility. While there had been numerous people moving about the castle, none of them had been Lady Macbeth. Sam hoped he was worrying over nothing.

The king's guards, when he approached, were no longer talking. Not about the wind or ghosts or anything. Neither were they standing at attention like stalwart Beefeaters. They were sitting on the floor, slumped against the corridor wall, legs splayed out in front of them. For a moment Sam feared they were dead, but was disabused of that thought by the sonorous whistles of snoring.

Between them lay a jug and two cups. Sam could tell from the smell it was wine. Strong wine.

He stared at the sleeping guards, then the door, remembering now from Shakespeare's play what had happened. Lady Macbeth had brought the guards wine. Probably commended them for their diligence in guarding the king so professionally, but feeling sorry that their duties denied them the privilege of indulging themselves at Casablanca along with everyone else.

"But your duty now is done. No trouble shall attend the king here. Partake of the wine as is your due and on the morrow, none shall be the wiser."

Yeah, Sam could just imagine what the woman might have

said. Lady Macbeth seemed good at convincing people what they should do. Maybe *she* should be king.

If the play held true, Duncan could still be alive behind the door. One small knock and Sam could explain . . .

Yeah, what could he explain? How he, a foreigner, was standing in the corridor outside the king's guest room next to the king's guards, drugged by person or persons unknown? Offering a wild tale of how the king's cousin and loyal general planned to murder him, but in two stages. First by getting the guards drunk. Then coming back later to finish the job. Right. Who'd believe it? Sam knew he wouldn't.

Standing there in the hallway, invisible, he rubbed his ear.

There was another way. All he had to do was convince Macbeth not to go through with it. Or, failing that, foil Macbeth's attempt at murder. That would probably be easier.

24
IS THIS A DAGGER I SEE BEFORE ME?

By the time Sam got back to Casablanca, the evening was winding down. The lion's share of guests had retired for the night, taking their good spirits and loud voices with them. Just Sam sat on his stool, playing an encore on his harp for the few stragglers that remained. Sam wondered if the big man ever got blisters on his fingers. Sacha was keeping himself busy by stacking used cups onto trays and arranging empty casks and jars into the larger crates they had arrived in.

Most of the remaining guests were gathered around the poker table where Sapphire was closing the night as dealer. As luck would have it, one of the last players was Thane Macbeth. Or maybe not luck. Maybe he was consciously or unconsciously putting off his promise to his wife for as long as possible.

By the look on the would-be killer's face, the thane's hand was at best mediocre. Maybe three of a kind or two pair. The other players, though Sam could tell they'd had a lot to drink, hadn't drunk enough to be suicidal. The fellow seated with his cards facing Sam had a full house, tens over eights, but opted to fold rather than bid against Scotland's champion of the battlefield. Smart. The two players who failed to fold had empty hands, allowing Macbeth to take the pot with a pair of jacks.

As the wannabe king watched his opponents sign the requisite promissory notes, Sam clapped his hands. "Sorry folks, but the party ends here. It's late and your wives and loved ones will be waiting for you. Come back tomorrow evening and we'll pick up where we left off. Consider Casablanca your home away from home."

Sam could see an argument forming on Macbeth's lips, but the other chairs slid back and were vacated before he could speak. The ambitious thane cast about himself in frustration, then sighed and stood.

For the first time since they had met at the edge of a forest near the cavern of the weird sisters, Macbeth looked at Sam and spoke. "You have done well here. Your sponsors spoke truly of your talents."

Sponsors. He meant Morgan Le Fay and her two witch friends. Sam felt his cheek twitch. "Happy to help." He'd hoped to say the words with more enthusiasm, but it was late and he was tired, and he still had a lot of work to do.

Macbeth seemed not to notice the slight. Sam figured the murderous thane's thoughts were on his own dark work that lay ahead that evening. There was no room to consider the impertinence of a temporary subordinate.

With most of the other guests already gone and Seyton nowhere in sight, Macbeth stalked alone toward the nightclub exit.

Sam waited until the would-be king disappeared into the hallway before turning to Sacha. "I should walk our host to his rooms. He's had a bit to drink and doesn't seem in the best of spirits."

"You are the boss," Sacha said.

Sam sighed. "Yeah. Sad, but true. Hey. Drinks for everyone on staff. On the house. Since I'm the boss, I can do that."

Just Sam must have heard him from across the room. The big man ceased playing, stood, stretched, and rubbed his fingers together. He had probably played them raw. The smile on the harpist's face was brighter than it had been all day. For his part, Sacha let out an exuberant whoop. Sam's precious gems, however, seemed indifferent. Perhaps they were teetotallers.

Leaving his staff to sort themselves out, Sam made for the exit. The corridor outside Casablanca was dark and quiet, with less than half the usual number of lit lamps. Even so, Sam could make out the shape of a murderer with a mission walking slowly toward the castle's main foyer, a rough beast slouching toward Bethlehem.

Slipping Le Fay's ring onto his finger, Sam followed, catching up to the Thane of Glamis as he climbed the spiral staircase. Instead of turning toward the royal guest room where King Duncan lay sleeping with his two guards passed out outside his door, Macbeth went the other way. At a branching corridor, the thane turned and continued walking until he came to the furthest door. Sam hurried his step and managed to squeeze himself inside the room before the door closed.

Macbeth's apartment was more spacious than Sam had expected, certainly larger than those he'd encountered in Camelot Castle. Like Camelot, there was an outer chamber and an inner bedroom, the difference being the outer chamber here was at least three times larger. You could comfortably set up two regulation billiard tables and still have room for a bar area.

In place of pool tables, the living room was furnished with several cushioned bench seats, hardback chairs, tables, and cabinets. Tapestries covered the walls, except where a window let in natural light during the day and cold air at night. Grudgingly heating the room, several logs crackled in a stone fireplace. A half-dozen candles sat about the apartment providing additional light.

"There you are." Lady Macbeth sat primly on a cushioned bench, an embroidery loop in her hands and a scowl marring the cool features of her face.

For a moment, Sam was afraid she was speaking to him. But the magic of Le Fay's ring was intact, keeping him invisible just beyond Macbeth's shoulder.

The scowl tightened. "If you dawdle much longer, the guards shall awaken."

"So," her husband said in a low voice, "you have done your part."

"And more," Lady Macbeth said. "I entered Duncan's chambers and almost did the deed myself. But he looked so old and frail lying there. He reminded me of my father on his deathbed. Even so, my blood ran hot from the wine I imbibed in that silly nightclub you commissioned, and the knives were warm in my hands. It would have been so easy."

"Why did you not persevere?" Macbeth demanded. "The old man may remind you of your father, but he is my cousin and I have loved him all my life."

Lady Macbeth threw down her needlework and rushed to her husband, enfolding his slight frame in her arms. "It must be you. How can you take Duncan's place if another clears the way?"

Macbeth shook off his wife's embrace and stepped back.

The Lady of Inverness snorted, then turned and picked up two knives from the top of a dresser. "Your destiny lies in the moment. If you would be king, choose your path." Then she threw the knives onto the floor and rushed into the back bedroom, slamming the door behind her.

Sam stood watching as Macbeth stared at the two blades. The aspiring murderer then turned toward an elegant side table that held a pitcher and several goblets, and poured himself a drink.

Sam couldn't help himself. He bent down and picked up one of the knives. The dagger weighed more than he had expected and fit snuggly in his hand, the blade separated by a cross guard and maybe two thirds the full length. If, after Duncan was killed, Sam returned to Hartford with one of the knives actually used in the murder, how much would it be worth? But, of course, if he prevented Duncan's murder, the dagger would be worthless.

A gasp caused him to look over at Macbeth, who held a cup in his trembling hands and stared at the knife. "Is this a dagger I see before me?"

Sam sighed. Now he'd done it.

Macbeth blindly set his cup on the table. "The handle toward my hand?"

What? Sam stared at the knife. The handle was pointing nowhere near Macbeth. It was facing more toward the door to the hallway.

"Come," Macbeth whispered. "Let me clutch—"

"Are you still here?" Lady Macbeth shouted from the bedroom. "I am coming out there, and if you and the daggers are not away, you and Duncan both shall feel their blades."

Macbeth hesitated, then lunged toward the knife in Sam's hand.

Sam let go and stepped back, then watched as the Scottish thane juggled the knife as it fell toward the floor, at last catching it by the hilt with both hands.

Even as the bedroom door swung open, Macbeth snatched the second blade off the floor and lunged toward the exit to the hallway. Transferring both blades to one hand, he batted at the latch with the other and yanked the door open.

Sam managed to follow at his heels out into the corridor before Lady Macbeth pushed the door shut behind them. Despite having escaped the apartment unscathed, Macbeth continued to race along the corridor. Sam followed after. The Scottish thane appeared to be mumbling. To himself or to the daggers, Sam wasn't sure.

"I go," Macbeth whispered. "And it is done."

A church bell, or something very much like it, sounded somewhere in the castle. A single, resonant gong. Midnight?

Macbeth paused, listening. "The bell invites me. Hear it not, Duncan, for it is a knell that summons thee to heaven or to hell."

Then he was off again, sprinting along the shadowed castle corridor.

25
BLOOD IS A WONDERFUL SIGHT

As Sam pursued a maniacal Macbeth through the castle, he pondered the various ways he might prevent Duncan's murder.

He could trip up Macbeth, but in his current befuddled state the thane might fall on his own knives and kill himself. What would Morgan Le Fay say to that? Or do?

Or he could try what he did with the two guards. Be a ghostly voice in the night. He could be to Macbeth what Jacob Marley was to Ebenezer Scrooge, and admonish him not to do it. Be a better man. But wouldn't that just befuddle Macbeth further? And he was armed. The madman could lash out at the ghostly voice and have two murders on his hands instead of one.

Or, Sam figured, he could shout for help. Rouse someone along the corridor to step out and see what was happening. But if the other apartments were as spacious as Thane and Lady Macbeth's, any alarm he raised might not be heard.

He was still dismissing potential solutions when they arrived outside Duncan's door. The two guards sat slumped on the floor, snoring, just as he had seen them earlier that evening.

Sam watched as Macbeth stepped over the two men's legs without giving them further notice. The two knives were clutched in the thane's left hand as his right descended toward the apartment's door latch. Sweat dribbled down the would-be murderer's face, and mumbled words fell from his lips. "Now half the world lies asleep and are deceived by evil nightmares. Old man murder, having been roused by the howl of his wolves, walks silently to his destination."

Sam felt he had to do something, so he kicked one of the guards. Nothing. He shuffled over and kicked the other one. Also nothing. Instead of rousing themselves to confront Macbeth, the two guards continued snoring. That wine must have packed quite a punch.

The impending murderer had ceased his mumbling and lifted the latch. As he pushed open the door, Sam opened his mouth to speak, to say something, anything, to prevent Macbeth from entering the apartment. But before words came, the would-be assassin slipped through the doorway.

Sam ducked inside after him, bumping the door as he did so. Macbeth hesitated at the sound, then whispered at the floor. "Hear not my steps, which way they walk, for fear the very stones reveal my whereabouts." Then he was moving again.

The layout of Inverness Castle's presidential guest suite was similar to the apartment Sam had just left, but looked less lived-in. The tables and cabinets were, for the most part, uncluttered. Candles sat unlit, the only light coming from several logs in the fireplace that had burned down to mostly embers.

Macbeth, undeterred by the darkness, was opening the door to the back bedroom. Sam had no plan for stopping him apart from tackling him to the floor, but then what? Throwing caution to the wind, he followed Macbeth into Duncan's bedchamber.

The King of Scotland lay on a king-size four-poster bed, complete with canopy. The mattress was elevated, so the old man would be hard to reach. If Macbeth was going to kill rather than injure the man, he was going to have to all but climb onto the bed first.

"So still a moment," Macbeth whispered. "A silence so appropriate for what I am about to do." The would-be murderer raised the two daggers, one in each hand, then slowly lowered them again.

Sam recognized the move. Hesitation. Reluctance. Second thoughts. Back when he was a cop, he'd seen this in half-baked criminals all the time. They would boast and bluster and drink to work up the courage. But when push came to shove, they couldn't go through with whatever hateful act they'd intended. That was a line that, once crossed, couldn't be uncrossed. Macbeth had brought himself to that line.

"Witches," the hero of the recent war muttered, "offer sacrifice to their goddess, Hecate. And while I stay here talking, Duncan yet lives. The more I talk, the more my courage cools."

And then, before it even registered to Sam what was happening, Macbeth threw himself against the giant bed, his arms raised, his feet leaving the floor, and his torso flying across the blankets. Extending both arms as far as they could reach, the murderer swung the twin daggers downward into Duncan's heart.

"No!" Sam shouted. But it was too late. And if Macbeth had heard him, the madman gave no sign.

The newly made murderer lay across the bed, his weight pressing down against the mattress, his two fists resting over the dead king's heart. Just as blood leaked out from where the knife blades pierced the old man's chest, words leaked out from between Macbeth's ragged lips. "It is done. The king is dead. Long live the king."

Except Sam knew it was far from over. Duncan's cowardly son, Malcolm, was set to be the next king. Why Macbeth hadn't plotted to kill him instead probably had something to do with medieval Scotland succession. Sam figured Duncan would name his younger son, Donalbain, should Malcolm die. And who knew who would be named after that?

A sound of weeping came from the bed. Sam watched as Macbeth struggled to extract the daggers from the old man's chest. They refused to move. The crying murderer tugged and pulled and wept until one, then the other, bloody blade came free. Macbeth then rolled himself off the bed and staggered out of the room.

Sam followed, through the austere living area, past the still-snoring guards, and down the short hallway to the main corridor. Macbeth walked like a zombie in a monster movie, his arms extended before him, a bloody dagger in each hand. He kept repeating the words, "It is done. It is done."

The murderer came to a halt outside the door to his own

apartment, but couldn't lift the latch with his hands full of bloody daggers. Sam slid along the wall to where he could reach out with one hand, lift the latch, and nudge open the door.

Macbeth seemed oblivious to how it had happened, but as the door creaked open, he pushed it further with his foot until he could squeeze in through the gap. Sam followed. There was nothing he could do at this point, but he wanted to see Lady Macbeth's reaction to the murder having been done.

Upon seeing his lady wife, who had resumed her needlework on the bench, Macbeth's voice rose above a whisper. "It is done."

"My husband!" Lady Macbeth cried. Then a smile gave her sultry lips a rictus grin. "My man."

"I have done the deed," Macbeth said. Then, as though coming to himself, he looked at the daggers in his hands. A drop of blood fell from the tip of one of the blades and made a precise circle of red by his foot on a throw rug. "This," he said, "is a sorry sight."

"Don't be a fool," Lady Macbeth growled. "Duncan's blood is a wonderful sight. But why did you return with the knives?"

"I . . ." The murderer had no answer. He simply stared at the daggers in his hands.

"Take them back," Lady Macbeth insisted. "Smear Duncan's guards' clothing with his blood. Then return the blades to their home in the dead king's cold heart."

"I dare not," Macbeth whispered. "I am afraid to even think it."

Lady Macbeth threw down her embroidery loop and rushed toward him. Instead of offering an embrace, she slapped her husband's face. "Coward. Give me the daggers. I shall take them to their place. We cannot incriminate Duncan's guards if the tools of murder go missing."

The woman plucked both blades from Macbeth's hands, then rushed out the door.

Sam was tempted to follow, but he knew where she was going and what she would do. And it would only take a minute. Instead, he watched Macbeth, who continued to stand, arms outstretched, his eyes bright with terror as he stared at his empty fists. "Whose hands are these?" he whispered. "Will all of great Neptune's ocean wash this blood clean? No. Instead, the seas shall become stained, my hands turning the waters red."

And then Lady Macbeth was back. "My hands are now as red as yours," she announced, "but I do not share your weakness. What is done is done. We now have other work to do."

Her husband seemed to snap out of his funk. He lowered his arms. "Other work?"

Lady Macbeth picked up a cloth from a stack on one of the cabinets and began wiping blood from her hands. As she passed the cloth to her husband, she said. "You must convince the thanes that you are a better choice for king than Duncan's brat."

"And your work?" Macbeth asked.

Lady Macbeth snatched up a second towel. "You left a trail of blood from Duncan's apartment to ours. I go to clean it up."

26
KNOWLEDGE IS POWER

It must have been one in the morning if not later by the time Sam returned to Casablanca. All but one of the candles had been doused, Sacha and Just Sam had returned to whatever places they called home, and the nightclub should have been empty. It wasn't. At a table below the single lit wall sconce, their arms folded across their chests and giving him cold looks, sat Sam's three precious gems. It was like coming home late from the pub to an irate wife. Times three.

"And where have you been?" Sapphire demanded.

Sam responded with the first lie that occurred to him. "I went for a walk. It's been a long day and I needed to shake loose some stress."

Ruby, her voice equally cold, said, "When you left here, it was to accompany Thane Macbeth to his apartment. That does not take an hour. More than an hour."

"And after that, I walked," Sam said, smiling. "I didn't think anyone would miss me."

"We were concerned," Emerald said in a voice as cold as death.

Sam felt his cheek twitch. It didn't sound like any concern he was familiar with. "You ladies did a wonderful job today. Macbeth couldn't have been happier. He told me that himself. But we get to do it all again tomorrow, so I suggest we get some sleep."

The three young helpers the witches in the cavern had provided him said nothing to that. Neither did they move from where they sat.

"Suit yourselves." Sam continued walking, all the way to his private apartment where he opened the door, stepped inside, then stood in the pitch darkness.

"Oh crap," he said aloud. He was still wearing Le Fay's magic ring.

Sam paced the floor in darkness, trying to decide if he should go out and challenge his precious gems with what he knew. Or should he keep it to himself? Knowledge is power, after all. He'd heard that somewhere. What had him riled up is that he should have known. There'd been something off about the three young women since he'd first seen them standing at the edge of the forest. They'd been more out of place than he was. And they'd only gotten weirder since. The blasted witches! They hadn't sent spies to keep an eye on him. They'd come themselves.

Slowly, Sam untied his shoes and stripped off his dinner jacket, pants, and shirt. He left his socks on; the castle was too cold to go barefoot, even in bed.

Morgan Le Fay had been watching him almost every minute since she'd pulled him away from Hartford. But which of his precious gems was she?

He lay down on the cot and pulled the blanket over his head. What he wanted, was to crawl under a rock, but this was the best he could do. He'd have to be careful what he said around the young ladies. Or more careful than he had been. Finding a way back home that bypassed Morgan Le Fay had grown that much more difficult.

Despite what he'd told his precious gems—the witches—about needing a good night's sleep, Sam tossed and turned for the next several hours. Giving up on the idea of getting any rest, he got up, dressed in the dark, and crept back out into the nightclub. The single candle was still lit, but his precious gems were gone.

Taking the candle from his office, he stepped back out into the casino and lit it off the burning one, then busied himself with his stacks of promissory notes, including the unsorted additions Sacha had left him. Seyton was going to demand his completed accounts first thing in the morning, and since sleep wasn't in the offing, Sam planned to surprise the puffed-up butler by having them done.

27
A TASTE FOR BLOODSHED

By the time servants arrived to light the candles and leave breakfast on the bar counter, Casablanca's paperwork sat in neat piles on his office desk and the summaries were complete. Sam had no idea what a silver merk was worth, but he now knew that Macbeth's countrymen owed the wily thane an awful lot of them. And that was after just one night. Sam should have known that Le Fay, the consummate conman, or con woman, wouldn't have come up with a crappy scheme.

Sacha showed up and helped himself to breakfast. A few minutes later, Just Sam joined them. The nightclub wouldn't reopen until evening after the castle bigwigs had had their dinner, but his employees didn't seem to mind pitching in all day.

"We went through almost all the alcohol last night," Sacha said, his face split in a wide grin. "Unless we restock today, tonight we shall have a riot on our hands."

Sam looked at Just Sam for his input.

The harpist shrugged. "I do not require restocking."

They finished breakfast with still no sign of Sam's precious gems. Perhaps the witches were sleeping in. Or perhaps, now with Duncan murdered, they had gone back to their cave. But no, Macbeth wasn't king yet, and Sam wasn't that lucky.

Seyton strolled into Casablanca and glowered at Sam. "You

have my accounts?"

Sam pulled two sheets of parchment from his dinner jacket pocket. "The proceeds from the bar," he said, offering the first sheet to the steward.

The haughty butler ran his arrogant gaze down the page to the sum at the bottom. His expression softened. "This more than covers the cost of the drink and crackers."

"And the poker receivables," Sam said, passing the tall man the second sheet.

Seyton spent noticeably more time taking in Sam's chicken scratches. "You have accounted for what you paid out yesterday?"

"Of course. That second last line is the balance of your coin bag."

Seyton's eyes snapped up. "Where is it?"

Sam's cheek twitched. "In my office. I'm going to need a safe or something I can use to secure the promissory notes and any coins I have on hand." He didn't know if safes had been invented yet.

The castle steward pulled on his beard. "Of course. You have faith these numbers are correct? They are rather high."

Sam shrugged. "Some of your guests lost big at the table. Others won big. They'll be back tonight to try to win even bigger or to recover their losses. Such is the way of casinos. The house, of course, wins either way. Though I suggest you don't let the debts get too big before trying to collect. Some may be unable, or unwilling, to pay."

Sacha cleared his throat.

Sam nodded. "We need to restock the bar. No one is going to stick around gambling if they can't get a drink."

Seyton folded the two sheets of parchment together and slipped them into a fold of his expansive robe. "Alcohol is already on its way. You are required to open early today."

"Early," Sam said. "How early?"

The steward was distracted from answering by a shuffling of feet near the nightclub entrance. Everyone watched as a trio of overdressed, serious-looking men arrived, glanced about the place, then sat at a table near Just Sam's harp.

"Now," Seyton said.

"What's this about?" Sam demanded.

The steward raised his nose in the air, then let out a sigh. "It is nothing of concern to you, but since Casablanca shall host a vigil throughout the day, I may as well say. There was a death in the night."

"Oh," Sam said. "If you're holding a vigil, it must be for someone important."

"Yes," Seyton answered. "Someone important." The snooty butler turned and left.

While Sacha served the new arrivals what little drink they had on hand, Sam and Just Sam cleared away breakfast. A door opened, and Sam's precious gems emerged from their apartment. The young women seemed unperturbed by the activity and made no mention of missing breakfast.

As he brought his helpers up-to-date, Sam did his best to hide what he knew about them. "There was a death in the night. Casablanca will be hosting friends and family throughout the day."

The disguised witches nodded before turning to help Sacha with serving drinks.

Sam knew what they were really doing—eavesdropping on the arriving guests to discern what they knew of Duncan's fate. And if Macbeth had gotten away with it.

Making up an excuse to inspect Just Sam's harp, Sam walked past the dour men's table and overheard one speak. He had a deep voice and a head of thick hair with a full beard to match. Sam remembered seeing him at Forres Castle but couldn't remember his name. "I discovered the horrible business myself," the man rumbled, "when I went to rouse the king."

"But Thane Macduff," one of his companions demanded. This was an ugly brute with unusually pale skin and a receding hairline. "Who could have done such a thing?"

A younger man with black curls and piercing eyes answered. "Can you believe it, Thane Ross? It was his own guards set to keep watch outside his door. God knows why they were still at their post, their faces and uniforms badged with blood, their blooded weapons at their feet."

"Thane Lennox has the truth of it," the man named Macduff said. "His Grace's guards were asleep. Sound as babes."

The brutish man, Ross, nodded. "Wine. After doing the deed,

the scoundrels paused to celebrate before making their escape."

"The audacity," Lennox added.

"I smelled the wine," Macduff continued. "As did young Lennox here. Finest quality. Strong. Stronger than the constitutions of simple soldiers are used to."

"Stolen most like," Ross insisted. "From Duncan's own room."

"The spoils of murder undid them," Lennox agreed, nodding.

Ross brushed a hand across the remnants of his hair. "What did these traitors say under questioning?"

"There is the rub." McDuff scowled at his companions. "Our Macbeth was so incensed that such a deed was done under his own roof, he executed the traitors on the spot."

Ross shook his head. "That is troubling. A confession would have smoothed matters."

"Thane Macbeth repented his fury," Macduff said. "As little good that will do us. Our fellow thane shall address us anon."

Sam had loitered near the harp for as long as he thought he could get away with. But what he'd heard worried him. As he sat on a stool at the bar, he recalled Macbeth's reluctance the night before to commit murder. And now this morning he had executed the guards? The innocent, sleeping guards? Could the man have acquired a taste for bloodshed? As a cop, Sam had encountered it many times. A man's first kill was the hardest. Each one after that came easier and easier.

28
BETTER FLED THAN DEAD

Over the next few hours, more guests wandered into Casablanca. Generals. Thanes. Who knew who else? Sam took a double take when the head carpenter who had built the bar counter poked his head in through the entryway. The man frowned slightly at seeing the small crowd of people, then marched into the nightclub followed by four men pulling and pushing a loaded cart with wheels that squealed beneath the weight.

"Your requested safe has arrived," Sacha announced from behind the counter, stating the obvious.

Sam watched as the workmen rolled the cart past him on their way to his office. The strongbox was the size and shape of a steamer trunk and made from some kind of dark hardwood. Filigree moulding covered the sides and much of the top. "A bit ostentatious for a simple safe, don't you think?"

Sacha laughed. "Your standard Celtic knot pattern. I imagine this chest has been borrowed from a castle apartment reserved for royal guests."

Sam threw the bartender a look. "Duncan's room?"

The barman shrugged. "Possibly. There will not be many such strongboxes in the castle. Commoners have no need for one."

"Bad luck," Sam said, rising from his bar stool, "receiving goods from the scene of a murder."

"In my experience," Sacha said, "one makes one's own luck."

Sam followed the procession into the gloomy half-light of his office and watched the workmen jog the heavy strongbox onto the floor in a corner of the room.

"You are familiar with keys?" the head carpenter asked Sam.

Sam took the heavy, oversized skeleton key from the man's hand, flipped it into the air, caught it, then tested it in the safe's lock. Unlike modern safes, where the door is on one side, the lock mechanism unlatched the top of the strongbox which, though heavy, Sam was able to lift. The empty space inside was wide enough for several stacks of promissory notes. "This should work fine."

By the time he relocked the safe and straightened, the workmen and their cart were gone.

"Not even a kiss for luck," Sam said as he dropped the key into a pants pocket where it sat like a paperweight.

When he returned to the casino, the workmen were trooping out the entryway only to be replaced by half a dozen servants carrying heavy crates.

"We shall require more ale than this," Sacha told them after inspecting the crates' contents.

The servants grumbled as they left, almost colliding into two well-dressed men who entered from the hallway.

Sam let out a laugh. "This place is busier when it's closed than when it's open." The laugh became a smile when he realized the elder of the two men was Banquo.

"Ah, Mr. Spade. Well met. Or not so well, considering the circumstances. Either way, it is good to see you." Macbeth's good friend joined Sam by the bar, then tilted his head this way and that. "This is your nightclub? I fully intended to arrive last evening for the grand opening of your establishment, but the weather on the road . . ."

Sam waved away the apology. "The opening went fine, all things considered. Who's your friend?"

Now that they stood closer, Sam could see that Banquo's companion was more of a teenager. How old, Sam wasn't sure. But the boy was one of the few men in the room without facial hair.

Banquo stood a bit taller, and his face split in a wide grin.

"May I present my eldest son, Fleance."

Sam automatically stuck out his hand. The boy stared at it a moment before reaching out for a firm handshake.

Banquo laughed. "Have no fear, my son. Mr. Spade is a foreigner. You have not just agreed to something untoward."

A nervous smile touched the boy's lips, followed by an awkward silence. Fortunately, Just Sam chose that moment to strum the strings of his harp. After a few notes, he began crooning something unintelligible to Sam's ears, but that turned the heads of every man in the room including Banquo and his eldest son.

Macbeth's good friend turned back to Sam. "You have a minstrel?"

Sam shrugged. "You can't have a nightclub without music."

Banquo nodded. "Sadly, I admit that, in regard to nightclubs, I remain unclear on the concept."

Sacha, who had been listening from behind the bar, laughed. "A round of drinks and a go at the poker table, and all shall be revealed."

In short order, Banquo had a drink in his hand and sat at the poker table with Macduff, Lennox, and Ross. Sam stood behind him, interested in seeing what Macbeth's good friend thought of the game.

"Remind me, Thane Macduff," Banquo asked. "Does a straight conquer a . . . what do you call five cards in the same suit?"

"A flush," the gruff man answered. "And no, a flush diminishes a straight."

"I see." Banquo stared at his cards. "Perhaps I shall add two merks to the pot and hold, shall I?"

The other three players threw their cards onto the table and ordered more drinks.

Sam smiled to himself at how quickly Banquo had picked up on how to control the table. The Thane of Lochaber's hand was a busted flush—four spades and a club. He could have folded and lost his stake. Instead, he bluffed and took the pot.

The ugly one—Ross—cast a stony gaze about the room. "Where have Malcolm and Donalbain wandered off to? We are here today for them."

Banquo took a sip from his tankard, then wiped a few errant drops from his beard. "Fleance will know. My son was sitting with them." He called his son's name across the room to be heard above the harp.

The boy rose from where he sat by himself at a table and approached his father.

"Where are your companions?" Banquo asked.

Fleance's eyes widened. "What?"

"Your companions. Malcolm and Donalbain."

The youth looked about the room. "I do not know."

"But you were sitting with them."

"I was," Fleance agreed.

"Cease this dithering," Macduff grumbled. "Their father was cruelly murdered in the night. They should not be left on their own."

Fleance regained the nervous look he'd had after shaking Sam's hand. "The brothers took their own counsel, speaking between themselves. They did not include me in their plans."

Macduff rose from the card table. "Then we must find them. Once the other thanes arrive, we shall proceed to Scone Abbey where Malcolm shall take his seat on the Stone of Destiny and be named King of Scotland in his father's stead."

Lennox looked up and wagged his head. "Sit, my friend. Duncan's sons are safe. Safer than had they remained in this cursed castle."

Macduff frowned and returned to his seat. "What say you?"

Thane Lennox lifted his ale cup and turned it in his hands. "It is passing strange the king's trusted guards of many years should slay their master then fall asleep at their post, only to be slain in return by Thane Macbeth. In truth, both boys fear for their own lives. Donalbain has fled to Ireland where he has distant family on his mother's side."

Macduff continued frowning. "And Malcolm, the heir to the throne, accompanied his brother?"

"No." Lennox smiled. "I advised them to travel apart. Far safer to separate their fortunes."

Ross leaned across the table. "You advised them?"

The younger thane shrugged. "'Twas more a caution. With the father murdered, who is to say the sons shall not be next?"

Ross shook his head. "But the king's guards—"

"Served their master faithfully," Lennox interrupted, "and had no cause to do him harm."

"Enough!" Macduff cried. "Where has Malcolm run off to? Forres?"

"The logical destination," Lennox agreed. "Should there be pursuit, Forres Castle is the first place one would go."

The gruff thane sighed. "So not Forres. Where then?"

Lennox sipped from his tankard. "England."

Macduff's eyes widened. "You sent the Prince of Cumberland to England. We are not on the best of terms with our southern neighbour."

A grin slipped across the younger thane's face. "Better terms than with Ireland, who Macbeth recently defeated in battle."

Macduff ground his teeth, but said nothing.

Thane Ross cleared his throat. "My good friend, Lennox. You may have just facilitated the escape of our king's true murderers."

Lennox slammed his tankard onto the table. "What? Do you suggest patricide? Good gods, why?"

Ross wagged his head. "Malcolm, having recently been declared heir, may have grown impatient waiting for his father's life to run its natural course."

"And Donalbain?" Lennox asked.

"Would do whatever his brother told him. The lad has not been able to think for himself since—"

"His accident," Lennox finished. "Yes. Yes. You are suggesting Malcolm convinced his father's guards to do the old man in?"

"Or paid them. And promised them no retribution, which would explain why they did not flee."

Macduff shook his head. "Ross, I know the lads. They would never . . ."

The balding thane drew in a noseful of air. "Whatever the case, we can hardly crown an heir who is not even in the country."

"Agreed," Macduff said. "Neither can we leave the throne vacant. Our enemies shall rise up against us while we are in disarray."

Lennox rubbed his bearded chin. "That is a valid point. What are we to do?"

The conversation had paused the game. Though Ruby had shuffled and dealt, none of the thanes picked up their cards. Sam felt his cheek twitch as he kept a watchful eye on Banquo. Would

Macbeth's good friend make the obvious suggestion?

Ross drew another noisy gust of air into his nose. "There has been talk."

"Talk?" Lennox echoed.

The older man nodded his hawk nose. "This last conflict with Norway—"

Macduff slammed his hand down on the table. "Norway? What does Norway have to do with anything?"

Ross wagged his nose in Macduff's direction. "Malcolm spent much of that battle hiding in a tent."

Lennox shrugged. "Duncan's son pulled a muscle."

All four thanes at the table stifled a chuckle.

"Whatever the reason," Ross continued, "'twas Thane Macbeth carried the day."

Nods all around.

Ross leaned forward and lowered his voice to a near whisper. Sam had to take a step closer in order to hear. "Whilst our king sat by the fire warming his ancient bones, 'twas Thane Macbeth who fought for Scotland, besting foreigners and traitors alike."

"What are you saying?" Macduff grumbled.

Ross blew air out his nose. "That there is talk. Among the soldiers. There are those who would see Macbeth sit on Scotland's throne."

Macduff leaned back in his seat. "Ridiculous. The next King of Scotland has been named. To set anyone else on the throne is treason."

"I would agree," Ross said, turning his gaze on Lennox, "were the heir not fled to our enemies in England."

Lennox pursed his lips. "Better fled than dead."

It was at that moment that Macduff raised his heavy eyes to stare directly at Sam.

Sam straightened and forced a smile onto his face. "Gentlemen. Is everything all right? I couldn't help but notice that you have paused the game. Is there a question about the rules?"

29
A NEW DAY, A NEW KING

Pour me a short one."

Sam stood leaning against the bar counter while Sacha slid over a clay bowl that was barely wet at the bottom. Lifting the makeshift cup, Sam peered into it. "I didn't mean that short."

Sacha chuckled. "It is still early in the day. You shall require your wits about you if you are to come out ahead."

"You're probably right." Sam lifted the bowl and collected the few drops of fermented barley onto his tongue. It hardly seemed worth the effort.

Casablanca had grown more crowded while he'd been eavesdropping on the thanes. If he'd heard right, Scotland's movers and shakers were gathering, not to mourn the passing of King Duncan, but to form a procession to somewhere named after a pastry where new kings were crowned. Only now the old king's heir had fled the country, leaving Scotland in a bit of a pickle.

Pushing away the empty bowl, Sam turned to look out over the casino and watched as the various discussions around the nightclub grew louder and the expressions on bearded faces less friendly. He also watched as Just Sam gave up trying to compete with the rabble and parked his harp in favour of a full tankard of barley ale. Apparently, Sacha was less concerned about

Casablanca's minstrel keeping his wits than he was its manager.

But the bartender was right. Sam needed to keep a tight rein on things. In addition to watching Casablanca's guests, he kept a close eye on his precious gems. The two serving drinks went about their task with warm smiles and, he assumed, innocent suggestions calculated to stir up the aggressive discussions. Duncan was dead, but the witches' agenda wasn't over.

He'd just turned his attention to Sapphire, who currently manned the poker table and seemed a little too chatty with a new batch of players, when the loud voices in the room trailed off. Sam swung his gaze toward the nightclub entryway where five men stood in the open portal, the least promising of which was Macbeth. The others looked like guards, though two were better dressed. Officers, perhaps.

"We seem to be mostly arrived," Macbeth announced. "Though unfortunately,"—he turned to one of the better dressed guards—"Captain Renault tells me the purpose of our gathering has fled to England."

Sam observed the captain as he scowled at the room. Renault. The name sounded more French than Scots. The man didn't look Scottish either. He'd shaved his beard, and kept his hair short and his moustache neatly groomed. He also wore a round cap that Sam had only ever seen adorning the head of a bellhop. And the man was short. Possibly the shortest man in the room.

Macbeth interrupted Sam's appraisal. "You may ask," the wannabe king drawled, "why Malcolm should flee the country when his father's murderers have been identified and punished. Major Strasser, representing the office of the Sheriff of Inverness, has suggested to me an answer. Major Strasser."

Taller than Renault by almost a head, the other well-dressed guard stepped forward. He also wore no beard, and his moustache was almost non-existent. The major's hairline had receded so far that most men would shave what was left and sport the Yul Brenner look.

"I have reviewed the facts," Strasser said, putting emphasis on the word *facts*. "And have thoroughly investigated the late king's quarters as well as the remains of the two men tasked to guard those quarters. It is clear from the evidence that our good king was murdered by his own guards. What is not immediately apparent, is why. Or should I say, who? Who was it who induced these two loyal men to commit such a vile and treasonous act?"

A surge of mumbling flared up around the room, then died just as quickly at a scowl from Macbeth.

"Who indeed?" Renault, the other officer, remarked, the timing sounding rehearsed to Sam's ears.

Strasser nodded. "That the king's offspring should flee upon hearing my question, suggests guilt. Patricide."

More mumbling, though more shocked than questioning.

Sam glanced over to a nearby table, where Macduff and his card buddies now sat. The younger one, Lennox, cast Sam a knowing smile. Whether that meant the young thane's advice to Duncan's sons to flee was well founded, or if he now believed the king's heirs complicit in his murder, Sam had no idea.

Macduff rose from his seat. "Major Strasser, just to be clear, are you suggesting young Malcolm is responsible for his own father's death?"

Strasser nodded. "That is the obvious conclusion."

Macduff glanced at Lennox before returning his gaze to Macbeth's party. "But could you not equally conclude that the heir and his brother fled in fear that they, too, may succumb to the assassin's blade?"

The major dismissed the suggestion with a hand wave. "Right now, Inverness Castle is the most secure place in the kingdom. To flee can only mean one thing—guilt."

Sam watched as Macduff sat back down, though the gruff man looked anything but convinced.

"Sadly," Strasser added, "this places us in a quandary. The king is dead. The Prince of Cumberland is fled. A new descendant of House MacAlpin must be chosen to wear the crown."

Silence ensued. Sam noticed that no one stood to suggest Donalbain, Duncan's younger son. Though rumoured to be a few cigarettes shy of a pack due to an unfortunate encounter with a horse, the boy had seemed a normal teenager to Sam, if perhaps a bit introverted. He'd only seen him twice, of course, both times at his older sibling's elbow. There could be more to the story.

The silence continued. Then, from somewhere lost in the crowded nightclub, a timid voice said, "Macbeth is Duncan's cousin."

"And is thane of not one, but three thanedoms," another anonymous voice added.

"Macbeth defeated Norway," another voice opined.

"Macbeth!" shouted a fourth.

"Macbeth!" several voices answered in reply.

And then, as Sam expected, the shouts became a chant. "Macbeth! Macbeth! Macbeth!"

Sam had no idea how many of those voices had been planted by Macbeth, or how many resulted from innocent comments carefully introduced by his precious gems. But things were rolling along too smoothly for it to be mere accident. Le Fay had said Macbeth was destined to be king, but she had also gone to great lengths to give that destiny a leg up. Help that included stealing Sam Sparrow from Hartford Connecticut to reprise his role as Sam Spade.

The chanting quickly grew unbearable, echoing off Casablanca's walls in utter defiance of the tapestries placed there to prevent such echoes. Sam resisted the temptation to stick his fingers in his ears.

Macbeth, still lingering near the nightclub entrance, sported a Cheshire Cat smile while the two well-dressed guards held a mixed expression of pride and relief. Sam glanced at Macduff's table, where Ross was shouting as loud as the rest of them. Lennox, he noticed, offered mere lip service, while Macduff pursed his lips. Macbeth's good friend Banquo appeared embarrassed, but soon recovered himself and competed with Ross in a contest of who could shout the loudest.

This went on longer than Sam figured it should have before Macbeth raised his hands and was rewarded with silence. "Friends. Countrymen. You bring warmth to this humble man's heart on a cold, cold day. Your confidence pleases me more than I can say. Even so, should another heir be available, I would refuse your kind nomination. I am but a general, a military man who would move Heaven and Earth to protect my king and country." He paused to suck in breath, then let out a heavy sigh. "And yet, alas, there is no one else, so I must now protect my country by bearing the burden of its crown."

Sam knew the windbag had more to say but, thankfully, his fan club cut him off by rising from their seats and resuming their clamorous, if simplistic, refrain. "Macbeth! Macbeth! Macbeth!" Then Lennox jumped up from his seat, knocking the table and almost spilling his ale cup. "To Scone!" the younger thane cried, causing the chanting to wind down to a half-hearted effort. "We must ride to Scone Abbey. On the morrow, Thane Macbeth shall sit upon the Throne of Scone and arise therefrom as King Macbeth!"

The chanting resumed as men throughout Casablanca rose from their seats and marched toward the exit, only now they shouted, "Scone! Scone! Scone!"

Sam turned to Sacha. "Right. That was the pastry. Scone."

The bartender blinked in confusion.

When the room was mostly empty, Sam looked about and saw Macbeth's henchmen, Renault and Strasser, still standing near the entryway, though the conspiring thane himself was gone. Just Sam had left Sacha at the bar to return to his harp. And Sam's precious gems—the conniving witches—sat huddled at a corner table whispering among themselves. Lennox and Ross were gone from their table, but Macduff remained seated along with Banquo and his son Fleance.

The room was quiet enough that Sam could hear the two thanes' conversation from where he sat at the bar.

"Are you not coming?" Banquo asked Macduff.

"I think not," the gruff man replied. "Macbeth shall sit the throne whether I attend or not. I do not like this all happening in one day: the murder of a king, the flight of his heirs, and the crowning of his cousin."

Banquo rubbed his beard. "It is indeed an ill day. Yet the crowning shall be tomorrow. A new day, a new king."

Macduff raised the tankard he had been nursing and took a sip. "A new day, yes. But we have no guarantee the morrow shall be a better one."

The gruff thane rose from his seat, drained the last of his drink, then gave Banquo a stern glance. "I shall spend the remainder of this day in contemplation. Then I shall await whatever the future holds."

30
THE BUTLER DID IT

Casablanca was so empty the place might as well be closed. Well, not quite empty. Banquo, having been abandoned by his fellow thanes, joined Sam at the bar.

"Mr. Spade. Such odd happenings. Fleance and I intended to arrive last evening to enjoy the grand opening of your night club and to celebrate Thane Macbeth's victory over Norway. Now it seems we are off to Scone to witness the crowning of my good friend as king." Banquo shook his head. "The things that can change in the matter of a few short hours." He sighed and threw Sam a helpless look. "Had I not arrived late, think you I could have prevented Duncan's murder?"

Sam glanced past Banquo's shoulder and noticed his precious gems watching intently. His cheek twitched as he said, "I'm not really in a position to say one way or the other."

Banquo stared into his empty cup. "One would think it matters little who is king. Is not being a thane, or thrice a thane, station enough?"

Sam signalled Sacha to refill Banquo's cup and to pour a few additional drops of ale into his own meagre bowl. "I have no interest in politics. The problems of the world are not my department."

Banquo looked up. "There is wisdom in that. A man should be

free to live his life as he sees fit, and not worry about someone taking it from him."

Sam felt his cheek twitch again, then swallowed the meagre refill Sacha had accommodated him with. He flicked his gaze at his precious gems who still watched from their table at the other side of the casino. He figured the witches could hear their conversation because the room was quiet. Either that, or they were using magic to listen in.

He returned his attention to Banquo, who set his re-emptied tankard on the counter.

"Come, Fleance. We have a long ride ahead of us if we are to witness our good friend crowned king."

The teenager set his own half-empty cup on the counter and followed his father to the exit.

Sam eyed the cup, wondering if Sacha would notice if he adopted it.

But the barkeep pushed it out of reach before setting his elbows on the counter's surface. He leaned toward Sam and lowered his voice to a whisper. "That fellow seems to have mixed feelings regarding his friend becoming king."

"How about you?" Sam asked. "Do you have an opinion?"

The cheerful man grinned. "Yesterday Duncan was king and I was a bartender. Today we have no king, and I am still a bartender. Tomorrow we shall have a new king." His grin widened.

Sam sighed. "And you'll still be a bartender."

"As the man said, wisdom." Then Sacha straightened. "What can I get you?"

Sam turned his head and saw that Captain Renault had joined them at the bar. The unaccountably French henchman ignored Sacha and gave Sam a threatening look. "You are a foreigner."

"I could say the same about you," Sam said.

The man cocked an eye. "Do you disparage my father's heritage?"

"You didn't hear me." Sam rested one elbow on the counter. "I said I *could* accuse you of being a foreigner, but I didn't. You, on the other hand, outright called me a foreigner."

The captain sputtered and blinked his eyes, then raised one hand.

If he was going to throw a punch, Sam was ready for it. The elbow on the counter was his left, and his right shoulder was cocked and ready to block any assault.

Renault managed to calm himself, however. He got his fluster under control and displayed a smile. "Most crime in Inverness is committed by foreigners."

Sam returned the smile. "I assume that label doesn't include yourself."

The captain nodded, taking the remark in stride. "My father immigrated to Scotland from Paris. Whether or not he committed petty crimes when he arrived, I do not know. I only know he was never arrested. I, on the other hand, was born in Glasgow. Joined the military. Worked my way up through the ranks. And now find myself in this place as captain of the Inverness Castle Guard."

"And now," Sam suggested, "you want me to give you my pedigree."

Renault again nodded.

"It's not pretty, but you asked for it. My father died in prison. My mother abandoned me as a child. I was a cop for a while, but was forced to quit. Now I'm a gumshoe who solves other people's problems for a living. My current employer is Thane Macbeth. He hired me to set up and run this nightclub."

"Night club?" Renault's expression turned to confusion. "It is but mid-morning."

"Come back tonight," Sam answered. "That's when the party really starts."

Renault rubbed his jaw and resumed his scowl. Sam had no idea how much of what he'd said had been understood.

"Have you ever been arrested?" Renault finally asked.

Sam rubbed his ear. "Not as such. No."

"You are aware of last night's murder?" the captain asked.

"It's a sad business," Sam said.

Renault watched him so closely, Sam felt he was in a staring contest. "In addition to murder there has been a robbery."

Sam pushed out a breath of air. "And since I'm not from around here, I'm a suspect."

"Everyone is a suspect." Renault continued to ignore Sacha, who stood listening from the other side of the bar counter.

"What's gone missing?" Sam asked. He was tempted to add, Duncan's crown?

Renault lowered his voice so only Sam and Sacha could hear, not that there was anyone remaining in Casablanca by this time besides the staff. "Lady Macbeth receives letters from her husband whenever he is abroad. Several of her latest missives are now absent from her writing desk."

"Letters," Sam echoed. The ex-cop in him wondered what could be in those letters to make them significant enough to steal. Then the Sam Spade in him remembered Macbeth sitting at a writing desk inside the witches' cavern. He must have been bringing his wife up to speed on how the old crones had predicted he would be king. Yeah, that would definitely be steal worthy.

Renault continued to stare at Sam, expecting a response.

Sam rubbed his ear again. "Several letters, you say? Not all the letters?"

Captain Renault blinked. "Why would you ask that?"

"It just seems odd. Someone enters Lady Macbeth's apartment, finds a stack of letters on her desk, and takes some but not all of them."

Renault blinked again. "Yes, odd. But what does it mean?"

Sam couldn't help but smile. "It's obvious to me what happened."

"It is?"

"Sure. Someone with frequent access to the apartment has been reading her Ladyship's mail. And these select letters were interesting enough that our visitor wasn't content with just reading them. Something happened. Maybe something mentioned in the last letter. Or maybe some event in the castle that is relevant to the missing letters. Whatever it is, something triggered the theft. And, most likely, those letters are intended to be sold somewhere."

"Sold?" Renault asked.

"Letters have no value. Not unless they contain something interesting someone will pay for."

The captain frowned. "You seem certain of this. Perhaps this felonious reader of other people's mail is you."

"Me?" Sam laughed. "I've only been here three days. And I have no access to the apartment where the letters were kept."

"Exactly," Renault said. "The theft happened shortly after you arrived."

"You've got the wrong man," Sam said. "I didn't even know about the letters until you mentioned them. You should be looking for someone who knew about the letters and who knew to be selective about which ones to take."

"Who would you suggest?" Renault asked.

Sam figured the captain still suspected him, but at least he seemed willing to talk. "Whoever frequently visits the apartment while the Lady and her husband are out."

Renault's frown deepened. "And who would that be, pray tell?"

Sam was having trouble believing how this conversation was going. "Remind me, what are you captain of again?"

"Castle security," Renault said. "My station includes incarcerating troublesome foreigners in the dungeon."

"Right. Right. Just asking. You should be looking at the servants who clean Lady Macbeth's apartment."

"Servants?" Renault's brows lifted in surprise. "Servants." He rubbed his jaw again, and his eyes narrowed. "Servants."

Sam remembered where he was. And when he was. "Preferably a servant who can read."

Renault looked at him. "That would narrow the field. Butlers can read. It is part of their job description."

Sam barely controlled his laughter. "While it is possible the butler did it, I suggest you look at everyone who has access to Lady Macbeth's apartment while no one is there."

"You have piqued my interest," Renault said. "This does not clear you, but I shall question the servants. Many of them are also foreigners, after all."

No sooner had Inspector Poirot made his exit, when a troop of travel-weary soldiers wandered in through the nightclub entrance and gawked about the place. None of these wore kilts, but were dressed in yellow shirts and dark pants. "What does Casablanca mean?" one of them mumbled.

"I thought this would be a fancy garderobe," another answered. Most of the soldiers laughed. All but two.

Sam stared as he realized the two soldiers with higher standards of humour, though dressed like the others and likewise overdue for a bath, were in fact women. And not just any women. One had blue eyes, blonde hair, and a scar running down her cheek. "Effie?"

31
MARRIAGE WASN'T IN THE CARDS

Effie looked in appearance much as she had the last time Sam had seen her. The added years were visible in the lines around her eyes, but did nothing to diminish her beauty. If the time transitions for his past journeys held true, she would now be a couple of years older than him.

Sam dragged himself off his bar stool and stood, dumbstruck, as Lady Euphemia Peregrine grabbed her female companion by the arm and strode quickly to the counter. "My name," Effie said, with perhaps too much force, "is Ilsa. This is my husband, Victor. What do you have to drink around here?"

Sam blinked. "Ilsa?" Then he blinked again. "Victor?" Sam could see that Victor had flaming red hair, cut short at the back and falling down across her eyes, and perhaps more dirt on her face than slogging for a month through the mud might warrant, but he also knew a woman when he saw one. Effie had called the woman her husband. "Victor?" he said again.

Effie looked at him and shook her head sharply. "And my name is *Ilsa*. Can we get a drink, or what?"

Sacha was already pushing two tankards across the bar. Effie picked one up and took a deep pull. Victor retrieved the other and hid her face behind it.

Sam waited, and Effie finally lowered her tankard and cast a quick glance at her fellow soldiers, who had shuffled off to commandeer several tables near the harpist. Just Sam was strumming what was probably a popular fighting tune, given the soldiers' reactions. Effie turned back to Sam and whispered, "Sam Spade? What are you doing here?"

The use of Sam's borrowed last name was not a good sign. He thought they'd moved past that a long time ago. If ever there was a tale of unrequited love . . .

"Well?" Effie demanded.

Sam tucked his hands into his dinner jacket pockets. "I could ask you the same question, *Ilsa*. When last we were together, didn't I leave you sitting pretty as a Lady's handmaiden?"

Effie smiled, and her expression softened. "Marion and Robin were both perfect. Too perfect. They had no real need of a handmaiden, and I grew bored. Restless." She glanced around quickly to ensure no one was within earshot. Sacha had moved to the other end of the counter to pour ale for a new arrival, so there was only Victor, to whom Effie gave a fond, if not loving, look. "Then Victoria came through Locksley looking to recruit patriots to work with her as spies in the service of King Richard."

Sam blinked. "Spies?"

Effie fingered her scar. "You know I did that once before, when Mordred rode against Camelot."

Sam pulled his hands out of his pockets and reached for his ale bowl, only to find it empty. He returned his attention to Effie. "You missed the life that much?"

"Of course not." Effie wagged her tankard. "But Victoria captured my eye and then my heart. She stayed at Locksley for a time. Before we left, Friar Tuck married us."

Sam choked, nearly swallowing his tongue. Married? Effie hadn't been kidding when she called Victor her husband.

The woman of many of Sam's dreams must have noticed his reaction, but continued as though nothing had happened. "Several months later we were in Edinburgh gathering intelligence. King Richard had returned from the crusades, and was incensed that his brother, John Lackland, had hired Scots mercenaries to aid in his attempt on the throne. King Richard sent us to determine Scotland's mood.

"Somehow . . . someone . . . well, we were betrayed. Victoria and I were arrested and cast into Dundee Prison. We petitioned for our release and even spoke with an embassy from England, but were told King Richard had died and John Lackland was now king. Lacking land no longer, King John saw no reason to trade for us. He told the Scots we were Richard's spies, not his."

"You're married?" Sam blurted.

Effie's eyes narrowed.

Maybe not the best thing he could have said. "Hey, that's a shocking story. All of it. And I'm thrilled you two found each other." He looked at Victor/Victoria again, seeing the woman in a new light. "It's just . . . I'm surprised is all. You seemed so sure marriage wasn't in the cards."

"It wasn't," Effie admitted. "The Church is *violently* opposed to such practices." She put extra emphasis on the word "violently" and Sam wondered if that was why Victoria was masquerading as Victor.

"But Tuck had no problem with . . ." Sam waved a hand.

"Friar Tuck is singularly enlightened," Effie said.

"But you were in prison." Sam moved ahead in Effie's story. "That must have been awful." He'd seen medieval prisons. There was his brief stint in Camelot's dungeon. And the Sheriff's Keep in Nottingham, where Vaisey's throne room would rate only half a star on TripAdvisor. The cell area in the back could only be worse.

Effie smiled again at her partner. "We had each other. That is what counted. We lost track of time and wasted away at Dundee for months until, by sheer accident, the key to our cell fell from our guard's pocket and we were able to make our escape."

Sam felt his cheek twitch. "Accident?"

Victor/Victoria spoke for the first time, a husky baritone rising from her chest and bypassing her nose. It wasn't a bad impression of a man with a slight cold. "We may have set a distraction."

"I can imagine." Sam ran through several scenarios in which women in prison might relieve a male guard of a cell key. He wasn't surprised that Effie glossed over that part in her story.

"The nearest disguise we could find," Effie whispered, "were guard uniforms. After trading our prison rags for those, we avoided contact with anyone and stole our way to freedom. Once outside Dundee Prison, we traded uniforms at the city militia barracks and travelled north as common soldiers toward Aberdeen because—"

Sam interjected. "Everyone searching for you would look south toward England."

Effie and Victor/Victoria both nodded. Then Victor took up the story. "I cut my hair and put mud on my face, and we masqueraded as man and wife forced by poverty to sign on with the local militia. Near Stonehaven we encountered a rabble of soldiers who had lost their lieutenant in a skirmish with Danish pirates. I told them we were headed to Forres because King Duncan had put out a call for soldiers to join his castle guard. Several of the party preferred that prospect over fighting pirates again, and travelled with us."

"You didn't want to return to England?" Sam asked.

Effie avoided the question. "Though Edinburgh has a large militia, we learned little there regarding Scotland's intentions toward England. Our new plan was to gain acceptance in Duncan's court and listen for conversation between the king and his thanes."

Victor/Victoria cut in. "Lackland is despised in England. He will not last as king. We hoped to gain valuable information to offer his successor."

Effie continued the story. "When we reached Forres, however, we discovered Duncan, his sons, and his retainers had departed for Inverness. Rather than await their return, we followed. But when we arrived here a short time ago, we learned Duncan was dead and his sons fled."

Movement caught Sam's eye. He looked over Effie's shoulder to see the remainder of her and her husband's troop swaggering toward the bar. He pointed with his chin. "Looks like your friends have finally figured out there's alcohol to be had."

Effie hissed, "Pretend you do not know us." Then, in a louder voice, "And soldiers are welcome at Casablanca?"

"More than welcome," Sam said, also loud enough for the approaching soldiers to hear. He nodded at Sacha. "I'll be in my office if you need me."

32
A FREE AND EASY DOZEN MERKS

Because there was only one candle in the entire room, Sam's office felt like a morgue compared to the brightly-lit casino. His brain knew Casablanca was on the main floor of the castle, but the lack of even a single window convinced his gut he was in a basement. Who designed these crappy buildings anyway?

He left his door ajar so extra light could seep in, and sank into the hardback chair behind his desk. Leaning the back of his head against the hard stone wall, he closed his eyes. Idly, Sam wondered if he should start a sideline of crafting padded leather manager chairs. He knew building them would be child's play for the talented head carpenter. Maybe he could convince Seyton that the nightclub needed a comfy chair.

But, no. What he needed was to get back to Hartford. Nora was still in the passenger seat of his Volvo S60, driving off the road in the worst blizzard in a century. And he had yet to find a way to escape Morgan Le Fay's unfathomable scheme for Macbeth. To further confuse things, Effie, of all people, had turned up on his doorstep. Sam hadn't counted on running into the literal woman of his dreams or anyone else from his varied sojourns into the past. Not in Scotland. Yet here she was. Married, no less. And an escaped felon.

"Mr. Spade."

Sam cracked open one eye to find a smallish man standing in front of his desk. Given the inadequate illumination of his lone candle, and that his visitor blocked most of the light coming in through the doorway, there wasn't much more he could tell about his visitor except that his head was mostly bald and that his rasping voice suggested he was somewhat older.

"You found him," Sam said, cracking open his other eye. "I don't think I've had the pleasure."

"My name is not important," the man said.

"It is to me. I like to know who I'm dealing with."

"Very well. You may call me Ugarte."

"Ugarte," Sam said. "Is that a Scottish name?"

The man frowned. "Is Spade a Scottish name?"

"Touché. I guess that makes both of us foreigners. What can I do for you, Mr. Ugarte?"

Ugarte hesitated. "It is my understanding that you have a strongbox in this office."

Sam also hesitated. "Sure, as of an hour ago. You here to rob it?"

Silence. Then, "No. Of course not. I am here to rent it."

"You wish to rent my strongbox?"

Ugarte turned his head to peer back toward the doorway.

Sam saw now that he was indeed mostly bald and that his moustache and beard were trimmed to near non-existence.

Returning his attention to Sam, Ugarte said, "I am to meet someone later this evening in your nightclub."

Sam said nothing, but continued to assess the man.

"To exchange something," Ugarte added. "Something of value."

Sam continued to say nothing.

"With a buyer."

"I see," Sam said. "And you'd be more comfortable if your something of value was safely under lock and key until then."

Ugarte nodded.

Sam sat up straight and squinted at the man in the darkness. "And why would you trust me with your something of value? Because we're both foreigners?"

The man made a noise. It went on for a while until Sam realized he was chuckling. "Of course not. Mr. Spade, I have many friends in Inverness. But I am willing to trust you because, should anything happen to the lett—my something of value, my buyer will have you killed."

Sam leaned forward over his desk. "You're not making much of an argument for me to rent you my strongbox."

Ugarte retrieved a small sack from beneath his coat. "I am sure you will find that twelve merks in payment make a strong argument."

Sam leaned back into his uncomfortable seat. "This nightclub earned more than that in the past hour. And we're not even open for business yet."

"Those are Thane Macbeth's merks." Ugarte waggled the sack of coins. "These shall be yours."

Sam lifted his fingers to his ear and rubbed. This was a fishy deal, but a free and easy dozen merks could go a long way to helping him find a way back to Hartford.

Reaching out to accept Ugarte's payment, Sam couldn't help but mutter, "I know I'm gonna regret this."

As Sam rose from his uncomfortable chair and stepped around his desk, the man calling himself Ugarte appropriated his candle and closed the office door for privacy. The man watched, not saying a word, as Sam retrieved the skeleton key from his pants pocket and unlocked his newly installed safe.

"That is the only key?" Ugarte asked. He stood next to Sam, holding the candle out so he could examine the empty safe.

"The only one I know about."

With his free hand, Ugarte reached inside his coat and retrieved a thin bundle of papers. "I advise not looking too closely at what I am placing in your strongbox. Assuming, that is, you are able to read."

"I make do in the shopping aisle," Sam said.

The balding man leaned down and set the papers inside the safe. When he straightened, he wore a frown, probably because he had no idea what Sam had just said. "A little knowledge," Ugarte intoned, "can be a dangerous thing."

"I can live with a little danger," Sam said. "But I have enough of my own. I haven't the slightest interest in whatever you have there."

Ugarte watched closely as Sam lowered the strongbox lid,

locked it, and slipped the key back into his pocket. "Be true to your word. In this particular instance, curiosity is not your friend."

"I get it," Sam said.

With Lady Macbeth's stolen letters now secured in the safe, the thief, or more likely the thief's accomplice, set the candle back on the desk and left Sam's office. The day had just gotten a lot more complicated. Not something Sam needed right now.

After rubbing his ear for what might be a world record, Sam made a decision. It was a risk, but at this point, anything he did was a risk. Retrieving the key from his pocket, he opened and reclosed the strongbox. Then he went next door to his apartment.

After less than a minute, he returned to his office. He eyed the chair behind his desk, but didn't think his back would forgive him if he sat in it again. Instead, he pinched the candle's wick with his fingers and returned to the casino.

33
AS TIME GOES BY

Despite Macbeth's train of hangers-on having left for the pastry stone, more visitors to Casablanca had arrived, some of them townsfolk or castle residents, but also bands of mercenaries or soldiers. Since none of them were peers of the realm, they were paying with coin rather than credit. Several sat at the poker table where Sapphire entertained them with her sweet smile and dealing technique. A small pile of beat-up coins formed a pot at the centre of the table.

Across the room, Just Sam was entertaining a group of soldiers that included Effie and her friend—her husband—Victor. Sam strolled over and winked at Just Sam. "Remember that song I taught you?"

"I remember every song," Just Sam said. "I know the one you mean. You have asked me to play it many times."

"Then play it again, Sam." He glanced at Effie. "Play it for old time's sake."

Effie looked away, pretending not to notice his attention, but turned back and smiled as Just Sam strummed the strings of his harp and sang the words to Dooley Wilson's "As Time Goes By".

Many of the soldiers looked at each other in consternation since the melody was foreign to them and the words were English instead of Scottish, but some caught the rhythm and began swaying their heads from side to side.

Sam couldn't help but mumble along when the song reached the familiar chorus. Then he noticed what looked like tears welling in Effie's eyes, and lost it. He blinked as he realized his own eyes were unnaturally wet. Whatever Effie was feeling, which memories recent or distant the lyrics evoked, Sam knew what was missing from his own heart. Married. Effie had always been out of reach, but this last step came with a stamp of finality.

As Just Sam strummed the final notes, Sam mumbled, "Of all the gin joints in all the towns in all the world, she walks into mine."

"Mr. Spade? Mr. Spade!"

Sam rubbed his eyes and turned to find a fiftyish man whose tailored coat seemed ready to burst at the seams. Signor Ferrari, the owner of the Blue Parrot. Possibly the last person he wanted to see right now. "Whadda you want?"

Ferrari frowned. "Is that any way to greet a customer?"

"We're not open yet," Sam said.

Ferrari cast his gaze about the nightclub, taking in the crowd of soldiers around Just Sam, the four fellows playing poker, and various others seated at tables or sitting at the bar.

"For not being open, you have more custom than my own establishment, which is open."

"What can I say?" Sam said. "I'm a victim of my own success."

The older man harrumphed. "I have rethought the proposal I made you earlier."

"Yeah, I kinda suspected that."

"One hundred merks. Take it or leave it."

Sam noticed several of the nearby soldiers taking an interest, and felt his cheek twitch. "Maybe we should take this to my office."

Ferrari must have felt a deal closing, as he smiled the entire way there.

Once they were seated, Sam behind the desk, Ferrari in front, the tiny room cloaked in shadows because the only light came from the doorway, which had been left open a crack, Sam said, "Look, I'm not interested in money."

Sam heard a growl from where Ferrari was seated. Then the stout bar owner grunted. "You seek to barter a higher payment?

One hundred merks is a king's ransom!"

"I'm not interested in money," Sam repeated. When Ferrari growled again, he raised his hand. "Hear me out. I don't want to be here any more than you want me here."

That settled his visitor down somewhat.

"But I can't leave without a little assistance."

Ferrari reached up and stroked what little there was of his moustache. "I can hire men to take you anywhere you wish to go."

"It's not that simple." Fearing the weird sisters out in the casino could magically hear their conversation despite the noise of Casablanca's merry clientele, Sam leaned over the desk and lowered his voice to a whisper. "I need the assistance of magic."

Ferrari, who had also leaned forward to better hear him, got no further in reply than to drop his jaw.

"I know," Sam said. "Talking magic is taboo in these parts. But the simple fact is, it's magic that brought me here and nothing short of magic can let me leave."

The jaw remained dropped.

"Now, if you should happen to know someone, even someone who knows someone else who can help me out, maybe we can make a deal."

The jaw was still dropped. Sam wondered if Ferrari might have died.

Then, slowly, the jaw raised and Ferrari leaned back in his seat. The man's eyes were two cold stones as they examined Sam. Finally, the competing bar owner rose up from his seat and wagged a fist at Sam. "You are a mad man. Completely unhinged. I have no need to buy this place. They shall have you locked up or hanging from a gibbet in short order." Then the dumpy fellow stormed out of Sam's office.

Sam let out an airy sigh. "Well, that could have gone better."

34
KICKING AND SCREAMING

When Sam emerged from his office there was no sign of Ferrari, but Captain Renault was at the bar chatting amiably with Sacha.

"Ah, Mr. Spade! I have good news."

Sam signalled Sacha for a splash of ale. "I could use a little good news."

Renault leaned in conspiratorially. "I shall soon make an arrest."

"For the robbery? Or the king's murder?"

The captain frowned. "Your humour is ill advised."

"The thief then."

Renault nodded. "The thief is in this very room."

Sam took a quick look about the place. "I don't see any cleaning staff."

The captain snorted. "The maid in question has taken up residence in the castle dungeon. No, I speak of the man who hired her."

"Sang like a canary, did she?"

Another frown. "No. She did not sing. She spoke. After some prodding, she could not tell me enough about a certain sometimes bedfellow who took an interest in her extracurricular cleaning activities."

"Ah. Pillow talk."

"Mr. Spade, I ofttimes find your foreign speech somewhat confusing."

Sam continued to survey the nightclub. Besides himself and his staff, the only people he recognized were Effie and her spouse, a few castle functionaries who had attended Casablanca's grand opening, and then there was the man who called himself Ugarte. The balding purveyor of stolen goods sat by himself at a table, no doubt biding his time until his buyer showed up. How about that. Just like the Royal Canadian Mounted Police, it looked like Captain Renault was going to get his man.

"If your thief is in the room," Sam asked, "why haven't you arrested him?"

Renault smiled. "Because, Mr. Spade, he has been loitering about your nightclub for the past while and shows no inclination to leave."

"And you're wondering why."

"Why indeed."

Sam signalled Sacha for another few drops of beer. "Perhaps your thief enjoys the ambience."

Renault cocked an eye as the bartender tipped a jar briefly over Sam's bowl. "Are you rationing your ale?"

Sam raised the near-empty bowl in a toast. "I'm not one to let my drinking do the talking."

"It is just as well you are sober," Renault said. "There is another matter I wish to discuss."

After wetting his whistle, Sam set the empty bowl on the counter. "Go ahead. Make my day."

"It concerns Major Strasser," the captain said. "He tells me an escaped convict has been spotted in Inverness." After pausing for effect, Renault added, "A woman."

Sam glanced at Renault to see the captain turned in his seat, the Frenchman's gaze pointed in the direction of Effie's table where she sat with her soldier friends.

Renault continued. "I doubt she would be foolish enough to infiltrate the castle, though her crimes were of a political nature. Major Strasser believes she may seek a position among the castle residents in hopes of discovering some military intelligence."

Sam purposefully didn't look at Effie. "This castle has some of that, does it?"

"Your foreign humour strikes a false chord," Renault said.

"The only gifts I have are the ones my mother gave me. Do you have a description of this escaped convict?"

The guard captain turned back to the bar and lifted his tankard to his lips. "I am told she is stern-faced, with long red hair, and that her youth has left her. Her age approaches a fourth decade. She is also said to be somewhat skinny." The captain snorted. "Likely disguises herself as a washerwoman."

Sam stared at the man. "If I spot any washerwomen at my poker table, I'll be sure to let you know."

"Joke all you wish," Renault said. "You have enough problems of your own."

"You mean your letter thief?" Sam asked.

"He is here in your night club."

"Half the castle is in my nightclub," Sam suggested. "It doesn't mean anything."

"Perhaps. But if you are protecting him, it will not go well for you."

"You don't have to worry about me. I stick my neck out for nobody."

Renault looked at him. "No, you are not the hero type, are you?" He turned to Sacha. "More ale. And pour one for my friend, Mr. Spade. A real drink this time. He is looking a tad peaked."

Sam felt his cheek twitch. He wished there was a mirror behind the bar so he could see himself. He knew he wasn't ill, as Renault suggested. But he could have gone pale when the captain mentioned a female escaped convict while looking toward Effie's table. Why mention only one convict, not two?

As the two men sat sipping barley beer, Just Sam strummed a tune rife with syncopated and dissonant notes that provided a suspenseful atmosphere for Casablanca's general hubbub. Sam had no idea what was on Renault's mind, but his was in fifth gear searching for possible ways to get Effie and Victor/Victoria out of Dodge. There was also the matter of Ugarte's pending arrest. It would probably work in Sam's favour to get a warning to the man, but Renault was on him like a cheap suit.

The harpist finished his cacophonous tune and started in on another, a Celtic oldie but goodie that inspired some of the soldiers to sing along, raising the noise in the room by several decibels. To Sam's ears it sounded like a broken washing machine, but to each his own. Soon the entire room was singing and swaying and waving their tankards in the air. If things got any further out of hand, Sam would have to excuse himself from Renault to go break it up. In the confusion maybe he could flash Ugarte a signal to hightail it.

He was about to make his move when none other than Major Strasser marched in through the entryway and made his way to the bar. To Renault he said, "You have not yet made the arrest?"

Renault's reply was cool. "I have yet to determine why our thief chooses to sit and wait in this tawdry night club."

"Hey," Sam said. "Casablanca is the best nightclub in town. Actually, it's the only nightclub in town, the world even."

Strasser worked his lips into a sneer. "Even so, the captain is correct. Your establishment is not to my taste."

Sam waved an arm at the rollicking room. "Everyone else disagrees with you."

"Enough of this nonsense." Strasser's glare took in the entire nightclub. "There is no need to wait and see who this Ugarte meets with. He will tell us under questioning, as well as why he chose to spend his final hours in this—" He turned to look at Sam while blatantly stealing Renault's insulting description. "—tawdry night club."

Sam waved his arm again, taking in the roomful of happy customers, then shrugged. "I give up."

And giving up was all he could do as he watched the two men walk across the casino floor to Ugarte's table. Sam contemplated making a run for it, but that would make him look as guilty as the old king's two sons. It would also mean leaving Effie behind, and he still needed to warn her that Strasser was closing in on her husband.

Captain Renault and Major Strasser now stood by Ugarte's chair. Two additional soldiers had joined them, the guard captain's deputies, no doubt. Despite being outnumbered, Ugarte showed no inclination to rise from his chair at Major Strasser's command. When the two deputies grabbed him, each taking an arm, Ugarte continued to resist. But the guards were bigger than him, younger and more fit. Within a matter of moments, they were dragging him across the stone floor toward Casablanca's exit.

The balding purveyor of stolen goods turned his face toward Sam, his expression one of hopelessness and cowardice. "Mr. Spade! This is your establishment. You cannot allow them to take me away like this."

Sam raised his arms in the universal sign of helplessness, and watched as Ugarte was dragged, literally kicking and screaming, out the doorway and into the castle hallway.

35
I LIKE THE WAY YOU THINK

Turning his gaze from the doorless portal that served as the nightclub's only entrance and exit, Sam noticed Casablanca had grown unusually quiet. The soldiers no longer sang, and conversations had halted. Even Just Sam had paused his strumming. Everyone was staring at the exit where the local constabulary had dragged away a nightclub patron.

Sam rose from his barstool and smoothed his dinner jacket. "Sorry for the disturbance, folks. Seems we had a fellow who couldn't hold his drink. But things are fine now. He's been taken somewhere to sleep it off. You can return to your activities."

When no one moved, he added, "Hey, it's almost evening and we'll be open all official-like, so carry on and enjoy." He looked over at Just Sam and windmilled a hand. The harpist got the idea and began strumming another popular tune.

The casino was slow to return to normal, so Sam waited until the soldiers and civilians were chatting gaily or listening to the calming resonance of Just Sam's harp before attempting to warn Effie about Strasser closing in on Victoria. He was about to make his move when the last person he wanted to see appeared in the entryway.

"Mr. Spade, a word."

Sam knew what was coming and had no interest in getting

169

there. Even so, he joined the town Sheriff out in the hallway under the Casablanca sign. "For you, Major, I'll let you have two words."

Whether Strasser understood the sentiment or not, he let it slide. "Our friend Mr. Ugarte has some interesting things to say about you."

"He does?" Sam did his best to look surprised. "You've only had him in custody for five minutes."

Strasser smiled. "Mr. Ugarte, it appears, has a low tolerance for pain."

"Wow." Sam's cheek twitched. "Five minutes. You must be good at your job."

"I am very good at my job. But we are here to discuss you, not me."

Sam realized stalling wasn't an option. "Okay. Your thief doesn't know me from a hole in the wall, so I'm interested in what he had to say."

Strasser let that slide too. "Mr. Ugarte said he gave you some papers to hold for him."

"Ohhh," Sam said, nodding his head. "The papers. That would have to be it. Those papers were the only interaction we had."

"I am pleased you do not deny it," Strasser said. "But only for the expediency of time. I imagine if you resisted and I were to arrest you, you would put up more of a fight under questioning than your friend Mr. Ugarte."

"Your fella is no friend of mine," Sam said. "And you've got me all wrong. I'm a lover not a fighter."

Strasser let that slide as well. "If you would be so kind as to show me the papers."

Sam jerked himself backwards as though he'd been punched in the chest. "The papers? But I returned them to Mr. Ugarte."

Strasser blew out some air, then stood evaluating Sam. "Do you prefer to have your fingers crushed, or your eyes gouged out with a hot poker?"

Sam took a step back. "Now wait a minute."

"Mr. Ugarte chose crushed fingers. He told us everything after losing just one pinky."

"I'm telling it to you how it is," Sam said. "Ugarte paid me to store his papers in my safe. Then an hour later, he retrieved them.

I expected him to leave Casablanca at that point, but he joined some men at a table instead."

Strasser took a step inside the nightclub and cast his gaze about the room. "Which men?"

Sam wagged his head. "I couldn't tell you. They're not here now. They weren't soldiers like the rest of this lot. And they were dressed better than the townsfolk you see now." He was tempted to throw out a name. Ferrari would be a good candidate. But he didn't know if the podgy bar owner deserved the trouble that would bring.

Then the major said something unexpected. "Show me this safe."

Sam felt his cheek twitch. Strasser really was good at his job.

After arriving at his darkened office, Sam retrieved the strongbox key from his pants pocket.

"That key has never left your person?" Strasser asked.

"No, sir." Fun and games were over. Sam had to play this carefully, and he'd already poked the bear as much as he figured he could get away with. Leaning down, he inserted the key into the keyhole, turned, and swung open the heavy lid. Then he backed away.

Strasser stared into the strong box. "There is nothing here."

Sam rubbed his neck. "There are some receipts and coins behind the bar counter I should have put in there, but it's been a busy day. Despite Casablanca not yet being open for business, I haven't had a chance."

Strasser looked at him. "Receipts?"

"For the drinks and the poker game. My bartender collects them, and when there are enough to worry about, I put them in the strongbox for safekeeping. At least, that's what I'm supposed to do. Fact is, I haven't actually used the safe yet. It arrived just this morning. Seyton was good enough to—"

The major raised a hand, and Sam stopped talking. He knew from experience as a cop that the best way to fool the police into believing you had nothing to hide was to talk incessantly. Strasser knew someone was lying. But was it Sam Spade, nightclub manager? Or a nine-fingered man calling himself Ugarte who had already admitted to being a criminal? Sam was doing everything he could to make his interrogator believe the latter.

Strasser looked Sam up and down, taking in his week-old, though desperately in need of dry cleaning, tuxedo. "What did Ugarte's papers look like?"

"I never actually touched them," Sam said. He held out both hands, one over the other, with a gap between them the thickness of a peanut butter sandwich. "Ugarte placed them in the safe and took them out again himself. I think they may have been standard parchment sheets, but folded over. Oh, and I'm pretty sure they were tied together with string."

"You never handled them?" Strasser asked.

Sam shook his head. "Ugarte was pretty adamant about that. He seemed afraid of his buyer. Said the guy would have me killed if I so much as looked at the papers."

"He never said who his buyer was?"

"Not even a hint. Ugarte seemed to have a method. I'm sure he's done this before. When I saw him hanging around Casablanca, I figured he was keeping an eye on me, making sure I didn't return to my office and sneak a peek."

The major rubbed his face. "You never returned to your office while Ugarte's papers were in your safe?"

Sam waved a hand at the strongbox. "That's one of the reasons I'm late with the receipts. I figured Ugarte would follow me into my office and kill me himself if I opened the safe."

Strasser dropped his hand and let out a heavy sigh. "You are in the employ of Thane Macbeth?"

Sam nodded. "He hired me to set up and manage this nightclub."

Strasser considered for a moment. "Then you have bought yourself some time. I shall await Lord Macbeth's return before proceeding with this matter." The major grinned. "Besides, Mr. Ugarte yet has nine additional digits."

"Nineteen," Sam said before he could help himself.

The major let out a laugh. "Of course. We must not forget the toes. I do like you, Mr. Spade. I like the way you think."

Coming from this man, Sam wasn't sure it was a compliment.

He felt bad about Ugarte losing a finger, and whatever else Strasser might do to the poor sap, but the man was a criminal. It seemed to Sam that medieval Scotland was not a good place to be a criminal. He only wished he hadn't involved himself by taking Ugarte's ill-gotten goods.

36
A SHOUTING MATCH SET TO MUSIC

When Sam and Major Strasser emerged from his office, the nightclub was definitely more crowded. Castle officials and businessmen from the city now outnumbered the soldiers. Emerald sat at the poker table introducing several new arrivals to the game while Sapphire and Ruby delivered tankards to tables. The bar counter was also lined with customers.

Strasser stood evaluating the madness. "I may have to retract my earlier opinion of your establishment. Now that the room is full, it feels . . . comfortable."

Sam looked at his watch, which suggested it was now evening in Scotland. "It appears we are officially open for business."

"I should return to the dungeon," Strasser said, "and spend more quality time with Mr. Ugarte. However," a grin crept across the man's face, "Mr. Ugarte isn't going anywhere. What do you serve at this bar of yours that is fit to drink?"

"Sacha can tell you that better than I."

The major frowned. "Sacha?"

"That's what I call him. His real name is so Scottish I can't pronounce it."

"Perhaps he will share it with me," Strasser suggested.

Before the Major could speak with the bartender, however, Signor Ferrari came running up. "Major! Major! I must tell you something about this man." The burly bar owner pointed a pudgy finger at Sam.

"If you must," Strasser conceded.

"He's a witch!" Ferrari blurted.

Sam laughed.

The major raised a brow.

Ferrari's cheeks were flushed. Whether from exertion or drink, Sam couldn't tell.

"He . . . He claims to have come to Scotland by magical means."

Sam laughed harder, bending over because it was hurting his chest.

"Signor Ferrari," Strasser said. "How much have you had to drink?"

"I. What? No." The portly bar owner continued to wag a finger at Sam. "He told me. Told me straight to my face that magic had brought him to Scotland and only magic could take him away again."

Sam grabbed onto the bar counter to keep from collapsing to the floor. He was laughing so hard he could scarcely breathe.

"Would someone," Strasser demanded, "let me in on the joke?"

"I'm—I'm sorry," Sam wheezed. He raised a hand in the air. "Gimme. Gimme. A minute."

"He's a witch," Ferrari repeated.

"Shut up," Strasser growled. "Let the man catch his breath."

Sam slowed his breathing and stifled several chuckles that attempted to escape. "I'm sorry, it's just that, Ferrari here has come to visit me several times to try to take over Casablanca." He paused for breath. "First, he threatened me. Then he offered me cash. Then more cash."

Ferrari didn't try to deny it. It was true, after all.

Sam took another deep breath. "I couldn't get rid of him, so I told him some cockamamie story about witches, hoping it would scare him away."

"I imagine it worked," Strasser said, giving the red-faced and trembling man a cold look.

Sam smiled. "He was out of my office before I could blink. I never imagined he'd trouble you with it."

"It was all a lie?" Ferrari stared at Sam.

Sam shook his head. "I told you several times. Casablanca is not for sale. I don't even own it. It belongs to Thane Macbeth."

"King Macbeth," Strasser amended, "in a few hours' time."

Ferrari ducked his head toward the Major. "Your pardon." Then he was running for the casino exit.

"Yeah," Sam said. "That's just how he left my office."

Strasser let the matter drop and, over the next few minutes, learned Sacha's real name and acquired a tankard of Inverness's best ale. Then, to Sam's surprise, the man loosened up. Showing no interest in the poker table, the major joined the soldiers near Just Sam's harp and encouraged a singalong.

Sam figured Effie and Victor/Victoria had recognized the major as the local law by his manner if not his dress. They quietly excused themselves from their comrades and withdrew to join him at the bar.

Effie slid a coin onto the counter and said to Sacha, "Two of whatever this will buy."

Sam slid the coin back toward her. "The drinks are on the house."

Victoria, still playing the husband Victor, hissed at Sam. "You took Major Strasser into your office."

Sam smiled. "You know who he is? It was more the other way around. He thought I had some papers he was looking for. I had to disappoint him."

Victor/Victoria nodded. "If you were to come across these papers, you would do better to sell them to me than give them to Strasser."

Sam widened his smile. "You can't even afford a cheap beer. How would you pay for Strasser's papers?"

"Money can be raised."

Sam did his best to keep from laughing. The past hour had seen him lying more than he usually did in a year, and losing his fingers and toes was only a misspoken word away. "I'm sorry, sweetheart, but those papers are too dangerous, even for you."

Effie interrupted. "Sam, you're making *Victor* uncomfortable." She placed emphasis on her partner's alter ego name.

Though no one except maybe Sacha could hear him over the singing, Sam lowered his voice and leaned toward the two of them. He looked Victoria directly in the eye. "I'm not sure you're fooling anyone with that disguise. You're really not much of a man. That's a compliment, by the way."

Victoria gave no reply, but the woman's expression could have made a mugger back away. Sam did his best not to.

The staring contest lasted several seconds before Sam broke off. It was only then he realized that the singing on the other side of the casino floor was growing more boisterous by the second. He looked past Victoria and Effie and saw some kind of conflict. Whatever song Just Sam had been asked to play appeared to have two sets of lyrics, both incomprehensible to Sam. The castle staff and businessmen seemed to favour one set while Strasser had incited the soldiers, who were fewer in number, to belt out the alternative. The song had grown into a shouting match set to music.

"Who do you suppose is winning?" Sam asked the ladies, raising his voice to be heard.

Effie replied instantly. "The civilians."

"That's what I was afraid of." Strasser didn't seem the type to lose gracefully.

A moment later Sam was proved right, as the major jumped to his feet and pushed his way through the civilians, a wolf through a field of sheep. The singing fell silent, as did the harp.

"Enough," Strasser barked. "It has been a long day. Back to your homes or your hovels. This night Scotland has no king. We should not be rejoicing. Return here tomorrow after Macbeth has been crowned."

The soldiers grumbled, but climbed to their feet and made for the exit. Sam figured they were out of beer money anyway. The castle staff and businessmen were another matter. They moved more slowly, perhaps hopeful Strasser would leave ahead of them and they could get back to their entertainments. But the major stood his ground, waiting until no one was left but Sam and his nightclub staff.

"As I said," Strasser growled at Sam. "Tawdry." Then the major was gone.

37
GUILTY OF VARIOUS OTHER CRIMES

Sam stood alone in the darkened nightclub. Castle servants had come and gone, extinguishing all but one of the candles. Sacha and Just Sam had left for wherever it was they called home. His precious gems had retired to their room.

He found himself wondering what the witches might be discussing. Possibly they were deciding they no longer needed Sam or Casablanca. The task they had given him was to help Macbeth become king. That seemed to have happened just fine without the involvement of a kidnapped gumshoe. Duncan was dead, and tomorrow morning Macbeth would sit on a pastry somewhere in Scotland and be crowned king. Sam had no idea why he was still here.

Unable to ignore the twitching of his cheek, he stepped lightly across the stone floor to the apartment that sequestered the three witches, and cupped a hand between his ear and the door.

Nothing. Could they be using magic to conceal their conversation?

Tiptoeing back toward the bar, he retrieved Le Fay's magic ring from his shirt pocket and slipped it onto his finger. The witches had to know he had found them out. He'd been foolish enough to strut back into Casablanca still wearing the ring after his failed attempt to prevent Duncan's murder, and his three precious gems had seen him. Only they shouldn't have been able to, not unless they were really Le Fay and her two partners in coven disguised as cocktail waitresses. And of course, they were. Le Fay was a hands-on type of con artist. There was no way she'd send Sam off to do her bidding without some kind of close supervision. But why keep up the charade?

Made invisible by the ring, Sam stepped out into the castle hallway. Though the evening was still young, the hallway was nonetheless empty. And why not? There was nothing at this end of the castle besides Casablanca and a seldom-used exit.

Making his way toward the castle's main gate, Sam wasn't sure what he hoped to find. He assumed Lady Macbeth had left with the thanes and other VIPs to witness her husband's coronation. That left the mice in the castle with an opportunity to play. Perhaps they'd provide some amusement. Maybe even some useful information.

At the entrance hall foyer, the staircase at the back wall provided access to the upper floor, while a narrower stairway descended. Sam figured the dungeon was down there. And maybe the laundry. He had no wish to see how many digits Ugarte had left, so he decided to ascend the stairs and make his way to Macbeth's apartment.

There were no guards in the hallway in that wing of the castle, not that there had been any when the Macbeths were in residence. Perhaps it was only the visiting king who felt he needed guards. Or maybe Duncan had simply been paranoid, though not paranoid enough.

Sam worked the latch to Macbeth's apartment and eased open the door. It was pitch dark inside—something he hadn't taken into account—but a narrow table just inside the doorway held a handled tray holding a thick candle. Lifting the tray, he took the candle into the corridor and lit it from a burning wall sconce. He found it odd that Camelot had had matches—called lucifers—while Scotland seemed backward. Maybe King Arthurs's court truly had been an enlightened society ahead of its time.

The apartment was as he remembered—an opulent living space with a single door leading to the bedroom. Sam cast his gaze about looking for drawers among the various items of furniture. Where would Lady Macbeth keep her letters? There was a small writing desk complete with inkwell and blank parchments, but it contained no drawers, and there wasn't a written letter in sight.

Finding nothing, Sam stood in the middle of the room and rubbed his ear. No letters. No bloody knives. Nothing incriminating. The bedroom perhaps?

Lifting the candle from the table, he turned toward the bedroom door, then stopped. The fireplace.

Though small by Fairfield Connecticut standards, a woodburning fireplace had been built into the wall near the bedroom door. He could see the opening went all the way through to the inner room, allowing a lit fire to heat the entire apartment.

Sam stooped down and waved the candle above the ashes in the grate. Sure enough, bits of charred paper lay among the coals. Lady Macbeth had learned her lesson.

There didn't seem to be any reason to search the bedroom. Anything else the least incriminating had likely met the same fate as Macbeth's letters.

After replacing the candle where he had found it, Sam pinched the wick and slipped out into the hallway.

For the next half hour, he haunted the castle corridors, creeping up on small clusters of servants and listening to their conversations. Like Duncan's late and unlamented guards, they spoke with strong Scottish dialects, so not people Le Fay had intended him to eavesdrop on. But that was okay. He'd finally figured out why he'd decided to roam the castle. To find someone, anyone, discussing magic or, better yet, practicing it.

He hadn't forgotten that Nora was still caught in a blizzard on a highway outside Hartford in a driverless Volvo. Sam figured he had slowed the vehicle enough before his impromptu departure that, should it hit something, Nora wouldn't be injured, or at least not seriously. But he still had to get back. In the nick of time, if he could manage it.

Thinking of Nora brought his thoughts around to Effie. Lady Euphemia Peregrine. The woman of his dreams, almost literally. Worlds apart in so many ways. And now married to a woman she loved. Sam felt a huge sigh leave his chest, causing the two butlers he had been eavesdropping on to halt their conversation and glance up and down the hallway.

"'Twas the wind," one said.

"Or an omen," replied the other. "The king wis murdered wi'in these very walls."

The first one scoffed. "Omens occur afore whit they portend, nae efter."

"What happens after?" his companion asked.

"Evidence?"

Sam slipped silently away, but the exchange had given him an idea. If he could find someone suitably superstitious to play the ghost for, they might let slip what they knew of any magic in the area.

For the next few minutes, he dashed about the castle seeking servants, especially elderly ones whose knowledge might be broader. He made whispering sounds or moved objects short distances. It was like Halloween, only, instead of entertaining giggling children, he played his tricks on grown adults. He soon realized he had to stop, however. He'd never seen so many faces go pale, or chests clutched as though suffering heart attacks. He was scaring people half to death and not a one uttered anything helpful.

In his travels he discovered Inverness Castle's banquet hall, brightly lit and occupied by a bevy of castle residents laughing, singing, and basically enjoying themselves in their master and mistress's absence. Sam stepped inside and positioned himself against a wall.

The head table stood empty, but the one nearest it was occupied by familiar faces. Sam made his silent way over in time to hear Steward Seyton. "It matters not our opinion. What is, is. Ere this time tomorrow, Thane Macbeth shall be King Macbeth. What is done is done."

Captain Renault sat next to the pompous butler. "We have a serving wench in the dungeon who insists, under pain of death, that it was Thane Macbeth who plotted Duncan's demise. He wrote it in two letters to his lady wife. Along with some nonsense about witches, admittedly. But the evidence cannot be ignored."

Seyton considered his half-full tankard of ale. "Of course, it can be ignored. You should execute the serving maid immediately."

Renault's eyes widened, then turned to the man on the

steward's other side. "What say you, Major Strasser?"

The sheriff stroked his bare chin. "The maid stole not just from anyone; she stole from the First Lady of Inverness. Execution is her due."

"But the letters!" Renault hissed.

"Are best burned with the others," Strasser said. "And the man, Ugarte, must also die, but not before he names every soul who has seen those damnable letters. So, too, that foreigner in the night club. He is much too dangerous to keep around."

Renault's jaw dropped.

Seyton shook his head. "Mr. Spade was brought here by Thane Macbeth himself. Our new king may not take kindly to your efforts to protect His Grace's honour."

Strasser smiled. "Of course. Which is why I intend to let the matter drop until I have the king's ear."

"But," Renault said, then pressed on after Seyton attempted to shush him with a wave of his hand, "my good friend, Major Strasser, how do you intend to reveal to the king Mr. Spade's involvement with the letters without revealing your own knowledge of them? Anyone who knows what they contain is a liability."

Strasser chuckled. "I would never be so clumsy. The king believes we only know the letters were stolen, not what they contain. That belief must be sustained at all cost. No, without once mentioning the letters, I shall convince King Macbeth that our Mr. Spade is guilty of various other crimes."

38
A SCHOOLBOY CRUSH

Sam stood in invisible silence as the three men who were in essence the law in the castle, junior only to Macbeth himself, moved on to less evocative topics. When he felt there was nothing more to learn, he stepped away from the wall to make his way out of the banquet hall. He wasn't careful enough, however, and bumped into the back of Renault's chair.

The guard captain swung his head around, eyes wide, thinking perhaps one of the servants from a further table had come up behind him to eavesdrop. But there was no one there. Sam stood frozen, watching as Renault peered about suspiciously.

"Is somewhat amiss?" Seyton asked.

"Someone . . ." Renault shook his head. "I could have sworn someone was behind my chair."

"Do not be ridiculous," Strasser said. "I would have seen anyone approach."

Seyton spoke up. "This conversation is for our ears alone. Perhaps we should adjourn to a place more private."

Sam was tempted to follow the trio to this more private place, but it had been a long day with a short night before that. He was tired. Instead, he made his way back to Casablanca. In his head he could hear the ticking of a clock. Once Macbeth returned from his pastry stone, Strasser would have him arrested on trumped-up charges, and Renault would see him executed. Unless, of course, Le Fay decided she no longer needed him first and turned him into a newt, whatever that was.

His future did not look bright. He'd have to change that. Throw a wrench into the works to buy him some time. He just wasn't sure what wrench. Or maybe he should just fade away into the sunset. Then there was Effie. Her spouse, Victor/Victoria, was a wanted woman. And Strasser knew she was somewhere nearby. Maybe the three of them should pull a disappearing act. England would be nice. He could look for Merlin to send him home again. Or the Lady of the Lake. It had been a decade since her murder. Surely, she'd be back from the dead by now.

Sam laughed to himself, frightening a lone servant who glanced about for ghosts before scuttling away as quickly as his skinny legs could carry him. It seemed unreal but, despite hearing his doom only minutes earlier, Sam felt hopeful. Since Le Fay had first brought him to Scotland to do her vile bidding, he'd been without a plan. Now he had one: Run away. Admittedly, it wasn't a good plan. But it was better than nothing.

When he entered Casablanca, the place was still a shadowy mausoleum brightened by a single candle in a sconce on a central pillar. It was at times like these he believed electricity was probably the greatest invention of all time. He figured if he failed to find a way home, maybe he could remember some of his high school course work and invent it before Benjamin Franklin was a twinkle in his mother's eye. What these people wouldn't give for neon signs and a flashlight. He'd be rich.

But no. He would find a way home. Nora needed him, and besides, he had no clue how to build a flashlight.

Slipping the latch on the door to the closet that was his one-room apartment, Sam slithered inside and eased himself down onto the cot. He didn't bother lighting the room's lone candle or undressing, and he continued to wear Le Fay's magic ring. If he needed to make a quick getaway, he'd rather be ready to run for it. Being invisible would be a terrific advantage. Against all argument, he felt secure enough in his safety of the moment that he fell instantly asleep.

Sam wasn't one to dream, or at least, one to remember his dreams. But this night he did remember. All his dreams were of

Effie. There was a surrealism to it all, with Effie's features in sharp detail while everything else remained out of focus.

It is daytime, with sunlight angling in through a paneless window in Camelot castle. A young woman of seventeen, blonde, bright-eyed, and cleverer than anyone he'd ever encountered, waltzes into his life. Maid Euphemia Peregrine. Sam, almost old enough to be her father, flirts with her anyway, and she seems to enjoy the banter.

In an eyeblink Effie is twenty-three, their ages now only a decade apart. More serious, and still working as a clerk in a Camelot that is decidedly less friendly, she is still beautiful and smart. And still too young for Sam's comfort, though her father offers encouragement.

The castle morphs into a darkened storefront in Nottingham Town where Effie, now twenty-nine and battle-scarred, seems happier than ever to see him. And yet he has never seen her lonelier. Lonely. Lost. Directionless. Effie had been so much in control of her life while in Camelot. The daughter of a duke, working as a clerk, defying all calls to marriage. She had been alone, yes, but not lonely. Sam believes that has changed when Effie accepts Maid Marion's offer of serving as her lady-in-waiting. Only that doesn't last.

The lights come up and Sam sits on a stool at the bar in Casablanca. In walks Effie dressed as a soldier. Her hair is bedraggled and she has mud on her face. Though still the same woman, she is now thirty-five years young and older than Sam by two rotations of the sun. Battle-hardened and married, of all things, to a female spy and traitor, a regular Mata Hari. Or possibly a freedom fighter. Sam figured that after all the time he'd spent in the past, he'd have managed to become an expert on how these feudal systems work. But he was still clueless.

In quick succession, the four faces of Effie flash before his eyes: The bright-eyed young woman he first met, the more serious twenty-three-year-old, the twenty-nine-year-old beauty who considered herself hideous because of a scar she had earned in battle, and finally, the older-yet-happier married escaped convict. Effie.

The dream stayed with Sam as he rose from the depths of sleep to the realm of consciousness. His room in Inverness Castle lay cloaked in darkness, though that was no guarantee it was still night. He resisted the urge to get up, and instead reflected on the dream and what it might have been trying to tell him.

If Sam had ever had a high school crush it would have been on Effie, with the roles reversed—her the schoolgirl and him the teacher. He'd loved her in an unrequited way. From a distance. Had Effie felt the same, the old Sam Sparrow might have stayed in Camelot to be with her. And again in Sherwood. But not now. They were not a match. Different worlds. Effie knew. Effie had always known. Smarter than him in so many ways. Sam's meagre wisdom had finally caught up. He and Effie would have never worked, no matter their respective ages.

But it could work with Nora, who was like Effie in many ways, yet different. Nora lived in Sam's world. Effie was a dream; Nora a reality. Sam needed to find a way back to Hartford and keep Nora safe.

39
ON A DEADLINE

When Sam emerged from his cocoon, Le Fay's magic ring once again in his shirt pocket, he found Sacha restocking the bar and Just Sam restringing his harp. His precious gems where nowhere in sight, and Sam wondered if they had put on their hatchet faces and long dark robes and gone back to their cavern. Mission accomplished.

"You are a man who sleeps late," Sacha said, his smile indicating no criticism was intended.

Sam rubbed his eyes. "It's good to be the boss. No surprise meetings today?"

"I received word from Lord Seyton that we are not to reopen until after the supper tables are cleared in the banquet hall."

"Seyton's a lord now, is he? Not just a steward?"

Sacha shrugged. "Perhaps with Macbeth's elevation from thane to king, his staff received a likewise promotion."

"Yeah, well, I'm pretty sure our steward promoted himself, and that his new status will only last until the new king returns. Which should be when, do you think?" Sam hadn't forgotten Strasser's threats.

Sacha set down the crate he had emptied. "If my recollection of tradition serves me, the coronation took place at sunrise. A short celebration will have followed, and the king's train will already be on its return to Inverness. It should arrive late this evening, perhaps in time to drop by Casablanca before retiring for the night. The ride to Scone and back will not have been leisurely."

Sam nodded. "Scone. Right." The last thing he needed was for Macbeth to return that quickly. What he did need was to speak with Effie, but he had no idea where his escaped convict friends were.

Precious hours went by as Sam paced the room while Sacha and Just Sam looked on, their faces creased with concern. His precious gems emerged from their apartment, watched Sam for several moments, then entertained themselves with several friendly rounds of poker. The witches hadn't returned to their cave after all. Macbeth was now king, so what were they waiting for?

Sam wanted to walk up and demand to be sent back home. But the disguised witches gave no indication the mission was done. And he didn't want to show his hand that he knew who they were. Abandoning Effie didn't feel right either. Sam had never felt more like being pressed between a rock and a hard place. He continued pacing.

His eyes kept returning to the poker table. Shouldn't Alison have brought him a second deck of playing cards by now? It had been two days. A second game would bring in additional revenue. Maybe that was what Le Fay was waiting for. Maybe, like Kickstarter, her plan had a financial target. Once Macbeth's war coffers were full, the witches would send him home.

But he didn't need to speculate about that now. He'd take Effie and Victoria back to England, and find his own way home.

Occasionally, someone would poke their head in through the nightclub entryway, eyes wide with curiosity, then disappear again. But no one entered the casino. Lord Seyton's edict, likely influenced by Strasser's early closure of Casablanca the night before, had been heard by all and sundry.

Sam stopped dead in his tracks, however, when a familiar face appeared. Recovering himself, he hustled toward the casino entrance.

"Sam," Effie whispered.

"Outside," Sam whispered back, moving past her through the

doorless portal.

In the hallway, he took Effie's arm and led her toward the niche where Macbeth and his wife had held their assumed private conversation.

"What is the matter?" Effie asked. "Is it not safe to speak in your office?"

"It would be," Sam said, "if Morgan Le Fay wasn't sitting at the poker table."

Effie's eyes widened. "Le Fay? Here?"

Sam nodded. "She and two fellow witches. The three of them are disguised as cocktail waitresses."

Effie's eyes scrunched with confusion.

"The three young women in the blindingly bright dresses."

Effie's mouth formed an O. "Your staff? They must have seen me. It is unthinkable that Morgan Le Fay would not recognize me."

Sam remembered that Effie had been forced to work for Le Fay for a time in Camelot. "I'm sure she has recognized you. But she doesn't know that I know who she is. Who all three of them are. She can't do much about you without giving herself away."

Still confused, Effie shook her head. "Sam, what is going on here?"

"It's a long story, angel. I'll tell you about it while we flee to England."

"Flee to England? I cannot do that. This is now the king's residence, at least for the time being. Victoria intends to stay and continue to spy for England."

Sam rubbed his ear. Effie's husband had known about Macbeth's letters. "Victoria mentioned the missing papers. Is she Ugarte's buyer?"

Effie's eyes widened. "What? No."

"Then how did she know about them?"

"I believe most everyone knows," Effie said. "This Ugarte, if that is who has them, put word out that he has papers that prove Macbeth is unfit to be king. He was seeking bidders. Victoria has no means to raise money quickly, so we were outbid. We are ever watchful, however, for an opportunity to acquire the papers. We do not believe the transaction has yet taken place."

Sam's cheek twitched. "Major Strasser has his work cut out for him."

"What do you mean?"

"The major plans to arrest and execute everyone who knows the papers even exist."

Effie covered her mouth with her hand. "That could be half of Scotland by now. Is he so eager to protect Macbeth?"

"I think he just wants to protect the status quo. Look. Those papers are poison. Are you sure Victoria really wants them?"

"Our task is to help England against Scotland. Macbeth is a ruthless general proven in battle, while Duncan's son and heir, Malcolm, is a cowering milquetoast. Were you England, who would you prefer on Scotland's throne?"

Sam nodded. "It may be too late for that. Malcolm flew the coop."

"Even so," Effie said, "once the truth is out, Macbeth will be ousted and Scotland's thanes in disarray. Victoria needs that evidence."

"All right. All right. Don't lose your socks over it. I may be able to get you those papers. But first you need to tell me what Victoria will do with them."

Effie frowned. "Until we know what the papers contain, we will not know what course of action to take."

"I'll tell you what they contain. These papers everyone is falling over themselves for are two or more letters written by Macbeth to his wife describing his plan to take Duncan's throne."

A gasp escaped Effie's lips. "His plan? Do these letters state how he plotted to take Scotland's throne? Do they reveal his intention to murder the king?"

"I don't know. I haven't read them myself."

"Then how can Victoria know what to do with them? What would you do with them?"

Sam rubbed his face. "I'd have them printed in every newspaper in the country. But even that might not be enough."

Effie furrowed her brow. "What are newspapers?"

"Exactly. We might need time to decide what to do, and we don't have time. Macbeth gets back later tonight, and when he does, Strasser is going to put the hammer down. Look, I'll try to get Victoria the papers, but we need to leave town before Strasser makes his move."

"Tonight? You mean for us to leave Inverness tonight?"

"That's my price for getting you the papers."

"Sam, I thought you were my friend."

"I am your friend. That's why we need to do it my way."

Effie stood silent for a moment. "I trust you, Sam. I will convince Victoria this is the right thing to do. But she will not agree easily."

"That's just the way it has to be," Sam said. "We're on a deadline now. Literally on a deadline."

40
A DAMN FINE SOLDIER

Effie had said it could take as long as an hour to meet with Victoria, convince her of the plan, and return to Casablanca. An hour. Sam stared at his watch, which said it was roughly mid-afternoon. Death was on a horse galloping toward him. At the evening banquet, while they lingered over dessert, Strasser would convince Macbeth to have his casino manager arrested and executed. Sam had to make his escape before then. With or without Effie.

After a quick visit to the surgeon to get his face scraped, Sam returned to Casablanca where Sapphire set down her cards, rose from the poker table, and sashayed up to the bar to join him. "Some excitement in the hallway?"

Sam stood momentarily speechless. Since encountering his precious gems five days earlier, or the weird sisters as he now knew them to be, they had hardly said two words to him that might be construed as small talk. Rubbing his raw jaw, he replied, "Needed a shave before we open tonight. A nightclub manager's only strength is his presentation."

"That was your barber who came to fetch you?" Sapphire accused, not missing a beat.

"What? Oh, her." Le Fay had obviously recognized Effie. Was he speaking with Le Fay now? Or one of the other witches? Sam weighed the potential consequences of telling the truth verses a lie, and figured the truth might require some explaining he didn't want to get in to. "That was just a customer hoping we were open."

Sapphire's smile tightened, possibly suppressing a laugh. Then she turned and sashayed back to her sisters.

Sacha leaned across the counter. "I think she likes you."

Sam felt his cheek twitch. "I think she wants to kill me."

The bartender laughed. "You are not good with women, are you?"

"That would be the understatement of the century."

Sam settled himself onto a barstool and tried not to look at his watch every five seconds as time slowly drifted forward. Or at the raven-haired cocktail waitress he figured must be Morgan Le Fay. Ruby and Emerald would be the other two witches from the cavern. Were they here just to make sure he did what he was told? Or was something else going on? Something darker?

When an hour went by with no Effie, he grew worried.

"Pour me a drink," Sam told Sacha. "A real one."

Instead of finding him a cup, the bartender said, "We do not open for several hours yet. Why not go lie down?"

Sam looked at him. "Have you got something against my drinking?"

The bartender lowered his voice. "I worked bar for a drunkard once. Swore I would never do it again."

"I may be a lot of things," Sam said. "A drunk isn't one of them."

"In that case," Sacha said, "I shall pour you a finger of the good stuff."

Sam had no idea what the good stuff was, but after one sip he knew one thing. The good stuff was good. Throw in a steak and garlic potatoes, and it would make an excellent last meal for a condemned man. If he didn't leave Scotland soon, that appellation could apply to him. He looked at his watch. Where was Effie?

At a quarter past five, one of Seyton's henchmen stuck his head in through the entryway and announced that King Macbeth and his lady wife, the Queen, had returned from Scone along with Banquo, Lennox, Ross, and a list of others whose names Sam didn't recognize. "They shall sit dinner in the banquet hall, and afterward adjourn to Casablanca for a short visit. The nightclub shall open upon their arrival after dinner. Not one minute earlier."

Sam swallowed the last few drops of ale he'd been holding in reserve. Macbeth had returned earlier than expected. Sam now had the space of a meal in which to flee the castle and get far enough away so as to not get caught. He cast a glance toward his office. His fleece-lined trench coat would keep him warm, but it wasn't much of a disguise. Not in medieval Scotland. He should have thought about that earlier.

The servant had no sooner left, when Effie came rushing through the entryway with even worse news. "Victor has been arrested!"

"Calm down," Sam whispered, rising from his seat and turning their faces away from the critical eyes of his precious gems. He gently maneuvered Effie onto a barstool, then sat next to her. "Sacha, pour my friend a finger of the good stuff." To Effie, he said, "What do you mean Victor has been arrested?"

A sip of Sacha's special reserve seemed to calm her down. "I looked everywhere for Victoria, but she was not in the barracks, not on duty, not . . . not anywhere. Then one of my squad mates told me she had been arrested by Captain Renault."

Sam felt himself also calm down somewhat. At least it wasn't Strasser who'd arrested Effie's partner. "What was she charged with?"

Effie wiped a tear from her cheek. "Impersonating a man. My squad laughed as they told me. They said they knew all along Victor was a woman, but she was a damn fine soldier and that is what counted. Their words."

"We can fix this," Sam said.

"We can?"

"Sure. Strasser's the boogieman, not Renault. I'll convince the captain to drop the charges. Where do you think he would be right now?"

"At table," Effie said. "With the king."

41
IF IT IS A TRADE YOU SEEK

Talk about a rock and a hard place. Instead of doing the smart thing and fleeing into the night, Sam found himself walking toward the firing squad.

After convincing Effie to wait for him at Casablanca, he straightened his bow tie and ivory dinner jacket and hiked across the castle to the banquet hall. It felt strange trooping down the castle corridors without the magic of the ring. The servants all saw him and gawked at his peculiar attire. When he reached the hall, however, all of his courage and confidence had been used up.

"Hey," he said to one of the servants in the corridor. "Is that Captain Renault sitting with Major Strasser and Lord Seyton?"

The man's eyes boggled. "You dare not call Steward Seyton, lord. Not with His Grace, the King, and his lady wife, the Queen, returned to Inverness."

"Yeah. That's what I thought. But I need to speak with Captain Renault. Could you let him know there is a problem with one of his prisoners, and send him out here?"

"I can do no such thing. The king is about to give a speech. No one may walk out on the king."

Sam sighed. "Well, that's just great."

As if on cue, the conversations in the banquet hall quieted and

Macbeth rose to his feet. After offering a hand to Lady Macbeth, his queen joined him.

"Friends," Macbeth shouted, his voice carrying across the room. "My dear wife and I thank you from the depths of our hearts. It was good so many of you could join us at Scone Abbey this morning and share in the awakening of this new day for bonny Scotland. While we did enjoy a brief reception following the coronation, it is only fitting we host a larger celebration tomorrow eve. Thanes and generals from across the kingdom have been invited, including those who were unable to join us on this coronation day. We welcome you, one and all, to celebrate with us at our new nightclub, Casablanca. Especially," he turned to Banquo and Fleance who sat with them at the head table, "my good friend Banquo who fought at my side against Norway and Ireland."

The assemblage cheered and applauded. It was the kind of applause one gave at the end of a speech to let the speaker know you'd heard enough.

Giving no indication he could read a room, Macbeth pressed on. "To honour his bravery and prowess in battle, I wish to present Thane Banquo this small token." The newly minted king extracted from a pocket of his dinner robes a thin chain holding a silver disk the diameter of a golf ball.

Banquo's eyes widened with surprise, but he stood and accepted the gaudy ornament, ducking his head so Macbeth could drape the chain around his neck.

The crowd again applauded, then fell silent when the king indicated he wasn't finished speaking.

"If you have not yet enjoyed the pleasures of our nightclub, please join us this evening after dessert. There shall be ale." Cheers. "Music." Cheers. "And poker." Silence. "It is a wonderful game. You shall love it."

Once again, the hall soared with the applause of finality.

Macbeth opened his mouth to continue speaking, but Lady Macbeth—who apparently could read a room—tugged him back into his seat.

"Now," Sam said to the servant, "could you please fetch me Captain Renault?"

The man cast Sam a sour look that said one did not fetch a

captain of the guard. A few minutes later, however, he returned with Renault in tow.

"You?" Renault said.

"Me," Sam agreed. "Let's step over here for some privacy."

"What is this about?" Renault demanded. "I was told this was about a prisoner. I am missing my dinner."

"I know how tough it is to set priorities," Sam said.

"Enough of this nonsense." Renault turned on his feet.

"I understand you're looking for some stolen papers. Or Strasser is, anyway."

Renault froze, then turned around. "What do you know about it?"

"I know they were in my safe. For an hour, anyway."

"Yes." Renault wasn't going to give anything away.

"And I know a certain Mr. Ugarte took them from that safe."

"Go on."

"And I know you and Strasser arrested Ugarte a short while later, but he didn't have the papers on him."

Renault pursed his lips.

"I also know that, between Ugarte taking the papers from the safe and him being arrested, he never left Casablanca."

"So, what you are saying is . . . ?"

"Ugarte has to have hidden them somewhere in the nightclub."

Renault snorted. "You are a fool. He obviously handed them off to someone before his arrest."

"I don't think so."

"And why is that?"

"The person he was supposed to hand them to came by later looking for them."

Renault frowned. "You know where the papers are?"

"Not so I could say. But I'm sure I could find them."

"Then you must do so immediately and turn them over to Major Strasser."

"I could do that. But it occurred to me what a feather in your cap it would be if it were you who found them."

The frown deepened. "You have no wish to be the hero?"

Sam shrugged. "I'm a foreigner. When the king tires of me, I'll be gone. But you, you'll get a promotion. What comes after captain?"

Renault grunted out a word. "Major."

"Look at that. You'll be equal rank to Strasser."

The captain mulled that over. "Why would you do this for me?"

"Well, as it happens, earlier today you arrested a friend of a friend."

"I arrest many people."

"Yeah, but this is a nothing case. You see, she's a woman who was mistaken for a man by some idiot soldier who later realized his error and, to avoid embarrassment, reported it as a purposeful deception."

"You mean that Victoria woman?"

Sam nodded. "It can't be easy for a woman in this man's army, but there's no sense in locking her up over a misunderstanding."

Renault waved a hand. "The details are immaterial. This woman means nothing. If it is a trade you seek, in return for the papers I shall release your friend's friend."

"That's the deal. Then you can show Strasser how you found his purloined papers."

Sam could see the wheels spinning in the guard captain's head. Finding the letters for Strasser could get Renault a promotion. Or it could get him killed. No one was supposed to know about the existence of the letters. Renault might want as little to do with them as possible. Or, having them in his hot little hands could give him power. He was probably considering what might happen were he to give the letters to Lady Macbeth instead of Strasser.

Suddenly Renault looked up. "Who is this person who came to you looking for Ugarte's papers?"

So, he didn't miss that. "I asked the fellow his name, but he wouldn't give it to me."

"Describe him."

"Middle aged. Beard. Moustache. A little taller than you. Carries a few extra pounds. Newish clothes. Cleaned and pressed. Short on patience." Sam had described half the upper class in Scotland. He watched Renault weigh what that might mean. The man Sam had portrayed was no middleman, but someone who could use the letters against Macbeth. The end game, so to speak.

It was too bad the fellow didn't exist. Sam would have given him the letters in a heartbeat.

"How soon," Renault asked, "could you find these papers?"

Sam pretended to think about it. "The nightclub is closed now, so it should be pretty easy to search. When can you have Victoria ready for an exchange?"

Now Renault did some thinking. "I am tied up with the king for the remainder of the evening. The earliest I can manage is after everyone retires to their beds. Perhaps, once the nightclub closes, you could join me in my office. I'll have your friend's friend there waiting for you."

"Sounds reasonable. Where's your office?"

"In the castle's lower level, next to the dungeon. I can have someone bring you."

Sam didn't cozy to the idea of walking into the lion's den after dark. It would be an easy thing for the guard captain to take the letters and lock Sam in a cell next to Victoria. But he gave none of this away, instead offering the captain a country bumpkin smile. "That's okay. I'll find it."

Renault raised an eyebrow at the assertion, but spun on his heels and returned to his dinner companions, where he immediately initiated a discussion with Strasser. Sam hoped the captain was convincing Strasser to hold off a bit on his conversation with the king, though he could as easily be repeating everything Sam had said. Either way, he figured he had bought himself some time.

42
HOUSE ARREST

Sam returned to Casablanca to find his precious gems still playing poker. Effie, the nightclub's sole visitor, sat alone at the table closest to the harp, listening to Just Sam play melancholy tunes. Casablanca was still closed and would remain so for at least an hour.

"Did you find Victoria?" Effie asked almost before Sam could sit down next to her. From the quaver in her voice, he could tell she really cared for her spouse.

"I found Victoria's jailor and arranged to meet him at midnight for a trade."

"A trade? What could you possibly have that this gaoler would want?"

Sam lowered his voice to a whisper. "He's pretty desperate to get his hands on some certain papers."

"No," Effie whispered back. "You cannot! We need those papers."

Sam's cheek twitched. "Do you need them more than you need Victoria?"

Effie clenched her hands together and twisted her fingers. "I suppose not. I will go with you."

"Hold on there, sister. I don't exactly trust this jailer." He leaned toward her and lowered his voice further. "I'll bring

Victoria back here, then we'll make our escape."

"Here?" Effie glanced about the almost empty casino. "And this trade will not happen until midnight? That is hours from now. Anything could happen."

"It's the best I could do. After closing is the earliest the jailer is available."

"If you say so, Sam." Effie looked at once forlorn and dejected. Miserable wasn't far off the mark.

Sam glanced over at the harpist. "Whaddaya say, Sam. Play it again?"

"I do not know, Mr. Spade, sir. 'Tis a foreign song. I do not know if it sits well with . . ." He wagged his chin toward the casino staff at the card table.

So even the harpist had caught on that there was something off with his precious gems. "I've got eccentricities," Sam said. "They'll just have to deal with it."

Just Sam nodded. "Yes sir, Mr. Spade." Then he launched into "As Time Goes By".

Sam didn't sing along this time, but sat next to Effie, her head resting on his shoulder. He risked a quick sideways glance and noticed his precious gems pretending not to notice.

The two of them sat that way for the better part of an hour until Seyton's henchman stuck his head through the entryway and announced the king's party was on its way.

"I'm not sure how this evening is going to go," Sam told Effie. "Like you said, anything could happen. I'm thinking you should go lie down in my apartment, at least until we know no one is going to arrest me."

Effie's eyes widened. "Why would they arrest you?"

"I told you. Because those papers are trouble."

"I am tired," Effie admitted.

Whatever she thought of his makeshift apartment, Effie kept to herself. Sam took the room's sole candle out into the casino and returned with it lit. Then he left Effie to her own devices.

The first customers to arrive for Casablanca's third night of operation were none other than King Macbeth accompanied by Queen Macbeth, a cohort of thanes, and a concert of yes-men that included Seyton, Strasser, and Renault.

The newly made king led the royal procession to the bar. Sam had never seen Sacha pour drinks so fast. Tankards in hand, Macbeth led the train to the next stop—Just Sam and his standing harp, where they commented on the man's size, nimble finger work, and dulcet tones. Final stop was the poker table, where both Macbeths sat along with Lennox and Ross. The remainder of the king's party stood and watched while Ruby explained the rules.

Once the first game was underway, Seyton walked to the far corner of the casino to reserve several tables for Macbeth's party. Banquo took that opportunity to return to the bar. "Sam, it has been a long day."

"A long two days, I imagine. You and Fleance have been riding nonstop."

Banquo laughed. "Fleance is young yet, while I am stiff as a dolman."

Sam wasn't sure what a dolman was, but felt confident the word was somehow appropriate. He pointed at the medal hanging from the chain around Banquo's neck, close enough now he could make out an etching of Macbeth's psychotic features. "That's quite the gewgaw you picked up since I saw you last."

Macbeth's good friend reached down and clutched the gewgaw in question. "A military medal. A custom adopted from the Romans during their brief occupancy of the Lowlands. Personally, I find the custom distasteful. But if it is what the king wishes . . ."

Sam nodded. "We all have our crosses to bear."

Banquo let go of the king's gift and lifted his tankard, savouring a mouthful of whatever Sacha had served him, possibly the good stuff. The Thane of Lochaber then set his drink on the counter. "I have informed the king that on the morrow my son and I shall take a leisurely stroll along the river path, where I hope to work out some kinks from our travels and be in greater spirits for his celebration come evening."

Sam glanced about to make sure no one was listening. "You're happy with how things turned out? Macbeth as king?"

"Sam, you are a foreigner, so I shall forgive your naivety. Such questions should not be asked. Duncan's death was anything but natural. That his offspring fled is even worse. I am simply grateful that my friend Macbeth rose to the occasion to take on the burden that is Scotland."

"So, smooth sailing from here on out?"

"Smooth?" Banquo laughed. "Until Malcolm and Donalbain make peace with Macbeth, sailing shall be anything but smooth. Both have a claim to the throne and may cause trouble at any time." He set down his empty tankard. "I return to the king now. Whatever His Grace bids me do, I shall do, and he has asked that I stay close during these first few days of transition."

"Of course," Sam said. "Before you go, I wouldn't mind taking that river walk with you and Fleance."

Banquo grinned. "That would be wonderful, my friend. I shall find you here, shall I?"

"Rain or shine," Sam said, causing Banquo to frown with confusion.

"That means *always*," Sam explained.

"You foreigners," Banquo wagged his head. "Always so amusing." The Thane of Lochaber then went off to watch the king play poker.

Next to join Sam at the bar was Major Strasser. "Any sign of those papers?"

Sam paused for a moment, wondering if this was a trick question. Did the major already know of his conversation with Renault? It didn't matter, his answer would be the same either way. "I'm beginning to wonder if I ever saw these papers. Maybe Ugarte is a magician, making me see what wasn't there."

"Was a magician," the major corrected. "I am afraid Mr. Ugarte is no longer with us."

"The same for his friendly housekeeper?" Sam asked.

Strasser nodded.

This medieval prison system didn't fool around. As an ex-cop, Sam was all for law and order, but appointing one man as judge, jury, and executioner went beyond the pale. "So, what happens next?"

Strasser shrugged. "I wait and I watch." Then he smiled. "You were afraid, were you not? I know it is so. You were certain you would be our next resident in the dungeon. Tell me if this is not true."

"The thought had crossed my mind."

"And truly it would have been more than a thought. But the

king still has use for you, so today I shall not arrest you. And perhaps not tomorrow. But you will remain inside the castle. My men throughout Inverness have orders to indulge themselves should they find you outside the castle walls."

"I'm under house arrest?"

"House arrest." A smug look crossed the major's face. "I like that. Yes, indeed. Consider yourself under house arrest."

43

A SECRET EXCHANGE

The remainder of the evening passed quickly and without incident, which was just as well as far as Sam was concerned. His conversation with Strasser had been enough to leave his heart hammering. Renault, unlike his counterpart, had kept his distance, though the captain had turned his head in Sam's direction from time to time.

Sam had also noticed Effie peeking out from behind his apartment door a couple of times, but she had been wise enough not to come out. None of her soldier friends were around. Just a cadre of Scotland's top bananas and a few men who would be happy to arrest her.

Like Banquo, most of those present had been riding all day, returning with Macbeth from his crowning at the Throne of Scone. He'd finally remembered the name of the place, though it still made no sense.

It was still early when Macbeth stood up from the poker table and declared the evening at an end. Tankards were emptied, receipts were signed, and in short order Casablanca was as empty as it had been most of the day. Just Sam nodded a goodbye and disappeared through the nightclub's entryway. The weird sisters, maintaining their disguise as cocktail waitresses, deposited cups they gathered from abandoned tables onto the bar counter before retiring to their apartment.

Sacha, as usual, was last to finish work, setting empty bottles into crates and stacking cracker plates and drinking cups for the castle staff to haul away and clean.

"It has been a generous evening," the bartender said.

"Oh?"

"The various lords had busy pens and were eager to lose at cards to their new king."

Sam nodded. "Macbeth has this game figured out, hasn't he? If he can't win the hearts and minds of his thanes and generals, he can buy their loyalty."

Sacha turned his head. "Is that not what this nightclub business is about?"

"Yeah, but it was a lot more amusing when it was just a theory. Keep an eye on the place, will ya? I have to go out for a few minutes."

The bartender cast him a critical eye. "To see a man about a horse?"

Sam glanced toward his apartment and glimpsed Effie lurking behind the cracked open door. "Something like that."

Once he was in the hallway and confirmed he was alone, Sam slipped his hand inside his dinner jacket and into his shirt pocket to retrieve Le Fay's ring. He might be walking into the lion's den, but he had a few tricks of his own.

The pair of guards standing at attention inside the castle's main gate didn't see him as he walked across the foyer to the narrow stairway that led to the dungeon. Neither did the two guards at the bottom of the stairs. There were fewer sconces along the walls than there had been on the main floor, and the place stank of mould. Sam didn't know if the putrid ambience was natural, or if Captain Renault brought it in special for his guests.

A short corridor led to one turn followed by another, until finally the passageway opened out to a series of small offices, most of which were empty. An open doorway led to another corridor which led only to a single door at the far end, which was also open. The layout made no sense until Sam realized its chief purpose was to prevent noise from the cells rising to the upper floor.

As expected, the final door opened to a row of cells. There must have been a dozen of them, with the opposite wall housing an array of torture devices. Sam only knew what they were because he recognized a couple from an old Vincent Price movie. Apparently, the prisoners all had a front row seat to whatever amusements Renault or Strasser were engaged in.

Several of the cells were occupied. No sign of the dearly departed Ugarte, but in one three-by-five cage he spied Effie's spouse, Victor/Victoria, huddled in a corner. The captured spy showed no indication of having been introduced to the implements on the opposite wall, though her mercenary shirt and pants looked like they could use ten rounds of dry cleaning. The dungeon was cold enough to keep food from spoiling, and they hadn't even given her a blanket.

Sam examined the lock on the cell door, then looked along the wall for keys. Nothing. He went back to where he had passed the offices. Also nothing, though he did find cabinets filled with sheets of parchment and various articles collected from prisoners: empty coin purses, shoes, boots, caps, and cloaks. Sam figured some of the clothing might make for a good disguise when he, Effie, and Victoria made their escape. There were no keys, however.

He paused for a moment, then lifted a warm-looking cloak from a cabinet shelf before returning to the cell area, where he pushed the heavy garment between the bars of Victoria's cage. She didn't react, so he figured she must be asleep.

At least one of the other inmates wasn't sleeping, however. Sam had watched him stare at the floating overcoat, his mouth agape. Returning to the same cabinet, he pilfered a second cloak and pushed it into the jailbird's cell. The fellow continued to stare, wide-eyed and open-mouthed, but wasted no time wrapping himself in its warmth.

With nothing more he could do, Sam returned to the stairs and ducked and twisted, trying to see if the guards kept the cell keys on their belts or in their pockets. They didn't appear to be hiding anything.

A noise caught his attention, and he looked up to see Renault descending the stairs. Sam quickly pressed himself against the wall and held his breath as the captain rambled past. The guards acknowledged him with some kind of salute.

Renault paused to instruct his guards. "He should be here any time. Be ready."

That didn't bode well.

Sam followed Renault to one of the offices, where the captain sat in a chair, pulled open a drawer, and retrieved a leather flask. Once the cork was pulled, Sam knew the canteen didn't contain water.

The guard captain sat and sipped his beer, waiting for a naïve sap to deliver some stolen letters. Said sap being Sam.

Sam also waited. Waited until Renault let out a breath and lifted the flask to his lips. Sam pulled off Le Fay's ring and cleared his throat.

As hoped, Renault's chair skidded backwards, the flask went flying toward the opposite wall, and ale spewed like rain from the captain's lips. "Wha-Where did you come from? Where is your escort?"

Sam slouched against the wall inside the office. "Didn't need one. I'd comment on your digs, but my mother once told me that if I couldn't say something nice, I shouldn't say anything at all."

Renault sat in his chair, brushing ale from his lap with a now-damp hand. Then he stood and continued brushing. He soon gave up and cast his gaze about for something to dry his hands, eventually settling on several sheets of ale-stained parchment. He stared at Sam for a moment, then look past Sam's shoulder into the corridor. "Where are my guards?"

"I'm here to make a secret exchange," Sam reminded him. "Your guards would just get in the way."

Renault rubbed his bare chin, forgetting that his hands were sticky.

"My friend's friend." Sam glanced around the small office. "I don't see her."

The captain returned to sitting in his chair. "She is safe. Where are the papers?"

"Also safe."

"You did not bring them?"

Sam shook his head. "You don't appear to have brought my friend's friend either. Our new-found friendship appears to be getting off to a bad start."

Renault narrowed his eyes. "You did find the papers?"

Sam smiled. "That would be telling. Might I suggest we try this again? Only it might work better on my turf."

"Better?"

"Casablanca will be filled with clueless witnesses. They won't know an exchange is taking place, not unless one of us doesn't deliver our half of the bargain and the other draws attention to it."

Renault frowned, but Sam could tell he was mulling it over.

As a cop, Sam had learned to read perps and witnesses. He wasn't surprised the guard captain had reneged on his side of the deal. His cautioning his men to be ready only confirmed what Sam had expected. Once he turned over the letters, Sam would find himself in one of those empty cages. Renault would claim he'd been caught trying to sell the letters or some such nonsense.

No. The time and place Renault had set for the exchange wouldn't work. Sam's purpose in coming had been to renegotiate them. The new terms weren't perfect either. The guard captain could still arrive at Casablanca with a complement of guards and arrest anyone he pleased. The nightclub had the added problem of no back exit. There was only one way in and one way out. But such an arrest would be messy, and risked embarrassing Macbeth and his lady wife. Sam was sure Renault was considering all this.

"Very well," the captain said at last. "Tomorrow evening, when I can excuse myself from His Grace, the King, I shall retrieve your friend's friend from her cell and escort her to your night club."

"You'll clean her up first?" Sam suggested. "She'd draw undo attention otherwise."

Renault frowned. "She was dressed as a soldier when she was arrested."

"She is a soldier," Sam said, "but our exchange may go smoother if she's dressed as a servant."

"Very well."

"A senior servant," Sam added. "She should look comfortable as a guest in the nightclub."

Renault snorted. "As you wish."

Sam made a quick exit before the captain could change his

mind, and collected strange looks from the guards as he raced up the stairs. All the better to keep Renault off balance.

When he returned to Casablanca, he found all but one candle extinguished, and Effie the only person in sight. Under other circumstances—better circumstances—he might hope that combination would lead to something, but the look on Effie's face as she rose from a bar stool reaffirmed what he already knew.

"Where is Victoria?"

Sam held up a hand. "She's aces. Captain Renault, on the other hand, is disappointed his trap didn't pan out."

"Trap?" Effie's shoulders drooped. "You did see her?"

"Victoria is fine. Her accommodations could be better, but she seemed okay."

The full meaning of Sam's words must have sunk in, as Effie's eyes suddenly widened. "Renault set a trap? Are you all right?"

Sam smiled. "Couldn't be better. I convinced our conniving captain to bring Victoria here tomorrow evening during Macbeth's big shindig."

"Here?" Effie's forehead wrinkled. "Why?"

"Witnesses."

"Witnesses? What? You wish to have an audience as you are arrested? Or worse?"

Sam let out a soft sigh. "Maybe witnesses is the wrong word. What I mean is, we'll have a crowd we can use as a diversion."

"What kind of diversion?"

"We'll play that hand once it's dealt. You and Victoria just need to be able to make a run for it when the time comes." Sam knew he was risking a lot by staying at Casablanca for an additional day, but what choice did he have?

Effie took a step away, then turned around. "You believe we will need to run after making your exchange?"

"Oh, I think we can pretty much count on it."

"I will speak with my squad. They may be able to help."

"Only speak to those you can trust," Sam suggested. "Don't forget it was one of your squad mates who snitched on Victoria in the first place."

"I will be careful, Sam." Effie stepped away again, then kept on stepping until she disappeared through Casablanca's entryway. Vanished with the finality of a curtain closing.

44
IN THE GRACE OF GOD

Sam managed to tally the evening's receipts in under an hour. If his PI gig ever dried up, he could take a shot as accounting clerk at the Mohegan Sun casino in Uncasville. "Do I have experience? Sure."

He locked the stack of promissory notes and Seyton's sack of coins in the safe, then snuffed out the office's lone candle before retiring to his makeshift apartment. In the dark, he took off only his dinner jacket in case he had to disappear in a hurry. Then he stretched out on his tiny cot.

It was late. He was tired. But sleep wouldn't come. He knew what the trouble was. There were just too many hammers about to fall, and nowhere for him to duck out of the way.

If Effie's spouse hadn't been arrested, they'd already be miles away. That, or in one of Renault's cells. Or worse, Effie and Victoria could be returned to prison while he wound up stewing in Le Fay's cauldron back in her cavern. And it wasn't just the witches. Strasser was only waiting on Macbeth's okay before he started separating Sam from his fingers. And now Renault was playing a dangerous game that would go better for him if Sam was out of the picture. The more Sam thought about it, the greater the number of bad endings kept stacking up.

With everything that had happened in the past few days, his

misgivings about meeting Nora's parents for New Year's Eve dinner seemed childish. Hartford living had made him soft. Maybe that's why he kept getting drawn into the past. Whatever lesson the universe was trying to teach him, he hadn't learned it yet.

When he couldn't take lying on the cot any longer, Sam got up, fumbled for his dinner jacket, then stood for a moment in the centre of his pitch dark, one-room apartment. He couldn't sleep, but what would he do instead? Remembering he wore a watch, and that the luminous dial wouldn't illuminate again until he exposed it to sufficient sunlight, he stepped out into the empty casino. By the light of the single lit candle, his Rolex suggested it was around 7 a.m. Much later than Sam had expected. He must have nodded off, or been playing mind games longer than he thought.

Strolling over to Sacha's favourite bartending position behind the long counter, he scrounged through the previous evening's leftover booze and poured himself several fingers. He took a sip, sighed, then stared down into the cup. Speaking to the empty room, he said, "I told Sacha I wasn't an alcoholic. Anyone walking through that doorway right now would see evidence to the contrary."

"Ah, Sam!"

And there, standing inside Casablanca's entryway, were Banquo and his son Fleance.

Macbeth's good friend appeared refreshed and vigorous, the opposite of how Sam felt. The Thane of Lochaber strode into the darkened nightclub with purpose, a wide grin on his lips, Macbeth's medal hanging from his neck like an engraved silver albatross. "I was uncertain you would be risen yet." He paused and cast his gaze about the room. "Who is it you were speaking with?"

"Spirits," Sam said, thinking of the drink in his cup. But then he realized there were other kinds of spirits. "Tell me, Banquo. Do you believe in ghosts?"

"Ghosts?" Banquo echoed. "As in restless spirits of the departed?" He smiled. "Superstition. As all good Christians know, the spirit rises to God's bosom when the body is no longer able to offer it a home."

"Sure," Sam said. "But is everyone in Scotland a Christian? I mean, there have to be some pagans still about. What do they think?"

Banquo no longer smiled. "I cannot speak for any who may eschew the Grace of God. Why do you ask such questions?"

Sam set his cup on the counter. This attempt at prompting information on magic was failing just like the rest of them. "Nothing important. I thought I saw someone, but it turned out no one was there."

Macbeth's good friend nodded. "A trick of the light. Or wind brushing a curtain. There is always a rational explanation."

"I'm sure you're right," Sam said, not mentioning the absence of windows or curtains in Casablanca. "I take it you like to take your walks early in the day?"

Banquo nodded. "When the air is freshest. Do you still wish to join us?"

"Wouldn't miss it for the world," Sam said.

It wasn't until Banquo led him to a rear exit of the castle and they were following a path toward the riverbank, that he remembered Major Strasser's threat about not leaving the castle. Idly, he wondered what counted in the here and now for *indulging oneself*, as far as city guards were concerned. Just in case it hadn't been an idle threat, Sam reached into his shirt pocket and retrieved Le Fay's ring, crushing it within his palm so, at a drop of a hat, he could slide it onto a finger and become a more difficult target.

The sky was blue and cold, the early morning sun hidden behind the walls of the castle, which sat on a slight rise. The path Banquo took led them down a gentle slope to a wide river with dark water and a steady, slow-moving current. A distance downriver, he could see a wooden bridge with thick pylons that provided access to a cluster of buildings along the opposite bank. Several men on horseback were making their way across.

Banquo turned the other way and guided the three of them along the bank going upriver toward a thicket of trees, beyond which Sam could see a gravelly shore. There were no buildings along the grassy path, granting the illusion of having left the city that sprawled for at least a mile on the other side of the rise.

Sam kept a wary eye out for Strasser's men, but as near as he could tell, the three of them were alone.

"Does this path get any busier later in the day?" Sam asked. They were almost at the stand of trees, and he could make out what looked like a church dominating the opposite bank. There were no monks or nuns or whatever in the churchyard, and no bells were ringing. On his own side of the river, a low hillside continued to hide the town.

"Oh, yes," Banquo said. "This waterway carries traffic from the entire north coast down to Holm, Balchraggan, Drumnadrochit, and many other ports. But, as you noted, it is yet quiet. The boatmen are about their breakfast."

That was more than Sam had asked for, but it was encouraging. Stowing aboard a southbound boat seemed like a good option for a quick escape. "Does the river go as far as England?"

"England?" Banquo paused and looked at him. "My good man, we are in the Scottish Highlands. The River Ness would not take you so far as Argyll. You would then need to cross Fife and Lenox and then the border lands. Either that, or Galloway. Neither is hospitable. Are you truly thinking of visiting England? Now is not a good time. There have been skirmishes of late."

Yeah. Nothing ever came easy. "Just trying to get the lay of the land," Sam said. "I'm not exaggerating when I tell you I have no idea where I am."

Banquo laughed. "Worry not. There is no place better on God's green Earth than the Scottish Highlands. And here, in the home of King Macbeth, no harm shall befall you. Macbeth shall keep you safe. You have my word on that."

Sam fumbled for a response, but didn't think Macbeth's good friend would take kindly to his opinion of Scotland's newly crowned king. Instead, he said, "You're aces, Banquo. If only Scotland had more men like you."

The Thane of Lochaber's face visibly reddened. "Your words are too kind."

They had almost arrived at the copse of trees, and Sam saw it was thicker than he'd first supposed. The grassy path, rather than try to go through the wood, split and veered to either side. Banquo casually followed the route by the river, taking them to the edge of the water.

"To answer your question," Macbeth's good friend said, "England is a good 250 miles from Inverness. Several days' journey, depending on the horse. Relations with England have never been good, however, and I suspect they shall not improve with Macbeth as Ki—"

Sam didn't have to wonder why Banquo had stopped speaking mid-syllable. Trapped between the thicket and the river, the three men who leapt at them from among the thick trees had an easy target. The attackers were dressed head to toe in black and carried themselves as professionals. No warning shouts. No condescending challenges. No fumbling with the knives they carried expertly in their gloved hands.

Sam saw one of the blades enter Banquo's chest. But that was all he saw, as he quickly turned his attention to a second blade speeding toward his own. He considered himself fortunate that this wasn't his first assault, and that as a cop he had received extensive hand-to-hand training. Spinning on the balls of his feet, he twisted sideways and brought up his elbow, knocking his assailant's knife arm wide of its target. In almost the same movement, he slipped Le Fay's ring onto the middle finger of his left hand.

Banquo was down. There was nothing Sam could do about that. But Fleance was still standing. Whether his attacker had missed, or the teen's youthful reflexes had kept him safe, Sam had no idea. But Banquo's son now had two of the three attackers to contend with and, with his back to the river, had nowhere to go.

The third assailant was searching the trees, likely thinking that was the only place Sam could have gone. But these men were professionals. In a very few moments, Banquo's son would join his father in the Grace of God, wherever that was, then all three assassins would be searching the trees for the one that got away. Unless . . .

There was only one thing Sam could do. Rushing past the two men in black, he pushed Fleance in the chest with both hands and the two of them crashed into the icy waters of the River Ness.

Cold didn't begin to describe it.

The slow current swept them away from the copse of trees, out toward the centre of the river and back toward the castle. Sam had never been much of a swimmer, but he kicked his feet and pushed with his arms until, finally, he came to a place where he could drag himself up onto the bank. Then he lay, invisible but shivering, as Fleance swam with the current, angling his way to the opposite bank, where he climbed out near the churchlike building.

"Fly, Fleance, fly," Sam mumbled. "Avenge your good father someday."

Turning his head toward the copse of trees, he saw no sign of the attackers. Maybe while he'd been fighting the river, they had booked it past the castle to the bridge. He looked downriver but saw no one along the path. They'd never catch the lad anyway. Banquo's son was long gone.

After considering and dismissing the idea of searching through town for local clothes he might steal to aid in his later getaway, Sam decided he was too wet and cold to make the effort. Instead, he would hotfoot it back to the castle. If you were going to steal, steal from the best.

He did take a minute, however, to walk cautiously back to the copse of trees further up the river bank. As expected, there was no sign of Banquo, just a dark patch on the grass that could be mistaken for dew. Sam imagined the body of Macbeth's good friend floating down to Moray Firth, then out to the North Sea.

As he turned back toward the castle, a glint of metal caught his eye. Sam bent down and pushed aside the grass to reveal the silver medal Banquo had worn around his neck, the one Macbeth had given him for bravery and prowess. There was no sign of the chain, which must have broken in his killers' hurry to dispose of the body. Not wishing to leave the memento where anyone might walk off with it, Sam slipped it into his sodden trench coat pocket.

By the time he reached the rear exit of the castle, his clothes had ceased dripping but were heavy and stiff with dampness. His Thorogood Oxfords, especially, had seen better days. They squeaked when he walked on the stones of the castle floor, so he took them off and continued in invisible silence wearing only his wet socks.

Sam knew there had to be a laundry somewhere in the castle, but in his previous prowlings hadn't come across one. He also knew that, during the day, the laundry would likely be busy with servants. Sneaking in and out with an armload of suitable attire might be a challenge. Instead, he made his way up to the apartment where Duncan had been murdered three nights earlier.

The visiting dignitary's bedroom was pretty much as Sam remembered, though it did look more cheerful in the light of day. Both outer and inner rooms had a window with the curtains pulled back, bright sunlight revealing every nook and cranny in stark relief. The corpse, of course, was gone. Probably mailed back to Forres, first class. The bedsheets likewise had been taken away. As was the mattress, soaked through with blood and rendered unusable.

But Sam wasn't interested in taking a nap. He shivered as he chucked off his Burberry trench coat and draped it over a bedpost. Next came his Merino wool dinner jacket. He used his hand to smooth it out before adorning a second bedpost. His shirt, tie, and dress pants followed. His socks. His briefs. Even his Rolex.

Being naked didn't make Sam feel any warmer, so he searched the portable storage chests and the ornate standing wardrobe for something he could use as a towel. Somebody up there must like him, because he struck gold. The closet contained a collection of men's apparel fit for a king, though perhaps it should have. With Duncan's sons having fled the country, the disposition of the old king's belongings was likely up in the air.

Sam rifled through the treasure trove, pulling out the plainest clothing he could find—socks that reached halfway up his thigh, a loose-fitting shirt as black as his tie, a dull grey robe that felt like silk, a belt with a heavy buckle that probably was gold, and slippers that were a bit too large and would cause him to trip if he wasn't careful.

There was no mirror for him to see how he looked, but he wondered if it would matter. If he continued wearing the ring until his clothes dried . . .

Sam frowned. Would they dry? Despite the bright, sunny day, the apartment was cold as an icebox. He stood for a moment, staring at his wet clothes, before stepping into the outer room.

It hadn't escaped his notice that the castle staff, going about their duties, had set an arrangement of kindling and firewood in the fireplace. All he needed was something to light it with. Yeah, right. Though there were oil lamps and lit candles aplenty once the sun went down, daytime was another story.

Sam rubbed his ear. There was probably a fire going in the kitchen. Surrounded by kitchen help. Yeah, any daytime fire was there for a reason. People would be using it.

His gaze pondered the fireplace, then lighted upon a bucket containing several metal implements. He didn't recognize half of them, never mind know how to use them. Oddly, the bucket also contained a fist-sized quartz rock.

Taking the stone in one hand, he examined the other implements in the bucket. Most looked like rough versions of modern fireplace pokers, but one looked like a warped horseshoe. He couldn't imagine any useful purpose for it, so figured it must go with the rock.

At the centre of the kindling set in the fireplace was a pile of wood shavings. Sam was no boy scout, but he could put two and two together. Gripping the horseshoe in his fist, he held it above the kindling and began striking the rock against it. Sparks flew, telling him he had figured it out, but the kindling didn't catch fire. He continued to strike until his back and arms got tired, then at last the kindling caught. He remembered something from television about blowing on the flames, but was afraid he'd blow the budding fire out. So, he took small, short puffs, and was reward with growing flames.

The larger kindling caught, then the sticks, and finally the cut logs.

Sam sat cross-legged in front of the blazing fire, warming himself, then returned to the bedroom to ensure heat was coming out that side of the fireplace as well.

When the room felt toasty warm, he threw more logs from a neatly piled stack onto the fire and left the apartment. It would take hours for his clothes to dry, and he felt he should check on things in Casablanca.

45
WHERE EVERY SERVANT GOES

Though quiet an hour earlier, the foyer inside the castle's main gate was bustling with activity. The usual pair of guards had been tripled. Servants rushed everywhere. And Steward Seyton stood greeting a group of road-weary new arrivals. Though Macbeth had already been king for a day, his soiree later at Casablanca would be the real celebration.

Sam figured it was fortunate no one could see him. Dressed as he was in odds and sods stolen from the late king's closet, he probably looked like someone who should be arrested. Whatever uses Morgan Le Fay had intended for her ring, Sam didn't think this was one of them.

When he arrived at Casablanca, he found Sacha putting the finishing touches on restocking the bar. Just Sam sat by his harp, concentrating on tuning the strings. Sam's precious gems, after initially noticing him and raising a collective eyebrow at how he was dressed, gave no further sign they could see him, and resumed their poker game. Sam figured they weren't playing for merks. For all he knew, the witches were playing for much higher stakes.

Since everything seemed in order, he decided to lie down for a bit. After a night of fitful sleep, a Z or two would be welcome. He ensured no one was looking his way as he lifted the latch on the door to his apartment and slipped inside.

When he emerged an undetermined while later—he had foolishly left his Rolex in Duncan's apartment—little had changed. The poker game was still in progress, but Sacha was now sitting at a table having a one-sided conversation with Just Sam. The harpist was a man of few words, or maybe he preferred to save his voice for singing. Sam, still wearing Le Fay's ring, forced himself to not glance at the disguised witches as he stole his way to the nightclub exit.

The castle was still a hive of activity. Servants quickstepped along the corridors carrying baskets and boxes. Larger chests took two strong men to carry. Aromas of baking drifted out from the corridor that led to the kitchen. Sam quickened his step; with so many new visitors, it wasn't impossible that Duncan's apartment had been commandeered.

To his great relief, the royal guest accommodations appeared untouched and much warmer than when he had left them. The fireplace, its job done, held smouldering ashes. Sam's clothes were dry, but not in the best of shape. The wool dinner jacket and gabardine cotton of his trench coat had come through the ordeal of the river relatively unscathed, but his shirt was a mass of wrinkles and his slacks severely creased. He smoothed them out with his hands as best he could, and considered himself fortunate the dinner jacket hid much of the damage.

His Oxford shoes were still a bit damp, but at least they no longer squeaked when he walked. Sliding his Rolex onto his wrist, he noticed it was almost two o'clock, much later than he had expected.

Despite looking more or less his normal self, Sam continued wearing Le Fay's ring as he made his way back to the nightclub. It was bad enough he had to dodge the heavy foot traffic; he didn't need their incredulous stares as well. And with the added guards, some of them might be looking to throw some weight around. Better safe than arrested.

Just outside Casablanca, he pulled off the ring and slipped it into his shirt pocket.

"There you are," Captain Renault announced as Sam came through the entryway. "I was about to send my staff to look for you."

"I didn't know I was so popular."

Renault snorted. "Comhnall has been waiting for you for ages."

"Who?"

The captain indicated a younger fellow, hardly more than a teenager, dressed as a butler. "Three times Comhnall has come here looking for you. Three times he came away disappointed. Where have you been?"

Sam provided the first excuse that came to him. "The Necessary—I mean the garderobe."

"Three times?"

"My breakfast didn't sit well with me. Uhm, who is Comhnall? And why is he looking for me?"

Renault tried to stand a bit taller. "It has been brought to the attention of Steward Seyton and others that you have begun to smell a bit ripe. Comhnall was to take your clothing to the laundress for cleaning."

"Was?"

The captain snorted. "There is no time now. The king's celebration shall begin in a matter of hours. It takes all day for the sorting and washing and rinsing and drying and folding."

Sam grinned. "You sound pretty familiar with the job."

Renault's expression hardened. "I am sufficiently knowledgeable of the daily operation of the castle."

"Wow. That's a mouthful," Sam said. "Since I can't get my clothes cleaned, is there time for me to have a bath?"

"Of course."

"Uh, where would I go for that?"

The captain's lips twisted in a tight smile. "Where every servant goes. You shall bathe in the river."

The irony of the day wasn't lost on Sam.

After depositing his trench coat in his apartment, he returned to the casino to find Renault and Seyton's butler-in-training loitering in a corner. It should have been Seyton directing his own minions, not the guard captain. But Sam had a nose for ulterior motives, and could easily smell Renault's. Lady Macbeth's letters. The captain probably hoped to catch Sam unawares, and apprehend the letters without necessitating the exchange. But why? Victoria was a nobody. Unless. Unless Renault knew who she really was.

This was a dangerous game the captain was playing with Major Strasser. Did he chafe that much from having a lower rank? Sam watched Renault with greater care as the man glanced once more around the nightclub before leading the butler away.

Feeling a sudden need for a drink, Sam walked over to Sacha and leaned against the counter. "I think I need a strong one."

For once, instead of forestalling or pouring Sam an eighth of a finger, the bartender poured him a full finger of the good stuff. The Scotsman with the unpronounceable name slid the heavy tankard across the bar. "You have been away all day. You had us worried."

Sam took a slow swallow, relishing the burn before answering. "What? Did you think I'd been arrested or something?"

Sacha merely looked at him.

"Oh, I'm sure I'll be arrested at some point, but for now Macbeth still needs me."

"If you say so."

As Sam took a second sip, he noticed his precious gems watching him. If the young women's expressions hadn't been expressionless, they would have been scowls. The witches, of course, had observed him wander in and later back out wearing the recent king's lounging around clothes. Sam waved his tankard and smiled. They looked away.

This was all going to come crashing down. He just had no idea which straw would break the camel's back.

Nursing the remainder of his drink, Sam idled away the time until opening. When a train of servants trooped in carrying platters of fresh-baked breads, steaming meats, and pungent cheeses, setting them at one end of the bar counter, he knew opening lay only minutes away.

The train's caboose arrived in the form of Seyton. The steward looked exhausted but kept a stiff upper lip, calling out instructions and adjusting the placement of almost every tray.

"The crackers are looking especially formal tonight," Sam suggested.

Seyton wiggled one of the trays over a fraction. "The king wishes to make a good impression."

"I bet."

The steward leaned toward him and sniffed. "You smell of mildew."

"What? You don't like my aftershave?"

If the medieval Scotsman knew what that meant, he gave no indication. "You shall keep your distance from the king, his thanes, and everyone else."

"Maybe I should take a walk," Sam suggested.

Seyton's eyes darkened. "You are the host. You must be here to greet your guests."

Sam couldn't prevent a smirk from twisting his lips. "But not come near them."

"You shall greet them from a short distance. They shall arrive anon. Go position yourself near the entrance."

"But not too near." Sam chuckled as he strolled toward the entryway that was the only way in or out of the nightclub.

For the first time since he had arrived at Inverness Castle, Sam could hear noises in the outside hallway. He poked his head out through the doorless portal, and almost burst out laughing. Seyton had 'em lined up around the block. Lords in flowing robes with wide belts and oversized slippers. Ladies dressed much the same. Soldiers in military finest, even if all that meant was a kilt and a clean coat. There were even a few who appeared to be servants or personal assistants, ready at their masters' beck and call. All, apparently, were waiting for the king to arrive before entering the king's nightclub.

Turning back inside, Sam nodded at his various staff members, but gave no indication of the hellish evening they were about to endure. He walked over to Seyton, who stood at the bar finishing off a drink. "We're going to need more chairs."

The steward rested his empty cup on the counter. "They are already being collected from the banquet hall. Additional alcohol is being purchased from the city as well. But there is one matter that is not yet settled."

"What's that?"

Seyton glared at him. "When I arrived this morning to collect yesterday's accounting, you were absent."

Sam paused for effect, then said one word. "Garderobe."

Unlike Renault, the steward looked too tired to argue. "Get me those accounts. Now."

Relieved that he hadn't lost any of his possessions in the river, including the skeleton key to his safe, Sam entered his makeshift office and returned a few minutes later with the summaries and bundled receipts.

Seyton scowled as he reviewed the accounting. Then, without a word, he stuffed the paperwork into his robes and strode toward the outside hallway to entertain the king's guests.

46
BLOOD SHALL HAVE BLOOD

Macbeth and Lady Macbeth entered Casablanca without fanfare. They had probably made their way along the corridor as though it were a receiving line, collecting congratulations and words of support from the highest stations in the land. Then the royal couple rolled into the casino and commandeered a corner table from which to hold court.

People shuffled in quickly after that, several making a beeline for the poker table while most followed food smells to the bar counter where Sacha offered various spirits to accompany their snack grazing. Sapphire began shuffling cards while Emerald and Ruby escorted patrons to tables. Just Sam, who had been strumming a gentle melody before Macbeth's arrival, now played something popular and traditional.

The new king's celebratory soiree had begun. Sam was alive, and not occupying a cell in the dungeon. So far, so good.

Then he noticed a problem. Lingering near the Macbeths stood none other than Major Strasser. Sam had wanted a crowd that he could run as defence when Renault brought in Effie's Victoria, but Strasser could very well recognize her as his escaped convict. Victoria being arrested by Strasser was not the distraction Sam was going for.

He glanced around for Renault but didn't see him. Hopefully, the guard captain was still in the dungeon, perhaps releasing Victoria from her cell and getting her cleaned up.

Sam was torn. He could put on Le Fay's ring and make his way to the dungeon. Prevent Renault from bringing Victoria to Casablanca. There was even a chance—a small one—he could incapacitate Renault and run off with Effie's spouse, hide her somewhere in the castle. Duncan's room would do. But what if the guard captain and Victoria were already on their way? Maybe taking an indirect route? They could arrive at Casablanca while he was away. Then there would be nothing he could do to prevent Strasser from taking her.

There was no good answer, so Sam decided to try a little of both strategies. Stepping through Casablanca's entryway into the now-empty castle hallway, he retrieved Le Fay's ring from his shirt pocket and slipped it on. He then re-entered the nightclub and dodged patrons as he made his way to the king's corner.

Strasser had whispered something in Macbeth's ear. Sam watched as the newly crowned king rose from his chair to address those nearest him. "Please stay seated. I must take a moment to mingle with our guests and play the humble host. My sweet lady wife shall remain and keep you all entertained."

Lady Macbeth smiled and nodded at the various thanes and generals. Sam recognized Lennox and Ross among them. "My lord husband has many duties, as do I. Chief among them is to make our guests welcome."

Sam wasn't interested in anything the scheming murderess had to say, but he did want to see what Macbeth was up to, especially if that business resulted in getting rid of Strasser. Invisible, he followed the two men through the casino and out into the corridor. So much for mingling with guests.

"They await you at the south postern gate," Strasser told the king.

Macbeth thanked the major and began walking toward the quiet end of the corridor where he had whispered with his wife three nights earlier.

Sam waited to see what Strasser would do and couldn't have been more disappointed. The major re-entered Casablanca. Now there were no good options. His gut told him to follow Macbeth, so that's what he did, making sure to step as soundlessly as possible as he moved along the empty corridor.

Macbeth reached the alcove he had shared with his wife, but continued all the way to the end of the hallway, where he pushed aside a tapestry that hid a narrow, bolted door. The king slid back the bolt and cracked open the door a few inches.

Cold air swept in through the opening, sending a chill down Sam's back. Macbeth made no move to go outside, so Sam took two steps sideways until he could see a hooded cloak in the darkness.

"There is blood on your face," the king said in a low voice.

A man's voice answered. "I cut maself shaving."

"It is not Banquo's blood?"

"No. That blood is in the River Ness."

"All of it?" Macbeth asked.

"My laird, his throat is cut. That ah did fur him."

Sam knew that was a lie, but dead is dead and Banquo was that.

Macbeth let out a soft chuckle. "You have a reputation as the finest cutthroat in Inverness. If your friends are half the assassin you are, the blood of Banquo's son, Fleance, also flows with the river currents."

"Alas, m'laird, Fleance haes escaped."

"Escaped? There were three of you. And but two of them. You took your quarries by surprise, did you not?"

"Very much sae. Bit the younger o' the two wis wiry. 'N' quick. He abandoned his father 'n' jumpt intae the river. The water current helped his escape."

"You searched for him?"

"Of coorse, m'laird."

"Then search again. And do not come back until Banquo's whelp lies bleeding in a ditch. Fleance cannot be suffered to live!"

The hood ducked lower, then was gone.

"Idiots," Macbeth mumbled as he closed and bolted the door. "Three grown men cannot handle a single boy."

Sam followed the king back to Casablanca where he resumed his seat next to his wife. The man had just received confirmation that the hatchetmen he had sent after his best friend had succeeded, and here he was laughing and drinking with his sycophants as though nothing had changed.

And Banquo had been a decent fellow. Maybe the most decent Sam had met since Le Fay brought him to Scotland. Why he and Macbeth had been friends, Sam had no idea. The two seemed polar opposites. He wished there was something he could do to wipe the smile off Macbeth's face. Then he realized there was. There were any number of things an invisible man could do.

"My husband," Lady Macbeth said. "Your absence has been hard felt. Why not raise a toast to your good friends?"

"My dearest lady," Macbeth answered. "Your wisdom is only exceeded by your beauty." He reached toward his tankard on the table, but somehow managed to knock it over.

The tankard had had help, of course. Sam stood in the gap between Ross and Lennox's seats and had reached out to tip the cup before Macbeth could grasp it. He backed out of the way as Lennox jumped up. "No fear, Your Grace. I shall fetch you another."

Sam didn't stop there, however. Remembering he had found Banquo's war medal in the grass where he had died—the medal Macbeth himself had given him—he retrieved it from his pocket and set it on the table, making sure it gave a soft click to attract Macbeth's attention.

Perhaps the click was too loud. Ross leaned over and peered at it. "Is that not the honour medal? The one Your Grace conferred upon Banquo yesterday?"

Macbeth stared at the offending disc, then swallowed. "Not the same. I had several made."

"Is it Lennox's?"

"I." The word came out as little more than a squeak. "I have not presented Thane Lennox a medal. It must have fallen from my robe." Regaining his composure, and perhaps hoping to change the subject, the king added, "But where is Banquo? I would have all of Scotland's peerage under one roof on this special night. I hope he is merely late and that nothing untoward has befallen him."

Lennox returned with a fresh tankard for the king and set it on the table.

"Thane Lennox," Ross asked, pointing toward the disk etched with Macbeth's likeness. "Know you this medal?"

"Medal?" Lennox examined the tabletop. "I see not what you

speak of."

"There. Oh. What? It is now gone."

Not quite gone. Sam waved the metal disk in the air behind Ross's head, and almost burst out laughing as Macbeth's staring eyes tracked it.

Lennox noticed Macbeth's behaviour and turned to see what captivated the king's attention, but Sam palmed the medal, causing it to disappear.

"Thane Lennox," Lady Macbeth said, "do sit. My husband is often thus. Has been since childhood. He shall be well again in a moment unless you pay too much attention to him. That sometimes extends his convulsion." Then she hissed something into Macbeth's ear that none at the table could hear, including Sam.

"But . . . but . . . but . . ." Macbeth said, pointing at where Banquo's medal had danced in the air.

"Hush!" Lady Macbeth slapped her husband's wrist. "You have had too much wine. You are seeing things."

"But there it is!"

Everyone at the table looked, but Sam had cupped his palm holding the metal disc so only Macbeth could see it. He moved his hand so Banquo's medal danced in the air.

"There! It is there! Can you not all see it?"

The thanes and Lady Macbeth said nothing, but turned their gazes on the king. Half the nightclub had ceased their conversations and were also looking. Sam noticed Ruby glaring at him, but no one else seemed to see anything out of the ordinary.

Sam knew he was pushing his luck. If Lady Macbeth or Lennox leaned toward the king, they would also be able to see the medal. Quickly, he curled his hand into a fist, causing the medal to vanish.

Macbeth fell back into his seat. "It is gone."

Lady Macbeth slapped his wrist again. "Such is the way of hallucinations. Especially those brought on by drink."

The word *drink* must have triggered something. Macbeth reached for the new tankard Lennox had brought him and downed half of it.

Lady Macbeth smiled at the surrounding men. "It is a strange infirmity, made worse by strong drink." She glanced at her husband. "Also cured by strong drink. Come, let us have that toast."

Ross and Lennox lifted their cups, as did Macduff, who sat opposite Macbeth and had remained quiet up till now. "To what are we toasting?" the deep-voiced thane asked.

Sam lowered his voice and attempted a Scottish lilt. "To Banquo."

"To Banquo!" the thanes shouted.

Macbeth nearly dropped his tankard.

As the thanes lowered their cups, Sam stepped around behind Macbeth and leaned down to whisper into the trembling man's ear. "Why did you kill me?"

The new king jerked back with a start, almost bashing Sam's cheek with the back of his head.

Ross seemed to have had enough. He rose from his seat. "I, too, feel I have enjoyed perhaps too much ale. I take my leave. Good night, My King. I wish you improved health."

Lennox also stood. "We have all enjoyed ourselves perhaps too well. I shall also retire to my bed. Perhaps Your Grace shall follow our good example?"

Lady Macbeth rose from her chair. "I fear this new nightclub, in its eagerness to please its patrons, has forgotten to water the wine. I shall have words with the staff on the morrow. Thane Lennox, your advice is sound. I shall take my husband to our apartment where we shall share a pitcher of water."

Thane Macduff also stood, threw Macbeth a contemplative glance, then stepped away.

The table was now vacated, leaving only the Macbeths. Music continued to flow from Just Sam's harp. Shouts and laughter erupted from the poker table. The bar was abuzz with voices all along the busy counter. Conversations droned from the varied tables. The corner of the room where the king had kept court held the only quiet.

Lady Macbeth, standing next to her husband's chair, hissed into his ear. "Saftie! You are ten times a fool."

"Do not harass me, woman. I have done all you have asked. But there is a saying: Blood shall have blood. Gravestones have been known to move, and trees to speak. The craftiest of murderers have been exposed by mystical signs made by crows and magpies. The dead have returned to haunt me!"

Lady Macbeth snorted. "You are being ridiculous."

Macbeth shook his head. "Tomorrow I shall take some men and ride to Achindown to speak with the weird sisters. They shall give me counsel. Then I shall know my course."

"You require sleep," Lady Macbeth said. "Not the advice of hags. You take care of Scotland. The dead shall care for themselves."

47
LETTERS? WHAT LETTERS?

Sam pressed himself against the wall as Lady Macbeth helped her husband rise from his chair. Together, they made their way toward the nightclub entryway. No one seemed to notice as Scotland's King and Queen exited Casablanca. Or perhaps they merely pretended not to notice, busying themselves instead with table conversations, the bar, the poker table, or listening to Just Sam and his harp. Never mind that Macbeth seemed unable to walk on his own. The man's face was white as the ghost he believed had haunted him, while Lady Macbeth looked angry enough to turn the next person she encountered into a ghost. Better to direct your attention elsewhere and deny having seen anything. So much for the celebration of the decade.

Distracted by his own shenanigans, Sam had completely forgotten about Captain Renault, who entered the casino a few minutes later with a smartly-dressed redhead hanging off his arm—Victoria.

Sam's gaze immediately darted around the nightclub, searching for Strasser. But there was no sign of him. Sam couldn't remember having seen the major since following Macbeth to his assignation with the assassin.

Renault's cold glare also drifted about the casino. Sam figured the captain was looking for him.

237

Not wanting to risk the time it would take to walk out into the corridor, remove Le Fay's ring, and re-enter Casablanca, he snagged an empty cup off the table and ducked down toward the floor. Using the table for cover, he removed the ring from his finger, slipped it into his shirt pocket, then straightened and set the cup back on the table. After glancing about for other problems suited to a club manager, he pretended to see Renault for the first time.

With a nod and a wave of his hand, Sam acknowledged the guard captain and made his way among the tables toward him. "You'd think a club manager would be above picking cups up off the floor," he said, "but you'd be wrong." He turned his attention to Victoria. "Who's your lovely companion?"

Renault ignored his words. "Do you have the papers?"

Sam rubbed the day's growth on his chin. "There's a good chance that I do."

"No more games, Mr. Spade. We both have much to lose."

Sam took a careful look at Victoria. Her short red hair had been washed and brushed. Her face and hands were clean, and she wore a plain white apron over a blue floor-length dress. The outfit suited her height and demeanour, but Sam couldn't tell if she was supposed to be a head maid or a nun. "You doing okay, sweetheart?"

Victoria's eyes widened and her mouth formed an *O*. When she found her voice, she said, "I am well."

Sam smiled. "You didn't happen to see a contingent of guards out in the corridor, did you?"

"The hall was empty," Effie's spouse replied. "But there is a man over there you may wish to meet."

Sam shifted his gaze to the table Victoria indicated, and saw Macduff sitting with two of his attendants. Unlike Ross and Lennox, the Thane of Fife hadn't turned in for the night.

"Stop this nonsense," Renault said. "You will give me the papers now, or I will escort your friend's friend to a part of the dungeon prisoners do not return from."

"Cool your jets," Sam said. "You're going to attract attention. Hang on a minute, and I'll go see what I can do about your papers."

Sam left the captain and Victoria standing near the nightclub entryway as he walked past the bar counter to his apartment. It worried him that he hadn't seen Effie all evening. He hoped she was just keeping a low profile. He also wondered at Victoria's interest in Macduff. The deep-voiced thane was behaving oddly as well, saying nothing while sitting with the king and queen, then staying behind after the others had left.

The tiny apartment was dark, but Sam didn't bother with the candle. Instead, he got down onto his knees and reached underneath the cot. The mattress lay across a row of wooden slats that had been set with two-inch gaps. Pushing on two of the slats to widen the gap, he reached between them and the mattress to tug the letters free.

Hiding one's valuables under a mattress was a tradition that dated back at least as far as the Great Depression. Sam didn't know when the practice had started, but it might have been in Macbeth's day and in this very room.

After climbing back to his feet, he checked that no one was peering in through the partly open doorway, then slipped the letters into a pocket of his dinner jacket and brushed the knees of his slacks with his hands. Then he left the apartment and made a beeline to where Macduff sat with his fellows.

Keeping the letters had been risky. Sam remembered the Bogart film he'd named the nightclub after as having letters as well—letters of transit that allowed people to leave German-occupied Morocco. The man looking to sell those letters had been arrested, leaving Bogart holding the bag. Sam figured Lady Macbeth's letters were no less an invitation to getting arrested. So once Ugarte had left his office, Sam removed the letters from his safe and stuffed them under the mattress in his apartment. The gamble had paid off. So far. This next bit was also risky.

From the corner of his eye, he saw Renault stiffen as the captain realized Sam wasn't coming toward him.

"Thane Macduff."

The deep-voiced statesman raised his head at Sam's address, then stood and extended a hand. "Mr. Spade. I do not believe we have been formally introduced."

Sam smiled. "Normally I wouldn't intrude, but the guard captain asked me to hand you these." In one swift movement, the letters Macbeth had written to his wife were gone from Sam's dinner jacket pocket and sitting in the palm of Macduff's hand.

"What is this?"

"You should read them," Sam suggested. "And I mean right now." He glanced over and saw empty space where Renault and Victoria had stood. Turning, he saw Victoria making a dash for the apartment Sam had just vacated. Turning further, he saw Renault advancing on the bar. Strasser had appeared from somewhere and now lounged against the counter. He held a drink in one hand while chatting with a young woman Sam had never seen before.

Sam turned back to Macduff, and saw Macbeth's one-time peer leafing through the letters. He hoped the man was a speed reader, and wasn't just skimming through meaningless scribbles.

He received an answer of sorts when Macduff snapped at his men. "Come."

They paid no attention to Sam as they strode quickly toward Casablanca's exit.

So far, so good. Now the hard part. He loitered near Macduff's abandoned table until Strasser stood breathing into his face, Renault standing just behind him.

"You?" the major demanded. "You have the letters?"

Sam blinked. "Letters? What letters?"

"You know very well what letters. Captain Renault says you have them."

"Renault?" Sam made an attempt at looking mystified. "The Major mentioned some missing papers. I told him I would look for them. I didn't say I had found them."

Captain Renault huffed and whined like a spoiled child. "You did. You told me you were going to get them. Just now."

Sam shrugged. "I had an idea where they might be. Where I'd put them if I were going to hide something in the nightclub. You say these papers are letters? Unfortunately . . ."

"Raise your arms," Strasser demanded. "Hold them out."

"What? Are you going to search me?"

"Of course, I am going to search you."

Sam lifted his arms. "Okay. Just don't get too friendly."

The major's search was quick and professional. The only thing of note he found was Banquo's medal that was still in his dinner jacket pocket. "Where did you get this?"

"It was on the floor," Sam answered. "Over by that table where King Macbeth was sitting. His Grace left before I could return it."

Strasser gave him a peculiar look, then stuffed the medal into his own pocket. "And the escaped convict?" he demanded. "Captain Renault said you knew where the convict was."

"He did?" Sam peered over Strasser's shoulder at the captain, wondering what all the man might have blurted out while trying to prompt the major to action. "The only person I saw matching the description of your escaped convict entered the nightclub in Renault's company. Though when he asked me a couple of days ago to keep an eye out, he could have told me she was a looker. That might have helped."

The major turned to stare at Renault.

"That was my sister," Renault lied.

"And where is your sister now?" Strasser demanded.

Renault glanced about the room. "She must have left when I saw Mr. Spade with the letters."

Sam laughed. "You couldn't have seen me with the letters. I never had them."

If Renault was going to mention Macduff, this was it. Now would be the time. But Sam didn't think he would. Had gambled he wouldn't. A thane trumped a captain and if Renault implicated Macduff, well, that was suicide, wasn't it?

The captain worked his jaw. Then, "No, no. I have not seen the letters in Mr. Spade's hands. He only said he had them."

Sam raised his voice and gave Renault a hard stare. "I said I'd look for them."

"Gentlemen," Strasser cried. "Enough!"

The major waited until the rest of the club's patrons resumed their own business before wagging a finger in Sam's face. "Were you not the king's pet project, I would instruct Captain Renault to have his guards use you for target practice."

Sam displayed his palms. "I haven't done anything."

"You have aggravated me," Strasser said. "That is sufficient."

"Well . . ." Sam knew when to back off. "I'll try to do better."

"See that you do," Strasser said. Then the major marched back to the bar, retrieved his drink off the counter, and resumed his discussion with his mystery woman.

"I will get you for this," Renault hissed.

"You should drop it," Sam suggested. "Those letters are trouble. Forget you ever heard about them."

Renault lowered his voice to a whisper. "Lady Macbeth shall not forget them."

"In time," Sam suggested. "She will."

"You do not know Lady Macbeth," Renault said before storming out of the casino.

48
STARING AT THE CEILING

With the king retired to his bed, Casablanca's remaining guests began drifting away. There was only so much ale a man could drink, and the lone poker table only accommodated four players. It sure would be nice if illuminator Alison showed up with that second deck of playing cards sometime before the Spanish Inquisition.

Soon all that was left of Macbeth's coronation celebration was a half-dozen gamblers and a handful of drunkards loitering near the bar. Even Major Strasser and his *date* had staggered off into the night.

To Sam's thinking, the evening had been a success. He'd poked the bear and gotten away with it. Three bears: Macbeth, Strasser, and Renault. He'd recovered Effie's spouse from the dungeon, and hadn't ended up there himself. All that remained was to find Effie and get her and Victoria out of the castle. But where was Effie?

A lifetime of abuse by his family and peers had conditioned Sam to expect the worst. It was only after meeting Effie in Camelot, and then Nora after returning to Hartford, that his life had seen a little sunshine. His luck had turned and he'd become a successful private investigator. He'd even made a few friends along the way. Sam was almost beginning to believe he now led a charmed life. Clear skies and bright days.

Except for Morgan Le Fay. It was the sorceress-turned-witch's fault he was now surrounded by multiple rocks and hard places. And he couldn't trust her to keep her word and send him back to Connecticut.

Sam stood at the bar counter rubbing his ear. His only tenable option to get back home still seemed to entail fleeing to England and finding Merlin or the Lady of the Lake. And with Strasser and Renault breathing down his neck, flight was looking pretty attractive. But he couldn't leave. Not without Effie. Where was she?

Effie knew the exchange for Victoria was to happen this evening, yet she hadn't made an appearance in the nightclub. He couldn't imagine what would keep her away. Well, he could imagine. Either Strasser had grabbed her in his search for Victoria, or Renault had thrown her in his dungeon as insurance. Either way, he knew where to look first.

"Hey Sacha."

The bartender set down a cup he'd been wiping.

"Keep an eye on things, will ya?" Sam dug the safe key out of his pants pocket and slid it across the counter. "If I'm not back before our remaining patrons drag themselves home, drop the final receipts in the safe for me and I'll deal with them in the morning."

Taking the key, Sacha leaned toward Sam and spoke in a quiet voice. "Another trip to the garderobe?"

"Something like that."

The bartender nodded. "These nocturnal adventures of yours shall get you into trouble one day."

Sam felt his cheek twitch. "Trouble is hard to avoid when you're in the nightclub business."

After stepping out into the hallway, Sam waited while a pair of late arrivals entered the nightclub. Once the coast was clear, he again placed Le Fay's ring on his finger, then moved quickly along the passageway to the castle foyer. Six guards still manned the main gate, but there wasn't anyone else in sight. Invisible, he descended the stairway to the lower level two steps at a time. He needed to make this quick in case Effie was, even now, on her way to Casablanca.

On his last visit to Renault's home away from home there had been two guards at the bottom of the stairs. Now there were four. Squeezing past them was a bit trickier. He found three more guards loitering in the cell area. Sam checked each cell, but none of the current occupants was Effie. On the way out, he paused outside Renault's office. The guard captain sat slumped in his chair, frowning into an ale cup, no doubt contemplating his future should word of his failed exchange reach Lady Macbeth's ears.

As Sam ascended the stairs to the castle proper, he realized he was being too much the pessimist. Where would Effie be if she wasn't in trouble? She was acting the hired mercenary. Maybe she was on duty somewhere. Or stuck in the military barracks, unable to leave.

Sam hadn't run across any barracks yet. At Forres Castle they had been in the yard out back, but there had been nothing out back of Inverness Castle when Banquo had led him down to the river. There were stables in front. Maybe the barracks were there too.

When he reached the foyer, Sam considered the six guards standing near the main gate. He doubted they'd miss noticing the massive door opening and closing by itself.

There was the postern door he'd seen Macbeth open, and the back door Banquo had used. Neither had been guarded. He could leave one unbolted and look around outside. But he hadn't explored the north end of the castle yet. Maybe he would look there first.

Stepping quickly, he passed the side corridor that led to the kitchen and banquet hall. He found no other hallways, merely a few doors that opened into crowded storage rooms overflowing with goods that had probably been moved there from where Casablanca now operated.

The door at the end of the main hallway looked similar to the south postern gate, but there was no concealing tapestry, and no latch to secure it. Apparently, he was going to visit the stables sooner than expected.

When he eased open the door, however, he found it didn't lead outside. Instead, it accessed some kind of annex, possibly a later addition to the castle. He could hear voices, but they sounded a distance off. It seemed safe enough to crack open the door and slip through. The new hallway had a lower ceiling, and the walls, instead of being carpeted with tapestries, were bare stone.

Laughter emanated from a room up ahead on the left.

To Sam's immediate right was a garderobe followed by a storage closet filled with boots, cloaks, and assorted swords, bows, and arrows. Beyond that, the corridor ended at a well of stairs going down.

As Sam moved along the corridor, the voices grew louder, and seemed to emanate from an opening in the castle wall opposite the storage closet. He found it interesting that, like Casablanca, there was a doorless room at the opposite end of the castle.

Looking through the entryway, he expected to find a mirror image of Casablanca, but instead found a long, narrow room with rows of cots lining each of the longer walls. He realized he had found a bunkhouse for those using the equipment closet opposite. Most of the cots were occupied by soldiers in various states of alertness. Some talked. Some slept. Others lay on their backs staring at the ceiling. One of the latter was Effie.

Safe. That was good. But why was she here? Thinking back to the guests who had crowded Casablanca for Macbeth's celebration, he realized the only soldiers present had been senior ranks: generals, majors, maybe not even captains. None of the rank-and-file mercenaries he saw now would have been welcome. Maybe this was the only place Effie could be. She couldn't know the celebration had ended early, and that most of Scotland's movers and shakers had left the casino.

Sam wished he had a way to tell her. Whispering in her ear could result in hysterics. And leaving a note was out of the question. He had no way to write one and, more likely than not, it would be in modern English, nonsensical to anything Effie was familiar with.

It looked like their departure from the castle would have to wait another hour or two. Which might be for the best. There was only one magic ring, so the three of them couldn't slip away invisible in the night. They'd have to walk out of the castle, steal horses, and ride off into the sunset. The fewer witnesses to that, the better.

It would take several days to reach England and find Merlin.

Robin might know where the old goat was hiding. If not, maybe more than a few days before he could find his way back to Connecticut and Nora Clark. Well, no matter how long it took, he'd find a way back. Hopefully back to the moment he had left, so he could safely bring his car to a stop.

Leaving Effie to stare at the ceiling and count the minutes until she felt safe the celebration was over, Sam made his way back toward Casablanca. As he neared the foyer, however, the thought occurred to him to go upstairs and see if he could eavesdrop on Macbeth and his devious wife. He couldn't help but smile. The look on the murderer's face when he thought Banquo was haunting him. And his wife's embarrassing explanations for his behaviour. That was a marriage made in Hell if ever there was one.

But their apartment door would be firmly closed, and he already knew Macbeth's plan. He would ride back to the witches' cavern and have another go at having his fortune read.

Of course, the witches wouldn't be there. They were at Casablanca serving drinks and dealing poker. Macbeth was destined for disappointment. The play was one of Shakespeare's tragedies, after all. Macbeth was never meant to end well.

When Sam arrived at the nightclub, however, he learned that his evening wouldn't end well either. He had only just entered, ring in pocket, when Sapphire walked up to him and placed her hands on her narrow hips.

"Where have you been? And what trouble have you been up to this time?"

"I. Uh." Sam had no answer. "I was looking for someone."

"Cease this foolishness. Go get that long coat of yours. We are to leave at once."

"Leave?"

"You heard Macbeth as easily as I, what with you standing next to him with my ring on your finger."

Sam did his best to feign surprise. "Your ring?"

"Do not play the fool. You knew from the first who I and my sisters were."

Not from the first. Not by a mile. He made like Le Fay had caught him out anyway. "Three witches. Three precious gems. It was pretty obvious."

"Humph." Sapphire/Le Fay glowered at him. "And what have you been doing all this time? I brought you here to manage this casino and earn Macbeth a war chest."

Hoping to avoid having to answer, Sam answered a question with a question. "Does he need us now? The old king is dead. His heirs fled the country. Macbeth and his wife have been crowned king and queen, and he seems to have everyone's support. Why would he still need a war chest?"

Sapphire's eyes tightened. "You should know the answer to that. What *seems* and what *is* are rarely the same. There are men in this country who despise Macbeth. And others who seek power for themselves. No king ever sleeps easy. Besides, most of Macbeth's soldiers are mercenaries. If he does not pay them, someone else will."

Still not wanting to answer Le Fay's original question of what he'd been up to, Sam said, "Then why are we leaving? If you need the casino to generate funds . . ."

"It shall have to do so on its own. Macbeth intends to ride to Achindown. We must be there when he arrives."

"You must be there," Sam suggested. "You don't need me. I'll just stay and run the nightclub. Win-win for everybody."

Sapphire/Le Fay leaned toward Sam. "I do not trust you on your own. You shall accompany us to Achindown or you shall die."

49
IS THAT JEALOUSY I HEAR?

Sam sat down on a bar stool and rubbed his eyes. "Pour me a tall one."

Sacha looked at him, then reached below the counter for a bottle of the good stuff. "It has been a most strange evening."

"It's about to get stranger," Sam suggested.

Sacha cocked an eyebrow as he poured.

"My precious gems and I will be gone for a while. Maybe a couple of days. You and Just Sam will have to hold the fort."

"The two of us?" Sacha's expression suggested he'd rather endure the Black Plague.

"Do you have any friends you could hire for until we get back?"

The bartender set down the bottle and waved his hand. "I know people. But who shall welcome the king and queen should they visit? Or the thanes?"

Sam leaned against the counter. "I have it on good authority the king will be away as well. I don't know that Lady Macbeth will drop by on her own. She hasn't in the past. And the thanes tend to look after themselves."

Sacha also leaned in, whispering conspiratorially. "You travel somewhere with the king?"

Sam forced a small laugh. "That would be something, wouldn't it? No, my precious gems say their mother has taken ill. They asked for some time off for a visit. I volunteered to accompany them. Three young women on the road alone." He shook his head.

Sacha nodded. "Is that what Sapphire was scolding you about at the door?"

"More or less."

The bartender straightened and began wiping a clay cup with a rag. "I shall hire some help, but I will need to teach one of them this game of yours so he can manage the cards."

"Pay them from Seyton's coin purse in the safe," Sam offered. "And let the receipts pile up. I'll do the paperwork when I get back."

Turning on his stool to take in the casino, Sam sipped his beer and watched the remaining patrons leave the club. Not all of them looked thrilled about it. His precious gems had been busy the past few minutes urging them to finish their drinks and sign their promissory notes. It looked like he would be hitting the road sooner rather than later.

Sam turned back around on his stool. "Say, Sacha. While I'm away, would you mind sneaking some food and drink to the young lady hiding in my apartment?"

"I already have," the bartender said.

"You knew she was there?"

"I observed your friend duck in there after Captain Renault abandoned her in order to converse with Major Strasser."

Sam nodded. "A second woman will be looking for her."

The bartender grinned. "Your blonde friend with the delightful scar? Ilsa?"

"Yeah. Ilsa. Tell my friends they should stay hidden in my apartment until I get back."

Sacha's expression grew serious. "Should I provide them with a chamber pot?"

The term sounded familiar. Sam figured the correct answer was yes. "You bet."

"You lead an interesting life, Mr. Spade."

Sapphire chose that moment to step up to the bar and scowl at Sam. "I do not see your coat."

Sam let out a sigh. "I haven't eaten all day. I figured I should grab something before we left."

Sapphire/Morgan Le Fay pointed her chin at the cup in Sam's hand. "You still haven't eaten."

He downed the remainder of his drink, enjoying the burn as it slid down his throat, then set the cup on the counter and stood. "This ain't no restaurant."

"Fetch your coat," Sapphire growled. "We are leaving."

Sam shook his head and walked over to his apartment, where he blocked the door as he eased it open and slipped inside.

Victoria, still in her maid's outfit, was sitting cross-legged on his cot. Somehow, Effie's resourceful spouse had managed to light the candle. "Ilsa?"

"She'll join you shortly," Sam said. "Unfortunately, I have to disappear for a while. Sacha, the bartender, will take care of you while I'm gone."

The English spy nodded. "You gave the letters to Macduff."

"That's what you wanted, wasn't it?"

Another nod. "Thane Macduff is no friend of Macbeth. He will know what to do."

Sam retrieved his coat from where it lay draped across an empty clothing chest. "What do you have against Macbeth anyway?"

Victoria cast Sam one of those looks women give you when the answer is obvious. "Macbeth is a warmonger. As was Duncan. Power is all such men care about. It matters not one whit who gets hurt in the process."

Sam rubbed his ear. "And Macduff isn't such a man?"

Victoria lifted her chin. "Thane Macduff is a voice of reason in the midst of a storm. Duncan paid his advice no heed. Neither will Macbeth. Perhaps the next king will."

"And here I thought *I* was an optimist," Sam said. "We don't have much time. I don't know how long I'll be away. But don't worry, Sacha will take care of you."

"I am not worried. I have never needed anyone to take care of me."

Sam had met the type before. And he respected it. Nora was that type. Strong. Self-reliant. Capable. "Yeah, but you're going about a dangerous business, and you're married to a good friend of mine. I'd hate to see you have to escape from another prison. Just cool your heels here at Casablanca for a couple of days. It's not safe to show your face right now; Strasser and Renault are both out for blood. Don't give them yours. Sacha will bring you anything you need. And when I get back, the three of us—you, Effie, and I—will put this castle behind us and make our way to England."

Victoria's forehead wrinkled. "Effie?"

"Euphemia."

"Ah, yes, your pet name for my partner, Ilsa."

Sam felt his cheek twitch. "Is that jealousy I hear?"

"Do not be absurd."

Sam threw Effie's spouse a smile, then shrugged his arms into his trench coat. "Promise me you'll still be here when I get back."

"I may make no such promise. Not until Ilsa weighs in."

"Then I guess I'll just have to hope for the best."

50
A LONG NIGHT IN THE SADDLE

After opening his apartment door no wider than a foot, Sam slipped through and eased the door closed behind him.

Seated along the bar, his precious gems were waiting. Each held a cup of ale and wore dark cloaks over their colourful dresses. Apart from them, Casablanca was empty. Even Just Sam was gone. The only exception was Sacha, who was organizing the remaining alcohol and stacking empty snack trays for the castle staff to take away.

"And I believed snails were slow," Emerald said.

"I had to write up the evening's accounts," Sam answered, a convenient lie to allow for the time he'd spent conversing with Victoria. "Seyton will be angry enough when he discovers we've left the castle. If he doesn't get his accounts, he'll be fit to be tied."

Ruby rose from her bar stool and pushed herself away from the counter. "We shall deal with the steward as well as anyone else who interferes with our plans."

"Of that I have no doubt," Sam said.

Emerald and Sapphire downed their drinks like sailors, then joined their sister and trooped out of the casino. Sam threw a helpless glance at Sacha, and followed.

As a boy, he'd learned from television that a witch's preferred method of travel was by broomstick. Sam figured the only reason

Le Fay and her two faux-sisters had opted to ride horses instead was because they insisted on bringing their stooge with them. Their stooge being an untrained nightclub manager named Sam Spade.

After leaving the castle through the main gate, the four of them, cloaked in night's darkness, walked into town where they apparently stole four horses from a stable. Strangely enough, the stable included several smallish horses that were already saddled and ready to ride. If there were stable hands about, they were in hiding.

Streetlamps in Inverness were few and far between, but under one of them Sam managed to read a sign that said Kingsmills Road. Not surprisingly, the street was lined with cottage industry factories that he assumed ground flour, turned sheep's wool into cloth, blew glass ale bottles, and who knew what else.

The town ended where a sign renamed the street to Culcabock Road, and that was the last streetlamp Sam saw as the open road led them into absolute darkness. The witches seemed to know where they were going, however, driving the horses at a steady walk. An occasional lamplit window indicated a farmhouse to either side of the road, but there were no other travellers.

Soon even the farmhouses were gone, and Sam felt as though his horse's saddle was carrying him through the void. The night sky was overcast, revealing no moon or stars. And the air was chill, a slight breeze cutting his face like a knife. Except for the clomping of hooves on dirt, there were no sounds.

Idly, Sam wondered what would happen if he reined in his horse, waited a minute, then turned around. Would the witches notice he'd gone missing? Would the animal be able to find its way back to Inverness? Somehow, he didn't think it would be that easy. Le Fay would know what he was up to. And whatever reprisal she'd mete out would be uncomfortable.

Eventually, the witches brought the horses to a stop. Sam wondered if they'd arrived at the place they and Macbeth called Achindown, but it was only a creek bed where the horses dropped their heads to drink. The witches didn't dismount, so neither did Sam. A few minutes later they resumed their journey through the darkness.

Hours drifted by before the sky ahead grew perceptively

brighter. Dawn. The shape of trees took form in the darkness, then Sam could see the dirt trail they travelled on. As the sky grew brighter, he saw fields and forests to the north and south. A short while later they reached a jumble of boulders where the witches dismounted. Sam recognized the place. Had it only been a week since he'd emerged from a hole in the ground hidden by those very same boulders, and begun his Shakespearian adventure?

Climbing down off his horse, Sam crab-walked about in an effort to work out the kinks he had gained from a long night in the saddle. Ruby shook her head at him before leading his horse to where the others were being tethered a short distance beyond the boulders.

"What should we do with this one?" Emerald asked Sapphire, wagging her thumb in Sam's direction. "Stake him with the horses?"

Sapphire/Morgan Le Fay seemed to consider before answering. "I do not trust him out of my sight. He was always a sly one, but his peculiar antics at Inverness Castle went beyond what I expected."

"Do we have further need of him?" Emerald asked.

Le Fay considered further. "Despite everything, he has done well with the nightclub. Macbeth shall need it a while longer."

Sam continued to stretch, pretending not to listen. He couldn't imagine why the nightclub was the least bit important, never mind needed. The Scottish thane had succeeded in murdering Duncan and becoming king all on his own. Sam hadn't had to do a thing. At least, he didn't think he had done anything to help. From what he could tell, the Macbeths had planned and carried out the murders without help from anyone. The ambitious thane had even had his best friend killed. Who does that?

"Mr. Spade," Sapphire said, interrupting his thoughts. "You remember our little home away from home?" She pointed at the cave entrance.

Sam glanced at the horses. "Aren't our four-footed friends going to raise some eyebrows?"

Ruby waved a hand, and the animals vanished.

"What friends are these of which you speak?" Sapphire asked.

"I guess you don't really need a ring for that," Sam suggested.

"No, but you do. Use the ring now. Macbeth must not see you, yet I wish you to remain in my sight at all times."

Sam sighed and slipped Le Fay's magic ring onto his finger.

Sapphire pointed again at the cave entrance. "After you."

51
THE WELLSPRING OF ALL CURSES

The cavern was as cold as Sam remembered, but not as dark. The witches, following behind him, had raised some kind of ambient glow. Sam easily followed the curve of the natural passage and soon came to the large chamber with the cauldron at its centre. It occurred to him that he hadn't seen the writing desk inside the entrance.

Emerald waved a hand, and a pile of burning wood appeared beneath the cauldron. Some kind of steaming liquid also began bubbling inside the giant metal pot. Sam had to figure the lifestyle of the weird and witchy was a relatively easy one.

Or not. One by one, his precious gems threw off their black cloaks, and Sam watched as their bright dresses became rags and their lustrous hair turned grey and brittle. The women's frames lost their gentle curves, growing gaunt and lanky before rising in height until their presence dominated the cavern. Then the chalk-skinned hag who had been Emerald crowed, "Thrice the brinded cat hath mewed."

Ruby, whose grey hair contained a hint of reddish-brown, followed, "Thrice, and once the hedge-pig whined."

Then Le Fay, hollow-cheeked and heavily wrinkled. "Harpier cries, 'Tis time, 'tis time."

The three witches then did some strange long-legged dance

that took them around the cauldron three times. Together they chanted, "Double, double toil and trouble, fire burn, and cauldron bubble."

Sam wasn't sure what to make of it. Did they do it for fun? Or was it something witches had to do?

When they finished their strange dance, the contents of the cauldron flared like an oil fire. Smoke filled the cavern, and when it abated, there were two sets of witches, only the new trio stood like lifeless puppets. A seventh witch, taller than the others and somehow even less human, stood behind them. This one wore no flowing robe, but a voluminous black dress that appeared mouldy and rotted. She had spindly, yellow-grey hair like dead roots that was woven into a high crown. Her skin was bluish-grey, and her eyes amber.

"Oh well done!" this taller witch exclaimed. "I commend your pains. And every one shall share in the gains."

Then the apparitions were gone, and only the original three witches remained.

"What was that?" Sam asked.

"Hush!" Le Fay hissed. Her attention was on the passageway that led outside. The other two witches also stood watching and listening.

Ruby whispered, "By the pricking of my thumbs, something wicked this way comes."

"Really?" Sam said. "I thought all the wicked were already here."

"Hush!" Le Fay repeated.

Sam shook his head and watched as torchlight flickered along the passageway. A tall, awkward shadow moved along the wall on one side of the passage, then a smallish man holding a torch appeared.

"Is that a cauldron?" Macbeth asked. "Whatever you are cooking stinks to high heaven. What is it?"

Le Fay turned her gaze toward the giant pot, which Sam agreed did stink. "A deed without a name," the witch murmured.

Macbeth snorted. "You speak in riddles. I know not how you know what you know, but I demand you answer my questions."

"Speak," Ruby said.

"Demand," Emerald added.

"We shall answer," Le Fay finished.

Then Ruby let out a long cackle. "Would you hear from us? Or would you prefer to hear from our Mistress?"

"You have someone above you?" Macbeth said. "Call her. I wish to see."

Le Fay threw something into the cauldron, and again it flared. For a second time, the cavern filled with smoke, then the puppet version of Le Fay appeared.

"But that is you," Macbeth said.

"It is, and it is not," Le Fay hissed. "It knows your mind. Listen to its words, but do not speak."

"Macbeth! Macbeth! Macbeth!" the apparition said in Le Fay's witchy voice. "Beware Macduff. Beware the Thane of Fife. Dismiss me. Enough."

"Well, yes," Macbeth said. "But I had already guessed as much. What I need to know is—"

"Silence!" Le Fay screeched. "It will not be commanded by you. Here is another. More potent than the first."

Now Ruby threw something into the cauldron. More fire. More smoke. Then her puppet replaced Le Fay's.

"Macbeth! Macbeth! Macbeth!" this apparition said in Ruby's ancient voice. "Be bloody, bold, and resolute. Laugh to scorn the power of man, for no man born of woman shall harm Macbeth."

"No man," Macbeth whispered. "Then I need not fear Macduff, nor any of the thanes." He rubbed his bearded chin. "Even so, I like not the look in Macduff's eye. I shall not suffer him to live, and thus shall sleep easier at night."

Even as he was speaking, Emerald threw something into the cauldron and her puppet replaced the other.

"Macbeth! Macbeth! Macbeth!" this apparition said in Emerald's rasping witch voice. "Be lion-mettled, proud, and take no care who chafes, who frets, or where conspirers are. Macbeth shall never vanquished be until Great Birnam Wood to high Dunsinane Hill shall come against him."

As this apparition faded, Macbeth said, "I am to be attacked by a forest?" He glared at Le Fay. "Your riddles are meant to confound me, but even I know it is impossible for a wood to pull its roots from the earth and advance across the countryside. And I still have received no answer for the question which brought me here. Banquo's son, Fleance, escaped my assassins. Can your dark powers see if he shall rise up against me?"

The three witches glowered at him. Then Le Fay said, "The apparitions have answered that question."

Sam almost spoke up. If this was a quiz show, he knew the answer. But Macbeth beat him to the buzzer.

"Fleance is a man no less than Macduff. So, you say I should not fear him?"

The witches said nothing.

Macbeth took several steps toward the weird sisters. "I will be satisfied. Deny me, and an eternal curse shall fall upon you! Tell me—What in that cauldron stinks so? And what noise is this?"

Sam figured the noise that had been growing in strength since the last apparition disappeared was some kind of music. Hellish music, worse than rap, but music just the same. It had a cadence to it. Nothing you could dance to. Nothing that inspired fingers to snap or toes to tap. But music just the same.

Then, where the three apparitions had stood, came a fourth. It was the witch who had appeared earlier, taller and more menacing than Le Fay and her faux-sisters. The one who had praised their work and must be the mistress above them Ruby had mentioned.

"Who are you?" Macbeth demanded.

The impossibly tall witch bent down, her amber eyes scrutinizing Macbeth as though he were a bug. Then she straightened. "I have many names. The one you may use is Hecate. Ah, before you speak, I shall answer your question."

Macbeth was smart enough to hold his tongue.

"You, who have not the power to curse, threatened to do so to my servants." The tall witch wagged a finger. "You should know the power of Hecate, I who am the wellspring of all curses. It is I who chose you to usurp the throne of Scotland. To make a mockery of the Christendom that invades this land. Yet you are not the only evil man in Scotland. Not the only man with murder in his heart. I can easily choose another."

"But . . ." Macbeth muttered. "Fleance . . ."

The witch Hecate let out a harrowing scream that filled the cavern. "Concern yourself not with Banquo's progeny. Fleance shall never be king. Nor his children. Yet long after your corpse is feasted upon by flies, his children's children shall rise to rule nations." Then the witch laughed. "Do not stand so amazed. All I and my servants have spoken shall come to pass. Now leave this place and continue as you are bidden."

In a swirl of smoke, the witch calling herself Hecate disappeared. Sam, also invisible, to Macbeth at least, rubbed his ear. So, Le Fay wasn't in charge. Maybe he could use that to get back to Hartford.

Noticing the cave was suddenly darker, Sam looked around and saw that Le Fay and her faux-sisters were also gone. As was the cauldron. Even the burning fire. There was just him, standing invisible in the dark. And Macbeth with his flickering torch.

52

NINE PARTS CONFIDENCE

Where have those she-devils gone?" Macbeth muttered. The murderous king turned toward the cavern's sole passageway and shouted, "Get in here!"

Sam wondered who he could be calling to. Then Thane Lennox, also holding a torch, joined Macbeth in the witches' cavern.

"Did you see them?" Macbeth demanded.

Lennox's lips moved, saying nothing, like a fish. At last, he said, "No, Your Grace. You bid me remain outside."

"No one passed by you?" Macbeth demanded.

"Indeed not, my lord."

The murderous king fingered his beard. "Then there is nothing for us here. We return to Inverness."

"But the horses?" Lennox averted his gaze. "We have ridden the animals hard. Another ride so soon shall kill them."

Macbeth harrumphed. "For your peace of mind, we shall keep the horses to a steady trot. It means arriving late."

Lennox lifted his eyes. "Thank you, Your Grace."

Sam followed the two men to the cavern entrance and daylight. He'd never pictured the younger thane as such a toady. Maybe Banquo's unexpected disappearance had something to do with that. First Duncan dead, then Banquo vanished. Sam suspected all the thanes might be getting nervous. Whispers of Macbeth's possible involvement were probably making the rounds.

When he emerged from the cave, Sam saw that Lennox wasn't Macbeth's only companion. A half-dozen rough-looking men stood guarding as many horses. The saddles had been removed, and the men were brushing the animals down. Sam suspected the hard ride Lennox had mentioned began that morning, while he and the witches had travelled all night at a more leisurely pace.

Once Macbeth's party was on its way, Sam walked around the boulders to where his own stolen horse was staked. He wasn't surprised to see all three hags transformed back into their precious gems personas and already mounted.

"Make haste," Sapphire growled at him. "Dawdling here buys us nothing."

Sam did as he was told. Only when they arrived in the middle of the night to an abandoned Casablanca shrouded in the shadows of a single lit candle, did he remember he still wore Le Fay's ring that rendered him invisible.

"Best take care," Sapphire murmured as he removed the silver band from his finger. "That is not a toy."

"It would help," Sam suggested, "if you told me what I'm supposed to use it for."

"The ring is only to be used when we wish you not to be seen. It should be of no aid to you in managing this nightclub."

"But—" Sam began.

Sapphire didn't let him finish. "Your task is to entertain Macbeth's thanes and generals. Provide them with drink and amusements. Separate them from their silver. Our Macbeth has challenges yet ahead. He shall require silver and the arms of strong men who lack silver. That is your task. Your only task."

Sam nodded and watched as his three precious gems retired to their apartment. But secretly, he knew he'd ignore Le Fay's warning. He had every intention of using the ring to roam the castle, spy on Macbeth and his peers to learn what was going on, and to find a way back to Hartford.

Starting tomorrow. He hadn't slept in two days and could hear his cot calling for him. He was tired. So tired that, in the darkened room, he didn't notice until he sat upon its occupants, that his cot was occupied.

Instead of shrieks of startlement, however, he was met with an unexpected surprise.

"Is that a knife at my throat?" Sam asked. "Or are you happy to see me?"

"Sam?" Then the knife was gone.

He slid off the cot until he was sitting on the floor, his back pressed against the bedframe. "Sorry, Effie. I forgot I had houseguests."

"You were gone an entire day," Effie whispered. "We did not know if you would ever return."

Sam felt his cheek twitch. "My time isn't always my own. How are you and Victoria doing?"

There was movement as Effie's bed partner sat up.

"We grow tired of hiding," Effie said. "With evidence against Macbeth now in the hands of Macduff, we agree we must leave this place. Go to England. Or Ireland. Or France. We have stayed only because you bid us to."

"I appreciate you waiting," Sam responded. "I asked you to wait because I want to go with you."

"To France?"

"To England," Sam said. "I need to find Merlin."

"The Merlin? It is years since I have seen him."

"Yeah, well, unless you know someone else who can send me back to Hartford, he's my best bet."

"There have been whispers," Effie said, "that the Lady of the Lake has returned to Avalon."

"Back from the dead, huh? Great. We can go there."

"Well . . ."

Sam twisted his head to look up to where he assumed Effie's face was. With the door closed and the candle unlit, the room was so dark he couldn't even tell if his eyes were open or closed. "Is there a problem?"

"No one knows where Avalon is."

Sam leaned his head back against the cot. "That could be a problem. What do you say we sleep on it?"

"And tomorrow we leave?"

"At our first opportunity."

Silence. Then Effie said, "Where will you sleep? This bed is scarce wide enough for two."

"I'm happy right here," Sam told her. And he was. He felt tired enough to sleep standing up.

"Truly? Victoria and I could sleep on the floor."

If he wasn't so tired, Sam would have laughed. "Go to sleep. I'll race you."

He figured he must have fallen asleep then and there, as he registered nothing until a sore back and derriere woke him some hours later. Since the room was still pitch black, he pushed up his sleeve and examined the luminous dial on his Rolex, which he'd recharged during the bitterly cold ride back to Inverness. The timepiece said it was past nine in the morning.

"Are you awake?" Effie must have heard or felt him move to check his watch.

Sam climbed to his feet. "It's later than I'd hoped. I'll go see what's happening out there and then come back."

"When you do, we will be dressed and ready to leave," Effie said.

Sam had no idea how long Effie and Victoria had been awake. They'd probably lain there for hours letting him sleep. Well, he'd needed it. Taking it on the lam wouldn't be easy. It would be less easy if it began with exhaustion.

Easing open the door of his apartment, Sam discovered a hive of activity. Castle staff swarmed the nightclub, carting away tables and chairs and even the tapestries off the walls. Just Sam's harp was gone from its platform, and Sacha was piling blank bar receipts into a box.

Crossing over to the bar, Sam peered into the box and saw Brother Alison's deck of playing cards and a stack of completed promissory notes. "What's happening?"

Sacha paused to stare at him. "You do not know?"

"I was away yesterday. Remember? Looks like a lot happened while I was gone."

The bartender nodded. "We are moving. By order of the king."

"Moving? Where to? The banquet hall?"

Sacha grinned. "'Twould be nice. No, the royal party is leaving Inverness for Macbeth's thanedom of Glamis. He insists the nightclub come with him to his castle at Dunsinane."

"What? When did this happen?"

"The order came late last evening. Steward Seyton himself stormed into Casablanca, grinning like the devil himself, and announced to all and sundry that King Macbeth was moving court to Dunsinane Castle for the winter season. He and his entourage would depart for Dunsinane on the morrow—this very morning—and would take the nightclub with them. Those who wished to continue availing themselves of the king's good graces were welcome to follow the procession. Otherwise, they should depart and attend to their homes and houses." The barman leaned forward and lowered his voice to a whisper. "Steward Seyton is an odd fellow. I do not believe he appreciates you or your nightclub. He seems to relish making your life a misery."

"He's envious," Sam said, glossing over a much more complicated relationship. "I take it we're leaving right away?"

"The procession has already begun," Sacha said. "Sam—the other Sam—has loaded his harp onto a wagon and shall arrive at Dunsinane Hill ahead of us." The barman glanced over to the far wall where Sam's precious gems stood observing the circus. "The uhm, ladies, said they would wait and travel with us."

Sam felt his cheek twitch. "With us? Or with me?"

Sacha nodded. "They mentioned you, but I wish for your company on the road as well."

Suppressing a sudden desire to slip on Le Fay's ring and disappear, Sam said, "I need you to do me a favour. Well, another favour."

The barman whispered. "The two women in your apartment?"

Sam fiddled with a stack of receipts to make it look as though he was doing something useful. "I need you to sneak them into Dunsinane Castle."

Sacha took the receipts from Sam and set them inside the wooden box with the others. "I am but a simple bartender. What you ask is beyond my skills."

"Don't sell yourself short," Sam said. "Round up whatever beer and whatnot was left over from last night. Have Effie—I mean Ilsa—and Victoria help you load it into a cart, then have them sit in the back while you drive the cart to this Dunsinane place. If anyone asks, tell them the ladies are new hires to wait tables in Casablanca."

"You believe I can do this?" Sacha asked.

"Act like you can, and no one will doubt you. Accomplishing anything in this life is one part effort and nine parts confidence."

"Truly?" Sacha asked.

Sam smiled. "It's how I got to where I am today. Oh, hey, just one more thing. Where is Dunsinane Hill?"

53

HOW CLOSE TO ENGLAND IS DUNSINANE HILL?

The weird sisters seemed to almost know Sam had planned to escape. As the king's procession wound its way through the streets of Inverness, then along the same road they had used to reach the witches' cavern, Sam's precious gems, now wrapped in the bright cloaks they had worn from Forres Castle, kept pace a few yards behind him.

He found himself missing Banquo. The Thane of Lochaber would be full of advice on how to leave the procession without anyone taking note, and even what route to take to reach England. Macbeth's one-time good friend might have been curious as to why Sam wished to go, but otherwise would have helped. Banquo had told him the route south past Loch Ness was unwise. Perhaps the route to Dunsinane would work in Sam's favour. How close to England was Dunsinane Hill anyway? If the witches ever took a break from watching him like a wayward child, he'd ask someone in the procession.

Sam had no idea who all was leaving Inverness for Dunsinane. Given Seyton's glee at the departure of Casablanca, he'd assumed the Royal Steward was staying behind. But Sam had spotted the imperious butler on horseback, pontificating with his apprentices, so Sacha's assessment that the man's good cheer arose from turning Sam's life upside down was probably the correct one.

Most of the other staff probably stayed behind, such as Captain Renault, who was in charge of castle security and the dungeon, and Major Strasser, who seemed to be Inverness's excuse for a sheriff. Sam wouldn't miss either of them, but figured he'd have to deal with their counterparts at Dunsinane.

Then there were the thanes and generals and whole cadres of soldiers who were part of the procession. Some followed Casablanca for its amusements, but he figured many accompanied the king wherever he went, either at Macbeth's beck and call or looking for opportunities to prove themselves to him.

The bulk of the procession, however, appeared to be hangers-on—servants, merchants, craftsmen, churchmen, and who knew who else. He hoped Dunsinane Castle had room for them all.

Macbeth and company moved at a surprisingly quick pace, with the train lengthening every mile as those on foot or riding mules lagged further and further behind. Sam and his precious gems, having been provided decent horses, managed to keep pace a distance behind the vanguard.

Not long after leaving Inverness, the procession reached a fork in the road that turned south away from the path that led to the witches' cavern. They were now heading into unknown territory, at least unknown to Sam, that consisted chiefly of forested hills, though every now and then they crossed through fields dotted with farmhouses. Sometimes farmers paused from their planting of winter barley to watch the procession, reminding Sam of trainspotters.

The afternoon grew colder as the road approached a village of some kind. A sign clinging to the wall of a one-storey inn declared the place as Aviemore. Several riders dismounted at the village green to draw water from a well for their horses.

"Are we staying here the night?" Sam asked a hard-eyed groomsman who was taking care of not only his own horse, but several others whose riders had retired to an alehouse.

The man appeared startled. "Here? Nae here. Nae anywhere. The procession is much tae lairge. We ride tae Dunsinane na maiter howfur long it takes or the hour we arrive."

"That's just swell," Sam said. He'd spent the last two days on horseback, and his backside was feeling it. "How much further do we have to go?"

The man just shook his head.

Sam's precious gems continued to ride a short distance behind him as the countryside grew hillier and the road more winding. He could almost feel their eyes on the back of his neck.

After passing through a village called Kingussie, several riders retrieved torches from their saddlebags and lit them with stone and steel like Sam had done with Duncan's fireplace, only much more expertly. Raising the torches on high, they broke out in song as the train moved on into the night. Sam couldn't understand the words, but could tell from the deep-throated vowels and jarring consonants that it wasn't a lullaby. Maybe it was noise to scare away wolves and bears. Or maybe it was just something to do to keep sleepy riders awake.

More hours passed before they reached a place called Blair Atholl. Despite the darkness of night, Sam sensed they were leaving the mountains behind them. A short while later, they passed a village called Pitlochry. Another town appeared not long after. Logiertait. Sam hoped the more frequent indications of civilization indicated they were nearing Dunsinane.

The road continued without Sam seeing much of anything until they came to a somewhat larger village called Birnam. It was only then he remembered where he had heard the word Dunsinane before. Both it and Birnam had been mentioned by one of the apparitions in the witches' cavern. Is that why Macbeth had decided to go there, all of a sudden? But what little he remembered from Shakespeare's play told him those places had something to do with the evil usurper's death. Was Macbeth tempting fate?

As the procession continued, Sam heard what sounded like a river off to his left. The train followed the waterway for a time before slowing. Had they arrived? Sam waited. And waited. In fits and starts, the horses in front of him moved forward. Sam glanced behind him and saw, by the flickering light of a torch, his precious gems astride their horses. If they hadn't been there watching him, this would have been the perfect time to find Effie and Victoria, slip into the trees, and continue south until they found a road to England.

Eventually he determined what the holdup was. A bridge crossed the river, but was so narrow only one horse or cart could cross at a time. As the procession resumed, he wondered if this trip would ever end. The only upside was that they had to be getting closer to England.

The sky to the east began to brighten, and Sam could see they were now travelling in a southerly direction. Perfect. The further they travelled south toward England, the better. Once the sky was fully bright, they came to a village with the very English-sounding name of Stanley and once again crossed a river. Sam was unsure if it was the same one.

The road they found themselves on looked little used, hardly more than a farmers' path. It led them east past a village called Guildtown, again sounding somewhat English, and through several fields, until a low hill rose in the distance.

As they drew closer, Sam could see various farm houses and outbuildings, but no actual town. On the hilltop, however, stood a structure that slowly took on the appearance of a castle. Like Duncan's castle in Forres, Macbeth seemed happy to not have any neighbours.

A winding path snaked its way up the gentle slope, revealing a flat hilltop dominated by a five-storey castle much larger than the one in Inverness. As the procession rode around one side, Sam saw that only the centre of the structure was tall. Wings to the north and south were two storeys, punctuated by three-storey turrets on the outer reaches. The building was impressive but, apart from a few outbuildings that included a stable, stood alone. There was no town.

Except there soon would be. Travellers from the train were raising tents on every square inch of remaining space on the hilltop. If this really was to be the king's winter court, his courtiers were going to get to know winter up close and personal.

At the stables, Sam climbed down off his horse and stretched his legs and back. These trips to the past were getting frequent enough that maybe he should take riding lessons. He knew there were several good Equestrian centres near Hartford. He'd just never had cause to visit any of them. Although apparently, he did have cause; he just hadn't known he did.

His precious gems also dismounted, but looked fresh as spring daisies as they gave him looks that suggested they should make their way to the castle. Sam glanced about for Sacha and his cart, but couldn't see much of anything in the hustle and bustle.

"What are you looking for?" Sapphire/Le Fay asked.

Sam feigned an answer. "Is there no town? Like Inverness? Why does Scotland have so many castles in the middle of nowhere?"

Ruby pointed through the crowd toward the east. "The town of Dundee is but a dozen miles away and is the provincial seat. Hardly nowhere."

Sam shrugged. "Let's just say Hartford is a bit more noticeable. I'm used to busy cities."

"What you are used to," Le Fay said, "is not important. Now. To Dunsinane Castle. You must get your nightclub up and operating as quickly as possible." As her violet-eyed gaze took in the crowds unloading carts and setting up tents, the raven-haired witch smiled. "After their long journey, your customers shall seek solace in ale and in your poker game."

54
PRISON ISN'T THE WORST THING THAT COULD HAPPEN

At the castle's main gate, Steward Seyton was directing traffic.

"So, you survived the trip."

"Did you expect I'd fall into a river and drown?" Sam asked.

The steward scowled. "With you, I never know what to expect." Seyton's lips curled into a smile as his gaze moved to Sam's precious gems. "I see your delightful assistants decided to continue in your employ."

"We're a package deal," Sam said.

"Perhaps that is what Lord Macbeth sees in you. Very well. Comhnall shall show you to Casablanca's new home."

Sam's gaze took in the teenager who, had Sam's timing been better back in Inverness, would have taken his clothes to be laundered. "Here's looking at you, kid."

The kid simply stared.

Inside the castle, Sam discovered Casablanca's new home situated just off the main entrance in what looked like a banquet hall that had been cleared of long tables. Unlike the converted storage space in Inverness, which had been windowless, a row of narrow, barred openings lined one wall. Sam was glad for the light, but the absence of windowpanes allowed the unseasonably cold air from outside to infiltrate the room. Two dozen round tables had been brought in and arranged so as to leave a walkway below the windows, and a wide fireplace occupied a portion of the wall opposite.

Further along the wall with the fireplace, Just Sam was setting up his harp. The musician threw Sam a smile that seemed to indicate he was both happy and relieved to see him. Sam returned the gesture.

Along the same wall on the other side of the fireplace, a bar counter was being built by a small team of craftsmen. Hauling the long counter from Inverness must have seemed too daunting. Sam searched with his eyes for private rooms for himself and his precious gems, but found only one large, doorless alcove in the corner by the bar where Sacha, with the help of Effie and Victoria, was arranging stock. In the back corner of the alcove stood a desk and larger strongbox than the one in Inverness. The stockroom, apparently, doubled as Sam's office.

Comhnall made a nervous sound in his throat. "Sir, is something amiss?"

"Apartments," Sam said. "At Inverness, Casablanca included apartments for me and my staff."

The apprentice butler nodded. "Steward Seyton has reserved four apartments just down the hallway outside." His face reddened. "We were under the impression you had five staff members. I see seven." He glanced at Effie and Victoria. "Finding an additional accommodation will be a challenge."

"That's okay," Sam said. "The new recruits will stay with me."

The youth's face acquired a deeper shade of red.

"I assume these are real apartments? My staff will use the bedroom. I'll require a cot in the outer room."

"Of course," Comhnall said, though his cheeks remained red.

To escape the awkwardness, Sam added, "I should go help out in the storeroom."

The young butler ducked his head, and escaped Casablanca through the hall entryway at a near-run.

After taking a quick look around and not seeing the witches anywhere, Sam stepped into the alcove and inspected the crate Effie was pretending to be busy with. "Are you and Victoria okay?" he asked while slipping off his trench coat.

Sacha had found clothes from somewhere that made Effie look less the soldier and more the housewife. Her long blonde hair hung loose, partly hiding the scar she had earned in Camelot. Victoria, working with a different crate, still wore the housekeeper outfit Captain Renault had found for her.

Effie attempted a smile. "It was an uneventful trip which brought us halfway to England, if that is what you are asking."

"I'm asking if you're okay. I'm pretty sure we left Major Strasser behind in Inverness, but he's not the only one in Scotland looking for escaped convicts."

"That is true. Do you still intend for the three of us to make our way to England?"

Sam tossed his trench coat onto the same crate where his staff had piled their outerwear. "I thought that's what you wanted too."

Effie cast her spouse a long glance. "Victoria has decided she would prefer to wait to see what fruit comes of her passing Macbeth's letters to Macduff."

Sam felt his cheek twitch. Victoria had never touched the letters. She'd wanted Macduff to have them, but he'd been the one to hand them over. "I'm sure Victoria can observe fruit from England as well as from here."

Effie let out a soft sigh. "That is what I have been telling her. I have had as much of Scotland as I can stomach."

"You and me both, kid. You and me both." Sam glanced over his shoulder and could now see his precious gems sitting at a table that afforded them a view of the stock room. All three witches glared at him with cold eyes. "You need to convince Victoria it isn't safe for you here. Even if Major Strasser or others like him don't discover you, Morgan Le Fay knows who you are. I wouldn't put it past her to cause trouble."

From where Effie stood, she could also see the three witches. "One of those beautiful young women is really Le Fay?"

"Altering her appearance is one of her old tricks. What worries me are her new ones. Le Fay has taken to being a witch like a boozehound takes to hooch. Anyway, we'll have to make our move carefully. Those three haven't let me out of their sight since we left Inverness."

"I have seen that to be true," Effie said, "but what is their interest in you?"

Sam felt his cheek twitch. "They gave me an explanation, but I don't believe it. That's why we have to be extra careful."

Effie shuddered. "Should Victoria and I be here, out in the open? I do not relish the thought of continued hiding in your apartment, but that woman was a monster in Camelot."

"That cat's already out of the bag," Sam said. "If they ask, I'll tell them Sacha hired you to help manage the bar and that I was surprised as anyone to see you. That's true, by the way. When you and Victoria waltzed into Casablanca disguised as soldiers, well, I have to admit I was gobsmacked. I'd never expected to see you again."

"Nor I you," Effie said. Then she laughed. "Especially not here in Scotland. You do manage to turn up in the most unexpected places."

"Call it a gift." Sam glanced at the witches, who were still scowling. "Look. Let's keep our heads down for the rest of the day. Tonight, after closing, we'll make our escape. Then we won't have to worry about Strasser or Le Fay or anyone else."

"I still have to convince Victoria," Effie said.

"You do that. Our luck has held up so far, but that can't last. And prison isn't the worst thing that could happen."

55
THE CLINK OF UNCLEAN COINS

Despite riding all night, a nap wasn't in the cards. Even with the help of castle staff, it took several hours to get the new and improved Casablanca set up and guest-worthy. Not to mention he was two days behind on the accounts. Sam was so sleep deprived, he almost nodded off while sorting and tallying a mountainous accumulation of promissory notes. But he was glad he made the effort, if only to avoid a chewing out by Steward Seyton. He'd just finished, and had settled himself at the bar for a three-finger pick-me-up, when the devil himself walked into the nightclub.

"Good. Good," the puffed-up butler declared as he made his way to the bar counter. "All appears to be ready, Mr. Spade. Even your sign above the door. You shall open your establishment right away. The king has awoken from his post-procession nap and wishes to entertain his thanes for the remainder of the afternoon and into the evening."

Sam shook his head. "That's all well and good for those who spent the day napping, but my staff has been working nonstop preparing for an evening opening. We need to have our own nap for the rest of the afternoon."

Seyton stared at him. "Mr. Spade, I do not know how things work in your country, but in Scotland, when the king gives an order, it is obeyed."

"In my country things work much the same. But our kings know that servants can't work for days without sleep."

"Days?" The steward's eyes widened with incredulity. "You have spent but one night dozing in the saddle. Soldiers do that all their lives."

"We're not soldiers," Sam said. "We're talent. And talent needs its beauty sleep."

Seyton snorted loudly. "Nevertheless, I declare this establishment open and am ordering the first drink of the day." He stared pointedly at Sacha. "Bartender, your best ale please."

Sacha smiled apologetically at Sam and poured the steward his drink.

Sam raised his glass. "That's actually the second drink of the day." Then he took a swallow, relishing the burn as it slid down his throat.

Seyton glowered at him. "Why are you drinking when you are two days behind in the accounts?"

Sam had been waiting for that. Reaching into his dinner jacket pocket, he retrieved the folded account summaries and handed them over while enjoying a second swallow of ale.

The steward perused the accounts, saying nothing.

"We're running low on promissory notes and blank paper," Sam said. "If you're expecting brisk business today, we'll run out."

Seyton again said nothing, but stuffed the summaries into his robes and sipped the remainder of his drink.

Sam left the patronizing butler to it, and walked across the casino floor to inform his precious gems and Just Sam that Casablanca was now open for business. The harpist took the news in stride, while the witches seemed almost gleeful. Effie and Victoria kept to themselves in the stock room alcove, but Sam interpreted Effie's sanguine expression to mean she had managed to convince her spouse that flight was the better part of valour.

The fireplace had been lit sometime earlier and now provided the casino with a comfortable warmth and only a little smoke. Sam paused in front of the burning logs to enjoy the heat on his face, then stationed himself by the entryway where he greeted various lords and ladies as they began trickling in. Many of the guests seemed unfamiliar with nightclubs, the four-day stubble on the casino manager's chin being the least interesting thing to meet their gaze. Sam supposed these were some of those who hadn't made their way to Inverness after Macbeth's coronation.

A hush fell over the room when the King and Queen entered accompanied by Lennox, Ross, and several other familiar faces. Notably absent, was Macduff.

Macbeth and his lady wife made the rounds glad-handing the nightclub guests. They lingered briefly near the poker table, where Ruby served as dealer to a full complement of raucous poker players, before commandeering a pair of tables in front of the fireplace.

All of this felt very familiar, and Sam realized the king was holding court like he had in Inverness. Sam couldn't help but think he might learn something important if he could eavesdrop unnoticed.

With no new arrivals imminent, Sam stepped out into the empty hallway and slipped on Le Fay's ring. He then re-entered Casablanca and positioned himself behind Macbeth's chair.

"But where is Macduff?" Lennox asked. "Fife is but an hour's gentle ride from Dunsinane. Surely, he would have been here to greet you?"

Macbeth snorted. "You know as well as I that he has run off to join Malcolm in England."

"So, the rumours are true." The speaker, a man whose head and face were a thicket of black curls, was a thane Sam had not seen before. "I had not expected such cowardice from Macduff."

"'Tis not cowardice, Thane Angus," Ross suggested. "Surely Macduff seeks to return young Malcolm to us on bended knee."

Macbeth slammed his fist on the table. "Malcolm murdered his father. There is no place for him in Scotland. And frankly, England is not distant enough."

Lady Macbeth chose that moment to speak. "Macduff has forfeited his title and lands. My lord, you should honour someone loyal to you with a bequeathal."

"It has been but one day," Ross argued, his wide nose flaring. "Surely we shall await an explanation."

"Two days," Lennox corrected. "And Thane Macduff also

failed to present himself at Scone."

"Macduff does not concern me," Macbeth said. "He has made his bed. But what of Cathness and Menteth? I have seen neither since Scone."

"Business at home?" Ross suggested. "They, too, were away at the war. Their thanedoms run not themselves."

Macbeth glared at Ross. "Yours seems to run well enough on its own."

"I have sons," Ross said. "They are proficient stewards."

"Speaking of stewards," Lennox interrupted. "Seyton approaches."

"Your Grace." Steward Seyton bobbed his head toward Macbeth. "There is someone at the postern gate who carries word for you."

Macbeth frowned. "Can this person not come here to bend my ear? I do not even have a drink yet."

The steward glanced about the nightclub, then spoke with unusual care. "This person is not properly attired to enter such a magnificent place."

That didn't sound like Seyton at all. Sam figured it was some kind of code.

"Very well." Macbeth rose to his feet. "I shall attend to this courier. And when I return, there shall be ale at my table."

"Of course," Lennox said, also rising. "I shall see to it myself."

Sam followed Seyton and Macbeth as they left Casablanca and marched down a narrow hallway that seemed to go nowhere except to a shadowed alcove. The steward pushed aside a heavy curtain and tied if off. Like the tapestry in Inverness, the curtain concealed a door, this one secured by a thick wooden bar.

Seyton lifted the bar, cracked open the door and, apparently satisfied with what he saw outside, stepped back down the hallway several paces, almost bumping into Sam as he did.

Macbeth also peered outside, then leaned against the doorjamb, his ear to the great outdoors.

Sam set himself against the wall near the door so he could eavesdrop.

"It is done?" Macbeth murmured.

"Lady Macduff's death was exquisite," replied a voice.

"And the children?" Macbeth whispered.

"We suffered the mother to witness the death of her eldest. The younglings followed after."

"Were there witnesses?" Macbeth hissed.

"There were." A pause. "Servants. They no longer witness nor serve."

Macbeth seemed to slump against the doorjamb. "Then all is done."

"Except payment," the voice answered.

Macbeth pulled himself erect, then raised his voice so Seyton could hear him. "My steward shall pay you. Begone until I need you again." Then the murderous king stepped quickly down the hallway back toward Casablanca. Sam heard the clink of unclean coins in the steward's hand as Macbeth's paymaster dug thirty pieces of silver from his money purse.

56
METHINKS YOU HAVE DRUNK TOO MUCH

Sam found himself wondering what sort of lunatic would have a man's family and servants killed because he suspected the man had turned against him. If Macduff hadn't actually turned, he would now.

In his mind's eye, Sam pictured Macbeth in his Inverness apartment holding two bloody knives, stupefied by what he had done at the urging of his wife. The murder of Banquo and attempted murder of Banquo's son Fleance had come easier, but he hadn't done those himself. Now he'd had a man's entire family killed. Scotland's new king was a monster.

Sam was tempted to deliver retribution. Become judge, jury, and executioner. If he had his Smith and Wesson semi-automatic, he could shoot Macbeth. A bullet between the eyes. He was sure more people would cheer than weep over the incident. And he would get away with it, too. Rendered invisible by Le Fay's ring, there would be no witnesses. His sidearm, though, was locked in a safe back in Hartford. That meant he'd have to make it more personal. Use a knife. Or poison. Or he could push Macbeth off the roof of the castle. Make it look like suicide.

But no. He couldn't do it. Even as a cop, he'd never killed a man. Never been in a position where he'd had to. Sure, he'd tried to shoot Morgan Le Fay once. But even more than Macbeth, the woman had it coming. And that had been a spur of the moment thing. Not premeditated. Sam didn't think he was the kind of man who could plan and carry out an execution. He was not a man like Macbeth.

Besides, from what he remembered of Shakespeare's play, Macbeth would get his comeuppance soon enough. By Macduff, wasn't it? At least now he knew why. Macbeth had brought it upon himself.

Outside the nightclub, Sam found the Casablanca sign from Inverness fastened above the arched entryway. Despite the music and laughter emanating from within, the cheerfully-painted sign seemed lonely. The broad, cursive letters looked out of place, the white paint almost grey in the poor lighting.

But maybe there was nothing wrong with the sign. The wrong was with Sam himself, surrounded by murder and deceit. The world of Macbeth was a dark and foreign place. He couldn't wait to leave. With luck, once the witches retired to their apartment, he, Effie, and Victoria would escape this madhouse.

Or not. In the few short minutes he'd been away, the interior of Casablanca had become . . . well, a madhouse. Guests had risen from their seats and were waving their hands and arguing with each other. If Just Sam was still playing his harp, there was no hearing it above the uproar.

Sam followed Macbeth back to his table, where Lennox and Ross looked ready to come to blows.

Lennox saw Macbeth first. "My Lord! Your courier? Was it news of Fife?"

Macbeth said nothing as he took in the looks on everyone's faces.

Lady Macbeth had also risen from her seat. "Murder," she said. "Foul murderers entered Fife Castle and put the knife to all they could find."

Macbeth feigned surprised. "What of the guard? Where were they?"

It was Ross who answered. "Most of the castle militia were with their thane in England. Those who remained were the first killed. I am told the attack was by stealth, that the killers were cowards."

Macbeth pulled on his beard. "Perhaps it was the English. No soldiers are more cowardly."

"Why would English soldiers murder innocent women and children?" Lennox demanded.

"Children?" Macbeth again feigned surprise. "They murdered children?"

"And their mother also," Lennox said. "Lady Macduff and all her young."

"Thane Ross," Macbeth said. "You must go to Fife at once. Assess what has happened. Perhaps you shall discover who has done this thing."

"Yes, Your Grace. I leave at once."

Macbeth sat down in his chair and picked up a waiting tankard of ale. Instead of drinking, he held it in front of him, hiding his guilty face.

Sam saw the murderous king's hands were shaking. If he still had Banquo's medal, he'd play the ghost again. Instead, he crept up behind Macbeth's chair, leaned over his shoulder, and spat into his drink. The agitated king appeared not to notice.

Who did notice was Morgan Le Fay, who swept in as Sapphire and asked if anyone needed something more to drink. None did, as all their cups were full, but Sam saw the look she gave him. He shrugged and backed away.

The room, having processed the news, was settling back down as Sam made his way out into the empty hallway to remove Le Fay's ring. He'd learned all he could stomach for the next while.

Re-entering Casablanca, he abandoned his post near the entryway and took a stool at the bar. "Sacha, I need a finger of the good stuff."

When the bartender obliged, Sam downed it in one swallow.

Someone sat down on the stool next to him. Sam was surprised to see it was Victoria. "Is it true?" the English spy whispered. "Is Lady Macduff murdered? And her children?"

Sam blew out a breath. "Macbeth ordered it done."

He must have said it a bit too loud. Sacha blanched visibly, while several people along the counter slipped away.

The bartender's eyes were wide as he leaned toward Sam and spoke in a whisper. "You must not make such accusations."

Sam pushed his cup toward him and gestured for a refill. "It's not an accusation. It's a fact. I was there just now when the murderers reported to Macbeth and demanded payment."

"Just now?" Sacha appeared confused. "Were you not availing yourself of the garderobe?"

"I was," Sam said. "And I wasn't. Gimme another drink."

Sacha didn't move. "Methinks you have drunk too much already."

"Gimme another drink," Sam said, "and I promise I'll shut up about Macbeth."

Sacha poured.

57
SHALL WE LEAVE NOW?

Sam nursed his drink as a confusion of conversation swirled about Casablanca. The news may have been bad for a lot of people, but it was good for business. No one, it seemed, could get enough to drink. And the poker players seemed driven to take greater risks.

Macbeth, for his part, sat at his table holding court throughout the late afternoon and evening, discussing who knows what with his thanes and generals. Sam had no way of finding out. Every time he stepped away from the bar, one of the witches took it upon herself to follow at his heels. He figured if they ever got him alone, they would demand their ring back. No time would be too soon to leave.

At a word from Lady Macbeth, a bevy of servants brought food and distributed it around the nightclub. An offering to appease the agitated gathering of Scotland's movers and shakers? Or a MacGuffin to distract them from the latest in a series of murders? The meal was well received, but did little to quiet the various conversations.

Finally, Macbeth and his lady wife rose from their table and made their way to the exit. Lennox and Angus followed them out, but the rest remained to continue their discussions in the absence of their king. Sam, watching over the lip of his cup, could see the thanes were agitated. But he had no idea what they were discussing. Probably theorizing who was responsible for the killings, and who might be next.

Eventually, Sam rose from his stool and began encouraging those who remained to finish their drinks and come back tomorrow. It had been a long day, and if everything went well, the night would be even longer.

While urging people out the door, Comhnall, the apprentice butler, entered the nightclub. "You have a delivery from Beauly Priory." The youth held a sack away from his body as if it contained snakes.

"I didn't order anything," Sam said. "Wait. Beauly Priory?" He took the sack and loosened the drawstring that tied it shut. Inside was a stack of painted playing cards identical to the ones used at the poker table, only the back wasn't blank. Instead, a reasonable facsimile of the Resistol fedora Sam had left back in Hartford had been skilfully drawn on each one. "How about that. Alison delivered after all."

Happy to be rid of his package, Comhnall disappeared into the hallway.

Sam set the sack on the bar counter and smiled at Sacha. "Better late than never."

The witches seemed to have forgotten Sam's latest abuse of their ring, or were maybe preoccupied with plans of their own. The moment the last patron left, Sam's precious gems also headed for the exit, presumably to their apartment down the hall.

Effie poked her head out from the stock room alcove, then she and Victoria emerged to stand with Sam in front of the fireplace. "Your witches are gone," Effie said. "Shall we leave now?"

Sam was tired. And a bit drunk. But still level-headed. Mostly. "Let's give everyone in the castle a chance to wind down and get cozy in their beds. I found a nearby side exit we can use to avoid the gate guards."

"When did you do this?" Effie asked. "You haven't left Casablanca since we arrived this morning, except to visit the garderobe."

"I could tell you," Sam said. "But then I'd have to kill you." The joke fell flat. Sam really was tired. "I'll show you, but now's not the time."

Since the witches had run off before the tables were cleared, Effie and Victoria helped gather cups and tankards and food trays and set them on the bar counter. Sam secured the receipts in the safe, but didn't bother doing the accounts. There was no point. In the morning, Seyton would be advertising for a new casino manager.

After gathering his trench coat from the stock room and the new delivery of playing cards from the bar counter, Sam handed Sacha the safe key. "You should hold on to this."

The bartender gave him a curious look.

"I plan to be hungover in the morning, and may not make it back to Casablanca before Seyton comes looking for his pound of flesh."

"I knew it," Sacha said. "I should have cut you off."

"It's been a rough day for everyone," Sam said.

The steward's apprentice, Comhnall, had shown them their apartments earlier in the day. Sam's room was closest to Casablanca's entryway, while his precious gems were housed further down the hall. Sacha's and Just Sam's lodgings sat in between. Sam waved goodnight as the harpist entered his apartment, walking almost backwards in his reluctance to take his eyes off Sam and his two new companions. Sam then nodded at Sacha, who lingered in the hallway, likewise prying. The whole thing felt like a scene from a bad romantic comedy.

Once they were inside their apartment, a spacious room that basked in the glow of a single oil lamp, Victoria said, "Your friends are curious as to your appetites. They believe more is going on here than sharing a room."

Sam forced a smile. "Won't they be surprised come morning."

"So, are we to simply wait?" Effie asked as she hung her and Victoria's riding cloaks on a monstrous-looking wooden arrangement that may or may not have been intended as a coatrack.

"You two should catch a nap," Sam said, opting to set his trench coat over the back of a chair. "I'll go scout around. See what's what, and make sure we don't run into any surprises."

"How will you do that?" Victoria asked. "Do you intend to roam through the castle? An unescorted stranger?"

Sam nodded. "Pretty much. Look. I'm going to show you how

earlier today I found a way to leave the castle undetected. I know you don't want an unpleasant surprise, so I'll tell you up front that I'm going to become invisible."

Victoria laughed. "Invisible?"

Effie remained straight-faced. "I have told you, Vic. Sam is a man of exceptional and varied talents."

"Yes, but invisible?"

Sam produced Le Fay's ring from his shirt pocket. "The sorceress who brought me here from the future also created this ring. When I wear it, I become invisible."

Victoria laughed again.

"Really. I'm telling you so you don't scream or faint or anything."

"Go on," Victoria said. "Become invisible."

Sam turned to Effie. "Will you make sure your partner doesn't do anything that could prevent us from making our escape?"

Effie responded by placing a hand over Victoria's mouth. Her partner didn't seem to mind, and watched as Sam slipped Le Fay's ring onto his finger. Sam, watching back, saw Victoria's eyes widen, but the professional spy made no sound.

"Sam," Effie said, "you are invisible."

"You can hear my voice, though. And hear me move." Sam tapped a little soft shoe on the stone floor. He was no Fred Astaire, but figured he'd made a passable performance.

Victoria pushed Effie's hand away. "This allows you to roam the castle undetected."

"Pretty much," Sam said.

"Such rings," Victoria murmured, "would be invaluable for people in my profession."

"I'm sure they would," Sam said. "Also valuable for people trying to sneak away from a castle. Unfortunately, I have only the one ring."

"Go do your reconnaissance," Effie said. "When you return, we will be ready to leave."

Sam nodded before remembering they couldn't see him. "Get some sleep. I'll wake you when I get back."

58
OUT, OUT, BRIEF CANDLE

The hallway, thankfully, was empty when Sam slipped out of the apartment. He should have taken off the ring first, and told anyone who saw him that he was going to the garderobe, but he was tired and not thinking at his best.

First things first, he went down the hallway Macbeth had used for his clandestine meeting. The exit was still unguarded, and the bar securing the door had been replaced, probably by Seyton after he'd paid off the murderers. Sam considered taking a peek outside, but decided against it. The less he disturbed things, the better. Instead, he went back past Casablanca and down the corridor to the main entrance. This gate was guarded, so he continued on.

What he hoped to find was a room with travel bags and maybe a dark rainslicker to conceal his trench coat. A kitchen like the one in Inverness where he could fill said travel bags. And a back hallway where he could sneak his purloined travel gear back to his room. Unlike Inverness Castle, there was no city outside where such supplies could be pilfered. Unless, of course, the people in the makeshift tent town left such things lying about.

There was also the mode of travel. If he and his friends weren't able to steal horses from the crowded stables, the first leg of their trip would be on foot.

Dunsinane Castle was bigger than others in Scotland Sam had seen, perhaps a reflection of Macbeth's ego. It took him a while to find the kitchen which, fortunately, was deserted. As he loaded a cloth sack with bread, cheese, and dried mystery meat, he felt something touch his ankle. Startled, he looked down and saw a grey and white cat rubbing against him. Le Fay's magic ring, it seemed, wasn't proof against felines.

Ignoring his new friend, Sam finished collecting supplies, then hustled back along a deserted corridor to a closet he had found that was filled to overflowing with weapons, cloaks, boots, and other items that would prove useful in the great outdoors. Nothing resembled a travel bag, however, so he'd have to make do with the cloth sack from the kitchen.

He wrapped the food sack inside a bulky travel cloak, but didn't think he could sneak the floating bundle past the guards at the castle's main gate. Hoping to find an alternate route, he climbed a servant stairway to a higher floor where he hoped to find a corridor that crossed over the entrance foyer.

The cat followed him for a while before losing interest. Maybe it had spotted a mouse and went to catch its own provisions.

Sam found a likely corridor, but hadn't travelled far when he saw a woman walking toward him. She was tall, darkhaired, and wore voluminous flowing nightclothes that pitched and rolled in the flickering shadows produced by the candle she carried. He recognized her immediately—Lady Macbeth. He also recognized the shambling movement and the unfocused look in her eyes. His police training had taught him the signs, but he'd never witnessed it before. Macbeth's wife was sleepwalking.

Curious as to where she might go or what she might do, Sam followed.

The Lady of Inverness didn't go far. A dozen or so steps took her to an alcove where she set the candle on a narrow table. She then looked down at her hands and began rubbing them together. After a minute or more, she muttered, "Yet here's a spot."

The woman's words then grew angry. "Out, damned spot! Out, I say!" She rubbed harder. "One, two. Why, Hell is murky! Fie, my lord, fie! Who would have thought the old man to have had so much blood in him."

Macbeth's wife then laughed, and sang in a singsong voice.

"The thane of Fife had a wife. Where is she now?" Then more anger. "What, will these hands never be clean?" She stopped rubbing, and sniffed her fingers. "Here's the smell of the blood still. All the perfumes of Arabia will not sweeten this little hand."

Suddenly she looked up and spoke to someone who wasn't there. "Wash your hands. Put on your nightgown. Look not so pale. I tell you yet again, Banquo is dead and buried. He cannot return from the grave." Then she turned her head as though hearing something. "To bed, to bed. There's knocking at the gate. Come, come, come, come. Give me your hand. What is done cannot be undone." Picking up the candle, she turned and stormed back down the hallway, her lips mumbling, "To bed, to bed, to bed!"

Sam pressed himself against the wall, allowing her to pass. Well, at least one Macbeth was haunted by their actions. Maybe if he hung around long enough, he'd see King Macbeth also haunting the corridor with a candle and a guilty conscience.

The only way forward was in the direction Lady Macbeth had gone. But instead of a stairway down to a hallway near Casablanca, the corridor ended at an unlatched door that led outside. Sam shifted his burden against his chest so he could reach up with one hand and rub his ear. There had to be another way downstairs. Maybe the stairway down was outside? To further tempt him, the door sat open, swinging in the breeze.

As he knew he would, Sam stepped out through the doorway. Even if he didn't find an alternate way to Casablanca, it wouldn't hurt to check out the lay of the land outside the castle. Maybe there were enough fires lit in the tent city for him to get his bearings. Maybe he'd be able to determine the best route off the hilltop.

What he found instead was a broad terrace and Lady Macbeth standing at the edge of the roof. Macbeth's partner in murder held her candle high in the air and was muttering to herself. Though he stood several yards away, the night wind brought the words to Sam's ears. "Out, out, brief candle! Life is but a walking shadow, a poor player that struts and frets her hour upon the stage and then is heard no more. It is a tale told by an idiot, full of sound and fury, signifying nothing."

Then she stepped up onto the low parapet wall, let go the

295

candle, and fell forward off the roof.

Sam rushed to the parapet, but there was nothing he could do. The ground was at least three storeys below, and he wouldn't have seen anything in night's darkness if not for the candle that had somehow fallen to the ground without going out. Next to the candle lay the form of a woman, her limbs twisted at unnatural angles. Even in death, Macbeth's lady wife looked beautiful.

59
FORESTS DON'T MOVE BY THEMSELVES

The terrace afforded a second exit. Sam went that way and, minutes later, arrived back at his apartment outside Casablanca. If anyone had been lurking in the corridor, they would have seen the door to his apartment open all on its own, and a folded cloak float inside. After setting his pilfered supplies on a small table, he closed the door and slipped off Le Fay's ring.

Then he paused. There was no point in trying to leave yet. Lady Macbeth's corpse had been discovered almost immediately after her fall. The resulting cries had raised half the occupants of the castle, and probably all the occupants of the tent city. Death always attracts vultures. It would be some time before everyone was back in their beds and things would be quiet enough to slip away.

Or was now the best time, while everyone was milling about in confusion?

"Sam?" Effie stood in the bedroom doorway. By the light of the room's sole oil lamp, he could see she was dressed in boots, pants, and a jacket—her old soldier's uniform. "Is it time?"

Victoria joined her, also dressed as a soldier, but with her short hair swept under a hat. Victor.

"Let's go while the going's good," Sam suggested. "I should warn you. There's a big crowd outside. Someone jumped to their death from the roof of the castle."

"What! Who?" Victor/Victoria asked.

"That's not important. I've got us some food for the road. Let's see if we can steal some horses."

Without further word, Effie and Victoria retrieved the cloaks they had worn from Inverness. Sam grabbed his Burberry trench coat and shrugged it on over his dinner jacket. One side hung lower than the other, weighted down by Ugarte's sack of silver merks. He jammed the sack containing Alison's new deck of cards in the opposite coat pocket. It barely fit and caused that part of his coat to bulge out, but the young monk had gone to so much work Sam didn't feel comfortable abandoning the illuminator's efforts.

He then slipped on the dark brown cloak he had pilfered that should make him less conspicuous as they moved about in the night. Clutching the sack of food in one hand, he opened the apartment door with the other.

The corridor, thankfully, was empty. Sam proceeded to lead the two women to the narrow hallway with the shadowed alcove and hidden postern gate.

Despite the untimely death of Lady Macbeth, the gate remained unguarded. Sam tied back the curtain that concealed the exit, removed the security bar, and inched open the door. The immediate vicinity appeared clear, so they exited the castle into the night.

The hilltop on that side of the castle was relatively deserted, but Sam could hear voices echoing from the west wall where Lady Macbeth had made her own more dramatic exit. Additional voices disturbed the night from the east, where the tent city had been erected.

"To the stables," Sam said.

As they entered the tent city, everywhere he looked people were coming and going or standing outside the canvas hovels that stood close together leaving little room for navigation. Lanterns or torches bobbed in the night as people headed toward the west side of the castle to gawk at the tragedy of Lady Macbeth.

Effie and Victoria seemed content to let Sam lead the way through the maze of bivouacs and lean-tos, even though he was sure they had a better sense for these things, what with being born in this day and age and being spies to boot.

Victoria, speaking in a deep voice that sounded much like a woman with a lifelong smoker's cough, said, "We need not attain the stables. A collection of empty tents with horses staked nearby will do."

Sam nodded. "I'm not seeing any."

"Perhaps closer to the stables," Effie suggested.

Sam figured the stables they'd visited when they arrived that morning were ahead and to the left. He led his companions around a broad tent, only to find their path blocked by a motley crew of half-dressed soldiers.

"What is gaun on?" one asked his companions.

"Ah hear someone wis hurt," another answered.

"'Tis Birnam Wood," said a third man. "The trees! Thay march the fields atween Kirkton 'n' Collace!"

"Oh, oh," Sam said. "This is worse than I thought."

"What?" Effie asked. "Surely you do not believe such nonsense?"

"Sadly," Sam said, "I do. The English are coming."

Putting their mission as horse thieves on temporary hold, Sam led his companions back the way they had come toward the western edge of Dunsinane Hill. Though it was still night, the clouds that had cloaked the sky almost nonstop since Sam had arrived in Scotland had mostly cleared. A full moon, accompanied by a chorus of bright stars, now filled the sky. It was enough to reveal movement in the fields below the hill and out toward the west.

Sam looked, then looked again, but swore he was seeing a forest of trees creeping ever closer.

"A wood cannot move so," Victoria said in her faux male voice, apparently seeing much the same.

"Birnam Wood," said a soldier within hearing distance. "There is nought atween Dunsinane 'n' Birnam bit fields 'n' the River Tey. 'N' yit thare is a wood. 'N' it grows nearer by the minute."

"It is but an illusion," Effie suggested, "brought on by moonbeams reflected among the clouds."

"I'll take moonbeams over walking trees any day," Sam said. "But Le Fay and her odious friends mentioned something about woods coming for a visit. We might have picked the wrong night to go out for a stroll."

Effie looked around. "Is she here? Surely that wretched woman and her companions are asleep in the castle."

Sam waved a hand at the growing throng of people that lined the top of the hill. The crowd was growing increasingly agitated as the shadowed wood advanced toward them. "Honey, there ain't nobody asleep in the castle. Not anymore."

"But our escape?" Effie said.

Sam rubbed his ear. "Maybe we can make this work in our favour. Any minute now, people are going to realize that forests don't move by themselves, and what we have here is an army come to put an end to Macbeth's bloody rule."

"An army?" The soldier who had spoken earlier took a step toward him.

Wishing he hadn't let the cat out of the bag, Sam said, "That would be my best guess. But what do I know? I'm just a casino manager."

The soldier stared at him, then headed back toward the castle.

Sam spoke to Effie and Victoria. "I'm not sure if what I just said was boneheaded or brilliant. Either way, we should go find ourselves some horses."

60
MACDUFF'S DESTINY

Heading back toward the stables was like swimming against the current, as more and more people from the castle and tent city flocked to the western edge of the hilltop to see for themselves the rumoured walking trees.

Sam had finally spotted a horse among the tents, when the brassy blast of horns broke the night air. "And there it is. Now things should really get interesting."

"Is it truly the English," Victoria asked. "Or has Norway rallied for a second incursion?"

Looking around for more horses, and not spotting any, Sam said, "If I remember my Shakespeare, what we have here are the combined armies of Macduff, Duncan's kids, and a bunch of English nobles who are willing to fight in exchange for concessions from whoever replaces Macbeth."

"What kind of concessions?" Victoria demanded. "I am the one who provided the intelligence to enable this coup. I should have a say in the matter."

Sam regarded the shadowed face of Effie's partner. "I have no idea. I'm sure you'll be compensated for your efforts."

"Victoria," Effie said. "Is it not enough that Macbeth will be defeated?"

Her spouse lowered her gaze. "Nothing will ever be enough."

Sam figured there was more going on here than he'd been told, but now wasn't the time to dig for answers. Macbeth's soldiers were running through the tent city all around them. One grabbed the horse he'd been eyeing. "Come on. We need to get a ride and get out of here."

"We should stay and fight," Victoria said.

When Sam stared at her, the English spy raised her chin.

"I would fight with Macduff to end the bloody reign of Macbeth," Victoria growled.

Sam continued staring. "Bloody reign? He's been king all of five days."

"Macbeth should have been drowned at birth," Victoria said. "His evil wife also."

Sam felt his cheek twitch. "Something tells me we're not going to move from this spot until you tell me the rest of the story."

"Sam," Effie said. "You know we were held in Dundee Prison for over a year."

"That much you did tell me," Sam said. "I can't imagine what it was like. But what does that have to do with Macbeth?"

Victoria raised a hand and clenched her fist. "Do you not know where Dundee Prison is? But twelve miles from this very castle. It is the Thane of Glamis's prison. Macbeth's prison. Scotland's monstrous general and his foul wife made regular visits to their pet prison to taunt and torture the inmates. Sometimes they would cast stones or starve us for days, then give us vinegar to drink. And there were worse things."

Sam looked at Effie, but she had turned her face to the ground. He felt his cheek twitch, and suddenly had second thoughts on his inability to commit premeditated murder. "I'm sorry to hear that. Maybe it will brighten your day to know the person who threw herself from the castle roof a short while ago was Lady Macbeth."

Victoria coughed out a harsh laugh. "That is one villain. The other yet remains."

Effie raised her face, her expression determined. "We must find ourselves weapons."

Sam let out a sigh. He knew when to pick his battles. This wasn't one of those times. "There are plenty in the armoury inside the castle."

"You will show us?" Victoria demanded.

"I don't think you'd let me say no."

By now people were running everywhere, mostly toward the western ridge. Macbeth and his thanes and generals would have ordered their soldiers to make a defensive line along the hilltop. The high ground would give them an advantage, but Sam had seen a lot of trees moving in the dark. He felt certain the defenders would be outnumbered. Those who were not soldiers or mercenaries were racing back to the tent city and snatching up their belongings.

Sam fought his way through the crowd, Effie and Victoria at his heels, to the castle's main gate, only to find it clogged with battle-hardened soldiers pouring out into the yard. Each of them carried weapons they had probably claimed from the armoury. Sam worried there would be nothing left when they got there.

"Hold!" A pair of castle guards stood before them with crossed spears blocking the gate. "There is na place within the castle fur ye tae hide. Na supplies wi' which tae sustain yourselves. The king's order is tae return tae ye tents or tae bolt tae the east."

Before Victoria could attack the guard with her bare hands, Sam said, "We don't live in a tent. We have apartments inside the castle."

The second guard squinted at Sam. "Ah recognize ye. Yer the foreigner wha runs the nightclub, are ye not?"

"Sam Spade. At your service."

The guard squinted at Victoria and Effie. "Ah dae nae recognize either o' ye, bit yer dressed fer war. Ye shuid take position alang the western ridge."

Effie showed the man her empty hands. "We require weapons first. From the armoury."

The guard's squint tightened. "Yur a woman." He turned his beaded eyes on Victoria. "An' ye . . . Ah dae nae ken what ye are."

Victoria growled, "We fight for coin as vigorously as any man."

The guard backed away and moved his spear. "Go arm yourselves."

Before the other guard could interfere, the three of them pushed their way inside the castle.

"To the right," Sam said. "The armoury isn't far."

As they approached the weapons closet, the flow of armed

soldiers thinned.

"How did you come to discover it here?" Effie asked.

Sam clutched the sleeve of his pilfered cloak. "Where do you think I got this?"

The closet, which had been filled to overflowing hours earlier, was now almost empty. But there were still several cloaks, a mismatched pair of boots, and a single wide-bladed sword with a crossed hilt. It looked similar to the weapons the redshanks in Nottingham had used. There was also a long, plain-looking spear. Victoria went immediately for the spear, while Effie picked up the sword and tested its balance.

The English spy frowned as she examined the mostly empty closet, then looked at Sam. "We must look further to find a weapon for you."

"That's okay," Sam said. "My weapon of choice is back in Hartford. I'll have to settle for using my wits."

"You will need to defend yourself," Victoria insisted.

Sam retrieved Le Fay's ring from his shirt pocket and slipped it onto his finger. "They can't poke what they can't see."

"You have never been in battle before," Victoria insisted, her gaze slightly to one side of where Sam stood. "Blades fly everywhere."

"I've had my share of dustups," Sam told her. "Nothing like what's about to go down outside, but I'll make do."

"It is your life to lose," Victoria said, her gaze following Sam's voice.

"Sam," Effie said. "Perhaps you should stay in the castle while we search for Macbeth on the field."

"You may want to take your own advice," Sam answered. "If your plan is to hunt down Macbeth, you should start here in the castle. Sure, he was the big general on the battlefield when the king sent him off to war, but now he's the king. He's probably up on the roof right now overseeing the pending bloodbath."

"You believe the devil is on the roof?" Victoria asked.

Sam nodded. "There's a terrace up there with a club level view of Scotland's defence and England's offence. I'll bet you dollars to doughnuts that's where he is."

"Then we must go there," Victoria said. "It is my destiny to see that Macbeth departs this earthly coil."

"I'm pretty sure that's Macduff's destiny," Sam said, "but why don't we go take a look?" He turned and started walking toward the stairs he had used earlier that night. "Follow me. And keep those toad stickers handy in case we run into trouble."

"Follow you?" Effie said. "We cannot see you."

Sam stopped dead. "That could be a problem." He slipped off the ring and squeezed it in his fist. "Let's do this on the up and up for now."

61
THE WAY TO A MAN'S HEART

As they came to the top of the servant stairs, a soldier with a torch in one hand and a sword in the other turned toward them and brandished his blade. When he saw Effie and Victoria emerge from the shadows behind Sam, the weapon faltered but quickly rose again. "Halt!"

"We have halted," Sam answered. "There's nowhere for us to go until you get out of our way."

Upon hearing Sam speak, the soldier became a jumble of nerves, the blade of his weapon bobbing in the air like he was cutting vegetables.

"Hey. Watch it with that. Someone could lose an eye."

"You are a foreigner!" the soldier shouted as the erratic sword made even wilder swings.

Victoria tried to move past Sam, but there wasn't enough room. Even so, she extended the spear she'd taken from the armoury in an effort to fend off the soldier's blade.

"There's no need for that," Sam said. "We're all adults here. I'm sure we can reach a peaceful resolution."

"English!" the soldier shouted, noting the distinct absence of a Scottish accent in Sam's words. He took a step backwards to avoid Victoria's spear. "How have you penetrated the castle so quickly?"

"You've got us all wrong," Sam said. "I'm an American. Not English."

"American?"

Sam tipped his head and offered his most charismatic smile. "King Macbeth hired me to run his nightclub."

"Casablanca?" The sword ceased shaking, then the soldier lowered it a foot or so. "I have heard much, but have not been there myself. Duty . . ."

"Sure," Sam said. "Maybe if we survive this invasion, you'll get some time off. But first things first. Let's work on surviving the invasion. I have information for the king that could turn the tide of battle."

The soldier's good mood vanished. "Information? How does a nightclub manager come across information regarding an attack by the English?"

Sam attempted another smile. "People talk when they drink."

The smiles didn't appear to be working. The guard's expression soured, and the sword rose a few inches. "And what do drinking people talk about?"

Replacing the smile with an expression he hoped looked sincere, Sam lowered his voice. "Well, if you can trust the word of a drunkard, your king has a traitor in his camp."

The sword lowered again. "Traitor? Who?"

Sam paused for effect. "Given the delicate nature of this information, it's for the king's ears only. You understand that, right?"

And up went the sword. "You shall confide this information to me, and I shall inform His Grace."

Right. A glory seeker. "We could inform His Grace together," Sam suggested.

The guard didn't move except to shake his head.

There was another way to play it. Lowering his voice even further, Sam spoke the first name that came to mind, "Macduff."

The guard snorted. "All men know Macduff fled Inverness to join Malcolm in England, and is even now among the army below the hill."

"Sure," Sam said. "But I'm fairly certain Macbeth doesn't know that Lennox and Ross have also turned against him."

"That is absurd," the soldier said. "Thane Lennox and Thane

Ross are the king's most faithful servants."

"So was Macduff until Banquo was murdered. It took Macbeth murdering Macduff's entire family to turn Lennox and Ross against him."

The guard snorted again, but Sam could see doubt in his eyes. Sam needed to push the envelope further. "Angus, Caithness, and Menteth have also turned against the king." And that was the extent of thane names he had heard.

"Harrumph." The sword lowered again. "I have never fully trusted Thane Menteth," The guard slid the sword into a slim scabbard at his waist. "I shall take your intelligence to the king, but he will not believe it."

Sam wasn't so sure. Macbeth was paranoid. He'd believe all of it.

Sam and his companions watched the guard and his torch travel down the corridor, then disappear down a side passage, the same route he had taken when he followed Lady Macbeth to her attempt at unassisted flight. He beckoned his Amazonian warriors to again follow him.

"But we do not know where the guard went," Victoria said.

"Don't worry, sister. I know where he went."

Sam led them through the mix of corridors that led to the rooftop terrace. The door was unlatched, so the three of them eased outside and stood against the adjacent wall.

A dozen yards away, gathered near the crenelated parapet, stood a small number of guards and message runners. At their centre stood Macbeth. The guard turned messenger they had encountered stood to one side awaiting permission to speak. The entire party faced away from them and toward the ridgetop, so they could observe Dunsinane's defences as well as the enemy that extended to the horizon on the plain below the hill.

It took a moment for Sam to realize the reason he could see so well was because the sky was no longer midnight black, but the sickly purple of a week-old bruise. He glanced at his watch, and was surprised to find the luminous dial indicated it was 6 a.m. Night was drawing to an end.

Waving for his companions to follow, he sidled along the castle wall to the far end of the terrace before moving up to the low parapet that looked westward. Down below, the advancing

English had discarded their tree branches and were approaching the foot of Dunsinane Hill. Some carried red flags covered with golden dragons. Near the centre were blue flags with a large white X stretching from corner to corner.

"Those are Clan Duncan's men," Effie said in a quiet voice. "The yellow and red among them indicate clan Macduff."

"Do you see Clan Banquo?" Sam asked.

"I am unfamiliar with that clan's flag," she answered.

"Pity. Fleance should be here." Sam looked to Victoria for help, but Effie's spouse was staring at Macbeth and his inner circle.

"There are too many to rush," Victoria whispered.

"You got that right," Sam said. "Whaddaya say we end this foolishness and go find ourselves some horses."

"But—," Victoria said.

Sam raised a finger, then pointed below the castle to where the English had begun ascending the hillside, crossing swords with a Scottish line they knew they outnumbered. "We can see from here what Macbeth is up against. In less than two weeks he's managed to tick off enough people that thousands of armed men have arrived on his doorstep to set things right. If you really do want to kill Macbeth, there's a long line ahead of you."

Victoria looked undeterred, and Sam could picture the situation getting ugly real fast. As shouts and cries, and the clang of metal on metal rose up from below, he tried to think of what more he could say or do to get the three of them out of Scotland alive. Then, above the clamour of battle, came the growl of a raised voice. Sam turned his attention back to the cluster of men further along the parapet.

The voice was Macbeth's. The king was berating a bearer of bad news.

Leaning toward Effie, Sam whispered, "My bad. I hadn't planned on telling the king any of that nonsense we fed his guard."

Sam figured Macbeth would push the hapless guard off the roof to keep company with his tragic wife down below, but was impressed when the king succumbed to his better nature and had the guard escorted inside the castle instead. Given the escort consisted of six men, Sam didn't think they were taking him to tea. The good news was, that left only two armed guards to secure the safety of the king. Them and several unarmed teenagers whose sole purpose was to carry messages to the fight and back.

Sensing Victoria was about to charge the party with her pilfered spear, Sam rested a hand on the English spy's arm before strolling over to where Macbeth stood. "Thinking of joining your wife?" he said. "My condolences, by the way."

Macbeth frowned, seeming not to recognize him. The dark cloak covering Sam's trench coat could explain that. Then the Scottish play's leading man swayed back on his heels, his eyes lit with recognition. His frown deepened. "The hags' nightclub manager." The murderous king waved a hand at the battle below. "Is this their doing?"

"No," Sam said. "This is *your* doing. When you start killing everyone close to you, the survivors get nervous."

"A minor setback," Macbeth grumbled. "All may die here today, but I shall live. Your mistresses said as much. I shall die by no man's hand."

"Yeah, well, as to that. History has a bad habit of leaving out the women. Your wife, now. She'll be remembered. But she's an exception. Villains usually are. History tends to have selective memory, however, when the heroes are women."

"Women?" Macbeth pulled at his beard in bafflement.

Sam was going to say more, but lost the chance when a voice called out, "Turn, hellhound, turn!"

Sam and Macbeth both turned as Victoria came storming at the murderous king with her pilfered spear raised. Effie's spouse had removed her hat, allowing her short, flame-red hair to billow in the icy breeze.

Macbeth reached for the sword he carried at his belt. "You are no man—"

But the weapon was still halfway in its scabbard when the tip of Victoria's spear took him in the stomach. "There is much I would say to you," Victoria growled. "But I will let my spear speak in my stead."

"How about that," Sam said. "The way to a man's heart really is through his stomach."

Macbeth's eyes widened as he let go his sword and pressed his hands to his abdomen, his thumb and forefingers clutching the pole of the spear. "I. Will. Not. Yield. Lay on, Macduff."

"I am no Macduff," Victoria said. "I am but a poet who spent many a long month in a cage tormented by the likes of you. It is in that cage I learned that the spear is mightier than the pen. Now taste my spear!"

Victoria leaned forward, heaving the weapon deeper into Macbeth's gut. A groan left the murderous king's lips as he collapsed to his knees.

"I, also, was in that cage," Effie said.

Sam hadn't heard her approach, but watched as the once sweet-faced clerk in King Arthur's court lifted her borrowed Scottish sword high above her head. Effie's expression was grim as she swung the blade, down and to one side, neatly separating Macbeth's head from his shoulders. The hairy ball rolled along the terrace stones, coming to an awkward stop against the parapet wall just as the king's headless torso slumped to one side.

Sam understood why Effie had done it. He just didn't think the act would provide her any peace. It certainly brought no peace to Sam's stomach, which churned at the sight of the bloody king despite not even remembering when he'd last eaten.

"Time to go," he said, after pushing bile back down his throat. He had no idea when Macbeth's remaining two guards and the flock of runners had fled. Before, during, or after the ladies' assault on their king. But they could have gone for reinforcements.

"We are done here," Victoria agreed.

62

WE'LL ALWAYS HAVE CAMELOT

Leaving the castle was the easy part. With everyone hiding in their apartments or outside fighting or fleeing, the stairs and corridors were mostly empty.

Sam hoped his precious gems were doing that first bit—cowering in their cots—but couldn't picture Morgan Le Fay hiding under a bed, no matter her disguise.

He also hoped Sacha and Just Sam would come out of this okay. In the few short days he'd known them, he'd come to appreciate their company. The bartender's humour and streetwise common sense were a rare combination. And he'd never met anyone more easygoing than the harpist. Both men, he was sure, were smart enough to stay in their apartments and wait for the dust to settle.

Those worries took a back seat as he and his two warrior women almost tripped and fell down the stairs to the castle's main foyer. The grey and white cat he encountered earlier had appeared out of nowhere in the middle of the stairwell, and raced between their feet as it headed up the stairs. Perhaps it had its own ring of invisibility.

The guards stationed at the castle's main gate clearly knew nothing of what had happened on the castle roof. They motioned for Effie and Victoria to hurry up and get outside to join the fight, but frowned at Sam's lack of a weapon, then gazed curiously at the sack of kitchen provisions in his hands.

"I had this when we went in," Sam said as he rushed by, not giving them a chance to detain him.

Outside the castle, they found themselves in the world's largest mosh pit. People were running—or trying to run—in every direction. Most of them carried bundles of belongings or weapons or both.

Sam couldn't tell if anyone knew Macbeth was dead, or if the panic stemmed solely from the realization that the king's forces were outnumbered and losing the battle. It was even possible some of the king's soldiers and mercenaries had switched sides.

He called to Effie and Victoria over the general din, "To the stables!" His companions may or may not have heard him, but followed at his heels anyway as he zigged and zagged among the crowded makeshift alleyways between the tents.

Even though the fighting was on the opposite side of the castle, English soldiers must have flanked one or both sides of the hill, cutting off retreat. That could explain the general panic and people running in all directions. Sam hoped they weren't too late to escape. It would be a real shame to have come this far only to be mistaken for Macbeth loyalists and killed.

The stables appeared just ahead, and after clearing past a few dozen more panicked locals, they took shelter under a barn roof that stank of manure but was oddly empty of people. The three of them searched the place. There was hay, buckets, a few saddles and blankets, and plenty of manure, but no horses. Not even a mule. Which could explain why no one was there.

Emerging on the east side of the long wooden building, Sam could see any number of mounted horses, wagons, and heavily burdened Scotsmen on foot racing toward a bright sunrise. The English may have flanked both sides of the hill, but they hadn't yet completely surrounded the place.

"Looks like we're on our own," Sam said. "With luck, the English will be satisfied with Macbeth's death and taking the castle, and won't send anyone after the deserters."

"We have not lost all the horses," Victoria said, pointing further along the outside wall of the stables.

Sam turned and saw a team of horses rigged to a heavily-laden cart, its bulky contents covered by a heavy tarp. Stealing the cart would help their escape immeasurably, but whoever had loaded it was sure to put up a fight.

Victoria, with Effie in tow, was already approaching the cart. The thick wooden wheels had dug themselves into the soft earth, making Sam wonder what had been loaded. He lifted a flap and found a wide barrel filled with silver coins.

Someone pushed down the flap, and Sam looked up straight into Sapphire's blue-violet eyes. Morgan Le Fay's eyes.

Sam smiled. "I guess now I know the purpose of the nightclub."

Le Fay sniffed. "Had Macbeth been wiser, he would have used Casablanca's profits to hire mercenaries and expand his army, as I instructed him. But greed got the better of him. Then he grew cocky when we told him he would not die at the hand of a man. Macbeth chose to hoard the coins instead."

"As I'm sure you knew he would," Sam said. "I guess he has no use for them now, seeing as he's dead?"

Sapphire's full lips spread into a grin. "Of course. Hecate showed us Macbeth's death. I must admit it was inspiring. Girl power and all that."

Sam felt his cheek twitch. "That should mean Effie and Victoria aren't in any trouble. You'll let them go, right?" He could see that Ruby and Emerald now flanked his two friends. At some point in the last minute or so, his warrior women had lost their sword and spear.

Sapphire's grin widened. "Euphemia Peregrine, Maid of Earl. Who knew the young girl had it in her? And her friend? Victor? Victoria?" Sapphire shook her shoulders as though experiencing a sudden chill. "A force to be reckoned with."

"You'll let them go?" Sam repeated.

"Of course, we will," Sapphire said, then paused. "Provided you return with us to our cavern without giving us any trouble."

"I've done what you wanted," Sam growled. "You promised to return me to my own time and place. That was our deal."

"Of course," Le Fay repeated. "Once my sisters and I report to our mistress, your task here will be done. Only then shall I send you home. Everything in its own time."

Sam still didn't trust the woman, but that was a better answer than he had expected. He turned to Effie. "You and Victoria have to go. Make your way to England. And please, do me a favour—retire from the spy business, will ya?"

"You are not coming with us?" Effie pleaded.

"'Fraid not, angel." Sam could only describe his unrequited love's expression as crestfallen. "Maybe I'll catch up with you later."

"In six years?" Effie's tone suggested six years was far too long. At least, that was how Sam chose to interpret it.

He shrugged. "Time will tell."

Effie surprised him by stepping forward and embracing him in a tight hug. "I will miss you, Sam. As I have always missed you."

Sam suppressed a choking sound. "We'll always have Camelot."

"And Sherwood," Effie returned.

"And Scotland," Victoria added from where she stood just inches away.

Sam sighed and gently separated himself from Effie. "You have to go. I have to go."

"We all must go," Sapphire announced. "The English have secured the castle and are coming this way."

63
I CAN LIVE WITH THAT

Sam took one last look as Effie and Victoria joined hands and began running down the hillside. Then he climbed up into the back of the cart and sat on something that felt much less comfortable than a crate of coins. He shifted around until his seat was at least bearable. Meanwhile, his three precious gems climbed up onto the plank bench at the front where Ruby used the reins to get the two draft horses moving.

"You're not afraid of the soldiers catching us?" Sam asked. "They can't be happy to hold a war, just to have you make off with the spoils."

Sapphire let out a heavy sigh. "There is very little that makes me afraid anymore. Certainly not soldiers. For one thing, the soldiers are no longer able to see us. As we did with your ring, and with the horses when last we visited Achindown, we have rendered our conveyance and ourselves invisible. For another, should anyone in some unfathomable way impede us, I shall simply call down lightning and burn them from brow to toe."

"Right." Sam figured that, whatever happened in the next few hours, it might be best to keep his thoughts to himself.

When they reached the bottom of the hill, Ruby turned the cart toward a dirt track that ran to the southeast. Sam couldn't see anyone fleeing in that direction, but he did see what looked like English soldiers patrolling further to the east.

The cart continued south along the track before turning west at a crossing lane. Sam couldn't see any soldiers ahead and, after a few minutes, several buildings marked the beginning of a small town. As they passed through, a sign named the place Kinrossie, but Sam called it a ghost town since all the occupants had fled before the English. The track came to a T-intersection, but instead of going north or south, Ruby drove the cart straight ahead into a cultivated field. Several fields later, they came to a much-used dirt road and turned north. Sam figured the roundabout route was in order to avoid English patrols.

Soon they turned west again, and some of the landmarks looked familiar. An hour later they reached the town of Birnam, now missing much of its wooded forests.

The cart didn't stop, however, except to water the horses. In addition to coins and candlesticks, the witches' burglary back at the castle had included food and drink. Sam found it ironic that, while he had been trying and failing to sneak off to England, his precious gems had kept themselves busy preparing a much more successful escape.

He idled away the journey's long hours by hoping Sacha and Just Sam were all right, and that Effie was safe and on her way to England. He also ran scenarios through his head of how he would rescue Nora, assuming Le Fay kept her word. He even napped a little. By the time the cart rolled to a stop outside the now-familiar jumble of boulders, night was falling.

Sam felt a little off balance as he climbed down off the cart and stretched. The conveyance wasn't as bad as riding a horse, but his roost had been hard and lumpy. Something told him there was a chiropractor in his future.

The sky above was as stormy as ever, and a cold wind was picking up. Despite wearing a double-breasted suit, a winterized trench coat, and a heavy cloak, an uneasy chill haunted Sam's bones. This was it. Either Le Fay sent him home, or she turned him into a newt or something worse. He didn't dwell on the subject, despite a first-class ticket to Hartford being the least likely option.

Watching Ruby unhook and stake the two horses, it occurred to Sam that leaving the cartload of loot outside probably wasn't in the cards. Maybe that was why they'd brought him. Slave labour.

He needn't have worried, however. Once Ruby was done, all three precious gems dropped their sweet and innocent disguises, became loathsome witches once again, and raised their hands in the air. A low chant escaped their lips, but Sam couldn't make out the words due to the rising wind. Or maybe it was just that his attention had been waylaid by crates and barrels rising up into the air from underneath the tarp. Coins. Candlesticks. Picture frames. Anything that was gold, silver, or held some kind of value. It wouldn't have surprised him to see a kitchen sink or two. The witches had stripped Dunsinane Castle bare. The stolen treasures began moving toward the hole among the boulders and down into the cavern.

When the witches were done, Sam spoke without thinking. "I thought it was leprechauns who hoarded gold."

Le Fay smirked. "So long as the wee folk stay in Ireland, they may hoard all the gold they wish."

In for a penny, Sam thought. "Okay then, how about dragons?"

"Scotland has no dragons," Le Fay said, "unless you count the creature in Loch Ness."

"Never mind that." Sam waved a hand at the last of the floating treasure as it disappeared below ground. "What are you going to do with it?"

The one-time sorceress, now a witch, scowled. "Magic is transitory. Gold and silver are forever. Come the day I have need of it, I shall have it."

"You plan to live forever, huh?" Sam didn't see the point of Le Fay's current machinations.

The witches ignored his question as they filed into the cave, once again raising an ambient glow to guide their way to the larger cavern. Sam noticed that the cauldron and firewood that had vanished during his last visit were still missing, and the crates and barrels of riches from Dunsinane sat stacked against one wall.

"Now what?" Sam asked. "You've got your loot all safely delivered. Is it time to send me home?"

In answer, the cauldron reappeared in the centre of the

cavern, along with its boiling contents and burning logs. Sam hoped the pot was necessary to work the magic to send him back to Connecticut.

"Remember," he said. "It has to be the exact time and place I left so I can regain control of my car and prevent Nora from getting hurt."

All three witches burst out in cackling laughter. Sam didn't think that was a good sign.

Chalk-skinned Emerald danced toward him. "Perhaps," the hag crooned, "you have some familiarity with the appetites of witches."

Apart from the story of Hansel and Gretel, he didn't. Mentioning the Grimm's fairy tale didn't seem wise.

Ruby also swept closer, her rusty-grey hair swaying like dead seaweed. "My sister and I saw no need for your involvement in this endeavour, but agreed to go along with our new sister's wishes"—she glanced at Le Fay—"provided we were rewarded in the end."

"Oh, come on," Sam said. "The nightclub would have been a disaster if not for me."

The two witches laughed.

"We care not for gold," Emerald said.

"It is blood that delights us," Ruby added. "And much blood was spilled this day."

"Right," Sam said, thinking of the battle that morning. "It must have been a very good day for you."

"We crave one additional death," the two witches said together. "Into the pot you go."

Behind them, Morgan Le Fay let out a rapturous shriek.

Sam gave his nemesis a cold look. "So, your word isn't worth the breath that spoke it." Not that he'd ever believed Le Fay's promise.

The sorceress-turned-witch grinned. "What can I say? I am outvoted."

Then a fourth voice echoed within the cavern. "I have not yet cast my vote."

Everyone turned to see an apparition with a crown of yellow-grey hair and a rotting black dress—the taller, less human-looking witch who had appeared to Macbeth.

"Hecate?" Le Fay's mouth fell open, revealing stained and crooked teeth.

The towering giant of a witch strode closer. Glowering at Le Fay, she pointed a sticklike finger at the stacks of coins and candlesticks. "Is this what you sought all along? I took you under my wing to make a proper witch out of you. In return, you come up with this hairbrained scheme to fetch someone from a future time to open a casino, for the sole purpose of lining your pockets."

"Mistress—" Le Fay tried to interrupt, but the tall witch would have none of it.

"I was never convinced Macbeth was the right candidate to stir up trouble, but you assured me your casino would inspire war across all of Scotland. The opposite has happened. That skirmish today accomplished nothing. Macbeth is gone. Malcolm shall sit upon the throne as was intended. And Scotland shall carry on as though our influence meant nothing."

"Mistress." Le Fay again attempted to break in.

Hecate grew even taller, and her amber eyes flashed. "It is as though Macbeth never existed. History shall all but forget him unless I inspire a playwright to tell his story. This venture has been a complete waste."

"Mistress!" Le Fay broke in a third time, flinging a hand in Sam's direction. "It is this man's fault. He was to inspire Macbeth to hire mercenaries, to assemble a giant army to slaughter all who might oppose him."

"Whoa, whoa, whoa," Sam said. "That was never in my job description."

"No," Hecate agreed. "It was not. That task was up to my novice witch, to prove herself."

"But. I—I." Le Fay seemed unable to find words.

"But you failed," Hecate said. "Instead, our little general hired assassins to kill a handful of women and children."

"Macbeth murdered Duncan by his own hand," Le Fay insisted. "And the king's two guards."

Hecate snorted. "And that act, along with the slaughter of Macduff's household, drove his lady wife to take her own life. Very poetic. But not the task you were given."

"I-I'm sorry," Le Fay muttered.

Sam figured the conniving sorceress knew she was beaten,

and that continued repudiation would only make things worse.

"You have failed your first test," Hecate announced. "Perhaps you shall do better with the second. But before that, we must do something with this Sam Spade you have burdened us with."

"The cauldron," Emerald cackled.

"Yes," Ruby hissed. "The cauldron."

Hecate wagged her head. "If anyone succeeded at what they were set to do, it was this Sam Spade of yours. So, no, not the cauldron. How am I to punish him and not punish you? All three of you, as you were given this task together. No. This one has earned the promise made to him."

The towering witch turned on Le Fay. "Daughter—and I am reluctant to call you that until you have earned it—you shall return Sam Spade to whence he came, to the time and place promised. And do not attempt to deviate from that task. I shall know if you do. Deny my will, and Hell shall be your home for eternity!"

"Of course, Mistress." Le Fay ducked her head. Then she raised her eyes and glared at Sam. "If ever I see you again, I shall be the last thing you see."

"I can live with that," Sam said. Or thought he did, as the words turned to mud in his mouth. The cavern, with its cadre of witches, spun before his eyes, and he had the sense he was falling, falling, falling.

64
EVERYTHING'S ALL RIGHT

Suddenly, Sam was no longer falling. He was still. He was cold. And Bing Crosby was singing "White Christmas".

Collecting his bearings, he realized he was in the driver's seat of his Volvo S60. The engine was dead, but not the battery. The radio display was illuminated, as was the oil indicator and a few other lights. Through the cracked windshield, all he could see was blackness and falling snow. Both headlights must have been smashed when the vehicle hit the ditch. How long had he been gone?

As his head continued to clear, Sam realized the white sack protruding from the steering column was a deployed airbag. What the . . . ? The car couldn't have hit the ditch that hard. It must have struck a fence or a tree.

Nora!

Sam turned his head so fast, he pulled a muscle in his neck.

His partner sat belted in the passenger seat, a deployed airbag draped down over the glove compartment and across her knees. Her torso pressed forward against the seatbelt webbing, and her head was lolled to one side.

"Nora!" Sam said.

No response.

His own seat belt had retracted when he was pulled back in

time to Scotland, so Sam felt no restraint as he leaned over and lifted Nora's chin. His partner's complexion was pale, and her eyes were closed. Sam pressed his fingers to her neck, checking for a pulse. When he felt a slow, steady beat, he sighed with relief.

"Nora?" he said again.

No answer.

Sam leaned further toward the windshield, and saw a patch of blood above Nora's right eye. "What the . . . ?" Then he noticed his partner's phone resting on her lap, its glass screen cracked. He wasn't sure where the phone had been before the crash, but the impact must have sent it flying around the interior of the car. He hoped it was a collision with the windshield or door that broke the phone, and not Nora's forehead.

He took one of her hands in his and gently rubbed it. "Nora?"

No response.

Despite the travel cloak pulled over his trench coat, Sam was beginning to feel the cold. How long had it been since the engine died and the heater stopped? He was tempted to try starting the engine, but had no idea of the extent of the damage. The engine might not turn over. Worse, it might burst into flames.

Le Fay. The foul woman had returned him to Connecticut too late to prevent an accident. Of course, she had. Well, that wasn't important right now.

Reaching beneath the borrowed cloak, trench coat, and dinner jacket, and into his shirt pocket, Sam pulled out his cell phone. Before leaving Inverness for Dunsinane, he had retrieved the phone from his apartment, along with Ugarte's cloth sack holding a dozen thousand-year-old Scottish silver coins.

He powered up the phone and called 9-1-1. The battery was low but not dead, so he got through and explained his situation. He requested an ambulance and a tow truck.

"There have been a lot of accidents," the dispatcher answered. "What with the blizzard and it being New Year's Eve. I can't guarantee when you'll get a tow, but I can expedite the ambulance."

"She might have a concussion," Sam said. "The sooner they get here, the better."

"Hold tight and stay on the line. I can talk to you if you like."

"That's okay," Sam said. "I'm an ex-cop. I know the ropes. You should go help someone else who needs it. I'll take care of things here. Besides, my phone battery is almost dead."

Sam felt hesitation in the pause at the other end of the line. "If you're sure. Normally I wouldn't let you go, but my board's all lit up."

Sam felt his cheek twitch. "Happy New Year." Then he hung up.

As he slipped the phone back into his shirt pocket, it bumped against something. He reached in and found Morgan Le Fay's magic ring. How about that?

Leaving the ring in his pocket, he wriggled out of the borrowed travel cloak and then his trench coat. The coat was the warmer of the two, so he draped the fleece-lined Burberry over Nora and pulled the cloak back on over his dinner jacket. Then he snuggled in close to try to share his body heat while they waited for the ambulance.

Sam again took Nora's hand in his own, only this time he just held it. Feeling a peace he hadn't felt in a long time, he blinked back a tear. Seeing Nora there, unconscious and bleeding, he knew she meant something to him. Something more than a business partner. More than a friend. What, exactly, he'd have to discover. Sam was confident he'd figure it out. He was a detective, after all.

ACKNOWLEDGEMENTS

This book would be a weaker work if not for the tireless efforts of my beta readers Val King, Jan Serne, and Kim Greyson. Or my editor, Margaret Curelas. As the saying goes—It takes a village.

ABOUT THE AUTHOR

Randy McCharles is a full-time author of speculative and crime fiction, and is the recipient of several Aurora Awards.

Randy's recent publications include *A Connecticut Gumshoe in King Arthur's Court* (2021 Aurora Award finalist) and *A Connecticut Gumshoe in Sherwood Forest*, both from Tyche Books. *Much Ado about Macbeth,* also from Tyche Books, was a 2016 Aurora Award finalist. 2019-2020 also saw the release of the first five novels of the Peter Galloway private detective series. More adventures are on their way.

In addition to writing, Randy organizes various literary events, including the award-winning When Words Collide Festival for Readers and Writers.

CPSIA information can be obtained
at www.ICGtesting.com
Printed in the USA
BVHW042318191022
649881BV00003B/7